D0566745

FICTION RAN
Ranney, Karen.
When the laird returns

A Marriage He Never Wanted

Though a descendant of proud Scottish lairds, Alisdair MacRae had never seen his ancestral Highland estate—nor imagined that he'd have to marry to reclaim it! But the unscrupulous neighboring laird Magnus Drummond has assumed control of the property—and he will relinquish it only for a king's ransom . . . and a groom for his daughter Iseabal! Alisdair never thought to give up the unfettered life he loves—not even for a bride with the face of an angel and sensuous grace that would inflame the desire of any male.

A Passion They Never Dreamed

Is Iseabal to be a bride without benefit of a courtship? Though she yearns for a love match, the determined lass will gladly bind herself to Alisdair if he offers her an escape from her father's cruelty. This proud, surprisingly tender stranger awakens a new fire inside her, releasing a spirit as brave and adventurous as his own. Alisdair feels the heat also, but can Iseabal win his trust as well as his passion—ensuring that both their dreams come true . . . now that the laird has returned?

KAREN RANNEY

When the Laird Returns

BOOK TWO OF THE HIGHLAND LORDS

An Avon Romantic Treasure

AVON BOOKS

An Imprint of HarperCollinsPublishers

AVON BOOKS
An Imprint of HarperCollins*Publishers*
10 East 53rd Street
New York, New York 10022-5299

Copyright © 2002 by Karen Ranney
ISBN: 0-7394-2491-2

Printed in the U.S.A.

To Ginger Blythe
(who believes that every woman
should have a Highland Lord in her life)
and to Al, of course,
and Taco,
and Winnie
(who, despite having four legs and being Welsh,
thinks himself the grandest Highland Lord of them all)

Chapter 1

July, 1775
Scotland

There were no hints of what was to come on that perfect summer morning, no sign that in a few hours her life would be forever changed. But then, Iseabal was later to realize, momentous events are often heralded not by a thunderclap but by a sigh.

She bent over the neck of her horse, flying over the ground so fast that the grass was a green blur. A brilliant blue sky, cloudless and clear, was a backdrop for the craggy hills in the distance. To her left was Loch Euliss shining gold in the morning sun, and ahead was her destination, the ruins of Gilmuir. The ancestral home of the MacRae clan sat perched on a cliff-faced promontory overlooking Loch Euliss and connected by a strip of land to the glen.

The wind, brushing against her cheeks almost abrasively, made her feel free and brave. But the feeling was short-lived and edged with caution. Each time she'd engaged in secret rebellion, the act had been accompanied by a sour taste in her mouth. Even now as she slowed, her fingers began to tremble on the reins.

Her father and his entourage had left for Inverness not an hour earlier, but Iseabal knew better than to believe herself completely safe. Hesitating at the land bridge, she turned in the saddle, watching as the sheep behind her were being moved. The shepherd was not, blessedly, looking in her direction.

Dismounting, she tied the reins of her horse to a piece of iron bar, all that remained of the front door. Stepping between two leaning columns, Iseabal entered Gilmuir. Although the slate floor was covered in brick dust, the hallway connecting the main part of the castle to the priory was surprisingly intact. The curved roof still held and sunlight spilled through the trellis-like pattern of bricks on one side. Walking through the corridor, Iseabal stretched out her hand, touching the sun-warmed bricks in greeting or petition.

After all, she was a Drummond and a trespasser.

"It's the spawning site of our enemies," her father had once said about Gilmuir. "Just as well there are no more MacRaes about," he'd added grimly. "I'd have to kill them all."

Yet she could not find it in her heart to feel anger toward people she'd never known.

Reaching an opening in the corridor, Iseabal turned to her left, facing the ruins of the clan hall.

Summer had come to the Highlands, sending the warm wind soughing around corners and darting in playful gusts around the rubble. Gilmuir seemed saddest in this season, as if knowing that the world blossomed around it and life would never come again to this once grand place.

There was no sign of grandeur now. All of Gilmuir's walls had fallen but for one short section, and it leaned at an angle toward the cavernous space below the ruin, a framework of piers and vaults that had once supported the floorboards.

Her imagination, however, sketched in details long gone. Across the ceiling and against the walls, the banners of the MacRaes would have been hung. Below her feet, polished boards would have gleamed from a treatment of heated oil. At night, lamplight and the glow from candles would illuminate the painted walls and embrasures.

The wind swirled around her, brushing a tendril of hair onto her cheek as if admonishing her for this moment of pretense. Smiling, she thought that the breeze, too, would have been different back then, filled not with the scent of dust but with the smells of fresh herbs and flowers.

Her fascination with the old castle had begun as a child, watching as her father directed the removal of stone and bricks from both Gilmuir and the adjoining Fort William. From that moment on, the fortress and the promontory on which it stood had been a lure. Perhaps in some way, her fascination with Gilmuir had also been responsible for her love of working with stone.

Sometimes she lost herself in carving, the rigidity and rough texture of the stone representing the life she lived. The broad strokes of her chisel against rock embodied her secret wish to escape from such an existence.

Leaving the protection of the corridor, she walked out into the open air. Something caught the light as she skirted the edges of the chamber. Kneeling beside the open foundation,

Iseabal stared down into the forest of pillars jutting up from the earthen floor. There, not far from the base of one, was a stone block, not white or beige limestone, but something as dark and shiny as the eye of a conjurer.

Measuring the distance from the surface to the bottom of the foundation, she realized that it was too steep to descend. Resigned to being unable to retrieve the stone, she rose to her feet. Without warning, the earth crumbled in large chunks beneath her. To her horror, Iseabal was sent hurtling into the open pit.

She fell hard, the force of the impact stealing her breath. Stunned, Iseabal lay as she'd fallen, struggling to breathe. The earth, soft and powdery beneath her cheek, smelled sour, layered as it was with rotting wood. Darkness draped around the base of the pillars like silken curtains. Other than her harsh breathing, there was not a whisper of sound.

Each indrawn breath brought a piercing pain, each exhale an answering discomfort. Pressing her left hand against her ribs, Iseabal laboriously struggled to her knees, leaning her shoulder against one pillar. Carefully, she pushed herself up until she was standing.

How was she to find her way out of here?

Glancing up at the spot where she'd been standing, Iseabal began to realize how far she'd fallen. Puffs of dust filled the air as she wound her way through the pillars looking for a way out of the foundation.

What she needed was a stepping-stone. Walking back to the spot where she'd seen the black rock, Iseabal placed her hand flat against her side and slowly knelt. Not shale, she realized, stroking her fingers against the slick ebony surface. Black marble, cool to the touch and too heavy for her to move.

Tilting her head, Iseabal wondered what she could carve from it. *Get yourself out of here first, Iseabal, before you begin to envision what shape is hidden in this stone.*

Standing once again, she leaned back against a pillar.

"Help!" A call too faint to be heard. Pressing both hands against her side, she shouted again. The word, eloquent in its simplicity, seemed absorbed by the foundation. As if, she thought, Gilmuir wished her to remain in this prison of rock.

Weakly, she leaned her head back, wondering how long she would have to remain here. Gilmuir was deserted, a place avoided by the people she knew.

Hours seemed to pass, or it could have been only moments. Time had a way of lengthening when she was afraid. The sun was directly overhead signaling the noon meal and the beginning of her mother's worry.

As a child, she'd been entertained with tales of the Raven, a mythical figure who'd been credited with rescuing Scots in trouble. Iseabal suddenly wished that he were real. She needed the Raven to save her from the foolishness of her own actions. If she were not found, Iseabal thought, she might well die here, becoming one of Gilmuir's spirits.

"Please," she said, placing a hand against the wall and resting her forehead against it. "Please," she said again, her murmured word a prayer.

A mischievous breeze ruffled his hair and Alisdair impatiently brushed it back from his forehead, staring ahead at the fortress he'd heard about all his life. Perched at the end of Loch Euliss were the cliffs of Gilmuir with their striated bands of beige and glittering white stone. Topping them like a worn and rusty crown was the ancestral fortress of the MacRaes.

"A lonely looking place, Captain," said a voice to his side. Alisdair turned, glancing down at his first mate. Daniel's auburn hair and beard seemed afire in the afternoon light, lending color to his pale face. He had the complexion of a clerk, not a man who'd spent his life at sea. His face was a pleasant one, if unremarkable, but at the moment marred by a frown.

Alisdair had been subjected to that glower every day since they'd left Nova Scotia two months ago. The voyage had begun on a Friday, an invitation to disaster according to Daniel. But the most dire warning of all had come when Henrietta, the ship's cat, had begun mewing while they were still docked. A sure sign, according to Daniel, that the voyage would be long and dangerous. The fact that they had made Scotland so fast, and that the entire journey had been marked by tranquility, had no effect on Daniel's ill temper and oft-repeated warnings.

"Henrietta's been sneezing," Daniel said now, glancing down at the overfed, purring calico cat in his arms. "A sure sign of rain."

"Yesterday she was frisky, and a gale was supposed to occur," Alisdair said dryly, glancing up at the cloudless sky.

A sailor trusted in the wind and waves, entities over which he had no control. Rituals that promised safety and fair weather, the right amount of wind, and protection from sea creatures were part of a man's shipboard life. Daniel, however, took the custom to the extreme, seeing omens and portents where none existed.

Ordinarily one of his brothers would have occupied the role of first mate, but they were ferrying ships to French buyers. Daniel was a fine man who held the post well, and upon their return to Nova Scotia, would be given his own merchant ship to command. Aboard his own vessel, Alisdair thought, Daniel and Henrietta could foretell doom and gloom to their hearts' content.

Staring up at the ruins of Gilmuir, Alisdair considered Daniel's words. A lonely-looking place? He supposed it was. And majestic in its way.

The MacRaes were returning to Gilmuir, if only for a day or two. On such a momentous occasion, pipes should have been playing, but there was no stirring call, no cry of lamentation or joyful greeting. Instead, accompanying the *Fortitude*'s progress through the loch were the voices of the crew shouting responses to Daniel's commands, canvas sails snapping in the wind as they were being unfurled, and the splash of frothy waves against the ship's hull, proof of the strong current of Coneagh Firth.

His only duty had been to travel to London, and his decision to come to Gilmuir had been an impulse, one that felt almost like a summons. As they had followed the coast of Scotland, he'd felt an odd sense of homecoming. When they'd entered Coneagh Firth, Alisdair seemed to know every turn, every current, as the ocean met the freshwater lake. Sailing through Loch Euliss was familiar and known, almost as if it had been imprinted in his mind and his heart.

Their ultimate destination was a hidden cove protected by a necklace of rocks, another of the tales told him in his childhood.

The ship he'd designed was fast, an ocean bird with her sleek prow and silhouette. Raising one hand, Alisdair gave the signal to lower the eleven-foot stern anchor, just until it broke the surface of the water. The drag would be enough to offset any of the *Fortitude*'s forward impetus.

Ahead was the chain of rocks. Unlike Gilmuir, both

erected and destroyed by man, this marvel of nature was unchanged, rising from the bottom of the loch like the jawbone of some mythical creature.

Creeping around the last rock, the *Fortitude* headed into the cove almost hesitantly, as if uncertain of her welcome. Encircled on three sides by high cliffs, this refuge was a silent place. No birds were calling out in warning from their nests tucked into the pocked stone. Even the water lapping onto the rocky shoreline was muted. The wind had subsided until it was no more than a tranquil breeze dancing on the deck of the ship.

Both stern and bow anchors were fully lowered as the crew began to make preparations for docking. But this visit would be, of necessity, a short one. Alisdair was due in London, a guest of the Countess of Sherbourne.

Giving the order for a boat to be lowered, he began to descend the rope ladder.

"Shall I come with you?" Daniel asked, peering over the side.

"No," Alisdair said, glancing up. For once, Daniel didn't question why, or offer any superstitions to fit the moment, seeming to sense Alisdair's need to be alone.

Daniel nodded, pulling back from the rail.

The trip across the cove was easily done. Alisdair pulled the boat up a few feet onto the shoreline, tying the rope around a large boulder. Straightening, he smiled at the curious sensation beneath his feet. The earth felt stolid and dead; there was no current, no feeling of movement as when a ship skimmed the waves.

Retrieving the lantern from the boat, he walked along the rocky shoreline until he found the entrance to a cave. Bending, he entered, then stood looking around him. Just as he had been told, here were the pictures drawn centuries ago, portraits of a woman beloved by a saint named Ionis.

"She's beautiful," his mother had once said of the drawings.

"Not as beautiful as you, my love," his father had interjected, smiling down at her. "But then, it's probably a good thing that you're not aware of your own loveliness."

He and his brothers had turned away, disgusted, Alisdair remembered. His parents were always losing themselves in a glance, or smiling secretly at each other as if the world around them had faded away. Only after he'd grown did Alisdair realize the depth of their love for each other.

But his mother had been correct. The woman in the paintings was lovely. Her long black hair was adorned with a wreath of daisies, her winsome green eyes and smile seeming to welcome him. Ionis's lady.

On the other side of the cave was the opening he sought. Staring up at the steps, Alisdair realized that he didn't need the lantern. Leaving it on the bottom step, he started upward.

The echo of his boots thudding against the stone steps marked his journey. A pleasing breeze accompanied his ascent, freshening the air. Near the top, he encountered broken slabs of chiseled slate, one bearing an iron ring. The answer to a riddle, then. Light filtered through the staircase because the entrance had been shattered. He pulled himself up with both arms, wondering at the destruction. Had the English, angered at their colonel's disappearance, hacked their way through it?

But it no longer mattered that the two secrets had been discovered. Every MacRae knew of the existence of both the cove and the staircase, having been either part of the exodus from this place thirty years ago or a descendant of those who had fled Scotland.

The priory seemed more suited to shadows than the bright sunlight. But there was no roof, no walls, and little more remaining of the structure than the slate floor beneath his feet. The atmosphere, however, was one of serene sadness, as if the death of Gilmuir had been expected but not unmourned.

A series of arches had once stretched across the back of the priory, facing Loch Euliss. Only part of one arch remained, framing the view. Loch Euliss stretched out before him, gradually narrowing until it flowed into Coneagh Firth and from there to the sea. On either side of the lake were thickly forested glens, the trees appearing more black than green.

Turning, he entered a hallway that had been described to him numerous times. The fortress had originally been built in the shape of an H, with the priory and castle connected by a covered corridor. But there were few signs remaining of what Gilmuir had once been. There were no tall chimneys, steeply pitched roofs, or towering walls aged by the passage of centuries. Instead, he viewed a crumbling ruin.

His father had spent years of his youth at Gilmuir, and later his mother had been held hostage within these walls, before becoming a rebel and then a wife to an English colonel engaged in treason. Here, his great-grandfather had ruled as laird and tragedy had swept over the clan, beginning with his grandmother's death.

Reasons enough for feeling an affinity toward the old castle. Or it could be that the answer lay in his great-uncle Hamish's words to him as a boy. "It doesn't matter where you're born, lad. If there's a drop of MacRae blood in you, you'll always be from Gilmuir."

Unexpectedly, Alisdair heard a soft, keening cry, as if Gilmuir's ghosts rose up to greet him. He shook his head, amused at himself and the fact that he'd momentarily allowed tales from his boyhood to overshadow reason.

Striding through an opening in the corridor, he found himself standing beside mounds of rubble and one weak-looking wall leaning precariously over a pit. He heard the sound again, but this time, instead of inciting his curiosity, the plaintive cry irritated him.

"I don't believe in ghosts," he said loudly, staring down into the opening. But the skin on the back of his neck tightened when something moved in the shadows.

"I am very happy to hear that," a female voice said weakly.

He frowned, studying the darkness.

"Show yourself," he said.

She stepped out of the shadows into the afternoon light, glancing up at him, a solemn expression on her face.

He wondered for a fleeting moment if it was true, after all, that there were spirits at Gilmuir. The intruder was the image of Ionis's love, the woman painstakingly crafted in the cave portraits.

Not a ghost, but human.

Her long black hair seemed part of the shadows, her eyes as delicately green as the stem of a flower. Her mouth was solemn but seemed to hint at smiles. An arresting face, square in shape.

Smudges of dirt marked her cheek as well as her pale blue striped petticoat. Her soiled white kerchief was hanging loose, held at the ends by a double brooch pinned to her yellow jacket. Her long black hair was tied at her nape with a ribbon of dark blue, the same shade that bound the hem of her skirt.

"Well?" he asked finally. "If you're not haunting Gilmuir, then who are you and why are you here?"

* * *

Slowly, her gaze traveled up from his black boots with their tops folded down at the knees of his buff breeches. His short waistcoat of plaid wool was topped with a buff cutaway jacket, the cuffs and lapels wide and folded back to reveal crimson facings. His brown hair was tied neatly at the nape of his neck, the high collar of his coat framing a heavily bearded face, thick brows, and eyes a shade of blue so light that looking at them was like viewing a dawn sky.

An imposing rescuer.

Iseabal took one step back.

"Are you a soldier?" she asked, having never seen the tartan worn by anyone other than the military. Once, in Inverness, she had watched as a troop of men assembled in strict formation, their attire no less resplendent than this man's. A regiment of Highland soldiers, off to fight for the English king.

"No," he said shortly. "And you? Who are you?"

"I am no ghost," she said, bending carefully to retrieve her leather sling. "But I might well be one if left here." Looping the ties over her shoulder, she looked up at him again. "Will you help me?" she asked.

Unfolding his arms, he knelt on one knee, studying the distance before lying flat on the ground. Reaching down with both hands, he waited until she stretched upward, then gripped her wrists. Rising first to his knees and then to his feet, he began pulling her free.

As he lifted her, Iseabal willed the pain away, but found that it was better simply to pray for the ability to bear it. Her knees bumped against the smooth stone of the wall and a moment later she felt the solid earth beneath her feet, the warming sunlight like a benediction against her face.

Taking a cautionary step away from the edge of the foundation, she glanced up at him. His size dwarfed her, and she was a tall woman. There was an air of command to this stranger, especially standing as he was with feet planted apart and the fingers of one hand wound around the wrist of another.

Only one other person in her life had demonstrated such force of presence—her father. Magnus Drummond was a short, bandy-legged man who nevertheless carried himself as if he were king.

"Who are you?" she whispered.

"A MacRae," he said, his frown not easing.

"There are no more MacRaes," she said, placing one hand against her chest.

"You are looking at one," he said. His voice sounded almost Scot, but there was a tinge of accent that flattened his words. "And you?" he asked again, taking a step closer. "Who are you?" He reached out one hand as if to touch her and she jerked away, the sudden twisting movement resulting in a spear of pain in her side.

"You're hurt," he said, his fingers brushing against hers, sliding to the back of her hand where it rested at her waist.

"I'm fine," she said, taking another step back. He followed her, implacable in his kindness.

A miscreant would be hesitant to have him as judge. But her lie had been a small one, Iseabal thought as his eyes, soft disks of pale blue light, seemed to bore through her.

Taking one more step away from him, Iseabal hoped he would not follow.

"How did you come to be in the pit?" he asked. "Why do you trespass at Gilmuir?" Once again he closed the distance between them.

Again she moved away from him, and this time he seemed to understand. Another step and he remained where he was.

Reaching her horse, Iseabal untied the reins, knowing that riding would not be wise with her side hurting so badly. Resigned to walking back home, she turned, heading for the land bridge.

"Why are you on MacRae land?" he asked again.

Iseabal faced him, answering him finally.

"It's no longer MacRae land," she said, wishing that it were not true. "There haven't been MacRaes here for years. It's owned by Magnus Drummond," she added, before leaving both Gilmuir and the man.

Chapter 2

Twice she turned and looked back at him, her face flushed and deepening in color as he watched. Her eyes, green and solemn, looked away before returning to him as quickly. Almost, Alisdair thought, as if she could not believe he were real.

They'd not exchanged names, but they'd touched as intimately as man and wife. He could still feel her pressed tightly against his body in that last second before her feet had touched the ground.

Her slender figure was framed against the whitish blue of the summer sky, her hair flowing against her back in a delicate fan. She crossed the land bridge keeping the horse at a walk, making him wonder again at the state of her injury.

Despite her claims, he'd seen pain in her eyes.

Who was she? A cautious woman, evidenced by that

slight change of expression from curiosity to wariness. A lovely woman, an enigma who spoke troubling words.

He raised a hand and scratched his beard with his knuckles. Now, that was probably why she'd run from him. But it was a tradition of his not to shave until he had finished his voyage and was home once more.

What did she mean that this was Drummond's land?

He glanced to the side, distracted by a blur of color. An ocean of sheep filled the glen, their lean bodies showing pink through their sparse tan fleece.

Frowning, he took a few steps forward, only to be called back by a voice.

"It's a fine place," Daniel said. "For all that it's nearly gone."

Turning, Alisdair faced his first mate. Most of the crew had followed him and were now roaming through the ruins. They, like him, were descendants of the people of Gilmuir, and the sights they saw today would be told in a hundred tales back home.

"The fort's not there," Daniel said abruptly, his voice tinged with amazement.

Alisdair spun around to discover that Daniel was right. He'd been so distracted by the woman that he'd never realized that Fort William had vanished. Built after Culloden, the fort had been an English stronghold for this part of the Highlands.

"It's an ugly thing," his mother had said. "A blight on the landscape."

"A fortification built in the style of English forts," his father had contributed with a smile. "We used the design in our first settlement here."

With Daniel at his side, Alisdair walked across the barren

earth that separated the two structures. An outline of bricks marked where the building had once stood, but there were no walls remaining, no doors, only a few wooden supports where he imagined the stable might have been.

"It looks to have simply disappeared," Alisdair said, startled to feel a surge of satisfaction.

Daniel nodded, studying the layout of the fort. "I wonder why they left?"

"Why stay?" Alisdair asked with a small smile. "They had already accomplished their aim." His own dislike of the English was due more to their encroachment in Nova Scotia and their paternalistic attitudes in the Orient than to the Crown's behavior in Scotland. His father was half English, a fact that most of the MacRaes of Cape Gilmuir conveniently ignored.

"What do you know of the Drummonds?"

"A thieving bunch, I've heard," his first mate said. "They were forever stealing our horses and our livestock."

Alisdair stifled a smile. The MacRaes had claimed this land centuries ago, had fought to keep it, had built from stone a fortress that commanded the surrounding countryside. People with such determination would have been as fierce as the Drummonds and no doubt as guilty of their own reiving.

Turning, Alisdair walked across the land bridge, leaving Daniel behind. The land was no longer a lush green; the voracious sheep had transformed the grass beneath his feet to dusty earth.

"Get off MacRae land," Alisdair said, reaching the shepherd of this damnable flock.

The man was dressed in brown breeches, a tan shirt, and boots that looked worn enough at the seams to fall apart with each step. His hair was a muted blond, his face not yet formed with character, and his brown eyes shone with a cool arrogance, betraying his youth as nothing else could.

"You'd be Magnus Drummond, then?" the shepherd asked, his gaze traveling from Alisdair's boots to the top of his head. "You'll not be looking like him."

"I'm a MacRae," Alisdair said, capable of his own arrogance.

"And why should I care?"

"Because this is MacRae land," he said, his irritation growing.

"There haven't been MacRaes here since the old times," the young man said. "Or are you thinking I should go back to Drummond and tell him that I've seen a ghost?"

"I'm thinking," Alisdair said carefully, "that you should get off my land."

He glanced around, searching the flock. There, on the periphery, was a belled ewe. Sheep were not stubborn as much as stupid, an entire flock following a leader unquestioningly, even occasionally to their death. Sheep were raised at home, not only for food but to supply his mother and the other women with wool for their looms.

Striding now to the edge of the flock, Alisdair gripped the ewe's bell collar and began walking her toward the southwestern corner of the glen.

"You can't do that," the shepherd said, coming up behind him and waving his staff.

"Get them off my land," Alisdair replied calmly. The sheep followed in an arrow shape behind him, drowning the shepherd's protests with their bleating.

The young man grabbed Alisdair's sleeve, pulling on his coat. Alisdair brushed the dirty hand away and continued walking.

"Drummond's not going to like this," the shepherd shouted.

One eyebrow rose, Alisdair's disregard for Drummond's opinion implicit in the gesture. He stopped, facing the shepherd. "Where is this Drummond of yours?" he asked.

"You mean to tell him it's your land?" the other man asked incredulously.

"I do," Alisdair said tightly.

The young man studied Alisdair for a moment, as if measuring the breadth of his resolve. "That's one meeting I'd like to see," he said. "I'll gladly give you directions to Fernleigh."

"And take your sheep from here," Alisdair added.

He nodded, hooking the curved end of his staff in the ewe's collar. Smiling broadly, he led the sheep away.

Alisdair watched him for a few moments before beginning the walk back to Gilmuir. The sun tinted the old ruins gold, and for a second Alisdair could almost believe the place whole again. The crew of the *Fortitude* still milled about, or stood transfixed on the headland, gazing down at the loch. Their presence gave the castle life, summoning a vision of what it might have been like to live here before the English bombarded Gilmuir.

His home in Nova Scotia had begun as a settlement of clustered wooden huts, gathered together in the shadows of a fortress. Over the years, the huts had been replaced by stone cottages offering more protection against the severe winter winds. Homes were adorned with animal skins and the bright wool of newly woven tartans. There was a smell of newness to each house, filled as it was with recently hewn wood crafted into beds and chairs and tables.

There was nothing about Nova Scotia that was old and revered or hinted at timelessness like this old castle. Yet the

MacRaes who lived there had willingly given up their past to guarantee a future not only for themselves but for their children.

Perhaps it was foolish to care about Gilmuir, to want it left sacrosanct and untouched. He didn't live here, nor did he plan to, his home being either aboard ship or on an island named for this somber and deserted ruin. But Alisdair couldn't shake the notion that this land and its fortress belonged to the MacRaes, whether absent or not.

Her home was only a few miles away, perched upon the highest hill on Drummond land. Originally, Iseabal had been told, Fernleigh had been nothing more than a mound of earth encircled by a deep trench. Over the centuries, the Drummonds had added a wooden fortress, then framed it with stone. That structure had stood until her father had rebuilt the outside walls with brick taken from the English fort.

Fernleigh towered over the landscape, a square red sandstone box. Her home was not a cheerful place, or a happy one. While laughter rang within the stone walls, it was a response to a drunken jest, or an uneasy chuckle at her father's wit. Most commonly heard through the narrow hallways and drafty rooms of Fernleigh were her father's shouts of anger.

"I'm an important man," he'd told her once. "A man feared and respected throughout Scotland." Not an idle boast, she suspected, since many a visitor from Edinburgh or Inverness came to their home, spending days in conversation with Magnus Drummond.

Life at Fernleigh was not wholly dour. There was luxury in their garments and their choice of meals. But such sparse pleasures never made up for the fear.

Iseabal couldn't remember a time when she'd not been

cautious of her father in a visceral way, one that dampened her palms and set her stomach to churning. For the most part she remained out of sight, having discovered that the fewer times he saw her, the less she was punished.

He was a man who sought out his enemy's weaknesses and used them to his advantage. Such cunning had kept the Drummonds safe over the years. But her father extended his wariness to his family, and saw a foe even in her mother and herself.

As she grew, Iseabal realized that her father would never soften and she could never be a daughter who pleased him. They would never come to understand one another. With that realization came a curious freedom. She was released from the obligation of trying to love her father.

She gave the reins to Robbie, and the stableboy took them, not questioning why she'd returned home walking her mount. Robbie was her companion in misadventure, never speaking of her secret visits to Gilmuir. Nor did he tell anyone of the stones he hid away for her or of the many times he'd reported her father's movements.

"He's back early," Robbie whispered, glancing around.

Forcing a reassuring smile to her face, Iseabal nodded. "Keep these for me," she whispered, handing him her leather sling holding her tools.

He ducked his head in agreement, having done so often enough in the past.

Iseabal headed for the kitchen entrance. Neither the cook nor her helpers acknowledged Iseabal's presence as she passed through the large chamber. A sign, she noted, and not a good one.

All the corridors of Fernleigh led to a small, round room, probably the original keep. Now it acted like the hub of the structure, connecting corridors. Built into the curved wall was a staircase winding up to the second and third floors, the steps rounded and worn.

The only illumination in the keep was from the archer's slits high up in the brick. In the summer a soft breeze sighed through Fernleigh, but in the winter the cold was nearly unbearable.

The staircase, the two entrances to the hall, and the front door were each guarded by a young man attired in black breeches, white shirt, red vest, and a black coat with shiny silver buttons bearing the Drummond crest. A costly uniform for a parsimonious laird, but sometimes her father's penury fell victim to his pride.

The men were handpicked for their stature and courage in addition to their prowess in battle, the latter ascertained not through war, but in the taverns of Inverness. If a man was willing to fight for a slur, or use his fists to solve an argument, then Magnus Drummond secured him in his service.

Iseabal passed in front of the guards neither expecting nor receiving a greeting.

Her mother's chamber was on the second floor, while hers was on the third with the servants. She began to climb the worn steps cautiously, her shadow dancing on the curved wall behind her.

"Where have you been, daughter?"

Iseabal stared down at her father, dread escalating to panic. He was dressed in a similar fashion as his guards, but instead of trousers, he wore knee breeches and richly patterned stockings. He had removed his coat, a familiarity that would never be permitted the other men.

His clean-shaven face might have been pleasant at one time, but a lifetime of anger had stamped itself on his features. His hazel eyes, ringed with wrinkles, were hooded and unreadable. Long lines bracketed his cheeks as if pointing down to a sullen mouth or upward to a deeply furrowed forehead.

"Come and talk with me," he said, almost affably. Turning, he entered the clan hall.

His geniality didn't reassure her. Iseabal took a deep breath, willing herself to be brave, and made her way down the stairs, one hand braced against the wall for support.

The clan hall was an ugly place, but it had not always been so. Once, the stone blocks of the walls had been painted a pale blue, a color that softened the angles of the room. Over the years, the paint had faded to expose splotches of gray. The flooring beneath her feet, made of rocks hewn into a square shape and then mortared with dirt, had been worn down until the corners were rounded and the surface dangerously uneven in spots.

Above the arched and cavernous fireplace was the only thing of beauty in the room. The whispered tale of this first Drummond said he was a knight, a pilgrim of sorts, coming to Scotland from England. As a child, she had come to the hall and stared up at the figure backlit by the sun.

The knight was pictured kneeling on the ground, the sunlight illuminating him as if in benediction. Beside him on the ground was a reed basket signifying, she'd been told, that he'd come to his new home with few possessions. His sword was planted in the ground, his forehead leaning upon the hilt. Etched into the gold and silver was one word in Latin. One of her innumerable suitors, a man learned in such things, had translated it for her. *Loyalty.*

Once, she imagined, the colors might have been vibrant. Cobalt and crimson, golden yellow and purest white. But age had dulled the colors, rendering the lead holding the picture malleable. Consequently, there were missing sections that had been patched with iron plates, the result being a crude yet impressive work of art.

Through the years, Drummond men had taken his oath of loyalty as their own, their fealty sworn to Scotland and their clan. Her father, however, seemed to have twisted the tradition and now swore allegiance only to himself and his money.

Iseabal glanced toward the corner. Her mother was not in her customary chair. Had she chosen to absent herself? Or had Leah been banished from the hall during Iseabal's punishment?

Yet another sign, one that settled like ice in her stomach.

She reached the table where her father sat with another man. The shepherd glanced at her only once before turning away.

Resignation surged through her. She'd been seen after all. If so, why hadn't he come to her aid?

"Where have you been, Iseabal?"

"Gilmuir," she said quietly, bowing her head. Her hands clasped themselves together at her waist of their own accord, all too familiar with this pose of submission.

He stood, the legs of the intricately carved chair scraping against the stone floor.

"Have I not forbidden you that place?" he asked, approaching her.

"Yes," she whispered, hearing the fear in her voice.

"Hold out your hand," he said, almost kindly.

She extended her arm, her fingers unclenching so that the palm was exposed.

As he retrieved the dirk tucked into his boot, Iseabal

closed her eyes, searching for that warm, dark place where she hid in moments like these.

She felt the knife point against the fleshy part of her hand at the base of her thumb and willed herself not to pull away. Her punishment was only greater if she fled from it.

"Tell me of the man you met," he said, sliding the blade smoothly from wrist to the tip of Iseabal's longest finger. There was not enough pressure to slice into her skin, but the threat was there nonetheless.

Her eyes flew open. "The MacRae?"

"The one," he said, resting the knife point against the base of her finger. As if, she thought in a surge of wild panic, he meant to slice it off.

"He is a man like any other," she said, trembling.

"His appearance?"

"Tall, with a full beard. Blue eyes," she added. "So lightly colored they seemed almost clear."

"MacRae eyes," he said, staring off into the distance as if seeing the man she'd met. Moments ticked by ponderously before his attention returned once more to her.

"What shall your punishment be, Iseabal?" he asked, staring down at her hand. "Shall I cut a few fingers or remove one? Tell me, how shall I teach you to obey me?"

Her hand trembled, but Iseabal remained silent. The ice in her stomach flowed outward to her toes and fingers at the same time that she began to taste the familiar sourness of fear.

"Perhaps a nick here," he said, making a mark on the base of her thumb. Instantly blood welled up to fill in the curved pattern. A D for Drummond? Or for defiant? *Desperate*, her mind contributed.

"The maids will search your chamber and bring everything of value to me. Perhaps being forbidden to leave your room until you're wed will teach you to obey me. Not the lesson you deserve, Iseabal, but one that will remind you who I am."

He could not beat her, she suddenly realized, or cut her. To do so would be to affect her worth to a future husband. She should have known that her father's greed would be greater than his rage.

Iseabal remained silent, a lesson she'd learned as a child, never to challenge her father. Yet even if her occasional rebellions were no longer possible, her thoughts were secret and her own.

Slowly, he removed the knife from her hand, dismissing her with a gesture. She clenched her hand tightly in order to stop the bleeding, escaping her father before he could change his mind and make the punishment worse.

Chapter 3

"At least we know what happened to Fort William," Alisdair said, staring up at the south face of the Drummond fortress.

"I never thought that a Scot would use the bricks of an English fort to build his home," Daniel said disgustedly.

They approached Fernleigh at a leisurely pace, giving Drummond's people enough time to send word of their arrival.

"Are you certain you wish to do this, Alisdair?" Daniel asked worriedly. "We should have brought the entire crew."

"I doubt Drummond is as ferocious as all that, Daniel," Alisdair said, smiling.

"What makes you think he'll listen to you?"

"What makes you think he won't?"

"He's a Drummond," Daniel said simply. "That's why."

They halted before the front door, made of oak and

banded with iron. Oddly enough, it didn't seem designed for the structure, causing Alisdair to wonder if Drummond's greed had extended to taking not only English bricks but part of Gilmuir. Perhaps the final destruction of the old castle was not due to the English at all, but was the work of another Scot.

"You can't be so foolish as to go in there alone?" Daniel asked incredulously when Alisdair waved him back.

Alisdair nodded, gripping the iron knocker. The door opened slowly, as if Fernleigh welcomed visitors only grudgingly. A young man stood before him, his face stiff and expressionless.

"I'm here to see Drummond," Alisdair said.

"And who would you be?"

"Alisdair MacRae."

A moment later the guard was pushed aside. An older man stepped into the threshold and stared at him.

The wrinkles on his face marked him at near Alisdair's father's age, but while Ian MacRae still drew the eyes of the ladies, Alisdair doubted a female would look twice in this man's direction. His nose, pocked and swollen, sat in the middle of a face weathered and burned brown by the sun. His brown hair, laced with gray, fell to his shoulders untied, and bushy eyebrows sat atop deep-set eyes now narrowed in instant dislike.

Magnus Drummond.

"It's you who've banished my sheep from their own grazing ground," he said roughly.

There were to be no pleasantries, then, which was just as well. Alisdair had no time to waste on false courtesy.

"If they were grazing on my land," Alisdair said, crossing his arms over his chest.

"What reason do you have for thinking it's yours?" Drummond asked, frowning.

"The reason is that I'm a MacRae," Alisdair said firmly, stepping forward. "The descendant of the old laird."

"If you're truly who you say you are, then where have you been all these years?"

"Over the sea," Alisdair said, not wishing to give Drummond any more information than that.

"Well, you can just go back there," Drummond said. "I'm the owner in the eyes of the law. The English ceded it to me years ago."

"Then they gave something away that they never owned," Alisdair said, pushing back his irritation. "If a thief steals a cow from one man and sells it to another, it only means that both men have been cheated."

"I care not if you are a MacLeod or a MacRae or a MacRath," Drummond said stonily. "The land is mine."

The men aligned behind Drummond took one step forward.

"My family has lived here for six hundred years, Drummond. I think that claim outweighs your gift from the English," Alisdair said tightly.

"Shall we send it to the courts, then, upstart?" Drummond asked, looking pleased.

Alisdair must have betrayed something in his expression, because Drummond began to smile. "Did you think it would be that easy? March in here, declare yourself a MacRae, and have me weep at your feet?"

"I haven't got time for the courts," Alisdair said stiffly.

"Then you should count your losses now, before they grow even larger. It'll be a waste of time for you anyway, since I've never lost a claim."

The older man's smile was grating, Alisdair thought, as if Drummond knew and enjoyed his growing anger.

"Do you make a point of stealing land from your countrymen, Drummond?" Alisdair asked, clasping his hands behind him. The pose was a natural one for him, revealing him as a man of the sea.

"You'll find that the Highlands are better suited to sheep than men, MacRae," Drummond said, beginning to close the door.

Alisdair slapped his hand on it. "Sell it to me," he said impulsively.

Drummond's lips twisted into a grin. He waved his men away and surveyed Alisdair with narrowed eyes. "A MacRae buying land he claims as his? Why?"

"Because I've no time for courts or judges," Alisdair said shortly.

"And you're not sure you'll win?" Drummond stepped aside, inviting Alisdair into his home with a sweep of his arm.

Alisdair turned and looked at Daniel. His first mate was standing with arms crossed, a frown on his face. His foot tapped impatiently against the dirt, a sign he was not pleased.

"If you don't come out in an hour," Daniel threatened, "I'm fetching the crew." Alisdair nodded, but doubted that Drummond would kill him, especially not since he'd tapped the other man's greed. But it was wise to be cautious. Alisdair entered Fernleigh, following Drummond, the man's two guards behind him.

Fernleigh's curving stone steps hugged the wall, wound up into clouds of shadows. Walls and floors, staircase and roof, were all formed of the same dull gray stone, lit now by slanting rays of sunlight entering from high windows.

Drummond led the way to another room, a hall that bore an aura of neglect. "My wife, Leah," he said gruffly, kicking out the chair at the head of a long, rough-hewn table. "Alisdair MacRae," Drummond added, the introduction swift and grudgingly made.

Alisdair turned in the direction of Drummond's wife. She was seated beside a cold fireplace, her head bent as if she diligently worked on the needlework in front of her. But her hands had stilled and she sat so stiffly quiet that he could almost feel her tremble.

"Thank you for your hospitality, madam," he said, walking to her side and bowing slightly.

She glanced up, obviously surprised.

For a moment Alisdair thought she was the woman in the ruins. But she was much older than the girl he'd seen, even though their coloring was the same.

"You are a MacRae?" she asked, her voice little more than a whisper.

"I am," he said.

Laying her needlework in her lap, she tentatively smiled up at him. A wisp of greeting in that look, one that charmed him.

"Who is your father?" she asked unexpectedly.

He hesitated in answering. Any questions about Ian MacRae were always viewed with suspicion.

"My mother is Leitis MacRae; my grandmother was Moira," he said instead.

"I knew your uncle," she said, her voice low.

"Did you?" he asked, surprised. Two of his uncles had died before his birth and the third only a few months ago, prompting his errand to London.

"Fergus," she said simply.

His mother's brother. Alisdair wanted to ask her about the man whose name brought such sadness to her face, but he was only too conscious of Drummond standing behind him.

"You are welcome here," she said softly, smiling up at him. "Could I offer you some ale, or perhaps some wine?"

"What are you gabbing about, woman?" Drummond demanded brusquely. "He'll drink good Scots whiskey or he'll go thirsty."

Glancing quickly at her husband, she nodded. "Of course," she said. Gripping her needlework tightly, she stared down at the delicate stitches.

There was a woman at home who'd appeared often in public with bruises on her arms and neck. "The cow kicked me," she would say, or claim it some other clumsiness on her part. But the truth, well known throughout the village, was that her husband beat her. Alisdair had offered him a berth upon *The Thistle*, a new ship whose voyage to the China Sea guaranteed that the man would be away for months at a time.

His wife had met Alisdair in the square one day, pulling his face down so that she might kiss his cheek. The dead look in her eyes was gone and her face aglow with happiness.

Leah Drummond reminded him of that woman, especially in the furtive way she glanced in her husband's direction.

Alisdair bowed once more and walked back to Drummond, sitting on one of the narrow benches flanking the table.

Neither spoke until the whiskey was brought.

"You'll buy the land, then?" Drummond asked, his hand held tight around his tankard. He pushed the other cup across the table to Alisdair.

Not a bad blend, he thought, tasting the drink, but not as

good as that distilled on Cape Gilmuir. The people of Scotland had not lost their talent for whiskey simply because they'd left their homeland.

"On one condition," Alisdair said, placing the tankard on the table and leveling a look at Drummond.

"You're not in a position to argue terms, MacRae," Drummond replied contemptuously.

"Give me your oath that you'll leave MacRae land free," Alisdair said.

"Do you trust my word, MacRae? It's the first time one of yours has ever done so."

"Is your oath of no value?" Alisdair asked.

The other man's face seemed to darken. Drummond's mouth pursed, his brows coming together in a frown that rivaled Alisdair's long-dead great-uncle's, and the old man had been master of the glower.

Before he could utter either an insult or a demand, Leah spoke. "If our guest is wealthy enough to buy Gilmuir, husband," she said, lifting her needle in one long stroke, "then perhaps he is in the market for a wife."

"I'll not marry my blood with that of the MacRaes, woman. Speak when you're told and not before," Drummond said roughly.

"Yet you've found no one else to afford the bride price you demand for Iseabal," she said serenely. The thread quivered in the air, leading Alisdair to wonder if her hands trembled. "For a few more coins, he could obtain his lands and a bride."

"I need no wife, madam," Alisdair said kindly.

"Then you are married?" she asked, glancing over at him briefly, an expression of disappointment on her face.

"I am not, nor do I plan to be soon." He had a shipyard to expand and ships to design and build before he took a wife.

"Have I your word, then?" he asked, his gaze returning to Magnus. "You'll not use Gilmuir land for your grazing?"

"A bond of kinship would strengthen the matter," Drummond's wife said from her perch beside the fireplace.

Drummond said nothing, considering his wife with narrowed eyes. Leah looked up and the two Drummonds exchanged glances. Slowly the other man nodded, beginning to smile.

"For once, you could be right, woman," Drummond said, leaning back in his chair before turning to Alisdair. "I'll not sell Gilmuir to you for any amount," he said, his smile part cunning, part amusement.

Alisdair took another sip of whiskey to hide his anger. He was not in the mood nor did he have time for Drummond's games.

"Instead," the older man said, "I'll sell you Gilmuir and my daughter."

Iseabal watched as the servant girls left her chamber, hearing the bar being lowered outside her door. They'd found little of value; her most cherished carvings were hidden in the stables with Robbie as their guardian.

The thought of being kept here for weeks or months was almost intolerable. Yet Iseabal realized that praying to be quit of Fernleigh would not be wise. When she was led from her room, it would be to attend her wedding.

The afternoon sun, streaming in through the small window, touched upon the furnishings of her room: a wardrobe, a squat bureau, a bedside table, and the small bed that had been hers since childhood. All of the pieces had been crafted by the carpenters employed at Fernleigh. The only exception was the small bench beside the window, sturdy and old, the wood having darkened over the years.

Here she sat and struggled with her needlework or mulled over her life. Sometimes, when her father was gone from Fernleigh, she'd get a stone from Robbie and begin to work on it, muffling the sharp pinging sound of the chisel beneath a cloth.

A basin stood on her bureau, the matching pitcher filled with cold water. Her father refused to have the servants engaged in pampering, as he called it. Even in winter there was no hot water for washing. The only respite from the cold of Fernleigh was to gather around the fireplace in the clan hall.

She washed her hands, noting that the cut on her hand was not deep and would heal soon enough. Iseabal wasn't as certain about her side.

Unfastening her canvas stays, Iseabal inspected them as she did every day. The straw stuffed into the narrow pockets would need to be replaced soon. Putting the stays on the chair as a reminder, she began to remove her shift.

Dipping a cloth into the cool water, she wrung it dry before placing it on the swelling at her side. The pain was manageable, but only if she did not move quickly or bend sharply.

A sound at the door alerted her, and she quickly wrapped herself in the blanket from the end of her bed. Settling on the bench, Iseabal gripped the rough wood at either side of her hips with both hands. Pressing her lips together tightly, she murmured a quick and familiar prayer. *Please do not let it be my father. But if it is, help me to be brave.*

But it wasn't Magnus Drummond, only a servant girl.

"You're to come to the hall, miss," she said, staring down at the floor.

Iseabal stood, wrapping the blanket tightly around her. "I'm to be shown again?" she asked, resigned.

For two years men had visited Fernleigh on all matter of business. Iseabal had been paraded before them like a ewe at auction, her virtues extolled and her bride price announced to any who would listen.

The majority of the men her father deemed wealthy enough to afford a Drummond daughter were in their middle years. Their faces had marked them as older; their wealth had indicated their success in business. In too many cases they'd spoken of dead wives and scores of children needing a nurse, mother, and maid.

The girl smiled kindly as if understanding the apprehension behind Iseabal's question. But her words did nothing to ease Iseabal's mind. "Your father bids you to dress in your finest garments, miss, because your new husband awaits."

An oath trembled on Alisdair's lips, but he held it back. He'd bartered all over the world, knew the value of a bland expression, an air of restraint. But hiding his emotions had never been as difficult as now.

"I've no wish for a wife," he said curtly. "Only ownership to land that is mine."

"Then wait until the courts decree it yours," Drummond said, looking beyond Alisdair. He raised his hand, wiggling his fingers in an impatient beckoning gesture.

Alisdair glanced over his shoulder. There, standing in the doorway, was the woman he'd seen in the ruins. Her black hair fell loose to her waist, acting as a frame for her pale face. Her lips, tightened in a grim look of purpose, fell open at the sight of him, then just as quickly closed again. Her hands, clenched together at her sides, loosened, then gripped the material of her blue-and-red-striped petticoat. Her short jacket, buttoned to her neck, seemed immobile for a moment, as if she'd taken a breath and held it to test her ability at such a task. A second later she breathed again, her breasts pressing against the material to prove she was not a statue but a living person caught suspended in a moment of surprise.

They shared startled looks before each glanced away.

"My daughter," Drummond said, although it was hardly necessary. She looked the image of her mother.

She didn't move or acknowledge the halfhearted introduction, only stared at the floor as if the worn stones were fascinating to behold.

"Iseabal," her mother said, summoning the younger woman with a gesture of her hand.

Alisdair watched as she made her way across the room. Iseabal. The name suited her. Forcing himself to look away, Alisdair faced Drummond again.

"I'll not bargain with you, MacRae. You'll take the land and the girl for the price I gave you. But if you haven't the money, then it's no matter to me. I'll be the same as I am now."

Suddenly, Alisdair understood that Drummond would be just as satisfied if he left empty-handed.

"I'll take the land," Alisdair said crisply. "I've no use for a wife."

"She's healthy and she's docile enough," Drummond said, as if describing a horse. "I've no doubt she'll breed well, being heartier than her mother."

He snapped his fingers in summons and Iseabal made her

way to her father's side. Drummond grabbed her petticoat, pulling her closer.

"She's got good teeth," he said, reaching up to grip her jaw and force her mouth open. "She had the pox as a child and won't get it again. She's got a good figure with enough padding that a man won't be stuck on bones, but not so much that you'd suffocate."

Iseabal's eyes fluttered shut even as her face began to flush.

Alisdair stood, pushing the bench back. "Enough, Drummond," he said, disgusted with the other man's crude display of his daughter. "I've only come for MacRae land."

"They come together, MacRae, for the price I stated. Without one, you'll never have the other."

A threat he didn't doubt Drummond would keep. Turning from the sight of Iseabal's mortification, Alisdair stared up at the ruin of the stained-glass window. He noticed the motto etched on the sword. *Loyalty.* How far did his own loyalty extend? To marrying a woman he'd no wish to wed? To beggaring himself in order to safeguard land his family would never hold?

The money he'd saved from his voyages had been set aside to expand the shipyard. He wanted to build faster ships incorporating the ideas of the *Fortitude.* If he altered the hull design, he could create a swan upon the water, a silent, beautiful, and speedy vessel that could outrun and outmaneuver anything currently afloat.

The decision had been made, Alisdair realized, the moment he'd stepped onto MacRae soil. Or maybe it had come before then, when he'd been a boy sitting on the floor beside his brothers in front of the fire, listening to his mother and father tell stories of Gilmuir. Or perhaps it was not a decision after all, but a gift to his parents and the others from Scotland who had made such a sacrifice in order to survive.

Alisdair turned, encountering the older woman's glance. There was panic in her eyes and a supplication as heartfelt as any prayer. She wanted her daughter gone from here, and it was not difficult to understand why. Drummond had treated Iseabal with such easy disdain that it must have been a habit of a lifetime.

"Well?" Magnus asked, the word more a demand than a question. He stood, pushing Iseabal away from him. She stumbled, falling to the floor with only a slight gasp of alarm. Alisdair reached her in seconds, bent down, and placing his hands on her arms, helped her rise.

She got to her knees, her face only inches from his. Her lips were white, but she uttered just one small sound as he helped her stand. "You're not well," he said quietly.

"I'm fine," she whispered, her gaze meeting his in a swift plea before glancing toward her father.

What sort of man engenders such fear in his own daughter?

"I'll pay your price, Drummond," he said reluctantly. "For Gilmuir and Iseabal."

"Then we'll draw up a bargain between us," the other man said. Drummond's glance at his wife was evidently command enough. Leah rose, placing her needlework on the chair before moving to her daughter. Together the two of them left the room.

"How did it go?" Daniel asked when Alisdair emerged from Fernleigh an hour later.

"I've bought the land," Alisdair said, frowning at Daniel. The transfer of his funds had been made by letter, the wedding bargain reached, both deeds done with such dispatch that he was still reeling from the speed of it. He glanced back at the Drummond fortress.

"I'm also to be married," he said, astonishment coloring his voice. "Tomorrow."

Chapter 4

Today was her wedding day.

Iseabal stood staring out her bedroom window, wondering if the weather was a portent for her marriage. The dawn mist had given way to a heavy shower that thundered against the roof, slanting against the windowpanes in watery disapproval.

Those passing between the outbuildings and Fernleigh did so quickly, their hurried footsteps marking the sodden path. Even the walls of her room seemed to weep with the dampness, as if subtly chastising Iseabal for her resolve.

She would not cry.

Any wish not to be married would be futile. This was the way of the world, after all. Daughters were to be wed, as profitably as possible. At least this bridegroom was young and healthy.

She had, at least, a passing acquaintance with those men who'd made a bid for her hand. She'd known the name of the palsied old man who'd tried to grope her, and the character of the toothless magistrate who'd been fascinated with her bottom. She'd been told where they lived, and what each man required for a wife—a fertile breeder, a mother to his children, or a nurse in his old age.

All she knew of the MacRae was that he felt a kinship to Gilmuir strong enough to pay a fortune for it and marry a stranger. A man of honor, perhaps. Or one whose stubbornness was the match of her father's.

Her prayer was simple. *Help me.*

God spoke to her, not in a booming voice, but in the sudden image of Alisdair MacRae extending his hand to her. The sun seemed to sparkle behind his beautiful eyes, and his smile was an answer of sorts.

A man who'd helped a stranger. One whose eyes had narrowed when her father spoke of her, who had halted Drummond's words with a curt command. A man to respect, perhaps.

Was it enough to respect a husband? Somewhere there must be another, softer emotion, one borne of laughter and friendship.

There were signs of love at Fernleigh, but it existed in the engaging smile of one of the maids as she waved to her sweetheart in the stables. Or when the cook kissed Angus, the carpenter, then shooed him from the kitchen with a pat on his rump.

But there was nothing of happiness in her mother's face and little amusement to be found in her smile. A lesson, perhaps, in that realization. Money, power, and privilege did not bring happiness.

Today, however, her father seemed pleased enough.

"The Drummond's being a right pleasant sort," one of the servant girls had remarked earlier in the corridor outside her room. "He even smiled at me when I brought him his porridge."

"It's best not to trust in his good nature, Mary," her companion cautioned. "His moods change with the wind."

But it seemed as if her father was not about to change his mind. She was going to be married in a matter of hours.

Turning away from the window, Iseabal walked to the rectangular straw basket that would serve as her trunk, holding her clothing along with the necessities of her wardrobe. In the bottom were the most precious of her treasures, her sculpting tools and those pieces she'd retrieved from Robbie this morning.

Her hands, lightly touching the flat top of the trunk, felt cold, her fingertips almost numb. But then her stomach whirred as if a thousand bees had taken up residence inside her.

What would marriage bring?

The sameness of her solitude, no doubt. A feeling of being alone in a vast sea of people. She would be expected to be pleasant and silent, smiling and mute. Not an appreciable difference from her current life, except for the added duty of the marriage bed. If she were lucky, her new husband would be kind. If not, she would simply accept her new existence.

But surely there was more to life than endurance?

She began to pace the length of her chamber, counting out the steps from one wall to the window and back again. From childhood she'd understood that the reason for a union mattered little, be it greed or pride or revenge, only that her father would choose and she would obey.

But it did not mean that she welcomed the future. She knew life at Fernleigh, accepted it as she did the changing of the seasons. Even her father's rages and the unforeseen nature of his cruelty were expected. She had learned the confines of her life as well as she knew the dimensions of her chamber.

Her mother entered the room suddenly, her face wreathed in a bright smile. In her arms she held a petticoat decorated with thin yellow stripes, and a dark blue shortgown, or jacket.

"I've finished," her mother said, spreading the garments carefully over the bed. On the cuffs of the coat and on the hem of the petticoat, Leah had embroidered tiny thistles and stalks of heather. A neckerchief of pale yellow, fastened with the Drummond brooch and her mother's blue beads, would complete her wedding attire.

Iseabal traced a finger over the silk threads, feeling the mist of tears. Perhaps she would cry after all.

"You must have been up all night," she said, talking past the constriction in her throat.

"My daughter is being married," Leah said softly. "I would gladly do as much a thousand times over."

Iseabal nodded, unable to speak.

"You are bound for a new life, Iseabal," her mother said, her smile oddly luminous. "Why do you look so miserable?"

Because I do not want your life. I don't want to be afraid all the time. Words she would never speak, because uttering them would wound the one person she loved.

"I am not miserable," she replied, forcing a smile to her face. "Just thinking that my prayers should have been more fully formed. I wished to be free of Fernleigh and now I find myself about to be wed. I wanted a man younger than my suitors and more handsome, but I never thought he would buy me in order to keep his land."

Her mother placed both palms on either side of Iseabal's face. "Love comes to most of us at one time or another, my dearest daughter. But you must watch for it, lest it slips past you unaware."

Pulling away, Iseabal stared at her mother. "You can say that, Mother, when he uses you so?"

"Your father has provided well for us, Iseabal," she said gently. "We live in luxury compared to so many others."

"Is it worth his cruelty?" Iseabal asked.

Leah gazed at her. "Your father does not think himself brutal, Iseabal, only strong. He does not see his cruelty, only his determination."

"Evil that does not recognize itself?"

"Is any man truly evil?" her mother countered, her eyes kind. "Or does each person hold within themselves a kernel of goodness? A seed that either grows or withers.

"It is enough, perhaps, to feel joy in your children such as you have given me," Leah said, placing her hand gently on Iseabal's cheek. "That brings a contentment all its own."

If her mother was content, why were there dark circles beneath her eyes? Or why was there panic on her face when her husband entered a room, sour-tempered and angry?

"Mother," Iseabal said gently. "You want to see goodness in him, and so you do. But have you never wished for more?"

"I had love once," Leah said unexpectedly, sitting on the bench. "A man I loved with all my heart," she added, staring down at her hands. She examined the backs of them, then turned them over, studying her fingers as if she'd never before seen them. "He was a MacRae," she said. "Fergus MacRae, of Gilmuir."

Shocked, Iseabal sat down beside Leah, stretched out her hand to touch her mother's wrist, a wordless comfort to counteract the sudden sad look on the other woman's face.

Glancing at Iseabal, Leah continued. "He was the most wonderful man I'd ever known. We planned to wed when the rebellion was over, when he came home."

"What happened?" Iseabal asked.

"A story repeated a thousand times. He never returned. I married your father only because it didn't matter. After Fergus died, I lived in a cloud. Nothing had the power to move me from my grief. Except you," she said, reaching up and brushing Iseabal's hair over her shoulder in a tidying gesture. "You have been my greatest joy."

"I thought you cried at night because of him," Iseabal said slowly.

"Your father?" Leah shook her head. "I never knew you heard," she said, standing and turning to the window. She gripped the sill as if to steady herself.

"He was a giant of a man," Leah said, staring through the window as if she could see him now. "Him, with his red beard and his way of walking as if he owned the earth below his feet. Sometimes I used to think that God Himself would look like Fergus, both fierce and kind."

"You love him still?" she asked.

"Love doesn't vanish when death appears, Iseabal. In my mind, I'm still that young girl who met him in the glens between my home and his. In my heart, I'm still his." Leah's words were laden with both love and sorrow.

"Is that why you welcome this marriage?"

Her mother glanced at her, smiling. "My one true regret

was that I never bore his child. Sometimes I pretended that
you were his, instead of Drummond's. But my prayers have
been answered in the best way. You'll marry the nephew of
the man I loved. If he is half the man Fergus was, then I'm
well pleased."

Standing, Iseabal kissed her mother's pale cheek. People
had always commented upon their similar appearance in that
both of them had been gifted with black hair and green eyes.
But her mother's hair had begun to whiten and her eyes
seemed to have become lighter in hue over the years. Almost,
Iseabal thought, as if she were becoming a pale version of
herself.

Iseabal could refute her mother's words in a hundred
ways, but the small smile on Leah's face discouraged any
spoken truths, even though they lingered in the air.

Gilmuir bound Iseabal and the MacRae together, not love,
however much her mother wished it different.

Alisdair stood beneath the stained-glass window in the
hall of Fernleigh, Iseabal silent beside him. She'd not spoken
to him once, and her only acknowledgment of his presence
had been a halfhearted nod when she'd appeared in the hall.
From that moment on, she'd stared at the floor as if the worn
stones held the map to heaven.

The rough planks of the table beside him were still littered with tankards, as if Drummond had spent hours celebrating his victory over the MacRaes. Whiskey fumes
permeated the room, mixing with the smell of a hundred unwashed Drummonds.

Despite the rainy day, no candles were lit, no lanterns
gleamed from the mantel, nor did a warm and welcoming
fire burn in the huge hearth. There was no priest in atten-

dance, or pipers playing the MacRae March. On such an important occasion as this, it was customary to wear the kilt, but even that had been forbidden him since the garment was still outlawed in Scotland. Nor was his family here to witness this ceremony.

Instead, his marriage was accompanied by a fetid and chilly gloom, being witnessed by his crew and the assembled Drummond clan, all of whom remained silent, as if realizing that this wedding was no cause for celebration.

The feeling of being pressed into this marriage only increased, like he was stepping into one of his brother's boots and finding it painfully small.

Turning to the assembled clan, Alisdair began speaking the vows given him only an hour earlier, then repeated them to the parents of his bride. Leah was smiling, her expression carefully directed away from her husband, whose bloodshot eyes were gleaming with triumph. Finally, Alisdair turned to face Iseabal. "I take this woman to my side, and bind myself to her," he said.

Her face was too pale, and her green eyes paler still, as if all the color had been leeched out of her by this ceremony.

All his life he had been surrounded by love. Passionate, endearing, humorous at times. He had never wondered about his own marriage, being certain that he would find that one woman to be his helpmate, companion, and lover.

One day he'd expected to marry a girl from the Cape. Noreen, perhaps, with her sunny smiles and her habit of teasing him. Or Sarah, who prided herself on her cooking and invited him for dinner every week, the meal shared with her father and brothers. But his heart leaned toward Hester, only because she was brave and daring and fearless. Women he'd known from his infancy, friends for a lifetime.

Not a woman who looked terrified of him, whose breathing was so rapid he wondered why she did not faint. Alisdair glanced at Drummond, thinking that being his daughter might well have given her a reason to fear all men.

The price for Gilmuir had been steep indeed.

Iseabal could hardly breathe, her heart was beating so fast.

The MacRae had shaved his beard, revealing a square chin and full mouth. But it was not his handsome appearance that caused her to look away, wondering almost frantically if there was a way to stop this marriage after all.

The scowl, forming over eyes the color of a pale blue sky, hinted at a formidable temper. He towered over most of the people assembled in the hall, and standing as he was with his hands clenched behind him, feet apart, he seemed to dominate the space with his presence.

The most imposing man she'd ever met.

He was dressed as she had seen him yesterday. His clothing was clean; even his boots were shined to a high gloss. Despite his fine clothes, however, he looked like a warrior, one of the legendary MacRaes, although she'd never met any of them. The clan had simply disappeared one day and there was no one left to tell where they had gone.

His voice boomed out his vows as if he were issuing a command. He paused, as if expecting her to acknowledge his words in some way. If she were truly as biddable as her father thought, she would have smiled at her new husband or appeared pleased to be marrying such a handsome and well-to-do man. But she did not, choosing silence instead, and focusing her attention on anything but him.

Her mother was thrilled with the match, simply because

he was a MacRae. Her father was pleased with the money he'd received and the fact that he had rid himself of a daughter. Even the Drummonds, murmuring behind her, did not seem averse to this union.

Evidently she was the only one with any objections, and they were not to be voiced. She was simply to acquiesce to everyone's plans for her and look overjoyed at the prospect.

The thunder was her only ally, booming overhead, rattling the stained-glass window as if in reproach for her submission.

The vows completed, her father passed a small silver chalice to Iseabal. The Drummond tradition of both husband and wife drinking from the same cup signified the joining of two lives. She took a sip of the whiskey before passing the cup to the MacRae. Her mother held out a sheaf of wheat and a square of woven cloth, symbols to indicate that each would provide for their home. She handed MacRae the cloth, while he took the wheat and presented it to Iseabal. The giving and accepting done, she waited for him to speak, a moment rooted in custom. The groom was supposed to praise his new wife and thank her parents.

Instead, the MacRae stepped forward, giving instructions for her belongings to be brought to the hall. There were to be no words of praise, no ceremony, which was as well, Iseabal thought. She disliked hypocrisy.

Her mother continued to smile at her, the look in her eyes one of joy. Behind her, the Drummond clan stood motionless and nearly silent, as did the men the MacRae had brought with him.

Her father made a gesture and one of his ever-present guards appeared beside him. "Fetch her trunk," he said brusquely.

With such simple words, she was acknowledged wife instead of daughter, and just as easily banished from Fernleigh.

Iseabal walked into her mother's arms, blinking back tears.

"I am so happy for you, Iseabal," her mother said gently. "You must be happy as well."

Iseabal nodded, turning back to her new husband. His gaze was fixed on the window above him, intently studying the glass rendering of a young knight. What did he see when he looked there?

She had not expected a display of emotion from her father, but her departure from Fernleigh was done without a word of farewell. One moment she was standing in the clan hall, the next she was at the door, swept along in a silent tide following the MacRae.

Glancing back at those who stood in the hallway, Iseabal felt a sense of loss she'd not expected. The servant girls she'd known all her life waved their fingers in discreet farewell. Robbie, the stableboy, smiled at her, but her father looked at her as if she were no more than an uninvited guest who'd outstayed her welcome.

Chapter 5

The MacRae took her arm, albeit gently, and walked with her from Fernleigh.

Her father had offered no horses, and the MacRae had arrived with none. She and her new husband were followed by two men who carried her straw trunk, and behind them at least twenty others, so orderly in their manner that they reminded her of the Highland Regiments assembling in Edinburgh.

The thunder roared again, preceding another cloudburst. In seconds she was drenched, rain soaking through her wedding finery. The MacRae acted as if the storm were nothing more than a minor inconvenience, and like their leader, none of the men behind them voiced a complaint.

They headed in the direction of Gilmuir, a journey she knew well enough. Iseabal was forced nearly to a run to keep up with the MacRae. His strides were long and impatient, as if he could not wait to reach Gilmuir. Or escape her presence.

The day grew increasingly miserable, with the chill bringing forth a fog that clung to the grass, shielding their feet from view. Occasionally Iseabal would push back her wet hair from her face, wipe her eyes dry, but the efforts were futile. The air was gray with rain and cold with the winds sweeping over the glen and through the branches of the trees.

After a quick sideways glance at her, the MacRae slowed his pace. Still, he walked ahead of her a few feet, with her trailing behind like a well-trained mastiff.

His sodden breeches could not hide the well-developed muscles of his legs any more than his coat could minimize the breadth of his shoulders. Even his hands were large, and she remembered the feel of them, warm against her palms.

What would it be like to lie with him?

She might be a maiden, but she was not ignorant of the deed. A few years ago she'd been courageous enough to ask a servant girl.

"Well, miss," Mary had said, "the man rises behind you, and inserts himself into your privates. All hot and bothered he is, miss, especially toward the last. Then he sleeps for a bit and wants it again. If you wish to know exactly how it's done," she'd confided, "watch the rams. They've the same bluster."

Iseabal had, secretly, taken the maid's advice. Not only had the ram acted as if the deed were owed him, but the whole coupling had been done in seconds, leaving the ewe bleating and rolling her eyes, for all the world like she was impatient with his posturing.

Surely she could be as placid as a sheep?

Halfway to Gilmuir, the MacRae turned to her. "Would you like to rest?" he asked.

"No," she said agreeably. She'd made the journey on foot yesterday, and she could do it again today. Nor would she utter a word of complaint about the weather or the cold. Slogging through the mud was not such a trial after all. The only difficulty was the pain in her side, but, Iseabal decided, she could bear it.

His expression lightened strangely enough, his scowl fading. "I meant to offer no insult," he said. "I only asked after your comfort."

She looked up at the sky, the rain pounding on her face. Comfort? Where was there comfort?

Despite the rain, and in abject disregard of the storm above them, the MacRae walked to stand beneath a gnarled old tree. Iseabal shrugged and followed.

"Are you not worried about lightning?" she asked.

He smiled, the expression out of place for this dreary day. "When you've been aboard a ship in a storm, you begin to think yourself invincible."

While she felt as vulnerable as the exposed root on which she sat. Spreading her filthy petticoat over the tops of her equally ruined shoes, she folded her arms across her knees and sat staring at the men around her. They stood uncomplaining in the rain, as docile as sheep.

"Who are those men?"

"The crew of my ship," he said shortly, then amended his statement. "The men of the *Fortitude*."

"Your ship?"

He nodded in response, leaving her to wonder if she should be satisfied with that.

"You are a sea captain?" she asked cautiously, wondering

if her prayers had indeed come true. A marriage to a man who was often gone from home would not be an onerous thing.

"I am," he said shortly.

Evidently, Iseabal thought, she was not to ask questions of him.

A few moments of silence passed before Iseabal stood, eager to complete the journey. At least at Gilmuir there was a spot or two that was still impervious to rain. And a fire would be doubly nice.

The remainder of the journey seemed to take hours, made in half steps through the mud. The fortress appeared suddenly, oddly surrounded by a white mist, as if Gilmuir were floating on a cloud.

They crossed the land bridge and only then did she begin to hear sounds from the men behind her. Some laughed; some uttered words of relief; still more began to talk freely, as if rendered mute in any place other than Gilmuir.

Iseabal walked inside what had once been the courtyard and beyond to the trellised archway.

"Prepare for departure, Daniel," the MacRae said to one auburn-haired man. He nodded and continued walking. Not one of the men was making an attempt to light a fire or prepare shelter for the night.

"Where are we to live?" she asked. She'd given no thought to the future, more concerned with getting through the ceremony to worry about more.

He looked at her with chilled eyes, as if she'd transformed herself into her father. "Not here," he replied curtly.

"Then why did you buy the land?" she asked, caution fading beneath curiosity.

"Because it belongs to the MacRaes," he said, striding

through the archway to the priory beyond. He turned to stare at her when she remained in place.

In her mind, Iseabal had always been brave. Her thoughts, reckless and occasionally daring, had been held within, where they couldn't lead to punishment. Rarely did she act upon them, having learned to be cautious and circumspect with her words and deeds.

She'd married a man she didn't know and had been led from her home uncomplaining, across the muddy glens to Gilmuir. All done without a word of protest. Surely she merited answers. Before her bravado escaped, Iseabal clenched her hands into fists and stared at her new husband. "We're to live aboard your ship?" she asked, confused.

"No," he said. "We're going to England."

She blinked, astonishment robbing her momentarily of words. England? A destination she would never have imagined.

The rain still fell, soaking into the ground of the promontory, pattering on the fallen bricks. At that moment it was as if Gilmuir were chattering around them, admonishment in every soft raindrop, a scold in the wisp of the wind.

He held out his hand, a dozen steps separating them. The journey, however, was longer than that, Iseabal realized. She was not yet a wife, but the man who stood looking at her was her husband. A man to whom she owed her allegiance, her obedience, her trust.

But she remained in place, her hands now at her sides, her face carefully devoid of any expression.

A moment later he retraced his steps until he stood in front of her. "There will be more comfort aboard ship, Iseabal," he told her patiently. "A shelter from the storm, at least."

Was she to sacrifice all she'd ever known? Give up her country as well as herself? Perhaps she was, and supposed to do so willingly, accepting her fate with quiet compliance.

A thought slipped from its sanctuary, one steeped in caution and restraint. *Ask him for the stone.* She had asked for little, no consideration, few answers. Her silence and her acceptance, Iseabal decided, deserved some reward.

"Will you grant me a favor?" she asked daringly. Cupping her elbows in her hands, she waited patiently for his answer.

"What favor?" he asked, frowning.

Turning, she walked back to the entrance to the ruined clan hall, hearing his boots on the brick flooring behind her. When he stood at her side, Iseabal walked out into the storm again, carefully skirting the edge of the pit.

Rain pounded the ground, creating pools among the pocked stone and a lake of mud in the courtyard. Streams of water poured into the foundation, flooding the base of the pillars.

"That," Iseabal said, pointing to the gleaming black stone barely visible above water level.

"A rock?" he asked, turning to her.

"A rock," she answered, surprised at the note of resolve in her voice.

"This is important to you, Iseabal?" he asked in amazement.

"Yes," she said, tightening her arms around her waist.

He shrugged but didn't question her further. Instead, he nodded, gripping her elbow and leading her back to the corridor. A request not to be granted, then. At his impatient look, Iseabal followed him into the priory.

This area of Gilmuir had become unsafe in the past years.

The yawning hole in the middle of the structure didn't surprise her. She'd heard her father crowing of his discovery and of the secret cove the MacRaes had hidden all these years.

This was how the MacRae had entered the fortress, yet she'd never questioned his sudden appearance. He'd simply been there, a rescuer not unlike the Raven, a Samaritan to help her from the consequences of her own folly.

The rain was louder here, slapping against the slate floor.

He sat, dangling his legs into the hole beneath him, his hands braced on either side. Slowly he disappeared into the blackness. Peering over the edge, Iseabal could see only a darkness that mimicked the grave. Unexpectedly, his head popped up, startling her.

She'd never taken the staircase before. But then, Iseabal thought, this day had marked a number of first occasions. She sat on the adjoining slate, dangling her feet just as he had. His hands wound around her legs, then to her waist as she slid down into his arms. Their soggy clothing did little to shield curves and angles, muscle and flesh.

His hands tightened against her waist, the unexpected pain surprising her. Drawing back, she pressed herself against the wall, taking shallow breaths to minimize the discomfort.

He seemed to stare at her in the darkness, but said nothing before turning and beginning to descend the steps. Once again he stopped when she made no move to follow him.

"Please, Iseabal," he said, evidently exasperated into politeness. "It is safe enough. Although the stairs are steep, all you need do is watch your footing. The passage is a narrow one, and you can hold onto the walls."

He thought her afraid. She should tell him of her injury, Iseabal thought. But this day had been marked by humilia-

tion and the surrender of home and pride. She'd just as soon
keep her pain to herself.

Slowly she followed, her right hand outstretched against
the wall, her left held tightly at her side. The staircase was
enshrouded in a darkness so profound that it made no difference if she closed her eyes.

"Take your time, Iseabal," he said, his voice disembodied
and echoing. "The rain has made the steps slippery."

A marriage to a pockmarked, toothless old man with a
bald pate seemed a blessing at the moment. At least an old
husband wouldn't march her from Fernleigh to Gilmuir in a
drenching storm, travel down this damp and pungent staircase, intent upon taking her to England.

Perhaps this was a dream and she lay abed now, recuper-
ating from her injury. The thunder was her father's roar. The
clammy wetness of her garments, the result of a breaking
fever. And this descent into the darkness was the embodi-
ment of her secret fear of going to hell for not honoring her
father. But the MacRae's voice, loud and commanding,
would have summoned her to wakefulness, which meant this
was real and not a nightmare.

At the bottom of the stairs was a cave, darkened by the
weather and the gathering storm. Two of his men stood beside the entrance, waiting.

"Are the rest of the men on board?" the MacRae asked.

"Yes, Captain," one said.

MacRae turned to her. "Iseabal," he said. Only that, a
summons in the speaking of her name.

Iseabal followed the three of them, ducking through the
rounded entrance to the cave and emerging into the cove
Drummond had discovered all those years ago. Ringed by

cliffs and guarded by a giant's teeth, the rain-dimpled water sheltered a ghost of a ship.

He turned to look at her, his smile undimmed by the storm.

"The *Fortitude*," he said, pride lacing his voice.

Chapter 6

Unlike the other merchant vessels Iseabal had seen in Inverness, the MacRae's ship was stretched at both ends until her bow and stern rose high above the water. Four towering masts spread the length of the ship, each intersected by thick horizontal beams holding huge swags of sails.

The *Fortitude*'s name in Gaelic was emblazoned in bold crimson lettering along her side. Iseabal knew little of the language, the Gaelic having been forbidden for decades now. In a strange way, she thought, the MacRae was more Scots than she. He wore the tartan, displayed the language of their ancestors, and no doubt spoke it as well.

MacRae led the way to a lone skiff on the shoreline. Without warning, Iseabal was being effortlessly lifted, her feet stumbling in the bottom of the boat before she was released. Stifling a cry of pain, she sat on the bench, surreptitiously pressing her arm against her side.

The MacRae sat beside her, one sailor behind her, the other opposite them manning the oars. Her sideways glance revealed that his lips had thinned, his face bearing a look of irritation. Was he a man of her father's temperament, slow to please and too quick to anger? If so, she simply didn't have the energy to care.

Iseabal sat on the rough wood seat, clutching her hands in her lap, choosing not to look at the MacRae, concentrating on the *Fortitude* instead.

Thunder boomed overhead; lightning appeared to sizzle from one cliff face to another. Rain had transformed the air into a gray, waterlogged blanket. Was it possible to be more miserable than she was at this moment? She was drenched and in pain, and even locked in her chamber Iseabal had not felt as isolated as she did at this moment.

The MacRae was as drenched as she, his hair slicked back in the pouring rain, yet he didn't look battered by the elements. Instead, he sat aloof and apart, as kingly as if he commanded the climate. Or perhaps a god of rain and storm, and in his eyes the promise of a fair, sunny day.

He turned, his gaze locking with hers for a moment before he looked away, gesturing to the man in front of them. The oars were stowed, the boat carried by the current until it nudged the *Fortitude*. One sailor reached out to grip the rope ladder, holding it steady for the other crewman. Then, Iseabal realized, it was her turn. Staring up at the distance to the railing, she felt unequal to the task. There was nothing to do but put her foot in one of the rungs and pull herself up the side of the ship.

Halfway there, Iseabal was certain she wouldn't make it. The pain in her side was as sharp and piercing as a knife point. Laying her forehead against the wet rope, she took as deep a breath as she could, gripped the rung above her, and began to pull herself slowly upward again.

The MacRae spoke from beneath her, but the rain abruptly increased in volume, rendering conversation impossible. Was he giving her words of condemnation or encouragement? Neither mattered at the moment. This ascent would be made with sheer determination and nothing else.

Iseabal gritted her teeth, ignoring the pain and the increasing violence of the storm, finally reaching the railing. The same two sailors helped her to the deck, a flurry of petticoats alerting her to the need for modesty. Such consideration, Iscabal thought, weighed less than her wish for warmth, shelter, and an end to the pain.

None of the sailors seemed to mind the storm or pay it any heed. A few of them bravely gamboled up the masts, untying the ropes that held the front sails furled.

Behind her, the MacRae swung a leg over the railing, speaking to Daniel before joining her. Gently, he took her arm and led her across the deck. Tucked into an expanse of well-polished wood was a door. He pushed it open, stepping back for her to precede him.

His hand on her back was both impetus and encouragement. Moving forward, Iseabal heard the door close behind her.

She entered, remaining by the door, hesitant to damage the flooring that gleamed beneath her feet. Water ran from her petticoat in rivulets and her shoes were caked with mud. But that wasn't entirely the reason she hesitated. The chamber was so small and crowded that her presence seemed intrusive.

At the end of the room, taking up the entire width, was a bunk built into the wall, framed with mahogany timbers and a curtain of red, black, and white plaid.

On the far wall was a series of shelves, each framed with a ledge, no doubt to prevent the books stored there from falling. To her right was a chest built in the shape of steps rising from the floor to the ceiling, each level containing a series of small doors or drawers bearing a small brass key adorned with a red tassel.

At waist level, a table jutted out from the chest. Designed, Iseabal realized, to swing back into the rectangular slit. When it was open, the table could act as a desk or a place to have a meal.

There was nothing on the left side of the room, which was just as well, since her trunk had been placed there. The woven basket looked waterlogged, absurdly forlorn, and out of place.

This room represented her marriage as nothing else could. She didn't fit into this man's life.

She turned, forcing herself to face her husband. Iseabal was certain that she had never looked worse. Her hair was hanging around her face in damp tendrils; her clothing was drenched. Even her shoes squeaked when she walked. The dye from the yellow kerchief was dripping steadily down her neck.

The MacRae retrieved a bit of toweling from his odd chest, startling her by wrapping the linen around her hair, and securing the ends of the cloth in a loose knot at the nape of her neck. His palm felt warm, as did his breath against her cheek as he bent closer.

She'd never before been so close to a strange man.

His presence had an extraordinary effect on her, but it wasn't dread fluttering in her stomach, or panic in her chest. Her breath felt tight, but that could be due to the pain in her side. Her heart pounded in her chest, due to the exertion of the journey, no doubt.

Once again he startled her by grabbing another length of toweling and beginning to blot her cheeks dry.

"You look miserable and exhausted, Iseabal," he said gently, placing a cloth on the table. "You're trembling."

"I'm cold." How tremulous her voice sounded, she thought. Almost faint, as if she were afraid to speak. Silence would be better, perhaps. Anything but conversing with this man the law had bound to her.

"You need to change your clothes."

"Yes," she answered, making her voice sound more firm.

Silence stretched between them, there being nothing more to say, no words to ease the awkward moment.

He walked to the door and opened it, the storm an oddly perfect backdrop to his appearance. Iseabal had the strangest thought that he could as easily be one of the early Scots, naked and painted blue, standing on a hillside with his arms outstretched as if to threaten his enemies with his very size.

Belatedly, she recognized that she should have thanked him for his kindness, but the words wouldn't come.

Crossing the cabin suddenly, he lit a lantern sitting on one of the steps of his chest. The soft glow illuminated the shadows as he hung it on a hook mounted on the wall.

"If the storm gets worse," he said, "extinguish the lantern."

"Where will you be?" she asked, swallowing heavily.

"I have an errand to perform," he said finally, shattering the silence, his eyes steady on hers. "After that I have a ship to command," he said, smiling. "We need to get out of the cove before nightfall."

Iseabal nodded, watching as the door closed deliberately behind him. For a moment she simply stood there, thinking that the magistrate from Edinburgh, with his tightly curled wig smelling of dust, wouldn't have smiled in quite that way. The merchant from Inverness, with his habit of rubbing his palms together, would never have made her think of pagan times. None of her suitors would have tenderly dried her face, his eyes intent on hers, his voice kind.

She began to unfasten her jacket, only now conscious of the movement beneath her. She had never been aboard ship before, and the experience was proving to be a disconcerting one. The *Fortitude* seemed to be alive in the storm, like a horse bound for a gallop.

Iseabal stood behind the door to remove her petticoat. There weren't any pegs or any other place to hang her wet clothing, so she draped it across her trunk. Next came her jacket, the effort of moving her shoulder resulting in a stabbing pain in her side. Resting for a moment, she wondered how long it would be until she felt more like herself again. The constant ache was debilitating, and her body seemed to be stiffening up in response.

The leather of her stays was soaked and so was the shift below them. She didn't remove either garment, not out of modesty as much as a very real fear that she wouldn't be able to don them again.

The light blue petticoat and jacket in the middle of the basket were slightly damp but in better condition than the clothing she'd removed. Dressing as quickly as she could, Iseabal began to rub her hair, wishing that, now she was partially dry, there was some heat in the cabin.

Moving to the lantern, she placed her palms over it, but the heat from the oil lamp was not enough to warm her.

Rain pelted the ship; wind swirled around the decks of the *Fortitude* and beneath the cabin door in a lamenting moan.

Iseabal sat on the edge of the bunk, her thoughts not on her wedding night or on the MacRae. Instead, she was wishing that she'd learned to swim.

There wasn't time to delay, Alisdair thought, climbing the stairs once again, two crewmen with lanterns accompanying him. The storm had darkened the afternoon sky and he wanted to be gone from the cove before the rest of the daylight vanished. Yet, for some reason, he felt compelled to do this task for Iseabal.

A rock. That was all she'd wanted. Perhaps a souvenir of Gilmuir or of Scotland. He would give her either or both. Not simply because she wished it, but more because of the decision he'd made on the journey from Fernleigh.

His was not the nature to accept what happened to him. Instead, Alisdair believed that a man made his own destiny. Somehow, he was going to obtain an annulment. They'd been wed outside his religion, in a ceremony unblessed by the kirk. Surely it would be easy enough to petition for his freedom.

Because of the amount paid to Drummond, he could barely support himself, let alone expand the shipyard. But he had enough left over to settle Iseabal in some other place. Some country far from Drummond, where she could live her life as she chose. As for himself, he'd made one fortune, he'd make another.

Peering over the edge, Alisdair reached for the rope ladder and, with the assistance of the other two men, pounded the metal hooks into the ground. He lowered himself over the side, each crewman holding a portion of the ladder to steady it.

Walking quickly to where he'd last seen the stone, Alisdair stretched a hand into the water and picked it up, surprised at its weight. Tossing it up to the side of the pit was easier than climbing the ladder with it tucked beneath his arm. At the surface, he rolled the ladder up again before retrieving the stone.

His boots sank into the waterlogged ground with each step as he made his way back to the priory. Turning to the men beside him, he nodded in thanks. Only then did Alisdair realize that this task had been performed in total silence.

The door opened so suddenly that at first Iseabal thought it was powered by an errant gust of wind. But in the center of the doorway was a boy not much older than ten, feet apart to brace himself, arms wrapped around her marble block.

Speechless, she watched him enter the cabin. He let the stone drop to the floor, the gesture accompanied by an oath so loud and foul that her eyes widened.

"You mustn't drop it like that," she scolded, standing. "Marble cracks."

"I'd not be criticizing me," he said, his scowl older than his years. "I hauled it from the boat, didn't I? And up the ladder? What the captain was doing fetching the stupid thing, I'll not know. Next you'll have him mucking about in the mud to find just the right pebble for you."

"Do you always talk in such a fashion?" she asked, startled. He was little more than a child, yet his vocabulary and demeanor marked him as older.

He stood, his legs still braced apart, his hands behind him, a pose she'd seen the MacRae assume.

"I'm Rory, the captain's boy, ma'am," he said proudly.

"His son?" she asked, confused.

"You're thinking I'm some by-blow?" he asked incredulously. "The MacRaes are honorable men," he said, making no effort to hide his derision. "I'm his cabin boy." With that, he stalked from the room, slamming the door behind him.

A gale had just passed through the cabin, Iseabal thought, a two-legged force of nature to challenge the gathering storm winds outside.

Lowering herself carefully to her knees, Iseabal placed her hands on the block, grateful to find no cracks in the surface of the smooth marble.

This was the errand the MacRae had spoken of, going back to the pit for the stone she wished. What kind of man grants a bride such a doubtful gift? Or who does so without a word of protest?

He was a man of fearsome stature, whose eyes had grown cold when looking at her father. The MacRae was not a man to challenge, yet he'd done such a thing for her. Nor was it the first time he'd shown consideration.

Who was her new husband? Iseabal suddenly realized that she wanted, very much, to know.

Chapter 7

The increasing wind buffeted Alisdair until his wet clothing was plastered against his skin. There was no reason to change; he'd only become drenched again. After the *Fortitude* made Coneagh Firth, he'd revel in dry clothes, and in the warmth of a brazier carried up from the galley. A promise to himself that led to another thought.

Where was he going to sleep tonight?

Sleeping below the stars was a nice respite from the closeness of his cabin, smaller than most captain's quarters due to the *Fortitude*'s design. On a fair night he would not hesitate to make a berth on deck. Nor was he adverse to sharing quarters with his crew. But he wasn't about to drown, and they were two sailors over on this voyage, the men drawing straws to see who won a hammock for the night. He wouldn't take a place not rightfully his.

The sails harnessed the wind in a whoosh of canvas. Below his feet, he could feel the *Fortitude*'s eagerness to escape from the cove. But Scotland did not release them easily, he mused, as the thunder growled over them and lightning struck too close to the necklace of rocks, as if warning them not to leave. The sheer cliffs curving to form the promontory that was Gilmuir were starkly illuminated by a flash of light even as Alisdair gave the signal for the anchors to be raised.

His most trusted pilot manned the wheel, easing the *Fortitude* around the natural barrier as he watched.

"Henrietta was right," Daniel said, coming to stand beside him.

"I thought that particular omen was for yesterday," Alisdair said, glancing at his first mate. "Or are there no timetables for Henrietta's omens?"

The cat might have warned him, Alisdair thought dryly, that he was about to be made a pauper and a husband.

"The cook wants to know if it will be a cold meal, Captain," Daniel said, not responding to his gibes about the ship's cat. When Daniel considered himself right, he retreated into a smug silence.

"Tell him to keep the stove cold until after the storm passes," Alisdair replied, annoyed.

Daniel nodded and left him. Alisdair turned, flattening his hand against the rail. Loch Euliss was a silvery gray, its waves quieted under the onslaught of rain.

The *Fortitude* was beginning to rock in the increasing wind, an indication that there was too much sail. Alisdair called out the order to Daniel and watched the men clambering up the mast. They were lost in gray shadows, as if they'd climbed into a watery cloud.

A gust of wind nearly felled him, as if in displeasure for his departure. Alisdair steadied himself, wondering if the storm would follow them all the way to Coneagh Firth. The MacRaes were once again leaving Scotland, and the rain and the thunder seemed to chase them on their way in punishment.

He had heard stories of the first exodus, when his parents had married aboard ship amidst the sound of bagpipes played by his great-uncle. Alisdair could almost hear Hamish's pipes now, the wind playing a tune as it whistled across the deck.

During the next few moments the elements became female, the wind careening around the mast, shrieking in high-pitched fury. The current from Loch Euliss churned below the *Fortitude*, slapping against the hull in an imitation of a barmaid's playful smack. Thunder, maternal and aged, boomed no farther than the top of the masts, and lightning, acting as a petulant daughter, illuminated the steep glens on either side of the loch.

They were too damn close to shore.

Alisdair made his way to Daniel's side, shouting at him as the rain pelted both of them with the surprising taste of ice.

"Have the men come down from the rigging," he ordered. The ropes were the most dangerous place for a man to be in a storm. Not only could he be swept out to sea by the force of the wind, but lightning occasionally struck the masts and spars.

"We're in for a night of it," Daniel yelled back. "Are we heading for the firth in this?"

"We'll sit here and wait out the storm." There was no other choice. They were too close to shore and could easily go aground in the darkness.

*   *   *

They were all going to die.

Iseabal sat on the edge of the bunk, gripping both sides of the frame with clammy fingers. The mattress smelled of herbs and pine, and would have been soothing at another time. But not now when a Highland storm, frightening enough on land, had been transformed into a monster that lived in the loch.

She'd taken the precaution of extinguishing the lantern and now sat in the darkness, a hundred prayers trembling on her lips. The Almighty was evidently on the side of nature as the ship began canting from side to side. Her basket slid across the floor, landing with a thump against the edge of the bunk. Even the marble block moved, crashing into the side of the wall. The other furniture, she suspected, was bolted down.

Gouging her nails into the wood of the bed frame, Iseabal held on. A violent shudder shook the ship, as if the ocean had gripped the *Fortitude* in its teeth, tossing the vessel from side to side like a cur with a bone. Iseabal lost her handhold and was suddenly tossed from the bunk, striking the floor with such force that she cried out in pain.

She had been wrong after all. God was not in the storm, but in her body.

Carefully, she rolled onto her stomach, each damp palm pressed flat on the floorboards, fingernails sliding into the joints between each plank. Turning her face to the side, Iseabal rested her cheek against the cold wood. Her mind was curiously empty, pain robbing her of thought and reason.

Her mind began to wander, following the pain around her waist and above to her chest and back again to her side, a torturous journey accompanied by short and laborious breaths.

Her stomach lurched, nausea spreading through her body like a wave.

There was no way to tell how much time had elapsed. The storm had darkened the sky until not even a sliver of light appeared beneath the door.

Twice she tried to move, and both times was halted by the pain. The third time, she managed to rise to her knees. She took one breath and released it, hands clenching and unclenching as if mimicking the throbbing of her side.

If pain were a color, Iseabal thought, grabbing the frame of the bed for support as the ship rocked again, then it was fiery gold and red. Courage must come in shades as well. Hers would be pink, perhaps, or a shade of coral. Nothing as vibrant as yellow or as brilliant as green.

Over the next moments the storm seemed to ease a little, the swaying not as violent as before. Iseabal lay her head on the mattress, knowing that she would have to stand in order to reach the bunk. The effort seemed beyond her.

The door opened suddenly, the gray and watery darkness a welcoming contrast to the darkened cabin. Out of the corner of her eye Iseabal saw a looming shape. Not the cabin boy with his arrogant disapproval, but the MacRae himself.

When he entered the cabin, the air seemed to change, growing heavier as if the space was further narrowed. Lighting the lantern again, he stared at her, the scene almost otherworldly. They might have been strangers coming across each other by accident, each seeking refuge from the storm.

"Are you ill, Iseabal?" he asked. The cabin grew increasingly brighter as he began flipping open the three closed wind shields. "The storm will ease eventually," he said, the tone one he might use to a frightened child. "You will soon become used to the feeling of the sea beneath you, and the nausea will pass."

As he walked to her side, Iseabal let her eyes flutter shut, unable to cope with both the MacRae and the pain. At the moment, her side demanded all her attention.

He placed his hand on her shoulder and she weakly shook her head. If he touched her she would scream. All her hard-won courage would come seeping out with her tears.

"Are you hurt?" he asked, bending close.

Again she shook her head, but he was not to be denied. Before she realized what he was about to do, he was lifting her in his arms. All at once she was adrift in a red haze so powerful and all-consuming that it robbed her of both speech and thought. She reached out and gripped his sopping shirt, pulling on the material with desperate fingers.

He bent his head and she whispered an entreaty in one word. "Please."

Laying her gently on the bed, he knelt beside her.

"What is it, Iseabal?" he asked. "The injury from your fall?"

Surprised that he had remembered, she opened her eyes to find him studying her intently. His face was wet with rain, his brows were drawn together, his mouth thinned, his eyes narrowing into slits.

"Does it still pain you?" he asked, reaching out to unfasten her jacket.

She felt as if she were floating with the pain, feeling his hands on her and being unable to prevent it. Her fingers found his, tangled with them in a weak effort to halt his actions.

"Iseabal," he said gently, making her name a whisper.

When his fingers moved steadily upward, her gaze locked with his. Surely he wasn't thinking of bedding her now?

"I'll not be forbidden this, Iseabal," he said grimly.

His hand slipped beneath her jacket, spreading it apart. When her stays were finally opened, and the leather frame separated to reveal her linen shift, embarrassment warmed her cheeks.

"You will need to sit up," he said surprisingly, standing.

Was a woman to assume the position of a ewe? The question was stripped from her the moment he placed his arm behind her neck and began to lift her.

She screamed, a zigzag of sound that began loudly and in surprise and faded to a gasp as he laid her back down on the bed. Withdrawing from her, he retrieved a knife from his boot, using it to slice through her shift.

"Merciful God, Iseabal," he said, staring down at her side. "What have you done to yourself?"

She followed his glance, feeling as if all the blood were leaving her head. Where there had been a faint shadowing the day before, now she was covered from beneath her left arm to her waist in one continuous dark purple bruise.

"Have you had no treatment for this?"

Because his voice was gentle and the look in his eyes almost kind, she forced herself to speak through the pain. "No," she confessed breathlessly.

Without a word, he began to slice open her jacket at the shoulder and sleeve. Iseabal closed her eyes, concentrating not on the MacRae, but on a trick she'd discovered long ago. If she focused on the pain, she could keep it contained and manageable. Otherwise, it crept through her defenses, taking command.

Slipping a hand beneath her back, MacRae pulled the stays out slowly and gently before tossing them to the floor.

Her shift was likewise disposed of, impatiently but with a dexterous touch.

She raised her right arm, laying it across her breasts, the fingers of her right hand resting on her left shoulder. Futile modesty, but an instinctive gesture.

Hearing the sound of something scraping against the floor, Iseabal opened her eyes to see him pushing her basket over in front of the bed with his foot. Once it was in place, he retrieved a ewer and basin from a shelf. After he'd set the basin down on the flat top of the basket, the MacRae went to the chest and opened the third door on the top layer of boxes. From that he took a length of linen and two amber vials, placing them next to the cloths.

Sitting on the edge of the bed again, he bent over her and placed his hand on her bare skin. Iseabal wished the pain would momentarily subside in order to allow her time to savor the curious sensation of being touched by another person. His fingers traced the outline of one rib, then another, his stroke light, almost delicate.

"Where does it hurt the worst?" he asked, gingerly probing the area.

Everywhere, she mentally answered, but discovered that was not quite true when he prodded an especially agonizing spot. "There," she said, her gasp released on a sigh.

"You've either bruised yourself badly, Iseabal, or you've broken a rib. Either way, it's painful." He leaned back, surveying her. "Why didn't you tell me?"

What could she have said?

"You might have said something, Iseabal, to alert me to your injury or the degree of it," he said. Cupping her chin with his hand, he turned her face, held his fingers beneath her jaw until she opened her eyes. "On the journey back to Gilmuir, for one."

"Then you will wait?" she asked. "Before we couple," she added, in case he did not understand.

His shoulders stiffened.

"I have no wish to bed you, Iseabal," he said tightly. "Only to treat your injury."

He removed his hand and stood, leaving her staring at him. She did not mean to escape her duty as a wife. Yet he'd sounded relieved more than eager.

Walking to his chest again, he opened yet another small door, retrieving a tiny stoppered pitcher. Pouring a small amount of liquid into a cup, he added water, stirring the mixture with his finger.

"It will greatly ease your pain," he said, moving back to the bed and handing the cup to her. "Drink it down as quickly as you can and you'll not taste the bitterness."

"What is it?" she asked as he held it to her lips.

"Poppy juice," he said.

She'd never heard of such a potion and eyed it with caution.

"I'll not harm you, Iseabal," he said softly.

She nodded, drinking the liquid quickly and wincing at its taste.

"The water's going to be cold," he said, filling the basin from the ewer. "The galley fires have been extinguished."

"That's fine," she said. How polite they were, she thought with a tinge of humor. He, soaking wet and dripping all over the cabin, yet insisting upon playing nursemaid. She, lying on his bed, black-and-blue with her breasts still showing beneath her shielding arm.

A strange wedding night.

Dipping one of the cloths into the cool water, he wrung it out only slightly before placing it on her side. She clasped her lips tightly against the delicate pressure.

As he bathed her, replacing the cloth often, she stared above and to her left, noting the details of the wood surrounding the bunk. The dark pattern of striated ovals contrasted sharply against a lighter background. Beautiful workmanship, evidenced throughout this cabin and no doubt the whole of the *Fortitude*.

"That isn't the worst of it, I'm afraid," he said, removing the warmed cloth.

Iseabal nodded, wishing that she could bear to speak. But each word felt nipped at its tail and held prisoner by a sudden overwhelming confusion. She was feeling strangely light-headed, as if the pain in her side were slipping away. Her fingers felt warm, as did her toes, and her teeth felt abrasive, like limestone against her suddenly sensitive tongue.

He set the cloth aside, reaching for one of the amber vials shaped in the form of a dragon, its back filled with sharp spikes, its mouth opened to reveal fearsome teeth. She could almost envision it writhing and curling, wrapping itself around the MacRae's hand. He captured it with his fingers, taming it and transforming it once again into glass. Uncorking the dragon's head, he tipped the vial until a creamy yellow lotion dribbled onto his outstretched fingers.

"What is that?" she gasped, her eyes watering at the stench of rotting meat and grass.

"I think it's best if you don't know," he said, a faint smile playing over his lips as he began applying it to her skin. "It's an old formula given me by a man versed in the Chinese healing arts."

His fingertips smoothed the cream against her skin in slow and gentle circles from her waist to just below her arm. A not unpleasing sensation, Iseabal thought, drifting in the feeling.

When he finished, the MacRae opened the second container, this one in the shape of a reclining rabbit, pouring an even viler smelling lotion into his palm.

Each of his fingers felt like a tiny brazier against her skin. His thumb heated the curve of her breast, then just as quickly eased the sensation with a long, soothing stroke.

Closing her eyes, Iseabal wondered at the strength of his poppy juice. "Warm," she said, the word languid and soft, as if having texture.

"It's supposed to feel that way," he reassured her, his voice low and lingering. *Your hands are warm*, she said in her mind. *Not the lotion.*

She blinked open her eyes to find him capping the vial. He placed it on the basket top before turning to her again.

"I cannot swim," she said sluggishly, feeling the gentle sway of the ship beneath her. She'd meant to tell him before, but just now remembered.

"Most sailors cannot," he replied reasonably. "But we're not going to sink," he added, "so it won't matter."

"Are you certain?" Why did her voice sound fuzzy?

"Imminently so," he said, smiling.

Raising her right hand, she cupped her fingers around his jaw, a gesture that evidently surprised him. His eyes flickered to her chest, then back to her face. The chilled air against her heated nipples reminded her that she was half naked.

"You're so beautiful," she said, the truth needing to be spoken. "Are all the MacRaes beautiful?"

He removed her hand, placing her arm over her breasts again, shielding her from his sight.

"I'm the least handsome of the lot," he said, a soft smile curving his lips. "My brother James is the handsome one."

"No," she said, wondering if her lips should truly be this numb.

"You will have to be wrapped, Iseabal," he said, his face somber. "And for that you'll have to sit up. Can you bear it?"

Iseabal nodded, thinking that she could bear anything at this moment, even her wedding night.

He began to tear a cloth into lengths, tying them together before folding them end over end. She watched his hands raptly, fascinated that a man's hands could be so large and yet so dexterous.

He was so close that she could see the pattern of his buttons, a raised fist holding a sword. An insignia not so much of aggression as of protection.

"What is this?" she asked, brushing the fingers of her right hand against his chest.

"The emblem of the Clan MacRae," he said, drawing her up to a sitting position.

She closed her eyes, the red mist threatening again, but warmth oddly seemed to replace the pain.

"What is your name?" she asked abruptly, obviously surprising him with her question. "What do your friends and family call you?"

"Alisdair," he replied. "But surely you knew that. I spoke my vows not once but three times," he added dryly.

Her gaze slipped sideways. "I was not paying much attention," she confessed, warmth heating her cheeks.

"What were you thinking of, Iseabal?" he asked.

"You," she said, leaning her forehead against his damp

coat. *You*, she whispered again in her mind. But nothing like the thoughts she was having now. He was parting the red haze with his fingers, his smile keeping the pain at bay, and she was almost desperately grateful to him.

Thank you, she said silently, brushing her lips against his coat.

Beginning at her back, he wound the cloth around her side, lifting her left arm carefully as he did so. His knuckles brushed the underside of her breasts as he rolled the cloth across her stomach and around to her back again.

Pressing the flat of one hand against her back, he held her upright. His palm was growing heated, or she more chilled. But she didn't feel cold. Instead, there was a warmth inside her, one that traveled from her nose to her navel and around to the backs of her heels to fly to her head.

Sighing, Iseabal breathed against him, finding the dampness of his clothing an irritation. She should take his clothes from him, place her hands upon his chest, and warm him, too.

Once again he raised her arm, his fingers brushing the inside of her elbow and lingering there.

A raindrop dangled precariously from his hair and Iseabal watched it in fascination, the sight of it filling her vision. Tinged blue and beautiful in the lantern light, it hung pendulous from one damp tendril before falling. She watched it float in the air for an eternity until it disappeared in a damp trail between her breasts.

Suddenly Iseabal was so tired that she could barely keep her head up. She pressed her face against his neck, breathed against his throat. He smelled of Gilmuir and himself.

Speech was beyond her, silence lingering and filling every nook in her mind.

His breath was warm against her chilled shoulder as he

bent to test the tightness of the wrapping. He glanced up at her and then away as quickly.

The procedure seemed to take an eternity and she reveled in it. A nearly inaudible voice from a far-off land whispered a tinny protest. She was not herself, but then she was. This woman whose lips were pressed against the MacRae's, Alisdair's, throat was not Iseabal Drummond, recently wed. Instead, this was a stranger, whose blood beat hot and whose skin shivered with a brush of his night beard against her arm.

The edge of his cuff touched her waist; the feel of the sodden cloth against her skin was too abrasive. How strange that she could feel so much.

As she watched him from beneath her lashes, her view of Alisdair was narrowed to his hands and his chest, but nothing more.

She was feeling exactly as she had when tumbling to the bottom of Gilmuir's foundation, as if her stomach were hollow and her limbs weightless.

"I do not feel quite myself," she said, her words slurred.

"It's the effect of the poppy juice," he said gently, tucking in the last strip of bandage. Tying it against her right side, he sat back to survey his handiwork.

"It is not, perhaps, as good a job as the physician could do," he said finally. "But at least the wrapping will support you until your ribs heal."

He stood, made his way to his chest, opened another of the doors to reveal a series of pegs on which his garments were stowed. Selecting one in a crimson color, he returned to the side of the bed.

Tossing the garment next to her, he bent and helped her stand. Her legs were suddenly so weak that she had to lean on him for support.

"You shouldn't wear anything constrictive," he was saying through the haze in her mind. "This should suit," he added, bending and holding out a voluminous nightshirt to her.

She nodded, the movement of her head making the cabin careen around her. Or maybe the storm was still raging and she'd not sensed it until this moment. Leisurely, she looped her arms around his neck.

"It's yours," she said, feeling as if some protest were necessary. All she truly wanted was to lie down in the bunk and surrender to this delicious feeling of languor.

"I never wear a nightshirt," he said, the words whispered against her temple. "This particular garment has only become a joke in my family. My mother weaves one for me every voyage in hopes that I will wear it." Pulling back slightly, he gently removed her arms from his neck.

"And you don't?" she asked, fingering a silver button.

"No," he admitted. "But I always tell her I have, and she always pretends to believe me."

He untied her petticoat, the fabric brushing her legs as it fell to the floor. The rest of her shift was next, the tattered linen drifting like a cloud away from her body.

Alisdair dropped the nightshirt over her head, helping her ease her left arm into the sleeve, and then her right. He said nothing when the heel of his hand brushed over the tip of her breast. She wanted to hold his fingers there, experience the sensation longer.

Kneeling at her feet, he slipped her shoes from her feet, and if he was surprised she'd not replaced her stockings, he said nothing. Censure would have been wasted on her at this moment.

He helped her sit again, lifting her legs until she was in the bunk. He covered her with the blanket, tucking it about her, then smoothing it beneath her chin. "You'll feel better soon enough," he said, the sound of his voice almost ethereal.

She nodded, Iseabal thought, falling into a delicious sleep, accompanied by the vision of eyes filled with the blue of a summer sky.

Chapter 8

Despite the fact that it was summer, the wind seeping in from below the door was chilled. Nor had the teak flooring of his cabin been designed with sleep in mind.

The storm had subsided enough that Alisdair was no longer needed on deck, and the night watch promised to rouse him if the winds showed signs of increasing. Now they sat in the middle of the loch, near enough to Coneagh Firth that he could feel the currents of both bodies of water surging beneath him.

The slow, almost rhythmic creaking of the hull timbers, the whisper of the wind either ruffling the sails or, as now, swirling around the deck with a mournful moan, were all customary sounds of night aboard ship. Here in this room, however, almost too small to be a cabin, and certainly not designed to hold two occupants, Alisdair found sleep to be elusive.

He studied Iseabal in the darkness, wondering at the confusion and interest he felt. Not once had she mentioned her discomfort, but from the looks of the bruising, she must have been in agony.

What kind of woman wants a rock for a gift and yet remains silent and stoic when she might have sought aid?

Iseabal breathed softly, deeply, almost as if she dreamed, but every so often she would hold her breath, those moments betraying her wakefulness.

"You shouldn't be awake so soon," he said, propping himself up on his side. "Are you still in pain?"

"A little," she confessed. "It's as if I feel it, but it doesn't consume me."

"Another effect of the poppy juice," he said, smiling at the wonder in her voice. "Some people like that feeling."

"I can't imagine why. It's as if you're walking about in a cloud. You hardly know what is real and what's a dream."

She'd pressed his hand against her breast, causing him to step quickly away. Did she remember that? Or of kissing his throat, her full lips pressed against his skin so fervently that she might have been a courtesan?

"Does the ship always seem to move so?" she asked.

Sitting up, he leaned against the door. "We're between the firth and the loch, and the currents are mixing beneath us. But I've always thought the ocean alive," he admitted. "As if there is a watery goddess spreading her arms beneath the waves. Sometimes the embrace is gentle, almost affectionate. But then she has moments of temper in which she crashes her fists against the hull."

"Are you a poet?" she asked quietly.

He laughed, drawing up one leg and propping his wrist upon it. "My brother James is the man of words in our family."

"Your brother?"

He nodded, then realized that she couldn't see him. "Yes," he said. "One of four."

"Five boys?" she asked, her voice sounding amazed. "Do you have any sisters?"

"None," he said. "At times there seems to be an army of us. It would be foolish to wish for more."

After a moment of silence he spoke again. "What about you, Iseabal? Did you not wish for sisters and brothers?"

"Always," she said, with a candor that surprised him.

He heard the sound of the covers rustling, then a faint noise resembling a moan. Standing, he went to the side of the bunk, sitting on the wooden edge.

"You must remain as still as possible, Iseabal," he said gently, touching her arm. His hand smoothed from elbow to shoulder, fingers splaying against the sleeves of the night-shirt. A sudden picture of her naked beneath the voluminous garment was supplanted by the realization that Iseabal was trembling.

He withdrew his hand and stood.

"Are we to live in England?" she asked. Of all the questions she might have posed, this one was the most difficult to answer.

"Perhaps it would be better not to talk of this now," he replied, feeling a discomfort that had nothing to do with her proximity and everything to do with his burgeoning conscience. Now was hardly the time to divulge his plans for an annulment. Time enough for honesty later, when she was feeling better.

"I have an errand to perform in London," he said, returning to his makeshift bed on the floor.

"What errand?"

What should he say? The truth, his conscience heralded. At least that much he could offer her.

"Before I answer, Iseabal," he said, "do I have your promise that you will not divulge what I tell you?"

The silence seemed to grow, expanding on its own until it filled the cabin.

"Do you ask for such a vow because I'm a Drummond?"

Perhaps he should have answered in the affirmative, but he had not been reared with hatred for her clan. They'd not featured in tales of Gilmuir, or in the heritage passed down by his kinsmen. The fact that he disliked her father intensely had nothing to do with Iseabal.

"No," he answered. "It is a secret that belongs to another."

Another interval of silence passed before she spoke again. "Then I promise not to divulge to anyone what you tell me," she said, her words solemn and having the import of a pledge.

The story was complicated, one that had been told to each of Ian MacRae's sons only when he was old enough to understand the need for silence.

"My father was born Alec Landers," he began. "The son of an English earl. But his mother, Moira MacRae, was a Scot, so he used to spend his summers at Gilmuir. From the day my grandmother was murdered, however, he refused to acknowledge his Scottish heritage. Only later did he return to Gilmuir, but as an English colonel commanding Fort William."

"You're part English, Alisdair?"

"I am," he said simply. "My parents fell in love when my father decided to be a rebel. He began to aid the people of Gilmuir, taking on the persona of the Raven, but he soon realized that any act of kindness was not enough to save the MacRaes."

He heard her indrawn breath and wondered at the cause of it. "The Raven?" she asked faintly.

"You've heard of him?"

"Every child in the Highlands has heard of the Raven," she said, her voice sounding as if it held a smile.

"I shall have to tell him, then," he said, amused. "He's a greatly respected laird, but I doubt that my father ever considered becoming a hero."

"Then he changed his name to MacRae."

"He did. Ian MacRae, the name his grandfather always called him."

"What happened to him, Alisdair? No one ever knew. Or, for that matter, what happened to the MacRaes."

"They escaped Gilmuir together. The world believes that he died at Gilmuir, but he's alive and well, living in Nova Scotia and still rebelling, in his way, against the English."

"And that's where you're from?"

"An island not far from there," he said. "We named it Cape Gilmuir in honor of the old place and Scotland."

"So that's where the MacRaes went," she said, her voice sounding increasingly drowsy. If nothing else, Alisdair thought ruefully, the tale had lulled her to sleep. "But why give out that he's dead?" she asked.

"Because the English would still pursue him as a traitor if they knew he was alive. He was an English colonel, after all." Stretching out his legs, Alisdair continued with his story. "Before he escaped Scotland, he succeeded to the earldom, yet surrendered the title to his younger brother. His stepmother was the only one in England to know he was still alive."

"And that is why you're going to England?" she asked. "To set the record straight somehow?"

"No," he said. "His younger brother has died and the title is vacant. His stepmother has it in her head that since my father cannot magically appear from the dead, the title should pass to his eldest son, a son whose existence had not been known of until now."

"You?" Iseabal's question sounded drowsy. He smiled, thinking that she would soon be asleep again.

"Me," he answered.

"You're going to England, then, to accept a title, Alisdair?"

"No," he told her softly. "I'm going to England to refuse it."

The galley was filled with a haze because Hamish was smoking his damnable pipe again. James frowned at his brother, but he only smiled in return. Sometimes, he thought, Hamish liked to rile him, receiving as much pleasure from the deed as he did in teasing Douglas or angering Brendan.

Turning away, James concentrated on the entries in his journal. Life aboard ship was tedious, for the most part, and he chose to spend his idle moments in writing down his thoughts while his brothers chose to play at cards. Brendan always won, and Hamish always halfheartedly accused him of cheating. At the end of the game, both brothers were circling each other like quarreling roosters, pleased with an excuse to fight. The winner of the bout would always concede graciously to the other, and for a week or so there was peace among the MacRaes while black eyes and bruises healed.

However their personalities grated against one another, the brothers were united in the front they showed the world. As if, James thought, listening to them quarrel now, each of them considered himself privileged to insult the other, but the world did not have that right.

Around them, the crew slept, the night lengthened, and still they debated the wisdom of their actions.

Douglas had started it all an hour earlier when he'd posed a surprising question.

"Since we're so close to England, why don't we meet Alisdair there?" the youngest MacRae suggested.

They'd been gone four months, ferrying two MacRae ships to the French. The transaction completed, and as profitable as Alisdair had promised, they were on their way home, slipping beneath the noses of the English.

Over the years, the Crown's military presence in Nova Scotia had grown alarmingly, a fact that greatly displeased his father as well as the older refugees from Gilmuir. The MacRaes had been careful to avoid being noticed.

Turning his attention to his journal, James began to write.

I cannot help but marvel at the irony of this family venture of ours. But then, rebellion is an old and honored tradition of the MacRaes.

Our minds are not on the journey home, but on the possibility of joining Alisdair in London. Doing so might lighten the burden of his task while allowing us some diversion. I have long wanted to see the sights of that great city and peruse its bookshops.

"I don't see why it's such a difficult decision," Douglas said now. "We're ahead of schedule," he added, trying to convince them. "London is not that far off course."

"It's more than that, Douglas," Hamish said, scratching his beard. "We're supposed to be neutral, and it's a bit like tweaking the noses of the English to sail into their port city after we've sold ships to the French."

"Ships that will be used against them," Brendan said, for once in accord with his older brother.

"And who's to tell?" Douglas said. "One of us? No one else knows."

"Is it that you're pining for Alisdair, Douglas?" Hamish asked with a smile, "or simply that you've a hankering to see London?"

"I thought his eyes would pop out of his head when we sailed into Calais," Brendan said.

"I'm not a world traveler like you." Douglas spoke angrily. "It's my first voyage."

"A true sailor," James remarked. "And not sick once, Douglas."

"Not like you, James," Hamish said.

James smiled ruefully as his brothers laughed. During that first voyage he'd not been able to raise his head above the bunk. He was not a born sailor, nor a man as suited to the sea as Alisdair. That first time aboard ship had been to the southern English colonies to purchase ironwood for the hulls of Alisdair's ships. Not like the ocean crossing that Douglas had endured, and well.

"I can't be the only one to want a glimpse of London," Douglas argued.

The four brothers glanced at one another, a grin playing over each face.

"Then what is to stop us?" Douglas asked, evidently sensing that the battle was turning in his favor.

"And you think a MacRae will be welcome in England, Douglas?" Brendan asked.

"All the more reason to join Alisdair," Douglas countered.

Brendan stood, placed his hands on his hips, and arched his back, stretching. "Who's to say he'll welcome our interference?"

"What interference, brother?" Hamish wondered, contentedly puffing on his pipe until his head was wreathed in smoke.

James stood and spoke to his brothers. "Since this is my ship," he said in order to forestall the budding argument, "I'll make the decision. We'll go to London, but we'll only stay five days."

"Why five days?" Brendan asked, frowning.

"Because that's how long the two of you can last before fighting," he said curtly, grabbing his journal and striding to the door.

Chapter 9

The calm water of Loch Euliss reflected streaks of orange and red from a reluctant dawn sun. The summer-
morning breeze carried the scent of flowers, grass, and the
pungent, salty tang of the sea.

Alisdair gave the signal for the sails to be raised. A flap of
canvas, the sound of the ropes tightening, and the creak of the
spars were signs that the *Fortitude* was waking.

She began to move, seeking the sea.

Planting his feet apart, Alisdair stood with hands clenched
behind him. The wind buffeted his face; his clothing was
moistened by salt spray as the *Fortitude* left Loch Euliss,
crossing into the firth. The current churned beneath his feet
as the two bodies of water met. Recalling his words of the
night before, Alisdair smiled. His watery goddess had become a shrew.

A thin yellow line on the horizon marked the division between water and sky. To his left were towering shale cliffs; to his right, an open sea the color of dull pewter. The *Fortitude* skimmed across the waves, her canvas shrouds full-bellied in the dawn light.

Behind him, men climbed in the rigging while others took their turns having their morning meal. Rations the night before had been paltry, limited to hardtack and jerky, but this morning the galley fires had been lit.

"A storm on your wedding night, Captain," Daniel said, coming to stand beside him. "An omen," the first mate added sourly.

Daniel's omens were almost as familiar as Henrietta's signs. "What is it now, Daniel?" he asked. "It's neither Thursday nor Friday, and we've fair weather with plenty of wind."

"It's a pity you'll not wear a hat," Daniel said, eyeing his captain's bare head. "We're guaranteed a safe voyage if you'd thrown it overboard."

"You'd render me poor, Daniel, constantly buying hats," Alisdair said dryly.

"I expect Drummond has already done that. Still, it's not wise to ignore the rituals of the sea."

Striding across the deck, Alisdair knocked on his cabin door to warn Iseabal, then walked inside at her soft welcome.

She wasn't in bed, as she should have been. Nor was she sitting on the edge of the bunk. Instead, she was attired in a pale blue petticoat and matching jacket, kneeling in front of her basket.

When she retrieved a small wooden box, he forgot his errand and strode to her side.

"You shouldn't be lifting anything," he said, taking the box from her. Placing it on the top of the open trunk, he bent, cupping her elbows with his hands, and helped her to rise. "You should be resting," he said, stepping back when he realized how close they were.

Sunlight spilled into the cabin from the open door, and a fresh wind swirled inside, bringing the scent of the sea and banishing the lingering odor of Chinese herbs.

"Are you feeling better?" he asked, brushing a tendril of hair from her cheek.

She nodded, her gaze never leaving his face.

"You were asleep when I left you," he said, the words conjuring up a picture of how she'd looked this morning, turned to her side facing him, her cheek pillowed on an arm, a small smile visiting her in dreams.

Stepping away, he handed the box to her and bowed slightly, thinking it wise to leave her.

"It's yours," she said, pushing the box back to him.

"What is it?" he asked, frowning. He wanted no bonds between them. No links or obligations.

"A wedding present."

Staring down at the box, Alisdair wondered if now was the time to tell her of his plans. This morning she was looking at him differently. Less caution and more affection. And, he thought, glancing at the flush mounting on her face, with more awareness.

He smoothed his hand over the top of the box, holding his palm there as if to refute his own curiosity.

"Please," she said, pressing her hand on the back of his.

A filigree plate connected the two halves, and was locked by a tiny brass hook. Flipping it open with one finger, Alisdair stared in wonder at the contents.

Before him lay a miniature of Gilmuir, carved from a block of stone and looking as it might have looked a hundred years ago. An oval drive curved in front of the castle, and the front door mimicked the texture of wood. The archway connecting the priory to the main structure was intact, as was the clan hall. The grass around Gilmuir had been carved so delicately that he could feel the spike of each blade against the tip of his finger. Even the cliffs, ribboned in brown and white, had been perfectly crafted. His thumb brushed against a steeply canted roof, each individual slate outlined in loving detail.

"It is not quite finished," she said, reaching up to touch one of the windows of the priory. "One day I would like to carve shutters there."

Alisdair glanced up, staring at her in amazement. "You did this?"

Her eyes widened at his tone, but she nodded, her gaze dropping to the miniature of Gilmuir once again.

Their fingers accidentally touched, and separated as quickly.

"I wanted you to have it. Besides," she added, "Gilmuir belongs to you now."

"But how did you know?" he asked, feeling stunned at the talent she displayed. "All these details," he said, touching the tiny gorse bushes emerging from the stone. "It's almost as if you saw it whole. How did you know how it once appeared?" He'd heard tales from his mother, his great-uncle, all those people who'd once lived in the old castle, but Iseabal had made those stories real in this rendition of Gilmuir.

She shook her head. "I didn't know for sure," she admitted. "But it was reasonable to assume from what was left in the ruins."

His finger rested upon a curved arch of the priory. "These

no longer exist," he countered. "Nor the roof. But it's just as it had been described to me."

He'd thought of her as a trespasser. Looking down at the work of art Iseabal had created, Alisdair realized that she had been more a steward, preserving the fortress as it had once been.

"That is why you wanted the block of marble," he said, understanding. "To carve."

She looked at him, her lips curving into a smile. "Of course," she said, chastisement present in that simple statement. "Did you think yourself married to a madwoman, Alisdair?"

Discomfited by her teasing, he concentrated once more upon the carving.

"My father thinks so," she said in the silence. "A woman should not wish to be more than she is. But sometimes the stones seem to speak to me, as if the images trapped inside wish to be released." Glancing up at him, she smiled again, a small, self-deprecating expression. "Perhaps I am mad after all," she added.

"I've heard my mother say the same about a length of yarn. She sees a pattern in her mind and must create it. She says it calls to her and she cannot rest until it has been born." He smiled, thinking of his mother and her passion for her loom, one of the first items crafted when the MacRaes reached Nova Scotia.

"Yes," Iseabal said, her eyes widening. "That's exactly how it is."

Alisdair slowly closed the lid of the box. "She is an artist and so are you. Thank you, Iseabal. I will treasure it always," he said, feeling duplicitous and awkward.

A few strides and he was across the cabin. Placing the miniature inside one of the tansu's doors, he retrieved a silver flask and his prized coconut cup. Heavily carved and surrounded by a chased surround, the cup had been given him for being part of the expedition charting the Sea of Japan.

Iseabal's eyes widened even further, and he wondered if she thought herself married to a tippler.

"My first mate relies on odd portents and strange signs to rule his life," he explained, raising his flask. "I'm merely trying to appease his superstitions."

Instead of speaking, Iseabal only nodded.

Too much of a gulf stretched between them, he suddenly realized. Background and dreams of the future, temperament and character. His was suffering at the moment, while hers shone clear and direct. She'd given him a gift to treasure, something she'd created herself with obvious love and even more apparent talent. He had given her nothing more than subterfuge and reluctance, tainted with anger for both Drummond and these circumstances.

Gripping the cup and flask tightly in his hand, Alisdair strode through the door.

"Here," he said to Daniel, filling the cup with a measure of rum and holding it aloft for his first mate to see.

Daniel smiled in approval as Alisdair walked to the rail and tossed the rum over the side. A pacification to the wind and waves.

He had no ability to see into the future, but Alisdair did know his first mate well. "Don't say a word about women on board, Daniel," he said in warning.

"It's not safe, Captain," Daniel replied, unrepentant. "Surely you know that."

"What do you suggest I do with her?" Alisdair asked, dismissing the sudden vision of Iseabal naked in front of him. "String her from the rigging? Tie her to the mast?"

"You shouldn't laugh at custom, Captain."

"She'll be gone soon enough, Daniel," he said, more annoyed at himself than at his first mate.

Daniel frowned, both eyebrows slanting downward as if pointing the way to his sharp nose.

"I'm not going to throw her overboard," Alisdair said, annoyed. "I'm simply going to find a way to have this marriage annulled."

"Can you do that?" Daniel asked skeptically.

"Surely that farce of a wedding was not valid, Daniel," Alisdair retorted tightly. "And for all that she's lovely and no doubt a paragon of all the virtues, I prefer to choose my own wife, and not have her thrust upon me."

"It seems to me the lass has little choice, either," Daniel observed.

Alisdair stared at him, feeling more irritated. One moment his old friend decried Iseabal's presence on board; the next, Daniel was castigating him for his decision.

"Are you going to leave her in England, then, Captain?" Daniel asked, his voice trailing off as he glanced behind Alisdair.

Alisdair turned to find Iseabal standing in the doorway of the cabin, staring at him. Her hands were clasped in front of her, her face serene, a small smile playing over her lips. But she was so still she might have been made of stone.

Her leather shoes made muted sounds on the wooden deck as she walked to him. He measured each hesitant step with an increasing remorse.

"Forgive me," he said. "I did not wish for you to learn of my plans this way."

Yet he'd ignored the opportunity to tell her in private, his conscience whispered. An uncomfortable position to be in, he thought, balancing on a fulcrum of his character, and knowing that he'd made the worst of mistakes.

"When were you going to tell me?" she asked calmly, blessing the training of a lifetime. How many times had she stood before her father, aching to say words she'd trapped behind restraint?

Something began to uncurl deep inside, a sense of shame so pervasive that Iseabal felt nauseous with it. Yet another emotion, as easily discernible, trod on its tail. Anger.

Her hands clenched into fists as she stared at him, Daniel fading from sight like a morning mist. The deck was so quiet she could hear her own breath, but a quick glance upward reassured her that no one watched them. Men climbed in the rigging, two stood at the double wheel, but not one pair of eyes was directed at her.

She knew instinctively that Alisdair MacRae was not a cruel man, nor did she think he had planned this public repudiation. He'd beggared himself for his heritage, maintained his temper although provoked, and looked after her last night as if she'd mattered to him.

Iseabal had begun to believe that Providence had smiled on her in bringing Alisdair MacRae to Scotland. For a few short hours she'd begun to believe that her future might be a happy one. Only to have this moment strip bare any illusions.

"Do you not want your freedom, Iseabal?" he asked, frowning at her.

"I have always been free," she said quietly. There were

her thoughts, rebellious and occasionally wicked, and her imagination, unfettered and soaring. Watching her words, measuring her moments of escape, were only the costs of such freedom.

"We do not know each other."

Most couples do not, she thought.

"I'm a sea captain and never home."

Only a benefit. She would be a happy wife never to be bothered with a husband.

"I'm from Nova Scotia," he said. "My home is lonely and cold. The winters are frigid and the winds never cease blowing."

She stifled her smile. Did he think winters in Scotland were any different?

"I am not prepared for a wife," he added, the words stark but ringing true.

While she was only too prepared to have him as a husband.

"I will provide for you, Iseabal," he said kindly. "You may choose where you wish to live and have enough funds to decide your own life. Your own freedom."

The MacRae wanted liberty of the will, and women rarely had such choice. Other wills prevailed over hers. A father decreed and she was married. A husband commanded and she was no longer a bride.

She looked at him beneath her lashes, as he remained standing there staring at her. She had a great many faults, Iseabal thought, but there were many attributes as well. Yet the MacRae had dismissed her from his life with surprising ease, as if she were no more than a wave upon his ocean.

Turning, she made her way back to the cabin, glancing over her shoulder at him before shutting the cabin door. He glanced away and she felt released, as if a bond stretching between them, one of emotions and thoughts, all equally unknown, had been severed.

"I've been discarded before, you know," she said softly. He turned his head and stared at her. "I've had a lifetime of practice at it." She was to blame for thinking there might have been more.

She closed the door behind her, wishing that she'd never seen Alisdair MacRae.

Leah would have liked to escape to her chamber, but Drummond ordered her to remain in the clan hall, a witness to his laughter and revelry. She herself would have rather been alone, reveling in the news that had come from one of Drummond's spies this afternoon.

The MacRaes had left Gilmuir.

Leah would miss her daughter, but offsetting that quiet grief was a greater joy. Iseabal would be beginning a new life.

Yet Magnus was celebrating not because his daughter had wed well, but because he'd gained a fortune and the use of MacRae land. With the news that Alisdair MacRae had left Scotland, Leah had no doubt that her husband would quickly issue instructions to send the flocks back to Gilmuir. A suspicion that was borne out by his next words.

"If the fool thinks I'll not take what is rightfully mine, then the MacRaes have bred idiots."

"Did he not pay you for the land, husband?" Leah said.

An expression of displeasure flickered over her husband's face. No doubt because she questioned him. Leah had not ventured a criticism of him in years, choosing instead to remain safe and silent. Now that Iseabal was gone, there was no such constraint on her words. What could he do to her that he had not already done?

Setting her needlework down in her lap, Leah gazed up at Drummond. Her eyes were open and direct, with no attempt to mask the loathing she felt for him.

For an instant he looked surprised; then his face fell into the usual stern lines.

The men sitting on either side of Magnus turned their heads and glanced at her. Two-legged curs, she thought, licking Drummond's boots as if he were their master. One of them was his cousin Thomas, linked not only by blood but by inclination.

His long, thin face reminded her of a starving dog, his rotting teeth sharpened and feral. Even his voice, raspy and hoarse, seemed less human and more like an animal given speech. He might have been a comical figure with those enormous ears of his, had not his character overwhelmed his appearance.

Thomas was the worst of them, even more so, perhaps, than her husband. He carried out Magnus's orders with both alacrity and enthusiasm. His hazel eyes, close together and too small for his face, stared at her now, his tankard halfway to his lips. They shared looks, neither hiding the antipathy for the other. Her aversion for Thomas seemed to amuse her husband, yet his cousin's insolence toward her was never remarked upon. Magnus reserved his loyalty for those who served him.

The remaining five men seated at the table were staring down into their whiskey, pretending that they did not notice her.

"What I do, or not do, is none of your concern," Magnus said curtly.

"You would go back on your word?" she asked.

"Who is to stop me?" her husband said. "Even if the MacRae sends part of his clan back to Gilmuir, I will force them out." He took a sip from his tankard, then wiped his mouth with the back of his hand. "Not with my sword, wife," he added, grinning. "But with the law."

As they stared at each other across the width of the hall, Leah abruptly wondered if she was partly to blame for Drummond's nature. She had married him willingly all those many years ago and had taken her vows to heart. Being a chaste wife had been easily accomplished, since she'd no wish to lie with another man. But Drummond had known that she'd loved another and that her heart was forever blocked to him.

Once, he had been a kinder man. Long ago he'd had other interests such as building and the writings of scholars to occupy him. Now, however, all his energies seemed narrowed and supplanted by his greed.

Would Drummond have been a better man if she'd been able to love him?

Leah stood and left him then, shocked at the thought.

Chapter 10

The day had passed quietly, the empty cabin a place of reflection and thought. Iseabal had had hours of solitude in which to contemplate the future. The longer she spent thinking of it, the worse her prospects seemed.

The door began to open, and Iseabal stiffened her shoulders. She wasn't prepared for any more of the young cabin boy's overt disapproval, nor did she welcome the MacRae's presence.

She winced at the sudden brightness, having become accustomed to the gloom of the windowless cabin. The MacRae stood there, one hand on the edge of the door, the other resting on his hip. His hair had been disheveled by the wind, and he'd removed the jacket he'd worn earlier. The bold colors of his tartan vest suited him, contrasting against the light blue shade of his eyes.

The fading rays of the sun spilled into the doorway, sending ribbons of pale light gleaming on each of her chisels. Arrayed from smallest to largest, they lay ready for her selection. She had spent most of the day examining the marble, trying to see what it might become. Nothing had occurred to her, and that realization had frightened her a little. But then, her thoughts were on her future, not on her carving.

"You didn't lift that yourself, did you?" Alisdair said, frowning at the block of marble resting on the table.

Staring down at the leather sling holding her tools, Iseabal could not help but wonder what kind of man wished to sever a marriage and yet worried about her health.

"Rory," she said, the one word an explanation. The cabin boy had opened the table and slid a chair beneath it, placing the marble block where she needed it. All these chores performed with a mulish expression and eyes that revealed, only too clearly, his disdain for her.

Iseabal had thought Fernleigh inhospitable, but it was nothing compared to the *Fortitude*.

"I need to treat your side," Alisdair said, closing the door. He moved to the lantern, lit it, opening all of the shutters. Iseabal wished, fervently, that he had left the room darkened.

"I feel much improved, thank you," she told him cordially, her smile hard-won but fixed in place.

"Nevertheless," he countered stubbornly, "I need to reapply the dressing."

"It's truly not necessary," she said, concentrating on the block of marble before her.

"It is, unless you've suddenly become able to move your left arm without pain," he said in a clipped voice.

He knew very well that she could not. The Chinese medications might have aided her, but they could not produce miracles. She would need longer than one day to heal.

She glanced up at him. "I truly do not wish your help, MacRae." *Nor would it be proper to have you treat me now,* she thought. She'd already bared herself to him, and could only pray that he would forget that incident quickly.

"Then I shall fetch Daniel," he threatened, standing with his feet braced apart, hands behind his back.

Her eyes widened at his words, but it seemed he was not finished with his intimidation.

"Or pick another," he continued. "It doesn't matter who as long as you're treated."

"Why do you care?" she asked curiously.

"Because you are my responsibility," he answered. "As long as you're my wife."

A burden, a millstone, an obligation. Irritation bubbled up again from beneath her veneer of composure.

"Thank you, no," she said, her voice even.

Instead of leaving, however, he wedged himself behind her, reaching around to the front in order to unfasten her jacket. She brushed his hands away, but they returned, implacable and as obstinate as the man.

She should stab him with one of her chisels, Iseabal thought. "Please leave, MacRae."

"After I've wrapped you again, Iseabal," he said, his voice as even as hers.

Her mother's oft-repeated remark echoed in Iseabal's mind. Men were warriors who had no hesitation in causing wounds; they simply did not wish to be around when they were treated. Such a statement might have been true at Fernleigh, but not here in this cabin.

Dressing had been a chore this morning, and donning her jacket had been a triumph of sorts. She'd relinquished wearing her stays, since she couldn't lace them over the wrapping.

MacRae, however, bent and removed the dirk from his boot, as if meaning to slice through her clothing again.

"Will you stand, Iseabal?" he asked, bending so that his mouth was close to her ear. "Or shall I simply cut your clothing from you?"

"Daniel," she said abruptly.

His hands stilled on her shoulders, making her wish he stood in front of her so that she could read his expression.

"I wish Daniel to help me," she said. The first mate's presence in the cabin would cause her only embarrassment, not this consternation of the senses, as her heart raced and her breath felt as if it were stolen from her.

He didn't say a word, simply moved to stand in front of her.

"Cut or remove it, Iseabal?" he said, his mouth thinned, his eyes narrowed in irritation. She felt the same but bit back her words.

That, evidently, was to be her only choice. Not who should treat her, but how she might be treated. Stubbornness would be impractical, since she had only one shift remaining besides the one she wore.

He was standing too close, his presence overpowering. Iseabal waved her hand in the air, a silent gesture for him to move back. He did so, and slowly she rose to stand in front of him.

"I will not hurt you, Iseabal," he said.

Merely discard her like an unwelcome parcel, she thought. Her father's sheep were treated with more prudence.

Closing her eyes, she stood compliant as he pulled her jacket free.

"Can you raise your arms a little?" he asked, his voice

sounding absurdly gentle for this moment and this occasion. And this man, she told herself.

She did so, feeling the soft shimmer of material over her skin. Crossing her arms protectively over her breasts, she stood uncomplaining and docile. Like a lamb, and not a ewe after all.

Carefully he began to unwind the wrappings, extending both hands around her. The fabric of his shirt brushed against her heated cheeks. He smelled of fresh air and salt water, and of his own scent, one indescribably male.

"Why did you marry me," she asked quietly, "if you planned to end the marriage soon enough?" Curiosity was unwise, but at least it would stop her from thinking of how close he was.

He straightened, and she opened her eyes to discover him staring at her.

"You could have claimed yourself affianced," she said. "Or even married."

"Neither of which is true," he said.

He would not be the first man who lied to escape his fate. Honor had made him her husband, yet it did not keep him one. Obligation placed him at her side, and responsibility had him standing too close, and too intrusive. If he had only been less noble, she would be at Fernleigh now, not standing nearly naked in front of a man destined to remain a stranger.

"Is the pain becoming more manageable?" he asked.

She nodded wordlessly.

"I'm going to press here," he said, gently placing his finger against her skin above her top rib. "Is there any pain?" he asked.

"No," she said. He was so close that she could see the

growth of beard on his cheeks. She wanted, rashly, to place her hand against his face, fingers following the edge of his jaw.

She wanted, also, to measure the breadth of his shoulders, and perhaps even trace her hands down his arms to gauge the circumference of his wrists.

His knuckles brushed over the swell of her breast and she held her breath at the touch.

"Forgive me," he said a second later, his voice sounding constricted.

Hurry, she whispered in her mind, truly wishing now that someone else were performing this chore. She bent her head, outwardly waiting in serene silence, the pose as much a sham as he believed their marriage.

More than once she'd seen a servant girl staring out the window at the carpenter's shed, her cheeks flushed and her lips swollen. Or a stableboy glancing up at Fernleigh's third floor, a look on his face speaking of his need. The emotion she felt was easily identified, but not so simply understood. How could she long for a man who had cast her aside before ever coming to know her?

The daring Iseabal, the one who explored Gilmuir and held great thoughts, wanted to bend forward and place her lips on his throat, right there where the pulse beat seemed the strongest. If he held the right to touch her by dint of obligation and responsibility, surely she could claim the same privilege, formed from inquisitiveness and an unsettling feeling of yearning.

Bending closer to untie the knot in the bandage, he brushed his chin against her shoulder. An abrasive touch, one that should not send shivers through her. Alisdair moved away, retrieving the strange bottles, placing them on the table beside her tools.

"Tell me about your carving," he said, pushing the chisels aside.

"There is nothing much to tell," she replied.

"When did you begin?" he asked, unstopping the dragon jar.

"When I was a child," she answered, turning away from the smell. "I used to make garden stones for my mother. Little frogs and toadstools," she added, smiling in memory of those years. Each and every carving, laboriously done with a piece of iron she'd taken from the smithy, had been greeted with enthusiasm by her mother. Some of her earlier efforts still remained in the garden, sentinels among the towering plants.

"Is that why you were at Gilmuir that day?" he asked absently, beginning to wrap her again. "To gather material for your carving?"

"Yes." Iseabal always found the best stones there, limestone in shades of brown and ivory, marble in variegated patterns. But she'd never before seen anything like the ebony stone she'd stared at all day.

"I thought you a ghost," he admitted with a small smile. She stared at him, bemused. His smile belonged to a troubadour, or to a young shepherd asleep on a hill and dreaming of his sweetheart. Iseabal glanced away, wishing that he were a different man. Crude and brutish and even cruel. Someone like Thomas, one of her father's kin and toadies.

I thought you were a god, Iseabal confessed in the silence of her thoughts.

For long moments there was no sound in the room other

than the sputtering of the lantern. He opened the rabbit jar and she tensed, expecting the heat of the mixture against her skin. But there was less burning than on the night before. Curious, she turned her head and glanced down at herself. The bruising had faded to a rainbow of hues, from gray to red to a mottled yellow to blue.

"There must be something magical in that potion," she said, amazed.

"Less magic than centuries of knowledge," he said, placing the stopper back in the jar. "The Chinese are skilled in the art of healing."

Without asking for permission, he untied her petticoat, letting it drift to the floor, then retrieved his nightshirt from where she'd hung it this morning. Bunching up the cloth, he draped it over her head, raising her left arm gently into the sleeve.

The back of his hand brushed over her nipple and it tightened in response, sending heat to her cheeks and throughout her body. She looked away, pretending that it had not happened, that the warmth of his hand was not so close that she could feel it still.

Finally, thankfully, the other sleeve was done, her hand peeking beyond the wrist of his nightshirt.

"Can you remove your stockings?" he asked. "Or do you need help?"

"I can do it," Iseabal said, shaking her head almost frantically.

"I've cleared off a space for you to sit on deck tomorrow," he told her, stepping back. "Behind the cabin, toward the stern."

So that she would not be seen and frighten his men?

"The area is sheltered from the worst of the breeze, and

you might wish to work there," he added, his words instantly shaming her.

"Thank you," she said quietly.

Nodding, he repacked the jars behind their doors, and left the cabin.

Shameless, Iseabal thought, to be repudiated and still wish to be touched.

She walked slowly to the door, daring herself to open it and call after him. If she did, would he come back? Or would he stand there and smile at her kindly as if she were an injured sparrow? What would he say if she spoke what was in her mind?

Kiss me, Alisdair. Give me that, at least. A memory to tuck away and savor when I'm no longer a bride. Rejection, she decided, was overwhelming when it fit inside a single word. Annulment.

If she were a woman of uncertain virtue, or one more courageous in deed rather than thought, she might have gone to him.

"Keep me with you," she would say, and then enumerate all the reasons he should. She would be a good wife, tidy and understanding and supportive. Complaints would never fall from her lips, and she would be content enough in their life together. Happy, perhaps.

Or she might claim his pity, but the idea soured her stomach. He either knew the truth and dismissed it or never realized what his decision would mean. From the moment he severed their marriage she would be a ruined woman. What man wanted a compromised bride? Her only salvation was to become a paid companion or a mistress to a man willing to give her that title, at least.

Opening the door quietly, she stared out at the darkness.

Dawn came without warning aboard ship, and night fell as quickly. There was no middle ground, no gloaming, no morning mist.

She fingered the wooden latch of the door, her hand slipping damply against it. Gradually she pushed the door closed, remaining there for a moment, staring down at the shadows of her hands in the lantern light. Before she could act upon her impulse, Iseabal pressed down until the latch engaged, the sound of the faint click a death knell to her thoughts of courage.

Fergus MacRae awoke as he usually did, before dawn. Sleep was never so valuable to him as the time awake. Once, he'd come too close to sleeping forever.

Sitting on the edge of the bed, he reached for his wooden leg, strapping it on with an ease that came from years of practice. He knew, from the pain in his limb, that he would only be able to use the wooden leg a day or so longer before trading it for his crutch.

Once, he had wished himself dead rather than maimed, but he'd been young and foolish. The time after Culloden had been difficult. Not only had he nearly died escaping Cumberland's troops, but he'd lost his leg from a musket wound. He'd taken nearly a year to heal and months after that in order to learn to walk again.

But he was more fortunate than all those who'd never returned from battle, and he greeted them every morning, along with all the ghosts of his regrets.

Standing, he took a few stumbling steps until he gained his balance. Catching a glimpse of himself in the fragment of mirror atop his bureau, he smiled. As a smithy, the muscles of his arms and chest had become powerful over the years. Dependence on his right leg had strengthened that limb, and his left thigh had bulked due to the effort of walking on a wooden leg. Consequently, he was a formidable figure of a man, if one could discount the fact that he was not whole.

He turned toward the window, pushing aside the draperies that the Widow McKinsey had made for him. His landlady was a sweet soul with a generous nature and two unmarried daughters. That state of affairs was to be expected in the Highlands. There was a dearth of young men in Scotland. Either they'd enlisted in the Highland Regiments or they'd been shaken loose from the land and sent fleeing from their homes for another country promising a better future.

As he did every morning, he watched the sun rise slowly over the rolling hills to the east. As the shadows began to lighten, he thought of his brother and father, lost to the world all those many years ago. His mother and sister seemed to stand smiling every morning, waving at him, their faces wreathed with smiles.

The sun stretched its arms until the horizon was filled with light, great orange-and-yellow streaks that heralded the morning. He felt his heart swell as the music of the dawn seemed to come to him in the sound of mythical pipes. Turning his head, Fergus glanced to the southwest, where Gilmuir lay. He'd been there only once since Culloden, but it had become a dead, empty place, solitary and abandoned. He'd never known if his people had been slaughtered by the English or banished like the men whose wrists were manacled with iron chains of his making.

He glanced in the direction of Leah McDonald's childhood home. She'd married a few years after Culloden, he'd heard. He'd never sent her word that he was alive, being ashamed of his condition, trapped by pride into silence. What woman would want a one-legged giant? A question he'd never asked Leah, and an omission for which he felt a daily regret.

If he had to relive his decision, he'd present himself in front of her, one leg missing and all, and see if they couldn't make a future for themselves. She might have been repulsed by his injury, but there was as good a chance that she would have opened her arms to him. He would never know now.

Fergus wondered if she thought of him occasionally, if she spared any time in memory of the boy he'd been. Too late now. That song replayed itself in his mind continuously. Thirty years too late.

In a few minutes the seaport he'd chosen as his home for the past ten years would be awake. Cormech was a pleasant enough place, less crowded than Edinburgh and closer to Gilmuir. There were opportunities for him in Inverness, but he had vile memories of that town during the war and would not return.

All in all, he enjoyed his work, finding pleasure in the small things of his life. The sizzle of water in the cooling bucket as he thrust the red-hot iron into it, the curve of a horseshoe appearing beneath his oak-handled hammer. One task he'd been given, however, disturbed him. Every few weeks he was to go to a ship and manacle the Scots in the hold. He'd done the chore, fixing the chains to both wrists and ankle, maintaining the required silence and grateful that he was not obligated to speak.

What could he say to these people? As the months passed and whole families were imprisoned, his sense of horror grew. When the guards turned away, Fergus had questioned a prisoner or two. Their careful whispers verified that they were not prisoners, or guilty of any crime. They'd been sold into slavery in order to make way for sheep.

The English had been more successful at conquering Scotland than they'd believed. The young ones were not speaking the Gaelic, a generation had been born that had never heard the pipes, and lairds were banishing tackmen from their homes.

Something had to be done, Fergus MacRae reasoned. He was one man, amidst a city of people who seemed to ignore what was before their very noses. What could one man do?

He smiled, looking out at the dawn sky. Perhaps it was for this challenge that he'd been spared, after all.

Chapter 11

Iseabal was seated in her nook on the stern, her attention directed once more to the block of stone before her. Over the past few days, she'd been working on it steadily, squaring up the corners with small, pinging taps of her chisel.

He'd never seen anyone as lost in her work as she.

From his perch in the rigging Alisdair watched her, wondering if she knew how often he did so. Iseabal was proving to be a mystery he very much wanted to solve.

Although she must have been in pain, she'd never complained, and not once had she asked what would become of her. He should have been pleased at her silence and acquiescence. Instead, he suspected that how she acted and what she felt were often at odds.

Perhaps it would be wiser to seek her thoughts in the flash of her eyes, looking past the façade of docility and serenity. In the deep green of her gaze she was neither. More than once he'd seen irritation there, and burgeoning anger. But these emotions as well as a surprising sadness were never given voice.

She was not unlike the women he'd known all his life, Alisdair realized. They had surmounted great hardships to found a colony far away from their homeland, carrying on with their lives in stoic acceptance of every burden given them to bear. But those women had been older, and experienced in life.

Drummond had done this to her.

A memory came to him then, of Iseabal standing mute and humiliated as her father extolled her virtues as if she were no more sentient than a rock.

Nor had he himself acted with greater honor, Alisdair thought, his mind furnishing yet another memory. Not that first night when she'd sat naked to the waist, innocently beautiful and in pain, but every night thereafter.

Every time he wrapped the bandage around her waist, he fought off the impulse to stroke her skin and feel the warmth of her flesh against his lips. And every night he helped her don the nightshirt, his hand brushed against her breasts, seeking satiation of a greater need. On each occasion Iseabal sighed in response, but never said a word in protest.

His conscience was nagging at him. A curious thing, to feel as if two separate parts of himself were warring. His mind stated emphatically that he was not willing or ready to be wed, especially to a stranger. Yet he hardened when he looked at her and had dreams featuring her soft smile and talented fingers.

She was injured, a stranger, bound by his protection. But a certain part of his body recognized her only as female, warm and fragrant and essentially lovely.

He should think of her as a troll, some sort of feminine monster with snakes in her hair. Not a woman with curving pink lips, a lulling voice, hair that was now snared in an ugly kerchief.

Turning away, he faced the bow, lacing his arms through the ropes and determined to think of something other than Iseabal. Some men saw to their physical needs indiscriminately at every port, but Alisdair had never considered himself a slave of lust or a creature subject to the whims of desire. Until now. Why else would he stand on the rigging day after day in order to watch her?

Alisdair had the odd and unwelcome thought that Drummond would be laughing himself silly if he knew.

The place MacRae had chosen for her was secluded behind the captain's cabin near the stern, and accessible only by a narrow walkway. Here, Iseabal was shielded from the sight of the sailors and their sometimes surprising behavior.

Most of them had dispensed with their shirts, revealing brown, hairy chests. Even the MacRae was tanned, but she resolutely pushed him from her thoughts.

The wind brushed playfully against her kertch, as if wishing to pull off her headdress and play among her hair. Irritated, Iseabal tightened the knot under her chin with an impatient jerk.

Two stacked boxes served as her table. Another wooden crate was her chair. And in front of her was the slab of marble, stubbornly quiet. She couldn't envision what it might be. A statue of a horse, perhaps. Or a replica of Fernleigh.

She picked up her largest chisel, its metal surface the width of three of her fingers, and continued with her task of removing the corners. Any occupation was preferable at this moment. She wanted to forget her surroundings and, most important, her circumstances.

This was the easiest work, yet the most treacherous. Too hard a strike in the wrong place and she could create a fissure in the stone. Or expose a cavity opening up where solid rock should be. But the ebony surface of the marble remained solid and intractable.

"Would you like tea?" Rory asked, peering around the corner.

Iseabal glanced over at him, shaking her head. Tea was evidently another custom borrowed from the Chinese, but unlike the men of the *Fortitude*, she did not enjoy it, finding it too bitter for her taste.

"Are you sure?"

Iseabal only smiled her denial. The cabin boy's antipathy had eased during the past few days, and from time to time he even deigned to grant her a smile. She wondered if the MacRae had spoken to him, or did the fact that his captain had an annulment in mind soften the boy's attitude?

Rory had acted as intermediary between the two of them for the past three days, ferrying questions and answers back and forth. Was she feeling any pain? Did she need anything? Was she hungry now? Did she have any preferences for her meals?

A surprise, that the *Fortitude* carried a cook on board, a man who reigned supreme, the power he wielded almost kinglike. His mop of red hair was his crown, while his scepter was the spoon he continuously waved in the air.

Iseabal didn't see the MacRae at mealtimes, choosing to eat alone in the cabin. She was more than satisfied with such an arrangement, thinking that the less she saw of her husband, the better.

Those moments when he changed her wrapping had become increasingly difficult to bear. Her curiosity, coupled with a loneliness she'd never before felt, made her want to act in daring ways. Stroking her hand on his chest, placing her palm on his cheek, smoothing her fingers down his throat, were all gestures forbidden yet enticing. Neither spoke during those awkward occasions, and the only movements between them were those necessary as patient and physician.

At night he would return to the cabin, make his berth on the floor, falling asleep without a word. And she, trapped in mute fascination, would lie there watching him in the darkness as if to learn about him while he slept.

Last night, however, he'd done something different. He'd pulled out the table and a chair, setting them up quickly before going to one of the little doors in his chest. He retrieved a bundle of wood tied with a bit of string, and another object that looked like an oblong bowl.

Without a word he placed the objects on the table, then opened another door, retrieving a set of tools not unlike her chisels, only smaller. Reaching into a compartment behind a sliding door, MacRae pulled out a small lantern and a glass vessel shaped like a teardrop, filled with a solid yellow mixture. Placing it on top of the lantern chimney, he lit the wick, then adjusted two vents.

His hand hovered over the selection of tools, as if he were undecided about which one to use. Finally he selected one and, spreading the wood strips side by side on the table, began to trim the pieces.

From her perch half concealed by the tartan curtain, Iseabal watched him, fascinated with his actions. He, in turn, was as silent as she, intent upon his task.

When the yellow mixture was liquefied, he poured it drop

by drop onto the ends of three of the shorter pieces of wood before affixing them to the oblong bowl. No, not a bowl, she realized as he added each piece separately. The wooden structure was beginning to look like the hull of the *Fortitude,* long and sleek, with an upturn on each end.

His head was bent, his attention on his work. As if he had, Iseabal thought, forgotten her very presence. She felt the same when lost in her stone carving.

In the faint light he looked larger somehow. Shadows fell over him, pooling around his shoulders and behind his head, dancing over his features.

Finally she could stand the silence no longer, curiosity prompting her to speak. "Is it a ship?" she asked.

He glanced up, turning his head slowly toward her. A lock of hair had fallen down over his forehead, as if pointing the way to his surprising blue eyes.

"Yes," he said. "I'm developing a new hull for a ship I'm designing."

"You build ships?"

"I did," he said, the words unspoken but lingering in the air between them. Before he had surrendered a fortune for Gilmuir and a wife he didn't want.

"You built the *Fortitude,*" she said, recognizing a similarity between the hull in his hand and the shape of the larger ship.

He nodded. "I'll build faster ones," he said. "Ships like birds that fly over the water."

"Is that a form of glue, then?" she asked, pointing to the lantern.

"A mixture of linseed oil, paraffin, and some other ingredients. It's more the consistency of wax, holding the wood together, but pliable so that I can move a piece if I wish."

"In this is how you build a ship?" she asked curiously. "From a replica?"

"This is how I do it," he said. "Only after I've tested the design do I put it on paper. The actual workmanship begins from that plan."

Iseabal had a sudden image of him as a boy, flattened on his stomach beside a stream, floating leaves in the water and testing each one to see which was faster.

The metal chisel ringing against inflexible stone was a familiar sound, one drawing her to her task and away from thoughts of the MacRae.

Placing her tools on the impromptu table a few moments later, Iseabal flexed her stinging fingers, still feeling the vibration of the stone in her bones.

This was a peaceful place to work, with the calm waves lit golden by the sun, and the sky a brilliant blue. She could feel the current, MacRae's sea goddess, beneath the *Fortitude* as they sliced through the water. The wind filled the sails, speeding them toward England.

A sound above made her tilt her head back, a hand shading her eyes. There on the rigging stood Rory, his bare feet resting on the ropes, his childish shoulders squared, his upper arms spindly in comparison to the MacRae's. He stood nonchalantly beside the boy, high above the deck, his right hand pointing upward, his left easily resting against the mainmast. He didn't seem aware of the danger, Iseabal thought, her heart beating furiously, both entranced and terrified as she watched him.

Again she was reminded of a warrior from earlier times. He looked as comfortable half naked as he did in his sartorial finery, and at ease with both the elements and danger itself.

Sound carried easily, their conversation wafting down to

the deck like a determined breeze. "Not until you've had more experience, Rory," the MacRae said sternly, shaking his head in obvious denial.

"I've been practicing, sir," the boy replied, his gaze one of entreaty. "Were you not my age, sir, when you first climbed the rigging?"

Alisdair studied the petitioner for several long moments. But the boy never looked away, only returned his gaze in equal measure. Finally the MacRae smiled, and with one gesture of his hand released the boy.

"Mind your feet, Rory," he said, staring after him. "And do not be in such a hurry that you don't see obvious dangers."

"Yes, sir," Rory said excitedly, bracing his feet on one of the iron bars embedded in the pitch-coated mast.

Tilting his head back, he watched as Rory rose to the next spar. His smile had disappeared and in its place was a somber attentiveness.

Iseabal turned away from the scene, from the sight of the MacRae, feeling suddenly overwhelmed. He was the MacRae, a man too large and strong to be denied, and her husband. Even if he did not wish it, he was forever bound to her. Perhaps one day, soon enough, he would declare himself released and sail back across the ocean, leaving her tied by tradition, ritual, custom, and ceremony to a man who did not want her.

Her left hand gripped the chisel, her right the mallet. At the moment, they looked like strange appendages. But it was better to concentrate on her tools than on her husband and his intentions.

Never a wife, always a bride.

She closed her eyes, banishing that thought. And the sudden image of the freedom he wished for her. Instead, she

craved the bondage he saw as matrimony, the feeling of be-
longing, the tandem of purpose.

What would it be like to be married to such a man? Someone who was protective, caring, and loyal?

He'd called her an artist. To most people, a piece of limestone was simply a rock, but to her, it held a magical promise.
There could be an angel trapped in a bit of shale or the image
of a face in marble. The first person who had understood how
she felt about her work was also the man who wanted to rid
himself of her.

Tracing the chips in the marble with one finger, Iseabal recalled the moment of their first meeting. Even then he had
fascinated her. Alarmed her, true, but incited her curiosity.

Glancing up, she realized that Rory was climbing back
down the iron rungs, more cautiously than he had ascended
the mast. But the MacRae was no longer on the rigging.

Instead, he was standing a few feet away. Her heart
lurched and then calmed, and her breath seemed absurdly
tight.

"Why do you wear a scarf over your hair?" he asked in
greeting.

"All married women wear a kertch," she answered, surprised. "It's a sign of modesty and decent conduct."

He began to walk slowly toward her, the journey measured not in moments but in elongated heartbeats. His tanned
chest was still bare, his shoulders naked, his stomach revealed as flat and rippling with muscle.

Iseabal looked away rather than stare, thinking that she
might still be a maiden, but she knew more of her husband
than she had of any man.

He reached out and touched the edge of her kertch where

it met her cheek. Her skin tingled as his callused finger began a journey down her jaw and then up to her temple. Iseabal felt her cheeks warm even as a path of chills followed his finger.

Only once before had they stood so close in the brightness of sunlight, on that first meeting days earlier. Each subsequent encounter had been in the shadows or illuminated merely by a lantern's glow.

Her knowledge was greater than it had been that day he'd rescued her. He was not simply a man blessed with a beautiful smile, or eyes as blue as a Highland sky. His character held as much fascination for her as his appearance.

I could love you. The thought caught her in mid-breath.

Slowly he untied the knot she had just tightened, his knuckles brushing the underside of her jaw.

Unable to look away, Iseabal watched as Alisdair lowered his head, his whisper traveling like a breath across her temple.

"I wish you wouldn't wear it," he said surprisingly, the low resonance of his voice causing another chill, this one through her entire body. "Your hair is too lovely to be kept covered."

Slipping the kerchief from her head, Alisdair speared his hands through her hair. As mischievous as the wind, and as determined, he pressed his hands against her scalp, the touch as strange and enticing as the smile he wore.

Reaching up and gripping his wrists, Iseabal forced his hands down until they stood linked only by the touch of their fingertips. A tentative joining, mimicking their marriage. Her thumb began to trace his index finger, then slowed when Iseabal realized what she was doing.

She pulled away, staring down at her hands rather than at

him. In the bright light her knuckles were almost bulbous, her fingers callused from years of using sharp tools and working on stubborn stone. She clenched them into fists.

"I am still a married woman, MacRae," she said softly. *However you might not wish it.*

"And I am still your husband," he countered, to her surprise. "Have my wishes no bearing?"

Glancing up, she saw that his smile had vanished, and his gaze, somber and direct, was filled with curiosity.

He gripped both her hands, gently turning them over. Embedded in her palms was limestone dust, the result of years of carving stone. On the base of her right thumb was a faint scar, the D her father had carved.

She tried to pull away, but he wouldn't release her.

"Talented hands," he murmured. "Those of a woman who chooses occupation rather than idle hours."

His words sounded absurdly like a compliment.

The shouts of the men on the rigging, the creak of rope tightening against the spars, Rory's triumphant whoop, the cook's shout to line up for the noon meal—all these Iseabal heard as muffled sounds. Even the air seemed thicker, heavier, laden with the taste of brine.

She was too fascinated with him, too curious, and too aware. He wanted nothing to do with her, wanted no bonds between them, yet now he stood as encapsulated in this moment as she.

"Please," he said, and it took a moment for her to understand. He didn't wish her to wear her kertch.

She nodded, reluctantly. He didn't know what he was asking, she realized. Not to wear her kerchief was to portray herself as a single woman. But perhaps it was right and proper for her appearance to mirror her status in the world.

Iseabal pulled away finally, bending to retrieve her tools. But he reached the leather sling first and passed it to her.

"Thank you," she said, looking anywhere but at his face.

"Iseabal," he began, only for her name to fade away between them.

She moved away from him, turning at the end of the passageway to glance back. He had not moved from his position and they exchanged long looks before she retreated into the cabin. Regret tasted like tears, she thought, closing the door behind her.

Chapter 12

London was a stain upon the horizon, great clouds of gray smoke looming over the city as if to mark it for the tired traveler. The harbor itself was a forest of masts, ships stacked together so tightly that Alisdair thought a man could reach the wharf by walking from deck to deck.

As was common in crowded ports, Alisdair chose to berth the *Fortitude* in the harbor, using her small boats to ferry the crew ashore. Giving the order to Daniel, he stood against the bow railing, watching as the anchors were gradually lowered.

Daniel was evading him of late, careful to carry out his orders, but just as cautious to avoid any personal conversations. In fact, he noted, his entire crew seemed to be going out of their way to avoid him. Which was just as well, Alisdair thought. He was in no mood for superstitions or portents or reportings of Henrietta's tail.

The ship's cat crossed his path, sending a sideways glance in Alisdair's direction as if amused at his growing irritation.

He had already dispatched Rory to the docks, to engage a carriage and driver for the journey to Brandidge Hall. According to his father's directions, the Sherbourne estate was not far from London, and the distance easily traveled in an afternoon.

Even though his cabin was located in the stern of the ship, he heard the door open. With his gaze now directed toward London, his senses were nevertheless attuned to Iseabal, making him aware of her in a way that surprised him. He could almost feel each one of her soft footfalls across the deck, hear her faint murmur as she greeted him. He should not have been able to discern the scent she wore over that of London's busy port, but he could, detecting something green and woodsy and smelling of flowers all at the same time.

Attired in a petticoat of red stripes and a jacket of red, she came and stood beside him. She had left her hair uncovered, spreading down her back like a thousand strands of ebony silk. Her face was pink with color, her attention directed toward London lying before them.

"There are a great many ships," she murmured.

"It is said that sooner or later everyone travels to London."

"Have you been here before?" she asked, looking up at him.

In the morning light she appeared almost radiant, he thought, then turned away before he could emulate James in waxing poetic.

"No," he answered. "I haven't."

"You don't like being in England," Iseabal said.

"No," he admitted. "I don't."

He had traded for silks in China, and for spices among the

islands of the Pacific. He had seen France, marveling at its castles and cathedrals. Spain and Portugal held an allure, as did the American colonies. But he had not, until now, felt uncomfortable in his travels or choice of port.

One of the *Fortitude*'s boats was returning, Rory sitting in the bow, a wide grin on his face. "I found a carriage and a driver, Captain," he called up, and Alisdair nodded in response.

"Will you be ready to leave in a few moments?" he asked, turning to Iseabal.

"Where are we going?"

"To Brandidge Hall. The Sherbourne estate."

"To refuse an earldom."

"Yes," he said.

"You're leaving me in London, then?" she asked, concentrating on the sight of her trunk being loaded into a second boat.

The question grated at him, coming as late as it did. She should have asked her fate a day ago, or a week. Not now, not when they were set to disembark.

"With the amount of money I intend to settle on you, Iseabal," he replied irritably, "you'll be able to choose your own destination."

Her glance was quick and shuttered, but instead of saying more, she moved to the side of the ship, peering intently over the rail. She looked, he thought sourly, as if she could not wait to leave the *Fortitude*.

The journey to the dock was uneventful, memorable only for its silence. Neither he nor Iseabal spoke, and even the voluble Rory remained mute, occasionally exchanging glances with the sailor at the oars. On the descent to the boat and in the ascent to the wharf, Iseabal merely took Alisdair's hand, nodding her thanks. But not once did she speak to him, as if she'd already dismissed him from her life.

Behind them, two sailors carried their trunks, Rory leading the way to the coach he'd hired. The boy glanced back from time to time as if wondering at the delay. Alisdair had issued orders that every man was to be given leave, except for a rotating watch left aboard the *Fortitude*. Rory was evidently eager to be about the business of proving himself man enough to consort with his fellow crewmen.

London's sky was gray, and the air seemed thick with the smells of a slaughterhouse, unwashed bodies, and smoke. Everywhere Alisdair looked there were people, crowds of them undulating toward their destinations. He took Iseabal's elbow, navigated beyond a small group of men talking vehemently in the middle of the street, their arms waving toward the harbor.

Carriages, drays, large coaches, and carts sat nose to nose along the wharf, waiting either for cargoes to be unloaded from an adjacent ship or for the transport of their wealthy owners.

Soldiers attired in their distinctive red coats stood in strict formation, ready to board one of the ships. Alisdair didn't doubt that their destination was the American colonies, their duty to act as a deterrent to the growing talk of rebellion.

Placing his arm around Iseabal's far shoulder, he pulled her closer to him, his annoyance growing with each of the glances sent in her direction.

Finally they were at the coach, parked away from the main wharf. He and the driver exchanged a few words while the trunks were being loaded.

"It'll take longer to get through London, sir," the driver

said with a gap-toothed smile, "than it will this place of yours."

He nodded, his attention caught by the sight of Rory opening the door for Iseabal. She entered the coach gracefully and silently, her quick smile one of thanks.

She smiled at his cabin boy and watched him with studied caution, Alisdair thought in disgust.

Rory stood at attention beside the coach, the pose difficult to maintain since his eyes were darting from sight to sight and his feet were impatiently tapping on the bricked pavement.

"You're eager to be off, then?" Alisdair asked with a smile.

"Yes, sir," Rory replied, with no attempt made to disguise his excitement.

Alisdair bent, grabbing the boy's hand and placing a few coins on his palm.

"Thank you, sir," Rory said, staring down at the money in awe.

"Your wages for the next month, Rory," Alisdair told him. "Have a care."

"I will, sir." Rory smiled brightly. In seconds the three sailors were gone, disappearing into the crowd.

Alisdair mounted the steps, settling himself into the coach with his back to the horses. As the vehicle lurched forward, the motion reminded him of a lumbering merchantman.

Flicking open the leather shade, Alisdair found himself unwillingly impressed at the sight of a large domed cathedral. He sat back against the cushions, feeling not unlike Daniel in the lion's den. Daniel might admire the predator's home, but it didn't mean that he felt comfortable as a guest.

Iseabal, however, appeared entranced with the view of

London. Her eyes widened; her breath seemed to stop before escaping on a sigh of enchantment. Not exactly Fernleigh, Alisdair thought, wondering at his foul mood.

"Have you never traveled before, Iseabal?" Alisdair asked. His voice sounded surly even to his own ears, so he forced a smile to his lips.

She turned her head slowly, her gaze measured. The hint of irritation, however, was in her eyes. "I've been to Inverness and Edinburgh, MacRae. But no farther than that."

"Why do you call me MacRae in that tone of yours?" he asked. "Have you forgotten my name again?"

She looked startled at his anger. Well she might be, he thought, and at other responses he was feeling at the moment. He needed to obtain an annulment, he decided, then ease his need with some willing woman. A female who did not look as equally alluring in sunlight or in shadow. And who did not, he decided, hide her thoughts behind such rigorous restraint.

"I call you MacRae," she said quietly, "because you've given me no reason to address you familiarly."

Her dignity shamed him at the same time that it fanned his irritation.

He should not wish for her to speak to him, to divulge all those secret thoughts she kept hidden. Instead, he should be grateful for her reticence. The less he knew of her, the better.

Yet a more ferocious part of him, controlled not by reason but by the more elemental emotions, wanted to hold her steady, place his palms on both sides of her face, and peer into her eyes until he found all the answers he needed. Who was Iseabal?

Alisdair realized that he still didn't know.

"We'll reach Brandidge Hall in the afternoon," he said.

She nodded, eternally accepting.

"My duties will take me no more than a few days to perform."

She didn't respond to that, merely kept her attention on the view.

"I'll be back on the *Fortitude* in a week," he added.

Still no response, almost as if he'd not spoken.

And Iseabal? What would happen to her? The thought was disconcerting. So, too, the realization that while it had been easy to make the decision to obtain an annulment, the execution was proving to be more difficult.

She was doing nothing to encourage him to remain her husband. She'd offered neither logic nor cajolery in an attempt to change his mind. Instead, her enticement was to irritate and confuse, to hide her thoughts and restrain her speech until he was mired in a curiosity that wouldn't cease.

He should simply kiss speech from her. Open her mouth and inhale her unvoiced words.

"Have you given any thought to where you will live?" he asked abruptly. "I will take you wherever you wish to go."

"You may as well leave me here," she said. "My father will have no qualms about declaring me a widow and marrying me off again. You and he are alike in your greed."

Startled, he stared at her, thinking that perhaps it had not been the wisest thing to wish speech from Iseabal.

"He would do anything for money, while you would do the same to obtain your freedom," she said at his silence.

"I've never thought to be compared to Magnus Drummond," he responded tightly.

She tilted her head, stared at him. "Outwardly you're nothing like him. Or any of the other men he's shown me to.

My candidates for groom have all been wealthy, but few of them had their teeth or hair."

"At least I have my hair and teeth," he said, annoyed in a way he could not articulate.

"Yes," she agreed, glancing at him. Only that. Just that one word uttered in such a bland tone that it had the effect of being among the most insulting remarks ever spoken to him.

The carriage was suddenly too small, the space so confining that he felt as if the air itself pressed in on his skin. Alisdair frowned, leaned back against the cushions, and feigned sleep.

Time had evaporated, and no great ideas had occurred to Iseabal about her future. Because her father considered her mother's relatives a drain on his finances, she'd not seen them often these past years. Yet word still flowed between Leah and her family, love having no barrier.

Her mother's sister lived in Inverness, but she had been sickly of late and it did not seem fair to appear on her doorstep without warning. A cousin living not far away from Fernleigh had borne another child. Perhaps she and her husband could use an extra pair of hands to help with the chores or act as nurse.

There were pitifully few choices for an unmarried woman. Nor did Iseabal have any talents that might support her. She didn't have her mother's ability at needlework or tatting lace. The making of bonnets was a tedious chore. The only true talent she had was in carving stone, and that was considered a foolish occupation for a woman.

How strange to be so unwanted in all ways.

From time to time she glanced over at the MacRae, realizing that he was not asleep, merely distancing himself by his position. He sat in the corner of the carriage, his arms folded against his chest, his long legs spread out before him. In this confined space he was too imposing.

Words might sway him from his decision, but she could not say them. *Let me stay.* A simple sentence, but one that was held in her heart, not to be voiced. Pride, it seemed, was all she had left, and it was not easily spent. Perhaps she was as much a miser as her father, Iseabal thought wryly.

Moments lengthened into hours and the view changed from thickly crowded London to a more pastoral vista. Softly rounded hills undulated around them, creating small, shadowed valleys. A gentle land, England. There were few people on the roads, and even fewer dwellings, as if this fertile earth stewarded itself.

Clouds began to obscure the sky, darkening as if in preparation for rain. She was suddenly amused by the hint of another storm. They had left Scotland in a torrent; were they to be welcomed in England by yet more rain? Even the breeze tasted of it, but there was neither lightning nor thunder to mar the perfect scenery.

Rain marked their passage, drumming on the roof of the coach in a strangely comforting sound.

There, in the center of a glen, sat a house, a structure reminding her of a great white eagle, its wings stretching out on either side of its body. Like that proud bird, the house seemed to declare itself as worthy of admiration.

"Is that Brandidge Hall?" she asked in amazement.

Opening his eyes without hesitation, Alisdair pulled the shutter away from the window, looking down at the house. "If it is," he said wryly, "I was not given to understand that it was quite so large."

An enormous white dome, its leaded glass winking in the

pattering rain, sat atop the center of Brandidge Hall. Above
the bowl-like shape, a tall, golden spire seemed to point the
way to heaven itself.

Flanking the house were great gardens, misted in the rain.
Hedges trimmed to form curves and winding, almost impossible, designs were interspersed with gravel paths and flower
beds rich with blooms. Iseabal recognized the pattern in the
center of one formal space as a Celtic knot, similar to that
found in her family's crest.

The carriage began to descend toward the house, taking a
road paved in glittering white stone. Just as suddenly as it
had begun, the rain eased.

"It seems as if we're being greeted," Alisdair said as the
carriage halted in the circular drive before the wide front
door.

At the top of the steps was an ancient-looking butler, hair
coiffed in an impressive white wig. Speaking to a footman
standing beside him, he pointed toward the carriage before
turning and walking back to the door in a shuffling gait. The
footman went quickly down the stairs, throwing open the
door and bowing.

Alisdair left the vehicle and held his hand out for her.

Climbing those steps would make one feel a penitent,
Iseabal thought, as if entering a great and noble cathedral.
The very last thing she wished to do was to set foot inside
that imposing-looking structure. But she forced her lips into
a faint smile and descended from the carriage.

Chapter 13

The majordomo stood stiffly inside the door, an ancient sentinel for Brandidge Hall. Alisdair wondered if the old man had known his father, but before he could ask that question or give him his name, the other man turned, leading them through the massive foyer and into a hallway.

His grandfather, he'd been told, had been a collector of sorts and Brandidge Hall mirrored his interests. Outside one door was a statue of a slender black dog, sitting with paws outstretched, muzzle erect, eyes blindly staring in eternal watchfulness. Egyptian, if Alisdair wasn't mistaken. Along one wall was a tansu, filled with dozens of tiny drawers, the key to each festooned with a golden tassel.

"It looks like the one in your cabin," Iseabal said.

"A Japanese tansu," he said, agreeing.

On an ivory pedestal stood a chest, a work of art intricately carved and lacquered in a brilliant crimson. Noting the dragons and the number of claws on each toe, Alisdair realized that the chest wasn't Japanese, but Chinese.

The majordomo stopped, glancing behind him with an impatient look. Alisdair knew he'd just been wordlessly chastised for dawdling.

Stopping in front of a large, heavily patterned door, the old man motioned to one of the two footmen standing guard on either side. The servant bowed, opening the door silently, and the older man shuffled in, announcing their presence in a voice that cracked with age.

"Your grandson, my lady," he said, standing aside. After Alisdair and Iseabal entered, he abruptly vanished, leaving Alisdair staring at the closing door.

"How did he know?" he asked, and heard a tinkling laugh.

"You're the image of your father," a woman said. "With your grandmother's eyes."

Patricia Landers, Countess of Sherbourne, was nothing like he had pictured her, Alisdair thought, glancing down at the diminutive woman who had been his grandfather's second wife. Although in her seventies, she seemed much younger. Her brilliant silver hair was arranged in a simple bun, her face only lightly lined and now graced with a radiant smile and faded, twinkling blue eyes.

She sat on the settee in front of the fire, one hand clasping a brass bird fixed on the top of a cane. Her attire was simple, the pale gray mourning dress reminding Alisdair that the man whose death had complicated his life had been her son.

"I'm sorry for your loss," he murmured softly, releasing Iseabal's hand to bow slightly in front of the older woman.

She took him aback by placing a hand on his forearm and squeezing lightly. "David had a rich, full life, thanks to your father," she said, her bright smile momentarily dimmed with sadness.

"Please join me." She motioned to the space beside her. "I trust your journey was an easy one," she added, glancing curiously at Iseabal.

Alisdair stepped back, also glancing at Iseabal. "May I introduce Iseabal Drummond to you, Countess," he said.

At her inquiring look, he hesitated. "My wife," he added.

"Not truly a wife," Iseabal replied, looking over at him. "Alisdair wishes an annulment."

Alisdair stared at her, unprepared for her candor and wishing she'd chosen another time to be so outspoken.

Patricia looked from one to the other, her brow furrowing. "I did not realize you were married."

"It's a recent event," he said, annoyed.

Iseabal glanced at him, her gaze filled with irritation. "We've been wed but a week," she contributed, turning to Patricia.

"I do not understand," the older woman said. "Why should you wish an annulment? Is there some impediment to your marriage? Some relationship that has just become apparent?"

"Our marriage was not a question of choice," Alisdair countered, "but of command. Her father's," he added.

He and his crew had fought bandits in the Orient and privateers in the Caribbean. Twice Alisdair had stared down the barrel of a pistol, certain he was about to die. But he'd never once considered that he might be at a loss with two women glaring at him as if he'd grown a horn in the middle of his forehead.

"What did you do, that he insisted upon marriage, Alisdair?" Patricia asked, her tone for all the world as if he were nine and had pushed James into the bay.

"It wasn't what I did, but what I wanted," he answered, disconcerted to see her lift an eyebrow imperiously at him. "MacRae land," he explained stiffly. "Drummond was using it for sheep fodder."

"You were married in Scotland, then?" Patricia addressed her question to Iseabal.

"Yes," she said quietly. "At Fernleigh, my home."

Patricia glanced at Alisdair once again and for a moment he thought she might say something else. But she clamped her lips together and reached up to take Iseabal's hand, drawing her down to the settee.

She bent and spoke in a soft tone to Iseabal, leaving Alisdair with the curious feeling of being dismissed.

He walked over to the blazing fireplace, staring up at the paintings mounted above the mantel. To his right was a portrait of a man of middle years, his sweet smile of contentment and look of vacancy in his eyes revealing his identity. The recently deceased Earl of Sherbourne had been a man in form, but a child in mind.

On the left was a painting of a man attired in a brilliant red tunic, a row of medals aligned over his heart. He was pictured mounted on a white horse whose bridle and saddle were laced with silver.

"Your husband?" he asked Patricia. She had married again after his grandfather's death. Due to the nature of David's malady, he guessed that this man had been the true steward of the Sherbourne wealth.

"Nigel Wescott," she said, glancing up at the portrait.

"General Wescott?" Alisdair asked, surprised. Wescott

was the man who might well have sent his father to the gallows, had the MacRaes not been able to escape.

"We struck up a friendship, the general and I," Patricia said, reminiscing. "The night your father and the MacRaes left Scotland, we discovered a great many things in common."

"Because of you, they were able to leave," he told her. "They never forgot your courage," he added. "A great many baby girls were named Patricia in honor of you."

Patricia smiled. "Thank you for telling me that, but I'm afraid it wasn't courage as much as fascination," she confessed, glancing up at the portrait with a wistful smile. "Nigel was a truly wonderful man. For years he acted as earl, since David held the title but could not perform the duties. He's been gone now for seven years and I miss him every day." She looked at Alisdair. "I loved your grandfather as well, Alisdair, but his heart had already been taken by Moira."

A footman entered just then, bearing a tray laden with a round china pot and matching cups and saucers, along with an assortment of pastries. A crystal decanter and matching tumbler rested on another salver carried by the second footman.

"Thank you," she said softly, smiling at the servants. "My butler took for granted that you would prefer whiskey over chocolate, Alisdair," Patricia said, her eyes teasing. "Was he incorrect?"

"No," Alisdair admitted, sitting in the chair next to the settee.

The fire was taking the dampness from the air, adding a cozy cheerfulness to the room. A brightly flowered rug in a Persian style covered the floor. Dozens of gilded sconces were mounted on the pale yellow silk walls, the beeswax candles lit against the gloom of the day. Elaborate plaster carvings of flowers festooned the corners of the ceilings. To complete the air of a feminine chamber, each table bore spindly legs, and each footstool arranged in front of the chairs was upholstered in needlepoint.

The only exception was the large wing chair in which he sat. The leather arms were worn and smelling faintly of tobacco. He couldn't help but wonder if the general had sat here at night in quiet companionship with Patricia.

"Is there a portrait of my grandfather?" he asked as the footman handed him a heavily cut glass half filled with whiskey.

She shook her head. "A small one," she said. "It was, after all, his duty to be pictured. Gerald did not approve of portrait painters, although he had your grandmother's likeness done."

"I've heard she was very beautiful," he said, glancing at Iseabal. She sat quietly again, her annoyance tamped beneath good manners. She was not unlike a volcano he'd once seen in the islands, Alisdair thought. Dormant and quiescent, it nevertheless had the power to crack the earth miles away. Sometimes steam erupted and large holes revealed secret rivers of molten lava.

What fierceness of temperament was hidden beneath Iseabal's façade?

Patricia stared down at the contents of her cup as if viewing something other than chocolate. Alisdair had the feeling that she was debating the wisdom of her words before continuing. Finally she replaced the cup in its saucer and gently set both on the table in front of her.

"Do you want to see Moira's portrait?" she asked. "It took months, I understand, until Gerald was satisfied. It's always hung in his chamber," she added, leaning on the cane and slowly standing. "Why don't I take you there now, and you can see it for yourself?"

Iseabal scowled at Alisdair, but he didn't see her, being so intent on assisting Patricia up the stairs.

Not once in her life had she ever deliberately harmed anyone, but at the moment, Iseabal wanted to hit the MacRae over the head with her mallet.

He'd introduced her nonchalantly, as if she were nothing more than an object. *This is a box, a trunk, a companion. My wife. Do not become accustomed to the fact of her; she is soon to be dismissed.*

Frowning at him, Iseabal trailed behind the two of them.

At the landing on the second floor, Patricia rested, one palm pressed against her bosom.

"I rarely come to this floor," she admitted after catching her breath. "My chamber is behind Nigel's library. A precaution my physician ordered."

"Then you should not have come," Alisdair said, his concern evident.

"I wanted to," she said gently, patting him on the arm in reassurance. "My health is an impediment to my wishes, a nuisance, nothing more."

Iseabal followed them down the corridor, tilting her head back and marveling at the rectangular sections of black-and-gold molding set into the ceiling. Painted inside each section was a vignette—tiny pointy-eared figures frolicking near naked in a glade, or toga-draped couples sitting amongst blue-edged clouds. The detail was apparent even from here, each separate painting unique and different.

"I have not been here in years," Patricia told him, slowly

opening the door. "But I keep it just as it was in your grand-father's day, Alisdair."

The older woman went to the window, pulling aside the green-and-gold draperies before opening one of the panes. For a moment, she stood looking out at the view of the lawn, sparkling with rain droplets, and thick trees, their branches laden with watery leaves.

The sun, diffused by the growing mist, was still bright enough to illuminate first Patricia, then the room, revealing its pristine condition. Almost, Iseabal thought, as if Gerald's chamber had been as carefully kept as a shrine. And the woman at the window, made young by the subtle shading of light, was its mistress and guardian.

There was something unbearably sad about the Countess of Sherbourne at this moment. As if the determined patter of the past few minutes had faded beneath the somberness of this place. Or perhaps, Iseabal thought, being in Gerald's room had simply opened up a store of memories, old and dusty and rarely recalled.

Dominating the room was the bed, draped in emerald fabric that shimmered in the faint breeze from the open window. Four tall and ornately carved posts marked each corner of the bed, and supported a tester elaborately shirred in the pattern of a sunburst. The headboard bore a crest of a lamb and a lion, each on a shield and separated by a diagonal line.

The other pieces of furniture, although smaller, were just as distinctive in style. The front of the armoire was decorated in inlay, both shades of wood, light and dark, portraying a landscape of willowy trees beside a tranquil river. The side tables and chairs were all crafted with slender legs that curved, bowed, and tapered to end in clawed feet.

Iseabal walked inside the room, her interest captured by the leather-and-gold-tooled top of a writing desk. Her fingers stroked over the deeply embossed pattern of green leaves and gold berries stretching around all four sides.

"Gerald shared this room with Moira," Patricia said, moving to the fireplace. No fire had been laid there, but the older woman extended her hands to nonexistent flames. "He continued to use it after we married." She glanced up at the portrait mounted above the white stone mantel. "I think it pleased him to remember better times."

The portrait of Moira MacRae was a simple one, that of a woman and her child. In the background was Gilmuir as it had once been. Moira's blue dress accentuated the color of her eyes, the same shade as Alisdair's. But that was not the only similarity between them. His grandmother's smile had been transferred to his face and the angle of nose and chin transformed to a masculine version. Anyone looking at them would know they were related, and closely so.

Moira looked down at her child with such joy on her face that Iseabal envied the long-dead woman. Would she ever feel that happiness?

Reaching up, Iseabal traced the line of the child's face a few inches above the canvas.

"Your father?" she asked.

Alisdair nodded.

"I love him dearly, even though he is not my own," Patricia said, smiling fondly. "My dream was realized when I received his letter all those years ago. You had just been born, Alisdair, and he was filled with tales of his bride and his son."

"There are five sons now," Alisdair said, turning his attention to her. "And all of us proud to call him father."

Patricia looked around the room, her gaze touching

fondly on one object after another. "Gerald would be pleased to know that his grandson has returned to claim his heritage."

Iseabal glanced at Alisdair, wondering why he didn't mention that he had no intention of accepting the title. Perhaps it was the sheen of tears in Patricia's eyes that rendered him silent.

Alisdair wordlessly followed the older woman out of the room, no doubt to assist her down the stairs. Worrying about a cabin boy's footing or an aged woman's health or her own injury made him the most unusual man Iseabal had ever known. A man who was so certain of his strength and power that he was not afraid to be seen as caring. Alisdair MacRae would never punish a woman because he was annoyed with her, or terrorize a child because it amused him to do so.

Iseabal didn't want to know more about him, didn't seek to measure the depths of his character. Otherwise, she would feel a greater sense of loss than she felt right at this moment.

Because, Iseabal realized, forcing her smile to remain in place as she stood staring at the portrait, he was the husband of her dreams.

Chapter 14

The chamber Iseabal had been given was lovely, but not as lavishly decorated as the public rooms of Brandidge Hall.

Directly opposite the four-poster bed swathed in yellow silk was the focal point of the room, a large mullioned window stretching from floor to ceiling.

Iseabal stood staring out at the view of rolling hills and lush green grass. There was nothing about the vista before her that was out of place. No sheep marred the thick meadows; the trees were large and majestic. A faint haze appeared in the distance as if God Himself had placed a foggy blanket over England so that she might sleep secure.

She didn't belong here, a feeling accentuated by the torpid descent of twilight. In Scotland, night came with a protest, wild slashes of orange and red appearing against the darkening sky as if the sun feared it would never come again.

In Scotland, vows were made and honored.

Turning away from the window, Iseabal walked back to the bed. The first time in a week she would have a solitary place in which to sleep, unburdened by the presence of another. For the first time in a week, Alisdair would not be forced to sleep on the floor.

Her hand slid over the counterpane, noting the fine quality of the fabric. A great deal of expense had gone into making the residents of Brandidge Hall comfortable. Not like her own home, in which repairs were grudgingly made and sparingly done.

The maid had spread her clothing on the bed, as if she had a selection from which to choose. Undressing, Iseabal gently folded each garment and placed it back in her trunk.

After washing, she dressed again, this time in a petticoat of tan with a pale blue ribbon hem. Topping it were her blue jacket and a necklace of stones graduated in color and in size, strung together with a thin gold wire. She had found the necklace among the ruins of Gilmuir and considered it her greatest treasure.

Her fingers trailed from stone to stone, each one of them in a shade of blue from the color of Scotland's skies to the exact tint of the MacRae's eyes.

Glancing at herself quickly in the mirror, Iseabal noted the paleness of her cheeks. Her eyes looked too large for her face, and her lips almost bloodless.

A knock on the door was an imperious summons to dinner.

There was no footman on the other side of the door to escort her downstairs. Nor was it Alisdair standing there. Instead, the Countess of Sherbourne tapped at the bottom of the door impatiently with the tip of her cane.

Iseabal stood back and watched as Patricia entered, along

with five servants, each bearing an object of clothing or a small chest.

"We've come to ready you for dinner, my dear," she said, smiling brightly. Her glance surveyed Iseabal, leaving her with the feeling that the countess disapproved of her attire.

Patricia sat on one of the chairs beside the large window, tapping her cane in a wordless signal. Two maids came forward, each intent on unfastening an article of Iseabal's clothing.

She brushed them away, and they glanced back at Patricia, who nodded in another signal, this one, evidently, to continue.

Iseabal stepped back against the wall, trapped between the armoire and the bed table, hands crossed over her chest.

"Your attire is quite lovely," Patricia said, "but not appropriate for the bride of the Earl of Sherbourne, my dear."

Iseabal stared at the older woman, uncertain as to what to say.

For a moment Patricia studied her, then raised the tip of her cane. Evidently, Iseabal thought almost frantically, each of her gestures was part of some secret language.

A woman of middle years came forward, a stack of clothing folded over one arm.

"The green one, I think, Jenny," Patricia said.

The garments were placed on the bed and again the two maids approached her. When one of the maids began to pull up her petticoat, Iseabal slapped her hand away and jerked the garment out of her reach.

"No," she said. "I appreciate your kindness, but I truly wish to wear my own clothing."

Again that silent nod. The door opened, and the maids slipped out of the room, leaving Patricia and Iseabal alone.

"Did I misunderstand, Iseabal?" Patricia asked, her voice taking on a cool tone. "Do you truly wish your marriage to be dissolved?"

"No," Iseabal admitted quietly.

"Then why have you done nothing to convince Alisdair otherwise? Pride is a foolish emotion, Iseabal. I spent a great many years being miserable, my dear. I was married to a man I desperately loved, yet was afraid to tell him so. Or," she said reflectively, "to demand the same of him."

Patricia smiled at Iseabal's silence. "Do you deny you feel affection for my grandson?"

What she felt was stronger than yearning, deeper than curiosity, yet Iseabal couldn't define it exactly. Perhaps it was affection, or something more.

"It is not a question of pride," she replied quietly. "Alisdair wants this annulment. He feels forced into our marriage."

"Was he?" Patricia asked, her gaze never leaving Iseabal's face.

"Yes," Iseabal answered simply. "He wanted Gilmuir; my father wanted a fortune."

Patricia's eyebrows rose. "And what did you want?"

"Does that matter?" Iseabal asked, unexpectedly amused. "My wishes are not capable of swaying either man."

"A man's pride is a brittle thing, my dear," Patricia said gently. "It breaks rather than bends. I am not surprised that Alisdair got his feathers ruffled at being forced to marry."

Iseabal doubted it was as simple a matter as his pride.

Patricia made an impatient sound. "Sometimes people are mismatched and refuse to admit it, or they're perfect for each other and cannot recognize that fact." She tapped her cane on the floor as if to accentuate her point.

Then she glanced over at Iseabal, her eyes twinkling.

"There are simply times when a woman must take a man's hand and lead him where she wishes. Get his attention, at least."

"I don't know what you mean," Iseabal said truthfully.

"I know you don't, my dear. But if you'll call the others inside, we'll show you," Patricia said, waving toward the door.

Over the next hour, Iseabal was prodded and pushed, her hair curled into absurd ringlets that were pinned at the crown of her head in an elaborate style. But the greatest indignity, Iseabal thought, was when her clothing was stripped from her as if they were rags and tossed to the bed, replaced by a garment from the countess's closet.

"I will agree it is not the latest fashion, my dear," Patricia said as Iseabal stared, dismayed, at the dipping bodice. "But it reveals a woman's figure."

The dress was of a deep emerald shade, the skirt draping in large swags over an underskirt of a lighter shade of green. But what material was used in the skirt was startlingly lacking above the waist.

The bodice of the dress fit tightly, leaving no room for her stays.

"What is that?" Patricia asked, pointing to her wrapping.

"A bandage," Iseabal answered, telling the other woman of her fall into the foundations.

"Very well," Patricia said, frowning, "I suppose it will have to remain. But your shift ruins the lines of the dress."

"I'll be naked," Iseabal said, beginning to panic. She couldn't appear at dinner with only the wrapping between the dress and her skin.

Patricia ignored her.

A tall, narrow-faced woman approached Iseabal, jerked down on the bodice until the tops of her breasts appeared like two round eggs sitting on a nest. She stared at herself in horror.

"I think we'll leave her hair unpowdered," Patricia said, waving away another woman bearing a box of powder and a paper cone. "But perhaps the smallest tint of rouge to her cheeks and her lips would not be amiss."

Iseabal shook her head, but her protest was disregarded.

Stepping forward, a maid opened the small mahogany chest she held, revealing a selection of jewels sparkling in the candlelight.

Wide-eyed, Iseabal turned to her hostess. "I can't wear any of these," she protested.

Patricia nodded. "Perhaps you're right, my dear. Your bosom will serve as a point of interest."

Finally she was done and being turned in the direction of a pier glass. Startled, Iseabal gazed at the woman reflected there.

Not Iseabal Drummond, modest and neat, but another female with ivory skin and an overflowing bosom even now turning pink with embarrassment. Her coloring seemed too vivid against the emerald fabric, her lips red, her eyes too deep a green.

And her hair. What had they done to her hair? Riotous curls were tucked into a torturous style, held aloft by pins that gouged her scalp. Even the slippers she wore, sewn around her feet by one maid as another burned her hair into place with smoldering tongs, seemed too tight and uncomfortable to wear.

The room fell silent as they waited for her reaction. No doubt they expected rapturous delight and overflowing thanks, Iseabal thought, unable to look away from the spectacle of herself.

"I'm without words," she said, speaking candidly. But it seemed to please them, because she was suddenly overwhelmed by the chatter of six women, all of whom were congratulating themselves on the success of her transformation.

She wanted herself back. Not the Iseabal who had stood before her father biting back words, nor the one who had silently married a stranger. Nor did she want to be the woman she had been on the voyage here. Instead, she wished for the girl who escaped from Fernleigh when she could, who conspired with a stable boy for freedom. The Iseabal who explored Gilmuir and dreamed of past glories, or of creating a masterpiece from stone.

Not this woman, laced and curled and painted to resemble someone else. Her hair was stiff with pomade, her face felt dry and powdery, but the Countess of Sherbourne smiled at her in approval.

"Let us go down to dinner, my dear," Patricia urged.

One last, disbelieving look toward the mirror made Iseabal recognize one simple truth. She had never been good enough for anyone. Not for her father, not for the Countess of Sherbourne, and certainly not for Alisdair MacRae.

There in the mirror stood a caricature, neither the woman she wanted to be nor the silent and acquiescent person she'd always shown the world.

Iseabal had never been as miserable as she felt at this moment. Or as angry.

Chapter 15

This sartorial splendor was hardly necessary, Alisdair thought, glancing at himself in the mirror. Whom exactly, was he trying to impress? His grandmother, perhaps. Certainly not the woman who had seen him at his worst. Grumpy, irritable, near sleepless as he lay beside her on the floor night after night.

He'd been placed in his grandfather's room, Gerald's chamber proving to be comfortable and welcoming. But as he closed the door behind him, Alisdair glanced at the bed, wondering why the thought of sleeping in comfort for the first time in more than a week was unappealing.

Two footmen at either side of the door stood like statues, their gaze fixed above him. Inscrutable and ever-present, Alisdair reflected, and as ubiquitous as the Sherbourne crest.

He entered the sitting room for the second time that day.

Walking to one of the long windows, he stood looking out at the night-darkened landscape.

Tomorrow, Alisdair decided, he would surrender all of this, but it was a sacrifice easily made. He had no connection to this land, no strange feeling of being pulled toward it as he had felt at Gilmuir.

The night was a silent one; there were no small cottages, no huddled dwellings lit brightly against an early dusk. Here, there were only the sounds of crickets and the plaintive bark of a fox hiding amidst the shadows.

In the darkness, the grass looked as black as the ocean at night. The great trees on the property appeared like shrouded giants.

The door opened and he turned to see a man enter. He was short, with a head of curling brown hair. His nose, hawklike and narrow, was accompanied by a thin mouth, giving him an appearance of an aesthetic who rarely saw humor in anything.

"Landers?" the other man said, inclining his head.

Legally, he supposed it was his name. Alisdair nodded cautiously. "And you are?" he asked.

"Robert Ames," the other man said, pleasantly enough. "Your grandmother's solicitor." The look he gave Alisdair was a sweeping one, ending with a tight little smile.

"I didn't realize you were to be here this evening," Alisdair replied, moving to the fireplace. New logs had been added and the fire burned bright and hot. A concession to Patricia's health, he thought.

"I've been in residence for weeks," the solicitor explained. "Waiting for this very moment. Your grandmother is very pleased you were able to arrive so soon. She isn't well, you know."

"Yes," Alisdair said shortly, the earlier visit to the second floor proving that. Her lips had been nearly blue when he'd escorted her to her chamber.

"You're a sea captain, I was told," Ames said, sitting in the wing chair with such ease that Alisdair suspected he'd done so many times before.

"I am," Alisdair said, gripping his hands behind his back.

"I was given to understand that the Orient is familiar to you. I take it, then, that you were engaged in the opium trade." The pleasantness of Ames's tone was not sufficient to offset the insult of his remark.

"I was not," Alisdair said tightly. "The English choose that trade, but I've no wish to carry death in my ship."

The solicitor's eyebrow arched, and his mouth turned down as if he doubted Alisdair's words.

"And what trade were you involved in?" Ames asked, the veneer of politeness falling from his voice one word at a time.

"Is it any of your concern?" Alisdair returned calmly.

"Everything to do with the Sherbourne estates is my business," Ames said curtly.

He should, Alisdair thought, simply tell Ames he'd no intention of assuming the Sherbourne title, and that the solicitor could take his questions and go to perdition. But Alisdair remained silent only because he was suddenly certain the information would please the other man.

"I was involved in mercantile trade, cloth and tea, in the East. I trust that satisfies your curiosity."

"And now you've come into quite an inheritance," Ames said. "How beneficial for you. A long-lost Lander's heir."

The door opened before Alisdair could respond, words stripped from him by the sight of Iseabal.

She looked like a different woman, one he might have noticed in a strange port, but only as a warning to his crew. Her ivory skin had been powdered, her cheeks and lips rouged, and if he wasn't mistaken, her eyebrows and lashes had been darkened.

Where was the woman who'd sat in the stern of the *Fortitude*, her eyes narrowing as she stared at the block of ebony marble?

Patricia removed Iseabal's shawl and for a moment Alisdair couldn't swallow. That dress was entirely too revealing, he told himself. No wife of his . . . the thought stuttered to a halt. Iseabal of the guarded glance and a world of emotions in her eyes was not going to be his to champion or guard.

Why the hell had he ever decided on an annulment?

Glancing at Ames, Alisdair decided to seek other counsel in the matter of his marriage. The less the solicitor knew of his business, the better.

Patricia held out her hand, leaving Alisdair no choice but to extend his arm to her while Ames escorted Iseabal to dinner behind them.

"How exquisitely lovely you are," Ames said, further irritating Alisdair. "If I may say so."

Iseabal should have smiled shyly, as she did with him. Instead, she spoke, her voice low and resonant. "I'm afraid I don't feel like myself," she confessed.

She didn't look like herself, either, Alisdair thought. Gone was the woman whose natural beauty was evident even when she stood drenched and shivering. In her place was a creature who looked as if she could cheerfully give a man the pox.

Unexpectedly, she laughed at something Ames said. Alisdair turned and glared at them both. Patricia patted his arm in a grandmotherly gesture, but her smile, he noted, broadened with his frown.

Iseabal had never laughed with him.

Most of the dinner was pleasant enough, the conversation desultory, concerning Patricia's health, the taste of various dishes, and the rebellious nature of the colonies.

During the meal, in which Ames uttered sycophantic pleasantries and never ceased in his visual admiration of Iseabal's most noticeable attributes, Alisdair decided that he disliked the solicitor intently. The man was a toady, one of those breed who make their living currying the favor of the wealthy.

He sat back in his chair, resting his fingers on the edge of the table, and began tapping an impatient tattoo. Would this meal never be finished?

"I am in the presence of a famous man," Ames remarked, suddenly turning his attention to him. Raising his wineglass, he toasted Alisdair with a sardonic smile. "I neglected to congratulate you earlier on your exploits," he added.

Alisdair said nothing, waiting for Ames to continue.

"Are you famous, Alisdair?" Patricia asked, her smile determined.

"Did you not know that your grandson is renown in seafaring circles?" Ames asked, turning to his hostess. "Have you ever heard of Antarctica?"

Alisdair remained silent, every nerve attuned to Ames.

Ames's smile broadened. "You stumbled upon a new continent."

"Other men found Antarctica, not me," Alisdair said, his composure never slipping despite his annoyance at the solicitor's remarks and the tone in which they were uttered. Alisdair wished, however, that the two of them were alone. He would be happy to divest Ames of that pleased little smile.

"But the notations in your log made it possible for them to do so. You saw something, didn't you? An island, I believe. Or was it a peninsula?"

For all the distances it covered, the sailing community was a small one and renown for its accurate news gathering. Two ships could meet in mid-ocean and before they separated, their crews would be more informed than the residents of adjoining towns.

Alisdair couldn't help but wonder, however, exactly how the solicitor had known of this little trick of his. Unless, he mused irritably, Ames had had him investigated. If that were the case, what else had he discovered? The fact that his father was still alive?

He took a sip of his wine, mentally cursing Ames. His irritation at the solicitor, however, was nothing compared to his sudden annoyance at Iseabal. Not only was she so exposed in that dress that he was amazed her breasts hadn't landed in the soup, but she was now looking at him as if he were a stranger.

The moment stretched out between them as Alisdair patiently waited, much as he did for the first hesitant puffs of dawn wind. She said nothing, trapped in her eternal silence.

Finally he inclined his head toward her. "I have an ability to see far distances," he explained. "That is all."

"Perhaps we should call you Argus," Ames said. "The Greek monster with a hundred eyes," he added, studying Alisdair for a moment. "Although, I confess, I see but two."

"What amazes me," Patricia interjected, smiling, "is that you have an affinity for the sea at all. As I recall, your father did not."

Alisdair smiled, but didn't answer. He didn't trust Ames, preferring not to discuss his father in front of him.

"The *Fortitude* is a beautiful ship," Iseabal said suddenly, addressing her remarks to Patricia. "And when she's under full sail, she feels like the wind itself."

"How poetic of you," Ames said, glancing at her with a thin-lipped smile. Alisdair sat back in his chair, suffused with a sudden wish to throttle the man and a longing to place his coat over Iseabal's bodice, sparing her one more leering glance.

"Do you enjoy poetry, Ames?" Alisdair asked, smiling. "If so, then there are many seafaring ditties you might enjoy. Shall I recite them to you in the privacy of the library? And while we're there," he said, standing, "perhaps you might tell me where you obtained all your information about me." *And just exactly what else you know.*

Patricia stood, leaning heavily on her cane. "The two of you will meet soon enough tomorrow," she said. "I think we should adjourn to the parlor. Only, however," she added, fixing a stern gaze on the two of them, "if you can promise to be amiable."

One of the footmen helped Iseabal with her chair, and she stood and joined Patricia, turning back to look at Ames.

He was once again, Alisdair suddenly realized, being dismissed.

Patricia led them to a chamber surpassing the luxury of the other public rooms Iseabal had seen.

The walls were covered in crimson damask, matching silk drapery framing both tall windows set into the longer wall. Like the corridor on the second floor, the ceiling was filled with rectangular panels, each one adorned with plaster frescoes. The floor beneath her feet was comprised of shining mahogany boards and covered with a pale ivory rug. At the shorter end of the rectangular room was a fireplace, surrounded by a wooden mantel heavily carved with trailing vines and flowers.

Patricia walked heavily to a settee placed opposite the blazing fire. She looked tired, Iseabal thought, but then, this day had been an exciting one for her.

Iseabal would have joined the older woman, had her attention not been captured just then by an object standing in the corner of the room. Alone in an alcove that looked to have been created especially for it was the most beautiful work of art she'd ever seen. In a room crowded with antiques, ancestral portraits, and indications of the Sherbourne wealth, the statue of a young man was quietly magnificent.

She heard the door clicking shut behind her, the muted voices of the others fading as she walked closer to the figure. Easily taller than the MacRae, the likeness was carved in a blue-white marble, the rust-colored veins of the stone revealing it to be of some age.

In his right hand the young man held a ball tucked beneath his chin. His left arm was stretched outward as if to help him balance, one foot drawn up at the exact moment of turning. Placing her hand on his knee, Iseabal could almost feel the joint move beneath her fingers.

Tiny ringlets of hair framed his face, accentuated the aquiline nose and a mouth thinned in grim determination. Eyes, sightless and blank, nevertheless seemed to stare out at the world, a mute witness to the centuries.

Her thumb fingered the detail of the short toga the young man wore. Somehow, the artist had managed to shape the stone over thickly muscled thighs and buttocks, yet still give the impression of a diaphanous garment.

Sliding her hand down the back of one knee, Iseabal marveled at the smoothness of the stone. Polishing often took longer than carving, requiring a dedication to detail and infinite patience. But perhaps the artist who had carved this work of art so brilliantly had had apprentices to perform this chore.

For a moment she stood in wistful silence, realizing that she would never have the talent to create something so exquisite. But she could learn, Iseabal told herself, hone her skills until she reached the pinnacle of what talent had been given her.

Turning, she almost bumped into the MacRae, his face as grim in purpose as this ancient boy's.

"You're falling out of your dress," he observed brusquely.

Iseabal told herself that the sudden warmth she felt at his look was from irritation, not embarrassment. Truthfully, however, she felt more uncomfortable than alluring. The dress was too tight, and there was too much of her showing. But she was not in the mood to agree with the MacRae and further shame herself with the truth.

"It was your grandmother's idea," she said curtly. "Offer your complaints to her," she added, her tone matching his.

"You shouldn't be laced so tightly," he said, his eyes narrowing. "You might do injury to yourself."

"I'm not wearing my stays," she said, wondering at the sudden flush on his cheeks.

Patricia was speaking to a footman, and Ames was examining a small bronze on the mantel. Neither seemed to notice her and the MacRae.

His face was once again closely shaven, his lips unsmiling as he faced her. His gaze slid between her and the statue, a muscle in his cheek flexing as if he held back his words.

"Besides, why should you care, MacRae?" she asked, tipping her head up to meet his gaze, wishing that he were not as tall or that she did not feel so insignificant beside him.

Iseabal turned abruptly and began to leave him. Out of the corner of her eye she saw him reach out for her. Pressing her arm closer to her side, she would have moved away, but he gripped her shoulder. His warm palm against her cool skin felt like a brand.

"Take your hands off me, MacRae," she said, anger surfacing from beneath a lifetime of restraint. "You've no right to touch me."

She jerked away from him and walked out of the room, leaving them all staring after her.

Chapter 16

The morning dawned clear, the rain the day before freshening the air. That gentle English storm made Iseabal long for those in Scotland. She missed the roaring thunder and the brilliant flashes of lightning as it scratched the sky.

The gardens of Brandidge Hall were even more impressive up close. On either side of the hedges grew a profusion of flowers. Rectangular beds, filled with roses in various hues, lined the gravel path. Some flowers, those she'd never before seen, waved their yellow petals in the morning breeze, a call to venture near and appreciate their beauty.

The garden reminded her, oddly enough, of her mother's embroidery, delicate and perfect.

Iseabal skirted the edge of the east wing, following the gravel path as the maid had instructed. Abruptly she stopped, startled at this new, more secluded enclosure.

This garden was a spot of wild beauty with plants growing

in a haphazard fashion. Rows of hedges had been planted years before to enclose the place in a square, leafy box. Obviously, gardeners did not venture here and what trimming or planting occurred was done by nature.

In the center of the space was a large pedestal topped with a bronze sundial in the shape of a laughing face. Beside it stood a wooden bench shaped like two semicircles resting atop each other, their bottom curves touching. There, the Countess of Sherbourne sat waiting for her.

Yesterday Patricia had appeared vivacious at times, as if she were a young girl peeping out from behind faded eyes. But now she looked frail, as if all the burdens and memories of her life weighed on her spirit.

"You wished to see me?" Iseabal asked tentatively, wondering what the countess wished of her now. After last night, Iseabal decided, she was not going to be transformed into someone other than herself.

Patricia patted the bench beside her. Iseabal walked over to her, reluctantly sitting. She tucked her feet beneath her, hoping for the right words to decline another metamorphosis. But the countess didn't seem interested in her attire. "This place reminds me of my childhood home," Patricia said, looking around her. "The older I become, the more I want reminders about me. Perhaps," she mused, with a small, self-deprecating laugh, "I wish to recall my youth in order to bear my old age."

"Or perhaps it's just nice to have things around you that remind you of easier times," Iseabal said. "Is that why there's a Celtic knot in the garden?"

Patricia smiled. "Moira had that planted, and it's been cared for ever since." She glanced at the sundial, useless in this shady spot. "Gerald found that for her," she explained, smiling. "Scotland has figured prominently in my life," she added. "But I truly thought that the last thread had been severed at Nigel's death."

She turned to Iseabal, reaching out to pat her hand. "Until you, my dear."

Patricia's fingers felt so cold that Iseabal covered the older woman's hands with her own.

"You're very kind," Patricia said, smiling faintly. "Which makes what I need to say even more difficult."

She seemed to sigh, then drew a deep breath. "I should have told you yesterday, my dear. But I am an old, meddling woman who saw the look in Alisdair's eyes and yours and hoped for a miracle."

Patricia looked off into the distance. "There is no need for Alisdair to obtain an annulment, my dear," she said. "Because you are not truly married to my grandson."

"We were married," Iseabal said, pulling her hands away from Patricia's.

The older woman nodded. "I know, Iseabal, but Scottish marriages have not been considered valid in England for a great many years."

Warmth left Iseabal's face, sliding down her body until it escaped through her toes.

English law did not apply to her, Iseabal thought. Unless she decided to remain in this country. Here she would be considered a woman without reputation or virtue, one of those shadowy creatures who were pointed at or whispered about. But in Scotland, she would be seen as married. A woman whose husband so disliked her that he had sailed away, leaving her a maiden wife.

Either way, she was caught in a situation even worse than marriage to a bald, toothless man.

"What will you do, Iseabal?" Patricia asked.

"I don't know," Iseabal said numbly.

"You're welcome to stay with me, my dear. I would relish a companion."

Iseabal forced a smile to her lips, grateful for the woman's generosity. But remaining at Brandidge Hall would be the worst thing she could do. Each day would summon up another regret. A whisper in the corridor would recall Alisdair's footsteps. A servant's smile, Alisdair's grin. This place itself, with its hints of Scotland and the MacRaes, would be a dubious haven.

"Thank you," Iseabal said. "I don't know what I'll do. But I can't stay here."

"The world is not always a kind place to women," Patricia warned.

Iseabal nodded. "I know," she said, not telling the older woman that she'd learned that lesson all too well at Fernleigh.

She'd always wished to be brave and daring, and it occurred to Iseabal as she sat there that now was a perfect time to begin.

The library at Brandidge Hall was a masculine domain, carrying the faint scent of tobacco and tanned leather. Tall shelves lining three of the walls were filled with books adorned with gilt spines. A fireplace flanked by two windows and a set of chairs looked to be a cozy place to read or converse.

Alisdair was early for the meeting with Ames, but the solicitor was there before him, occupying the massive desk in the library as if it were his domain.

For all his intentions of giving up the title and Brandidge Hall, Alisdair thought that until he did so formally, this was his room, and these were his books and his desk. He said nothing, however, simply crossed the wooden floor and stood beside the leather-tooled desk until Ames glanced up.

The solicitor had the grace to look embarrassed as he stood, pushing his papers to the other side of the desk. But Alisdair noted that not one word of apology crossed his lips.

Ames sat on one of the two chairs located on the opposite side of the desk, while Alisdair occupied the tall leather chair he had vacated. Atop the desk, was a leather blotter, a tray of quills, and an inkwell shaped like a frog.

"I imagine you want to get down to business as quickly as possible," Ames said, placing the papers in a leather portfolio.

Alisdair sat back, folded his arms, and stared at Ames. Had Patricia not employed him, Alisdair would have dismissed the man on the spot, if for no other reason than the leers he'd directed toward Iseabal. But there was also the question of his investigations.

"How did you learn so much about me?" Alisdair said, cautiously amiable. Demonstrating anger, or even irritation, was unwise in any type of negotiations.

Ames began to push the leather case across the desk, hesitating at the question.

"You can't imagine that I would turn over the Sherbourne wealth to anyone?" he asked.

"Is it yours to cede?" Alisdair asked calmly. "I believe it belongs to Patricia at the moment."

"You're wrong, of course," Ames said, smiling faintly. "She has no claim to any of the fortune. She's living here on your sufferance, but you're within your rights to banish her from Brandidge Hall."

Ames slowly slid the document case across the desk. "If you'll begin signing, then I shall attest as witness."

Alisdair opened the portfolio, beginning to read. All of the properties entailed with the title were listed in alphabetical order, along with the dates when they had been acquired. He was surprised to see that most of them went back hundreds of years.

"You'll find that everything is in order," Ames said stiffly. "Upon your signature, the Sherbourne wealth is yours."

Alisdair grabbed the quill, flipping open the frog's head with its beady emerald eyes, and dipped the nib inside. "What happens if I refuse the title?" he asked idly, tapping off the excess ink from the pen.

"Why would you do that?" Ames wondered, frowning.

"What happens?" Alisdair repeated.

"The title and the estates would go to your second cousin."

"Do you know him?"

The other man nodded. "I have had some acquaintance with him," he conceded. "A man of great nobility, who will hold the title well. Unlike your predecessor."

"I take it you did not approve of my uncle David?"

"The man was a simpleton," Ames said sharply. "He was most happy with his cats. Anything more difficult was beyond his comprehension."

Alisdair's dislike of Ames was growing with each passing moment.

"If I were to decline," he said, "I would want the countess to be able to remain at Brandidge Hall for as long she lives. And to have a sum of money settled upon her until she dies." His entire family owed her a debt of gratitude. Not only had Patricia distracted the English while the MacRaes escaped from Gilmuir, but she had been a guardian of their secret all these years.

"I would certainly state that in your letter to the new earl." At Alisdair's silence, Ames continued. "You must understand English law. It would be up to the new earl to decide what will be done. If you surrender your rights, you also give up the ability to dictate terms."

Alisdair lay the quill down and leaned back in his chair, wondering at the curious feeling of reluctance he felt. The words would be swiftly spoken. *I do not wish to be Earl of Sherbourne.* A simple declination of a title he never wished to have.

The idea, however, of a remote cousin dictating what would happen to Patricia and Brandidge Hall rankled him. He didn't like obstacles in his path. Nor did he like being dictated to. He wanted to live the life he'd chosen, not one forced upon him.

How many of the MacRaes had been allowed to do that? Startled by that thought, Alisdair stood, walking to one of the twin windows.

"Leave me alone for a few minutes," he said without turning.

"I cannot witness your signature if I'm not here to see you sign the papers," Ames said patiently, as if he spoke to a child.

"Then I shall not sign them until you return," Alisdair said. A moment later he heard the door open and then close.

The mantel clock chimed the minutes, a metronome of sound accompanying his thoughts. He turned, to find himself reflected in the convex disk of a sunburst mirror. Staring at his distorted image, Alisdair could not help but wonder at what the world saw.

A captain, certainly. A man to whom family was important. A MacRae, whose heritage was equally so. A builder of ships.

And a selfish fool? One who had forgotten all the deprivations his kinsmen had suffered in settling at Cape Gilmuir. Iseabal had called him greedy, her eyes changing to chips of emerald stone. Until this moment he'd never considered her correct.

As captain of the *Fortitude,* he was familiar with taking responsibility not only for his ship, but for what was more important, the men who sailed her. Yet he'd easily discounted his own responsibility in both his marriage and his heritage, thinking more of his own dislike of the situation than how his actions would impact others.

He couldn't leave Patricia unprotected, nor could he surrender his ancestry and his father's to the stewardship of Ames.

Most important, he could not abandon Iseabal.

I'll not harm you, Iseabal. Words he'd said to her. Yet he had done so in the worst way imaginable. Although she'd been roughly treated by her father, Iseabal had been protected from the world. Instead of the sanctuary of marriage, he had promised her money and the freedom of her future. But even he was not free, Alisdair realized, tied as he was to those he loved by invisible bonds.

He had thought to marry a woman from his homeland, but the images of his childhood friends had faded in the past days until they were now only faint ghosts of memory.

In the forefront of his mind, confusing and mysterious, was Iseabal.

Take your hands off me, MacRae. Her rejection of him had been all too apparent. Or perhaps it was only a mirror of his treatment of her.

Not once had he kissed his wife, the realization thrumming into his mind like an arrow from a tightly strung bow. Nor had he touched her as he'd wished. Not accidentally while treating her, but with purposeful intent.

He could still see Iseabal's fingers stroking a marbled thigh, indolently exploring the sleekness of a flank, the fullness of a buttock, the muscles of an upper arm.

Alisdair had never thought himself possessive or jealous, but last night he'd been both. An unknown model, dead a thousand years, had loaned his body to her callused fingertips and furnished knowledge to a mind previously innocent.

His should have been the body she touched, Alisdair thought, the ideas of protection and responsibility fading beneath a starker truth. He wanted Iseabal to learn from him, map the texture of his skin, smooth her hands over his buttocks with curved fingers the way she had that damn statue. He wanted to see that look of wonder on her face as she touched him.

Alisdair knew, instantly, what he was going to do. Striding to the door, he opened it, gesturing for Ames to enter the library again.

Chapter 17

⟨flourish⟩

Hearing the crunch of boots on gravel, Iseabal turned her head. Alisdair was walking between the ornate hedges, his destination obvious.

"Are you certain you will not reconsider my offer, my dear?" Patricia quickly said. "I would dearly enjoy you as a companion. Will you stay with me, Iseabal?"

Glancing over at the older woman, Iseabal smiled. "It's you who are kind," she said, wishing that she didn't suddenly have the urge to cry. She patted Patricia's hand, then stood, watching Alisdair approach. She didn't feel the least bit brave or daring at the moment. Regret, yes, she felt that, and a sadness that speared through her at the sight of him.

He was dressed formally, as he had been last night. Aboard the *Fortitude* he'd often been attired in nothing more than breeches and a shirt. Sometimes she'd seen him standing at the bow, the fabric of his clothing rippling with the breeze from the ocean. Once, Henrietta, the cat, had sat beside him, both watching the endless surge of waves. A companionable and charming memory she would hold in her heart.

Unbidden, another recollection flashed before her, of his shirt wetly plastered to his chest, his smile kind as Alisdair bent to dry her hair. She had wanted to put her hand on his chest and feel the beat of his heart even then.

Without his beard he appeared a different person, she thought. But the man who commanded the *Fortitude* was far different from this sartorial gentleman. She would never be a suitable wife for this man, but the captain touched something in her nature, drew her admiration and another emotion she dared not name.

He was all too human, her captain. Occasionally arrogant, certainly obstinate, he was also kind, protective, and caring.

Perhaps in time she might talk of him to matronly women she knew. *I was married,* she would say, *to a comely man with eyes like the sky. A man of honor and loyalty.* They would nod kindly, these women of her imagination, but perhaps not believe her.

He slowed, his footsteps oddly muted now. There was a smear of ink on his forefinger and thumb. He had signed away his heritage, then.

Go away, MacRae.

She focused her gaze on his boots, wondering how to say the words, thinking that they might well be the most difficult she would ever utter.

"Scotland," she said, forcing herself to face him. His blue eyes were now somber, his lips curved in a half smile. The closer he came, the harder it was for her to breathe.

"I want to go back to Scotland," she said before he could

speak. "You promised that you would take me anywhere. Take me home, then, MacRae. I'll bear my shame in my homeland."

"You think it shameful to be married to me?" he asked, the amiability of his expression instantly vanishing.

"We are not married, MacRae," she said, forcing a small smile to her lips. "At least not in England. Evidently, the English do not recognize a Scottish ceremony."

Brushing by him, Iseabal held her head high.

His hand reached out, gripped her arm. "What are you talking about?" he asked.

"You wanted your freedom, MacRae," she said. "It seems you have what you wanted. Now take it."

He was becoming damn tired of being dismissed by his wife. Spearing his hands through his hair, he turned to Patricia. "Is that true?"

Slowly she nodded. "Regrettably," she said. "There is no need for an annulment, after all, Alisdair."

"Then get me a priest," he said, annoyed with English law.

He caught up with Iseabal at the maze, once again reaching out and gripping her arm. She flinched and he jerked his hand back. "Did I hurt you?" he asked, fearful that he had caused her pain.

She turned and looked at him, then glanced away as quickly. Her eyes were deep with tears, her face brushed with pink across the bridge of her nose and cheeks. Like a butterfly, he thought nonsensically.

She wore her pale blue jacket today, he was grateful to see. Not something borrowed that revealed too much of her body and disregarded her true charms—eyes that sparked, a mouth that seemed made for laughter, a nature that hinted at both gentleness and strong emotion.

He turned her gently until she faced him, her back to the hedges forming the maze.

In the wake of her silence he spoke again. "What does it take to get you to speak?" he asked, frustrated that she would not answer him.

He placed his hands on either side of her face, tilted her chin up, and bent down to breathe against her lips.

"What must I do to coax you from silence, Iseabal? Should I feed you my own words, only to have you repeat them to me? Or," he said, placing his finger against her bottom lip, "shall I urge you to speech another way? Speak to me, Iseabal," he urged coaxingly, "and I will swallow your words so that they never breathe in the open air."

He lay his lips softly against hers, exerting no demand, simply familiarizing himself with the feel of her. Her skin beneath his fingertips felt like the softest silk from the ports of China, but warm and pulsing with life. Her lips were full and pillowy, immobile beneath his in an invitation as artless and intriguing as the woman.

"Am I supposed to be grateful for your permission to be free with my words?" she asked, pulling back. The question was surprising, uttered in a breathless tone but stinging all the same.

"I can say anything I wish, MacRae," she continued, frowning at him. "And have always been able to do so. It is the consequences of my speech that I must consider."

"Yes," he said, wondering if their kiss had loosened her words, testing the thought by bending forward to kiss her again. "But the consequences of your silences are even greater. I think I will kiss you each time you refuse to answer me."

She spoke against his lips, her hands smoothing up his arms before abruptly falling away. "Why?"

He drew back, glancing down at her with a rueful smile. "Because I've wanted to all this time. Is that not a good enough reason?"

Her eyelids fluttered shut, and her words, when they came, were oddly without emotion.

"I will not be your whore, MacRae."

"Stay my wife instead," he murmured, placing his lips against her cheek. Her skin was heated, but he felt her shiver as he kissed a path to her throat.

"We aren't married in England."

"Does that news please you?" he asked.

"No," she said breathlessly, the confession inspiring another kiss.

They could be seen from any window, he thought, smiling against her mouth. Alisdair MacRae, intent upon ravaging his wife in the gardens. Reason intruded. Here he was not a MacRae and she was not his wife.

He stared down into her lovely face. Her eyes had closed, her lashes long and feathery against her cheeks. In that moment she looked suspended and hesitant, poised upon a pinnacle crafted of both confusion and desire.

Cupping his hands around her face, he waited until she had opened her eyes and gazed up at him. To his delight, her cheeks deepened in color, her eyes widening as she stared at him. Speechless again, he thought, smiling down at her.

Brushing his thumbs against the corners of her mouth, he spoke again, his voice low and grave, the words those he'd never had a chance to speak.

"Marry me, Iseabal," he said.

She stepped back, her hands at her side. Her silence didn't surprise him. Nor did the fact that she seemed abruptly distant from him, as if she'd taken herself far away from this place and left only the shell of her body behind. He'd seen her do this before.

"Marry me, Iseabal," he said again.

She looked up at him, her face flooding with color. "Why?"

Her habit of restraint had unexpectedly become his. He wanted to know why her eyes looked sad at times, or what irritated her. Why she sometimes trembled when he stood near. What she thought of when she stared out to sea, and what her thoughts were when her gaze lit on him and her face stilled into a somber mask.

Curiosity, however, was not enough of a basis for marriage. Yet he felt that they had been bound to each other by ties neither understood. Not merely Drummond's command, or their mutual fascination for Gilmuir, but something else that he could not quite comprehend. Still, he could not tell her that, or explain his sudden confusion.

"Because you know how I awake in the morning?" he said, floundering for an explanation. "Or because we have such delightful conversations?" he added dryly.

She returned his gaze, her look as steady as his. By law they were not married, not in England or in his homeland. They were companions of a sort, only that. Escapees from a land that had nurtured her and beggared him. But he suddenly wanted more than that, and that was what he could not explain.

"What is your choice, Iseabal?" he asked again, impatient with himself. "Scotland or here? Marriage or no?"

"A woman has one choice," she said simply. "To be happy or not."

"And what would make you happy, Iseabal?"

"To be a decent woman. We are already husband and wife, MacRae. By Scottish law. How were your own parents married?"

She didn't look away and neither did he, stunned by the emotions she'd incited in him. Lust, shame, anger, and confusion.

"By decree," he admitted, beginning to smile.

"To think that Scots law is not valid, MacRae," she said, leveling a surprisingly stern look at him, "is to commit treason. What would the Raven think of that?"

Alisdair felt himself vacillating between an odd compulsion to comfort Iseabal and a wish to kiss her words from her. Her words had a way of puncturing his skin and his resolve with near-deadly barbs.

"My father doesn't belong here," he said, smiling. He reached for her, bending to kiss her again. "Not while I'm kissing my wife."

Her mouth fell open beneath his. One kiss and she'd learned to ensnare him. He smiled against her lips as he felt her arms looping around his neck. Softly, sweetly, Alisdair drew her closer to him, wondering how soon he could arrange another ceremony.

Chapter 18

The next week was spent on arrangements, not only for their wedding—done properly this time—but also for their return to Nova Scotia. Between the trips to London and the duties attendant upon assuming the earldom, Alisdair hadn't seen Iseabal for three days.

Because he was ennobled, Alisdair discovered with some amusement, doors were suddenly open to him, favors were granted, and a surprising amount of people proved to be ingratiating.

Leaving Daniel with a list of provisions for the journey back home, Alisdair returned to Brandidge Hall alone. A bit of vanity on his part, perhaps, not to invite his crew, but they had witnessed one wedding and had no reason to think it invalid.

There had been only one disconcerting experience prior to this, his wedding day, and it featured Ames once again.

This morning the solicitor had handed him a sheet enumerating not only the property valuations of those estates he now owned, but also a carefully detailed account of the fortune accompanying the title.

"Are you certain this is correct?" Alisdair asked, wondering at his ability to speak.

"Quite certain, my lord," Ames said, bowing slightly. Another change that had come with his title, the solicitor's unctuous behavior. Alisdair didn't bother telling Ames that it was a week too late, or that he was currently interviewing other firms just as capable but less intrusive. He didn't want any further investigations about his background or his family.

"My father was Patricia's adviser before he died," Ames was saying now. "And prior to that, General Wescott managed the funds for your uncle."

Alisdair nodded absently, staring at the account and once more tallying the figures in his mind. He'd just become wealthier than any man he knew. The money accompanying the title of Earl of Sherbourne was at least a thousand times greater than what he'd paid for Gilmuir.

He'd left the library without another word. Ames, no doubt, had wasted no time sitting in the earl's chair and dreaming himself master of Brandidge Hall.

Now he was dressing for his wedding again. The sky had darkened, but with night, not rain. Even if the heavens opened above them, it didn't matter. They could spend the rest of their lives in Brandidge Hall and never feel confined.

Alisdair glanced at himself in the full-length mirror, pulled down on the cuffs of his new black coat. His breeches were finished at the cuffs with silver buckles adorned with tiny diamonds. His stockings had been woven in France from the finest silk. A bootblack, attentive to detail, had given his diamond-buckled shoes a mirror finish.

He was dressed in the manner of a noble, one about to be married.

Before leaving the room, he walked to the mantel and picked up the candle, staring up at the portrait his grandfather had no doubt studied every day since his wife's death. Alisdair's attention was not drawn to his grandmother or his father, but to the fortress in the background.

The artist had depicted gray clouds rendered white as they drifted across the sun. Shadows hung over the landscape, but Gilmuir was lit by broad bands of light, touching upon the steep roof and towering walls, rendering the aged stones an old gold.

Alisdair had traveled the world and on those voyages had occasionally felt the longing for home. Yet he had never felt as he did now, sundered by his loyalties and the feeling that he was acting counter to a destiny previously ordained. All those people who'd ever lived and loved and died for Gilmuir seemed to call him, to tug at his sleeve and demand his attention.

A thought came to him with the speed of a storm on the ocean. He could rebuild Gilmuir, and barely make a dent in the Sherbourne fortune. And the sloping glens just outside the cove would make a perfect location for a shipyard. He could test the hull designs in the cove itself, even mount supports all around the shoreline to hold a half-finished vessel afloat.

The decision filled his mind, easing the feeling of something not yet accomplished.

Alisdair began to smile, thinking of Iseabal's reaction when he told her.

*   *   *

For the second time in her life, Iseabal found herself about to be married.

Her wedding dress had again been pressed upon her by Patricia, but this gold-encrusted garment was much more modest than the first gown Patricia had offered her.

"I'm sure that Moira looked as lovely at her wedding as you, my dear," Patricia said from her chair beside the window in Iseabal's room. She again commanded the maids, tapping her cane from time to time in approval or demand. She didn't look like an autocrat, Iseabal thought with a smile, dressed as she was in a gown of pale lavender adorned with trailing sleeves and a neckline of lace.

Nodding in approval as the maid adjusted the high collar of the garment, Patricia smiled. "The dress has held up well after all these years."

That Alisdair had accepted the title was another surprise to assimilate, along with the fact of this marriage. But when Fate holds out a blessing, only a fool declines. She was no fool, Iseabal thought.

She'd lived through the past week in a benumbed fog, remembering first Alisdair's kiss and then the look in his eyes, tender and gently amused.

He'd been gone for days, and except for this moment, attired in Patricia's wedding gown, Iseabal might have thought this a dream, a fanciful notion that she had wanted desperately enough to make it seem real.

She stood looking at herself in the pier glass once again, but the image reflected back to her was not shameful. The woman who stared at her did so with flushed cheeks, full lips, and green eyes wide with wonder. Her hair was left straight around her shoulders, in a maiden's pose. She looked different, Iseabal thought, almost beautiful. Happiness was a greater cosmetic than any paint.

In two weeks she had gone from dreading her marriage to wishing fervently for it to continue. Yet at the moment, she was filled with both anticipation and a strange sort of fear. She was about to become a wife, in truth.

This time the bridegroom was not a stranger, but a man she'd come to respect and admire. His appearance made her tremble; his touch incited other, stranger feelings, as if her body melted inside. He annoyed her occasionally, amused her at times, and endlessly occupied her thoughts.

Iseabal turned from the mirror to meet Patricia's smiling face. The older woman slowly stood, surveying Iseabal carefully.

"I never had a daughter, my dear," she said softly. "But if I had one, I could not wish for her to be more lovely than you. You are quite the most beautiful bride I've ever seen."

A mist of tears blurred Iseabal's vision. She blinked them away, impulsively reaching out to hug the Countess of Sherbourne.

A few minutes later Iseabal followed Patricia through the hallway, down the sweeping stairs, and into another long corridor leading to the private chapel. Her feet felt numb, her knees almost weak. Twice she had to stop, forcing herself to take a deep breath. Not because the dress was too tight or because she was afraid. Her breathlessness came from anticipation and a wonder deep enough to change her entire life.

She was marrying the man she most wished to have as husband. From this moment on, words would mean more, silences would be deeper, the capacity to be wounded would be greater.

Two footmen each opened one of the double doors, and she found herself moving down the aisle toward Alisdair.

Most weddings were performed in the morning, but Patricia had insisted upon this ceremony being held in the evening. Iseabal instantly understood why. The chapel was a blur of candlelight, a shadowed nook that gleamed with the gold of the plates and goblets on the altar and sparkled with a hundred crystal candleholders.

An enchanted place, she thought, walking toward Alisdair. Behind him stood a cleric dressed in white-and-gold robes, and no doubt there were people sitting in the pews of the private chapel. But she saw only him, smiling at her in wordless encouragement. What would he think, to know that what she truly wished to do was run down the aisle?

There was something in his eyes, an expression that tightened her breath even further and escalated the beat of her heart. An answering emotion swept through her so quickly that she was taken aback by it.

He stretched out his hand to her, and the tiny, delicate leaves of her love began to unfurl.

"Iseabal," he said. Just her name, no more an inducement than that. But the slow, dawning curve of his smile made her smile in return as she took one step forward, then another, until their fingertips touched.

He stretched one arm around her as they turned to face the altar. The ceremony was quickly done, the words she spoke more formal than in Fernleigh's clan hall. As they turned once more to face the back of the chapel, Iseabal realized that the pews were, indeed, filled. Patricia sat in front; Simon, the majordomo, beside her. Behind them looked to be the entire staff of Brandidge Hall beaming at the bride and groom.

A screeching noise unexpectedly swelled throughout the chapel. Startled, Iseabal turned. There in the corner of the room, shadowed by candlelight, was a man attired in kilt and sporran, a plaid draped over his shoulder. One of the Highland Regiment, she realized as he began to play. Never before had she heard the sound of the pipes, since they'd been outlawed in Scotland before she was born. The music was raw yet powerful in this place of worship, as if the tune were a summons to God Himself.

She reached out and gripped Alisdair's hand, and he squeezed back just once in wordless acknowledgment.

He had always been so certain of what he wanted in life, Alisdair thought, only to have another destiny foisted upon him. The strangest thing was that this life was proving to be more interesting than the one he had planned for himself.

Iseabal was trembling, her hand nestled in his. He had never seen a woman as beautiful as she was at that moment, limned by candlelight. Ionis's lady, he mused, had truly become his.

He doubted that Patricia's idea of a celebration ended with their wedding. But instead of leading the way to the dining room, or to another one of Brandidge Hall's cavernous chambers, she walked to the foot of the curving stairs, gesturing upward.

"You must pardon me, my dears, if I call it an early night. I find that all this excitement has left me exhausted."

Alisdair inclined his head, regarding her with a smile. At that moment Patricia looked like an aged elf. Her eyes twinkled with the mischief of a child's, and she appeared more enlivened than weary.

"Your wedding dinner will be served shortly," she said.

"Another tradition?" he asked doubtfully. But he smiled at her nonetheless, accepting her plan for the affectionate gesture it was.

"If you will come this way, my lord," Simon murmured, bowing in front of them.

Alisdair bent down and, kissing Patricia's cheek, whispered, "Thank you." She had been welcoming and open not only with her hospitality but with her love. Pulling back, he noted the sheen of tears in her eyes, and wordlessly acceded to her wishes, following Simon up the stairs, Iseabal at his side. Their destination was not, evidently, to be Gerald's room. Nor was it the chamber Iseabal had occupied since their arrival.

Instead, they found themselves before a broad set of mahogany doors, each elaborately carved with half of the Sherbourne crest.

"The royal chamber, my lord," Simon intoned, bowing slightly before opening the doors. In silence, the married couple entered the room, Alisdair closing the doors behind them.

Chapter 19

The royal chamber, like the chapel, was illuminated by dozens of candles, each pillar resting in a small silver plate. The walls were covered in ivory damask, and on either side of the room, mirroring themselves, were twin fireplaces, their ebony mantels sleek and polished. Covering one wall were dozens of gilt-framed miniatures, and below their feet, a heavily patterned carpet in ivory and blue. In front of a windowed alcove, curtains drawn for the night, was a small oval table set with gold-edged dishes, crystal stemware, and a vase filled with white roses.

The focal point of the chamber, however, was the wide bed covered in ivory fabric heavily embroidered with the Sherbourne crest in a deep blue. Standing on its own mahogany pediment, the bed was easily four times wider than Alisdair's bunk aboard the *Fortitude*.

Tonight would mark the tenor of their marriage, the

essence of it. He wanted the experience to be one of grace and favor, respect and humor, friendship and need. At least he had kissed her, he thought ruefully, glancing at her. Only a few moments had elapsed since they'd entered the room, but her cheeks had grown paler, and her smile now seemed forced.

There was something to be said for experience. Alisdair thanked God that he, at least, had enough to note that his bride was terrified. After all, words spoken before an Anglican priest and a room filled with observers didn't make them more married than they had been. Or this occasion any less awkward than their first wedding night.

"Why do you think it's called the royal chamber?" Iseabal inquired, moving to the wall of miniatures. He followed her slowly, wondering why he'd never watched her walk before. She did so with an alluring sway of her hips.

"No doubt because of the kings who stayed here," he said, noting the arrangement of the palm-sized portraits. "The Sherbourne earls evidently took this opportunity to remind each monarch of years of cooperation."

A chronology of history itself, with the depictions of England's kings hanging side by side with those of the Sherbourne earls who had served them. Strange, but he had never before given thought to these ancestors of his. His brother James took after their great-grandfather, Alisdair realized with a smile, and there was a touch of Douglas in one of the portraits.

His father was not pictured, and Alisdair had not expected it, but he halted at the likeness of his grandfather. One sat for a portrait grudgingly, if the stern, brown-eyed glare was any indication. If there was an air of sadness to Gerald Landers, it did not reveal itself. Instead, he had the appearance of a man who'd seen his duty and resolutely performed it despite any personal tragedy. Or perhaps Alisdair's grandfather had simply been adept at hiding his emotions.

In the next tier of paintings was David, his father's half brother and Patricia's son. Like the portrait in the sitting room, it revealed him as simple-minded, perhaps, but a kind man who lived in an isolated world, protected by his mother and stepfather.

"I wonder if life was kind to him," he said absently, touching the edge of the gilt frame housing David's portrait.

Iseabal glanced at him curiously, and Alisdair suddenly realized she didn't know the entire story. "He was the last Earl of Sherbourne," he explained. "A man who never grew beyond boyhood in his mind."

"He looks happy," she said, tilting her head to study him.

Alisdair nodded. "He was content enough with his cats and his picture books, I understand."

A knock on the door interrupted them. Alisdair strode to the double doors, opening the right side. Simon entered, followed by a line of footmen, each bearing a domed silver platter. One by one, they set their burden down on the small table.

When they'd finished and left the room, Alisdair extended his hand to Iseabal as Simon stood at the table.

"Will you join me?" he asked.

She nodded and came to his side, her heavily embroidered gown making a whispering sound as she sat. Simon began to serve them both, an honor, Alisdair supposed, since the man never unbent long enough to smile, let alone perform such a duty.

He waited until the butler had left, then picked up his wineglass in a salute to his bride. "To married life," he said softly.

Unexpectedly she smiled, the expression undeniably perfect. There was no self-deprecating humor in Iseabal's glance, no forced look of amiability. Only joy, sweet and sincere, dusting her smile and her eyes.

He wanted, at that moment, to give her the world. To set at her feet her deepest wishes and secret cravings.

"Would you like to live at Gilmuir?" he asked, lowering his glass. She did the same, her gaze wide-eyed, her flush deepening.

"In the ruins?"

"No," he said, wondering if she would have done so. "We'll build a little house to shelter us until the work is finished. I'm going to rebuild Gilmuir."

His smile increased as she simply stared at him, her eyes widening as the moments passed. "Rebuild Gilmuir?" she asked finally.

"From the foundations up."

Iseabal sat back in her chair, her fingers fumbling on the stem of the glass. Her gaze rested on the array of dishes and cutlery on the table, moved away toward the curtained windows, before finally returning to him again.

"Why?"

"Because it's my birthright," he said. "Perhaps it makes no sense," he added. "I only know I must."

"He'll never leave your land alone," she said faintly. "My father's greed knows no boundaries, Alisdair, not even those of birthright."

Abruptly he stood, striding to the door and opening it. Standing aside, he waved his arm impatiently as though ushering a ghost through the door. "I'll not have Magnus Drummond in my bedchamber, especially not tonight."

Her blush deepened, but so did her smile.

"Are you guarding us?" he asked incredulously, just now seeing the two footmen stationed in front of the door. "From whom?"

One of the men glanced over at him, bowing slightly. "We've been given orders, your lordship, to remain on duty."

"Here are your new orders," Alisdair said gruffly, striding back to the table. Grabbing the bottle of wine, he carried it back to the door and handed it to the surprised footman. "Go to your quarters and drink to my wedding," he said. "But do not stand there," he added, infused with a curious embarrassment. He'd never thought to have witnesses to his wedding night.

He closed the door against the flurry of thanks and congratulations, turning back to Iseabal. She was no longer seated at the table, but was standing behind him.

He pulled her close to him, wrapping his arms around her until they stood entwined in the other's embrace. They had never done so before, never measured the differences of height and breadth and shape. Her cheek lay against his chest, her feet between his, full breasts and womanly thighs pressing against him, an unnecessary reminder of hidden curves.

Bending his head, Alisdair rested his cheek against her temple. Her hair was imbued with a light and flowery perfume; her skin seemed anointed by ancient creams smelling of sandalwood.

She no longer trembled, but he could feel her breathing against his chest. Fast and unsteady, almost like his own.

"We should eat," he murmured.

"I'm not hungry," she said faintly.

"How strange," he said wryly. "Neither am I."

Moving his hands to her shoulders, Alisdair traced one heavily embroidered rose with a tender finger, following each curve of petal and arching stem until it led to her throat.

"You should be unlaced," he murmured, kissing the base of her throat as he spoke.

She nodded wordlessly.

"I doubt, however," he added, "if Patricia will send a maid to assist you."

She looked up then, her eyes sparkling at him. He had not seen her amused often, but in that moment Alisdair decided it was an expression he wished to see again. But not, perhaps, on his wedding night.

"Another of her ploys," Iseabal said, smiling gently.

Suddenly she turned and bent her head, sweeping up a few loose tendrils of hair with one hand in order to bare her neck to him.

The pose, both intimate and demanding, should not have had the power to arouse him. She glanced back at him curiously, and Alisdair found himself desperately wishing to be quit of gentleness and restraint. He wanted to pick her up in his arms, march to the bed, and bury himself in her. Weeks of hunger would then be eased, and this surprising need abolished.

But he bent and placed a kiss on the nape of her neck, praying for control.

The dress, in addition to being ornate in style, was laced in a series of tiny knots worthy of a sailor on his first voyage. Alisdair gritted his teeth as he worked his way from Iseabal's neck to her waist.

Once the garment was open, Alisdair reached inside her

dress with both hands. She held her indrawn breath, then released it on a sigh as he leisurely traced a path around her waist on both sides until meeting at the front. He began to unfasten her stays, his fingers growing increasingly dexterous as he continued with his task. After the unlacing was done, his palms splayed against her stomach, feeling the heat of her body beneath her shift. His thumbs were close to her breasts, an intimate pose they'd shared before.

Now, however, nothing restrained him.

Leaning forward, Alisdair whispered against her ear. "Are you in pain?"

"No," she answered, just as softly.

With great care, he began to pull her stays away from inside her dress. She was still fully clothed, still proper, still maidenly to the unseeing eye. But she was nearly naked to his fingers, her heart beating so fast that her breasts trembled.

His resolve to take this night slow was weakening by the moment.

Bending, Alisdair touched his lips to the warm skin between Iseabal's shoulders, feeling her tremble at the feathery touch. Her hand, pressed against her hair, clenched almost into a fist. Not repudiation, he realized, but reaction.

He moved closer and she leaned back, resting her head against his shoulder. Iseabal's surrender was an inducement to haste, but he steadied himself and pretended control while his mind urged him to take her to his bed now, love her with tenderness and whatever grace he could muster.

Threading his fingers through her hair, he forced himself to be less hurried, loosening the tiny hairpins from each temple and letting them fall to the rug with a muffled sound. Slowly he pulled her bodice free, pushing the voluminous gown to the floor in a whisper of fabric.

He moved in front of her, placing his hands on her shoulders and gently walking her to stand against the door. Raising Iseabal's arms above her head, he pressed the backs of her hands against the wood.

"Keep them there," he murmured, his nails smoothing against the center of her palms.

She nodded, turning her head aside and closing her eyes.

Her arm curved gracefully from wrist to shoulder, long shadows adding mystery to her inner elbow and armpit. Her talented fingers were long, her callused palms heated. The fine hairs on the backs of her arms seemed to be alert, and a soothing brush of his knuckles against her skin brought a shiver of response.

When had an arm ever been as alluring? Sweetly so, as if enticing him to explore other treasures. He traced a path with one finger from her inner wrist to the inside of her elbow, resting there as if to mark the spot. Bending his head, he pressed his lips there against her warmed flesh, feeling the pulse beat rapid and strong beneath his lips. He drew back and did the same with the other arm, this time brushing the tip of his tongue against her skin.

Still she remained as she was, a pagan sacrifice for his curious eyes.

Slowly he turned her face to his, bending his head to kiss her. "You're beautiful, Iseabal MacRae," he murmured, and her only response was to tilt her head, encouraging a deeper kiss.

Their kisses in the garden had been light, almost tentative. Here, in this room marked as theirs, they took on a more heady flavor. A sweet, almost helpless sound escaped her as his tongue touched the edges of her lips, then entered her mouth.

How had he lasted so long without the taste of her? Or without touching the silkiness of her skin?

Gently he brought her with him to the side of the bed, holding onto his restraint with an almost desperate grip.

"Do you know what will happen between us?" he asked.

She nodded, eyes downcast.

"Your virginity is a gate we must pass through," he said, wishing that he could ease the experience for her.

Leaving her at the side of the bed, he extinguished all of the candles until there was only one left on the mantel, enough light to lift the darkness but not so much that Iseabal would be embarrassed.

He felt both woefully inept and almost painfully aroused.

Aboard ship, the small confines of his cabin necessitated order. But at this time and place, regimen and routine didn't seem nearly as important as removing his clothes. He took off his stock, throwing it on the dining chair. His coat and vest soon followed. His shoes, normally easy to remove, were now proving to be a nuisance.

Iseabal stood beside him, a small, amused smile curving her lips.

Humor, he thought wryly, was not entirely appropriate to this moment. But at least Iseabal wasn't as afraid as he'd expected her to be. Instead, she stood there lit by the light of the solitary candle, her shift falling in wispy, drifting folds from her shoulders, The silk revealed rather than concealed, the hair at the apex of her thighs a dark shadow, coral-tinted nipples pressing against lace.

Clutching his breeches in one hand, he bent closer, kissing her lightly on the lips in appeasement for his delay and unaccustomed clumsiness.

Finally, he was naked, finding the position an awkward one, especially when his bride was staring at him, her gaze fixed on his rigid shaft.

Reaching out, he gripped her shift with both hands, sliding it upward over her knees, the length of her legs, the curve of her hips, the swell of her breasts. Graceful folds of silk were held suspended on her rigid nipples. He bent and tugged on the shift, replacing the silk with his thumbs and then his mouth. He bestowed a tender kiss to each heated nipple, her gasp of surprise his reward.

He knelt and leisurely rolled her stockings down, her legs as smooth as the silk that covered them. One garter, then another, each adorned with fabric roses and embroidered stems.

Finally, only her wrapping remained between them.

Standing, Alisdair placed both hands at her waist, moving closer until his erection brushed her naked skin. Her eyes widened even as he felt himself growing harder.

Now, now, now, a primeval need that echoed his heartbeat. A carnal whisper that urged him to fulfillment rather than prudence.

"Are you certain you're not in pain?" he asked again. As much as he wanted her, as desperate as he was beginning to feel, Alisdair vowed he would not touch her if the act would bring her discomfort.

"No," she whispered, her attention directed downward to where his erection lay momentarily quiescent against her belly.

He bent his head, his fingers trembling, and began unwrapping her bandage. Once around the back, and she was rewarded with a light, almost teasing kiss. Around to the front, and he kissed the tip of her breast, dampening it with his tongue. Another pass and the kiss deepened, his mouth opening around a tightening nipple, gently sucking.

She moaned, and the sound nearly drove him to his knees. *Now, please God, now.*

"I wanted to touch you that first night," he said, the words muffled against her warm skin. Alisdair closed his eyes, praying for restraint.

"I wish you had," came her whispered confession.

An oath escaped him, and he pulled her forward, his shaft slipping between her thighs like a ship finding a berth. *Almost home,* was his last cogent thought before sensation overtook him. He kissed her again, his tutelage finding an apt pupil. Iseabal was artless in her skill, rendering him breathless as her tongue found his.

He wanted to be inside her, the urge so powerful that he tugged the rest of the wrapping from her with trembling fingers, uncaring that it dropped to the floor. Tomorrow he would tear up silken sheets to treat her, biting the threads apart with his teeth if need be.

But now, dear God, don't let her be frightened of me. He would never last for hours. Or even for the next few moments, he thought as she moved closer, the gentle friction of her body leaving him awash in a feeling so painfully perfect that it weakened him.

He moved away from her, needing the time to calm himself. His body was heated and aching with a yearning he'd never before felt.

"Is it time?" she asked, the innocence of her question inflaming him further.

"Yes," he said tightly, wondering if a man could spill his seed at the sound of a woman's voice.

Iseabal turned, mounting the pedestal and then the bed. Her body gleamed with the luminescence of a pearl as she rose to her hands and knees, pert derriere in the air, the globes of her breasts hanging down, nipples pointing the way to the mattress.

"I'm ready," she said, looking at him. She glanced at his naked body once more, taking a deep breath before lowering her head between braced arms.

He closed his eyes at the temptation of her pose, wanting feverishly to position himself behind her, entering her deeply and fully until she could not tell where he left off and she began. He could almost feel the curve of her buttocks against his thighs.

And nearly lost his resolve at that moment.

Alisdair climbed up beside her on the mattress, gently pulling her from that enticing position to lie on her back at his side.

"Have I done something wrong?" she asked, looking up at him.

"Who taught you that a man and woman love like that?" he replied, the words coming with great difficulty. Conversation didn't rank high on his list of priorities at the moment.

Her hands were clutched together and nestled between her breasts in a penitent's pose. Placing a light kiss on her knuckles, Alisdair felt torn between lust and tenderness.

"They don't?"

"Although the position is one I certainly wish to experience with you," he managed to say calmly, "it isn't appropri-

ate for your first experience, Iseabal." He drew his finger over
her knuckles, up the swell of her breast to capture a nipple
against his palm.

She closed her eyes at the sensation, and he felt the same,
brimming with feelings that were new and startling but too
fascinating not to explore.

"I would enter you too deeply," he said, rubbing his palm
slowly across her nipple, feeling it tighten even more against
his skin. "We'll have to leave it for another time." *When
you're used to me.* The thought nearly had the power to un-
man him, as needy as he was.

"The maid," she said faintly, her voice sounding constricted. "She said that if I watched the rams, I would know
how it was done."

He stifled his smile, thinking that she would not appreciate his tender amusement.

Propping himself up on his elbow, he studied her, wishing
that he'd left all the candles lit. Her legs were together, her
feet pointed toward the ceiling, heels perfectly aligned. With
her eyes closed and the position she maintained, she might
have been laid out on her bier. Except that her breath came in
short, measured bursts and her hands were trembling despite
her convulsive grip.

"Are you cold?" he murmured, kissing the side of her
breast. His nose nuzzled against her skin as he lifted her
breast for his kiss. Soft and sweet and nearly his undoing.

She shook her head from side to side.

He wanted to place his mouth on her and make her moan
with desire. To enter her and coax her to fulfillment with his
will and his wish. Or scrape his teeth over her bottom lip in
an atavistic urge to mate and conquer. But he leaned over her,

clenching his fists in the sheeting, and contented himself with kissing her.

Desire did not come in measured doses, Alisdair discovered, however much he wished it. This urge did not ebb and flow like the tides, allowing him to ride it out. Instead, this hunger was a tidal wave, threatening to drown him.

Alisdair drew away from her, lying flat on his back, staring up at the ceiling, and praying for control.

Iseabal blinked open her eyes, feeling as if she were enveloped in a thundercloud preceding lightning and wild winds.

She wanted him to touch her again, to whisper words that heated her inside and made her breath tight. But he lay beside her on his back, one arm over his eyes.

"Touch me," he said unexpectedly. Not a command, but a request uttered in a voice unlike his own. "I want your hands on me, Iseabal. I have not tortured myself enough this evening," he added dryly.

Startled, Iseabal studied him in the near darkness, wondering if the hunger for touch could be a contagious thing. She'd never before considered that he might wish her compliance in this act. Mating was supposed to be quickly done, and simply executed, not touching and kissing and aching in spots that felt swollen and wet.

How delightful to be wrong.

How was she supposed to touch him?

Reaching out a hand, she let her fingers feel their way across his leg. Closing her hand around his erection, she was startled to realize that he was larger than her grip. Hotter, too, as if his flesh were a living brazier.

"Not there," he said in a choked voice as he removed her hand. "Like you did with that damnable statue."

She flattened her palm against his stomach, fingers splaying to touch the greatest area. Iseabal had never thought of exploring a man the way she did a block of marble. Nor had she known that her imagination could sketch in details that her fingers only felt. There was the straight line that ran in the middle of his chest as if to delineate both halves. Here was the nest of hair that rested at the base of his erection, and although she wished to linger there, his indrawn breath warned her that such exploration was unwise.

His thigh was hard to the touch, the muscles bunching beneath her fingers. His knees, his elbows, the bulbs of his shoulders, were all exquisitely formed. His flat stomach and broad chest were the reason his clothes fit so impressively. She had seen the same long line of muscle beneath the fabric of his breeches, but began to measure the corded length of his legs with stroking fingers. A moment later she felt the texture of the back of his hand, the strength of his arm, the warmth of a palm.

She played her fingers lightly over his nipples, feeling them rise, surprisingly, to her touch. His breath was held in abeyance for her to continue, it seemed, and she did, delicately tracing a line from one nipple to the other, then traveling down his stomach.

In such a way she was an artist of sorts, but instead of seeing the possibilities in stone, she traced the pattern of a completed masterpiece.

"Iseabal," he said warningly, as if divining her intent. But she could not help herself, fascinated as she'd never before been. Her hand closed around him again, measured his length, marveling at the firmness of him, as if he were, in truth, created from marble.

"You're the one who's beautiful," she said softly, remembering his earlier compliment.

He reached out and placed his hand on the back of her neck, pulling her over to him in a sudden, unexpected movement. In an instant his mouth was on hers, his tongue dancing across the seam of her lips until she gasped and welcomed him inside.

When the kiss was done, when both of them were gasping for breath, Iseabal lay at his side, whispering the words against his ear. "Touch me," she said.

For a moment she thought she'd shocked him in some way, because he didn't respond.

"Please," she said. "I want to feel your hands on me."

He made a sound, an oath or a prayer. But he pushed her gently onto her back. His hands learned her, his soft exploration of touch a feast of the senses. Had she made him feel the same?

Fingers lingering on the inside of her elbow and wrist caused her to wonder at the sensation. Even when he touched her there, almost innocently, her heart escalated and her breath tightened.

When she'd looked at him aboard the *Fortitude*, aloft in the rigging or standing at the bow, she had felt her heart flutter. But that feeling was nothing compared to what she experienced now, her body heating until Iseabal wanted him to hurry and at the same time wished he would linger.

One hand flattened on her abdomen, fingers trailing across the surface of her skin in an evocative exploration. He leaned over her, brushing the fingers of his other hand through the hair at her temple.

She wished there were more light so that she could study the expression in his eyes, know the reason for that somber look. For a moment, heedless in its length, they stared at each other, husband and wife, lovers for the first time. Impatient and hesitant.

He kissed her again, and she felt herself open up inside. Her heart seemed to expand to hold all these new, wondrous feelings. She'd never known intimacy, but at this instant of time, Iseabal felt it.

One finger, tenderly intrusive, entered her at a leisurely pace, his thumb sliding through her intimate folds. Molten heat both marked his passage and escalated at his touch.

"You're ready for me," he murmured, his voice sounding amazed.

"I've always felt this way around you," she confessed.

Alisdair lay his forehead down between her breasts. "Iseabal." Only her name, but he made that one word sound like a caress.

He raised up, knelt between her knees, entering her slowly. The pain she expected to feel was no more than a dull ache. Closing her eyes, Iseabal marveled at all the various sensations she was experiencing at this moment. An almost wanton pleasure wherever he touched her, a vulnerability for being so invaded, a wish to welcome Alisdair into her embrace and her body.

Once more his hands were on her, cupping her breasts and lifting them for the delicate branding of his tongue. He suddenly surged within her, and her body, knowing instinctively what he sought, rose up to meet him. Her fingers clenched on his shoulders as he filled her, her body accepting his presence in a muted delight and awed surprise.

The discomfort eased, the pinching feeling remaining, but

not unendurable. He invaded her, surrounded her, stripping every thought but of this moment and these feelings.

She wrapped her arms around his neck tightly as a rhythm began, a thrust and capitulation. He was elemental and primitive. She was yielding and accepting.

His head arched backward as Alisdair abruptly stiffened, a guttural moan escaping him. A moment later he placed his forehead on the pillow beside her, his breath harsh, his hair damp from exertion.

Iseabal lay dazed, confused, and more than a little uncertain about what had just transpired.

"Are we finished?" she asked hesitantly.

He lifted himself up on both forearms, staring down at her. Once again Iseabal wished she could see his face.

"For at least an hour or so," he said wryly.

She nodded as his thumbs stroked from the corners of her mouth to her temple.

He slid his arms beneath her, rolling with her until he held her tucked against his chest. Iseabal rested her cheek against his skin, hearing the booming of his heart.

Tears were oddly right at this moment, words being too much and not enough.

Chapter 20

A lisdair awoke to find Iseabal curled at his side, her hand curved around his body, a portion of which was fully engorged and eager.

Aboard ship, he would be up and about his duties by now, but he was a bridegroom and as such allowed, even expected, to be indolent. Lustful thoughts kept him occupied for a few moments before he reluctantly slipped from the bed.

Drawing open the curtains, Alisdair was surprised to discover a deep balcony extending the length of the room. Opening the French doors, he stepped outside, taking in the view.

An early-morning sun illuminated the rectangular lawn, neatly cropped and framed on both sides with a series of conical-shaped topiary bushes. At the end of the expanse, as if to catch the eye, was a large circular pool dominated by a fountain of bronze fish merrily spewing water into the air.

Perhaps this was why the room was called the royal chamber, he thought, smiling. The scene before him was fit for a king.

The vista was not all bucolic, however. In the distance was the home farm, its fields ripening and soon to be harvested. A grove of trees hid the sight of the stables and the large enclosures where horses from Brandidge Hall were trained and run.

All details he'd learned the day before, when he'd realized exactly what being the Earl of Sherbourne truly meant.

Turning away from the scene, he entered the room once again, leaving the doors open behind him. For a few moments he watched Iseabal sleep, reassured that he hadn't disturbed her.

His wife. She now lay on her left side, her legs drawn up beneath the sheet. Her cheek was cradled on her left arm, her right hand stretching out as if her fingers were reaching for him even in sleep.

At the moment, she looked like an innocent, yet she'd enticed him with the skill of a courtesan until he'd behaved like an untried youth. He'd taken more pleasure than he'd given, Alisdair thought.

The sudden knock on the door was peremptory, an almost dictatorial summons. Alisdair crossed the room, annoyed.

"A little less noise would be appreciated," he said, opening the door.

Simon stood there, his expression inscrutable as usual. Beside him stood a fresh-faced young footman bearing a tray piled high with domed dishes, a large china teapot, and two cups. The vase of roses, Alisdair suspected, was Patricia's addition.

Simon glanced at him, then away, as if he had never before seen a naked man. The footman, however, began to grin before being chastised by the older man's swift frown.

"Your breakfast, my lord," Simon intoned in that stentorian voice of his.

"Thank you," Alisdair said curtly, taking the tray. Without further comment, he closed the door with his foot. A sputter of sound indicated Simon's indignation well enough, but at least the fool had the sense not to knock again.

Halfway back to the table, he glanced toward the bed. Iseabal was awake, and leaning up on one elbow. Her hair was in disarray, a cloud of ebony falling over her shoulders, her eyes lambent pools of green. A beautiful woman, rendered doubly so by the faint morning light.

"Breakfast," he said, feeling absurdly awkward. "Would you care to join me?"

"Must I be naked?" she asked, smiling.

"It's not a requirement," he said. "But it might give new meaning to the word 'appetite.' "

She sat up, modestly arranging the sheet around her. He should have told her that her efforts were too late; he could still feel the heavy curve of her breasts, and the stiffening of her nipples against his exploring thumbs.

"I have nothing to wear," she said softly. Iseabal's cheeks were deepening in color as she threaded her fingers through her hair. A siren, a Circe, a sorceress of the most elemental kind. One who could lure a man, seduce him from duty into pleasure.

He was willing and more than ready.

After placing the tray on the table, Alisdair walked to the armoire. Iseabal's clothes had been placed beside his, a sleeve of her jacket brushing the cuff of his coat. Selecting the garment he wanted, Alisdair returned to her side, laying it beside her on the bed.

"If nothing else," he said, amused at himself, "the nightshirt will keep my mind on my breakfast."

She smiled at him in perfect accord, looking as pleased with herself as he felt.

Iseabal donned the nightshirt hurriedly, one rosy nipple peeping from beneath the sheeting. Before she could cover it with the red wool, he bent over, cupping one hand beneath her breast and placing a kiss on its tip.

"A good-morning kiss," he said, explaining.

Her blush deepened as his smile grew. Holding out his hand for her, he pointed the way to the dressing room, leaving her some privacy for her morning ablutions.

When she returned, her face had been washed, her hair brushed. The collar of his nightshirt was neatly arranged, the laces done up and tied with a pretty bow. She walked toward him, her hands gathering up the material, her pink toes showing beneath the voluminous garment.

He would need to add to her wardrobe and soon, he thought. Even a nightshirt was not covering enough.

In her absence, he'd moved the table to the balcony, taking away the dinner dishes and replacing them with the breakfast tray. He'd also taken the precaution of donning his breeches and a shirt. He didn't give a whit for modesty, but he wanted to restrain his physical reaction to her. Although, Alisdair thought as she smiled at him, it might well be that all he'd accomplished was to cause himself discomfort.

Pulling out the chair for her, he waited until she sat before joining her at the table. She stared out at the view before them, as entranced as he had been earlier.

"Can you truly leave all this?" she asked, awed.

"It isn't mine," he said, having realized that before she'd awakened. "I'm only one of the Sherbourne earls. My chief duty, I believe, is to leave the estates in no worse condition than I found them. For our son and his son, and so on."

Her wide-eyed stare made him want to kiss her.

"Had you not considered it?" he asked, concentrating on buttering his toast, thinking that he had been right in his prediction. The breeches were uncomfortable even now.

She shook her head, then glanced behind her in the direction of the wall of portraits. "You'll be there," she said, her voice sounding bemused. "And our son."

Somehow it sounded different when she said the word, inviting. Alisdair wouldn't mind beginning that particular son's creation right at the moment. Perhaps practicing the endeavor over and over again until he felt less callow and more in control of his reactions to her. He'd even bring her pleasure, he vowed.

He glanced at her, wondering how Iseabal would look when passion overcame her. Would she scream and hold him tight? Or would she simply hold herself restrained, feeling all those unbearable sensations secretly?

Why was it so damn difficult to swallow a bit of toast?

"Perhaps there is a gallery of Sherbourne countesses somewhere," he suggested, turning his thoughts to something less visceral. "We shall arrange to have your portrait painted as well."

"I sincerely hope not," she said, pouring more tea into her cup. She made a face at it, and he retaliated by dropping more sugar into the dark, bitter brew. "I'm not certain that I would want people to speculate on my life a hundred years from now."

"Then it is their loss," he said affably, considering her. "Perhaps they'll understand you if they look in your eyes. When you're angry, they flash with lightning. Or now, when they're soft and seem as deep as the ocean." He tilted his head, a smile curving his lips. "What emotion is that? I wonder. Happiness?

Or contentment? Or simply a good night's sleep?" Not the afterglow of satiation, he thought, once again chastising himself. He'd been too quick last night, but at least he'd climaxed inside her. He'd had grave doubts about lasting that long.

Her blush deepened, but she didn't look away.

He smiled, his hand pushing an errant lock of her hair behind her shoulder. "Perhaps my brother Brendan should paint you as you are now," Alisdair said. "With your face lit by the sun, and the smallest smile on your lips, as if you cannot decide whether or not to smile or frown." He continued to study her. Without warning, he leaned over and kissed his bride, surrendering to an undeniable impulse.

The sun was muted behind his eyelids, his breath cut short by the tender placement of her palm against his cheek. Once again he felt lost in her kiss, transported into desire so effortlessly it was almost magical. Finally he pulled back, the gazes they shared those of startled wonder.

She looked away, sitting back in her chair. Silence stretched between them, a thread so small as if to be invisible, but linking them all the same.

When had Iseabal's kiss become so necessary to him? Breath and food and water and Iseabal. From the first moment he'd seen her? Or at the first flash of her irritation at him? Or when she stood in front of him last night, silently encouraging him with her tentative smile?

"Is your brother an artist?" she asked after several minutes, seemingly entranced with the view.

"Yes," he said, grateful for the change of subject. "He sketches and sometimes works in oils. Hamish plays the pipes, and Douglas is the troublemaker," he added, thinking of his youngest brother. "In all fairness, Douglas is still too young to have formed his habits."

"A poet, a painter, a musician. Yet you all go to sea," she said, glancing at him.

"A man cannot provide for his family or his future without an occupation," he said.

"Yet you've given up yours," she said. "All to rebuild a castle."

"No," he said, gently correcting her. "A castle and a ship-yard."

She was surprised once again. "A shipyard?"

"The home of the finest ships in the world," he said, smiling. "MacRae ships that can sail across the oceans faster than any others."

"Is it true that you were an explorer?" she asked, fingering the edge of her cup. "Or that you found a continent?"

"Ames's words," he said. "He took a bit of knowledge and expanded it solely with the intent of goading me, I think." He uncovered a dome to discover porridge. Frowning at the two bowls, he covered them again. "I was part of the discovery, and a small one at that."

"Perhaps you're too modest," she said.

"No," he replied, "just truthful. It was an accident that I saw the peninsula. I was overdue for a meeting with my brothers and didn't pursue the matter. I wanted to get to port before they sailed."

"Won't you miss them if you live in Scotland?" she asked, tracing a delicate pattern around the rim of her plate.

"Yes," he said honestly, lifting the cup to his lips. "But Scotland is no more difficult to reach than China, so I expect them often enough at Gilmuir."

"And your parents? Will they come back?"

"The Raven returns?" Alisdair smiled, considering the question. "I doubt it," he said. "The danger for my father is still too great."

"Two more people to miss," she murmured, studying the silverware with intensity. He wondered if there would come a time when she'd look at him with such directness. "Yet you think of Gilmuir as your birthright, not this place."

He nodded.

"You love the *Fortitude*," she added. "And the ocean."

"While you love rocks and stones and Gilmuir."

She looked startled, the expression summoning his smile.

"We're not quite strangers after all," he said gently.

She blushed, the rosy tint not hard to decipher. Last night they'd come to know each other well. "What is your favorite season?" he asked to ease her embarrassment.

"All of them," she replied. "Spring is new life, the lambing season. Summer brings warm winds and the fullness of the flowers. Autumn is a long farewell, and winter only makes you grateful for the other months in the year."

"Autumn is my favorite," he said. "For the danger of it. Spring winds are gusty, but autumn brings gales and hurricanes."

She glanced at him, obviously surprised. "You like danger, Alisdair?"

He fingered the hilt of his knife, wondering if he could explain. "Not foolishly so," he said. "I like the contest of it, wondering if I can win, being willing to pit myself against a formidable foe."

"While I would much rather be a coward in a cave," she said ruefully.

"Women are to be protected, Iseabal," he pointed out. "Not expected to fight."

"But women have their own contests, Alisdair," she said, turning directly toward him. "Or do you think birthing a child an easy thing?"

Alisdair shook his head, realizing that he'd suddenly gotten his wish. Her look was level and direct, even though her cheeks were still blossoming with color.

"The only time I've ever seen my father unmanned," he admitted, "was when my mother was confined with my brother Douglas."

The thought of his child growing in Iseabal should have been a solemn one. A serious matter, this breeding of a heritage. Instead, his body fueled his mind with another image, that of planting his seed deep inside her.

He spread his legs even farther apart, easing the constriction of his breeches.

Several moments were devoted to eating, the clinking of utensils. He sipped his tea, easily identifying the Keemun Congou blend.

A quick glance revealed Iseabal smiling faintly, her chin propped on her hand, elbow resting on the table.

"Will you be unmanned, Alisdair?" she asked, her low tone ensuring that his breeches were suddenly painfully tight. "When I'm confined with our child?" she added.

"Aren't we being precipitous?" he said calmly, wishing that another topic of conversation would immediately come to his mind. But every memory, every thought, had been oddly expunged by her look. An awakening temptress.

"Last night you told me you always felt ready for me," he said boldly, remembering the moment only too well when his fingers had found her wet and hot.

She nodded, her gaze not on the table but on him.

"Do you feel that way right now?" he asked, his words grating, almost harsh.

She only smiled.

His hunger for food appeased, Alisdair stood, pulling

Iseabal up to him. He might as well be wearing no clothing at all. He could feel each of her curves and indentations, and the swelling of his joyful manhood, expectantly exuberant.

"It's too soon," he said aloud, hoping that she would disagree.

She startled him by pulling back and moving to the pedestal.

"Why?" she asked, climbing onto the mattress.

"You're too sore," he said. How quickly, he wondered, could he undress?

"Am I supposed to be?" she asked curiously, tipping her head to the side.

"I believe so," he said dryly. "Although my experience with virgins is somewhat lacking."

Iseabal shook her head, her hair falling over her shoulders in an ebony waterfall. "I don't feel sore," she said quietly.

"Thank God," he said, relieved, and was delighted by her smile.

He began unfastening his shirt, moving slowly toward her. "Do you realize what this means?" he asked, brushing a kiss against her cheek.

"No," she answered softly, looping her hands around his neck.

"Now the pleasure begins," he said with a smile, reaching for her.

Chapter 21

Iseabal leaned over the edge of the railing, marveling at the endless activity on the London wharf. The *Fortitude* had taken her place along the dock and now a procession of barrels was being rolled up the gangway.

All of the containers held supplies that would help them last through the winter. There would be no question of seeking support from her family, partly due to Alisdair's independence of spirit, and partly to his abiding dislike of her father.

Two weeks had passed since they'd been wed again, the time spent in preparation not only for this journey, but also for Alisdair's duties as earl. Although, she admitted, most of the hours had been given over to planning for Gilmuir's reconstruction.

More than once Alisdair had taken the miniature of the castle from her trunk, studying the detail of it. They'd spent hours talking about what it might have looked like when it was built, or before the destruction by the English.

The nights, however, had been set aside for the two of them, time in which each learned of the other. Passion was like sugar, she'd discovered. A taste of it on the tongue and her whole body noted it, stilled in appreciation, and craved even more.

The only sadness had been in leaving Patricia.

"Do not worry about me, my dears," Patricia said, her voice merely a whisper when she and Alisdair had bidden farewell. Reclining on a chaise in her bedchamber, a lacy shawl over her shoulders, the older woman appeared delicate and frail. As if she'd been strong until Alisdair arrived, only to fade when her duty was done.

"Thank you for granting an old woman's fondest wish," Patricia said, framing Alisdair's face with her hands. Next, Patricia hugged Iseabal, the embrace bringing tears to both women's eyes. But as she'd pulled away, Patricia began smiling, her whispered words full of mischief. "Happiness is a habit, my dear. Make sure you acquire it." Even then Patricia was giving advice.

Since they had returned from Brandidge Hall, the hours had been spent in a maelstrom of activity. Alisdair had hired a merchant ship to accompany them to Gilmuir. The *Molly Brown* looked like a squat brown duck swimming alongside the sleeker *Fortitude*. But what the merchant ship lacked in speed, she made up for in cargo space.

Now the other vessel was beginning to resemble an arc, Iseabal thought in amusement, watching as horses from Brandidge Hall, cows, goats, and chickens were all led or carried aboard. Grains and other provisions were being stored in the *Molly Brown*, as well as in the *Fortitude*'s limited hold.

Iseabal turned, bracing her back against the railing in a position she'd seen Alisdair assume many times before.

There was more activity aboard the other ship, the crew members of the *Fortitude* having gathered at Alisdair's request. They stood aboard the deck in lines four deep, their faces somber, as if they knew that their captain had serious words to say.

"Once," Alisdair began, "my father stood aboard a ship addressing the men and women of Gilmuir. He offered each one of them a choice of freedom versus privation. Each one of you is descended from those same men and women, just as I am. The choice I offer you now is a different, perhaps more difficult one. We have two homes, all of us. One where we were reared, and the other, the home of our ancestors. It is my choice to return to Scotland and settle there."

Silence greeted his words; then the first mate spoke.

"You're going to live there, Captain?" Daniel asked, evidently dumbstruck by the idea.

"I am," Alisdair said, scanning the face of every man who stood before him. Expressions of worry, irritation, even eagerness were easy to read on their faces. The MacRaes had not been beaten down or subjugated like some in Scotland and most at Fernleigh. A leader of such proud men, Iseabal thought, would have to be as respected and admired as Alisdair was.

"I intend to rebuild Gilmuir," Alisdair said. He moved his feet apart, placing his hands behind his back, a pose she'd seen often, especially in his role as a commander of men. Or when, she realized, he bore the weight of great emotion.

"If there are those among you who do not wish to remain at Gilmuir," Alisdair added, "then I will pay for your passage home. The *Molly Brown* will carry you back to Nova Scotia."

"The MacRaes are returning to Scotland, then?" a voice asked. Iseabal didn't recognize the speaker, but it was obvious, from their nodding, that he uttered the sentiments of his crewmates.

"As many of you as wish to, yes," Alisdair answered solemnly. "If you want to fetch your wives and children, Gilmuir will be open to them also."

All at once the men began to speak among themselves, the cacophony of voices traveling over the ship. One by one, they came and spoke to Alisdair. He shook each man's hand, either nodding solemnly or smiling when he heard his decision.

They'd decided easily, Iseabal thought, certain that most of them would choose to remain in Scotland. How many would stay at Gilmuir because of Alisdair?

He turned, then, glancing at her, his eyes warming in that look she'd come to anticipate. From virgin to wanton in only a fortnight, she mused, smiling. He nodded, one sharp acknowledgment of both her presence and his awareness of it. Someone called to him, and he smiled ruefully before moving away.

Iseabal walked the length of the ship, careful to keep out of the way of the sailors who were beginning to ready the *Fortitude* for her voyage. Instead of the cabin, Iseabal's destination was the stern and her little niche where she could sit and watch the activity in the port around them, and wait for Alisdair to join her.

To her surprise, a table had been set up, the marble stone atop it covered with a piece of oiled canvas. Beside it was the leather sling containing her tools and mallet. Alisdair's work.

He was always showing his consideration for her in little ways, such as bringing her tea in the morning or leaving a fresh flower on her pillow. He still insisted upon checking her ribs each day, although, she admitted, that chore often led to more delightful occupations.

Sitting at the table, she removed the canvas from the stone.

Fur rubbing against her ankle made her start. She glanced under the table to find the ship's cat leaning against her leg, purring loudly.

"Henrietta's approving, then," a voice said behind her. She turned her head to see Daniel standing there, a pack over his shoulder. "She's been playful this morning, a sign that the voyage will be a fair one."

Iseabal smiled, thinking that he'd never before spoken so many words to her.

"I just wanted to bid you farewell, mistress," Daniel said. "I'm to stay behind, you see. To fetch masons and mortar and such. And to find something called rice flour if I can," he added, a look of consternation on his face.

"Rice flour?" she repeated.

He nodded. "An old Chinese trick," he said. "Adding it to the mortar makes brickwork stronger, and the captain is determined not to allow Gilmuir to fall around his ears."

They did not know each other well enough to exchange embraces, but she held out her hand to him, smiling when he reluctantly took it. Was there a superstition to fit this occasion as well?

"I'll look forward to seeing you at Gilmuir, then," she said.

"I'll not be staying long, mistress," he said. "I'll direct the captain of that floating wreck to Scotland, all right." He stared at a second merchant ship berthed next to the *Molly Brown*. "But I've a wife and child at home and they'll be missing me."

"Perhaps they'll wish to come to Scotland."

He shrugged. "I doubt it, mistress. My wife's close to her mother and I'd not think Annie would want to come back to Scotland."

"Then fare well," she said, genuinely wishing good fortune for him.

He nodded and moved away, Henrietta trotting after him, tail high in the air.

"I've a legacy," his landlady said, staring at the letter in her hands. The paper trembled as she held it at an angle, the better to view it in the faint light from the window.

Fergus looked up from his task. He'd crafted a new latch, a replacement for the one on the front door, and was polishing the metal until the hinges turned easily.

The Widow McKinsey was a comely woman with hair barely graying and a sensitive, caring nature. From time to time he had the feeling that she might be holding out hope for him. He made a point of being scarce when her eyes softened and she arranged her hair differently. She would always gradually revert back to treating him as she would her other boarders.

In a way, perhaps, he was more her brother than a lodger. Over the years, he'd been almost an uncle to her two girls, and knew that they considered him part of the family.

"What legacy, Susanna?" he asked now, only vaguely interested in the answer.

"I've a fortune, Fergus," she said, holding out the letter to him. She startled him by beginning to cry, tears running silently down her cheeks.

He set the latch and oiled rag down, taking the letter from her. The lettering was cramped and ornate, but the gist of it was easily understood. Susanna McKinsey's great-aunt had passed away, leaving her a goodly sum and the house called Tyemorn Manor, not far from Inverness.

"You are, indeed, an heiress," he said, smiling and glad for her. She'd worried about her girls, and how she might help them acquire husbands. Now there was no need for concern. Nothing made a woman appear more attractive than a sizable fortune.

"Oh, Fergus," she said, clapping both hands against her reddened cheeks. "We shall go there immediately, all of us."

"Not I, Susanna," he told her, regretfully. "I've work here, such as it is. If I left Cormech, I'd be fortunate to find any labor at all."

"But you needn't now, Fergus," she said, her eyes still brimming with tears.

An attractive woman, he thought, but one who deserved more than he could give her. He'd not been a celibate man all these years, but his heart had never once been touched. Instead, it seemed destined to remain the property of Leah McDonald.

But because he liked Susanna, and had lived beneath her roof for many years, Fergus was kind in his refusal.

"I regret that I cannot, Susanna," he said gently, concentrating once more on the hinge.

Chapter 22

Sunlight danced on the water in a thousand golden winks. The sky, bright with an early sun, was a pale blue, the shade of Alisdair's eyes. Seabirds circling above screeched raucous cries as if envious of the *Fortitude* as she slipped along Scotland's coast.

Iseabal sat in the stern, glancing behind her from time to time at the *Molly Brown*. Ever since they had left London two days ago, the distance between the two ships had lengthened until the lumbering vessel was no more than a spot on the horizon. The merchant ship could not compete with the *Fortitude*'s speed.

There was something almost mystical about returning to Gilmuir, as if a long-held, but unvoiced, wish were being granted her. She smiled at her whimsy, flattening her palms on either side of the stone in front of her. The work was going well, the image she'd envisioned beginning to appear in the marble. She'd known, ever since arriving in England, what it would be.

She could almost feel Alisdair's face beneath her hands, the high cheekbones, the square jaw, his regal nose. Iseabal smiled, thinking that she had learned him through touch these past nights. But if this marble were to truly be Alisdair's likeness, she should craft it with his smile, his head tilted in that almost autocratic way of his, or with a light in his eyes as he posed a question she felt too tongue-tied to answer.

The master of Gilmuir, the MacRae, captain of the *Fortitude*, and now the Earl of Sherbourne. Although she doubted he would ever use the title, it fit him even so.

What must I do to coax you from silence, Iseabal? His words were so easily summoned, quick to recall. He had sought her thoughts and she'd begun to speak them to him, finding in her husband a confidant she'd never expected.

The stone sat inert beneath her fingers, patiently waiting for the moment when she would conjure up life with her chisel. She was almost afraid to do so, wondering if her talent would be great enough.

Praying for divine inspiration, Iseabal struck the marble with the second largest of her chisels. In the small space, the noise resounded like the peal of a bell. Taking a deep breath, she raised the mallet again.

Hearing the sails being unfurled, Iseabal glanced upward. He was in the rigging again, companioning Rory. But for all her fear of what might happen to him, it seemed somehow right to see Alisdair gamboling among the sails like his young cabin boy.

She glanced away, focusing on her work, becoming so fixed with it that time passed unawares.

Alisdair's hands on her shoulders pulled her from her concentration. He bent down until his head was beside hers, staring at the lump of black stone. At this stage, the marble looked as if it had been gnawed on like a bone, the gashes in its surface resembling teeth marks.

"Have you decided what it will be?" he asked, studying it.

"Yes," she said softly. "But I've always considered it unlucky to speak of something unfinished."

"So I'm to wait, then?" He smiled. Reaching out, he touched the stone, his palm resting on the front surface.

"Are you done climbing the rigging?" she asked.

"Rory needed a little assistance with his footing," he noted, his eyes dancing and his smile crooked.

She smiled, not believing a word. He had looked as young as Rory jumping from rope to rope.

"You needn't worry," he said. "I've been doing it since I was a child."

"I used to be afraid for you," she said. "Before I learned how well you climbed."

He moved away, standing against the rail. His arms were folded and he studied her as intently as she scrutinized her work. She could feel warmth travel from her toes to her cheeks in response to his scrutiny.

"I would not have done it if I'd known you worried," he said.

Iseabal could only stare at him, surprised that he might alter his behavior to ease her fears.

"Would you cease climbing the rigging if I asked you to?"

"Yes," he said easily. "But only if you could not be reassured that I was as safe there as standing here."

"Would you give up sailing?" She was testing the limits of her power.

"No," he replied quickly. "But I would take you with me."

"To the Orient?" The idea captivated her.

He nodded, unfolded his arms, and strode toward her. Smiling, he brushed at her cheek with the backs of his fingers. "You have bits of marble all over you," he said. "Perhaps I should be the one to worry that you might injure yourself with your chisels, or breathe too deeply of dust."

"I would teach you what I know so that you wouldn't be afraid," she said, lightly.

"Tell me," he urged, leaning against the railing once again. "I have no knowledge of carving."

"All I know is what I've done," she admitted. "My technique may be all wrong."

"You've never taken instruction?"

"My father would not have paid for such a thing," she said, smiling at the idea. "Perhaps you might hire a stone carver to replicate some of the more delicate work in the priory. I would be able to ask him some questions."

"Such as?" he asked curiously.

She picked up the mallet, hefted it in her hand. The instrument was made of old wood, soaked in a mixture of pitch and oil until the grain had turned black. She'd had the tool for five years and it appeared as pristine and unmarked as it had the day the carpenter secretly presented it to her.

"What is the best way to make a curved surface?" she said, answering his question. "Is there a method to it that's easier than what I do now? What do I do when a fissure appears in the stone? Is there a way to save my image, or is all that work destroyed?"

"Then I'll have to plan on an expert to come and work at Gilmuir and answer your questions," he said.

She smiled at yet another sign of his consideration.

He bent and took the tools from her, setting them down on

the table. Drawing her up slowly, he encircled her wrists with his hands. Gently, he slid his thumbs across her skin as they stood there watching each other.

"You look so lovely standing here with the sunlight in your hair and your eyes sparkling at me. Do you know what it reminds me of?"

She shook her head, bemused by the tender look in his eyes.

"When I first kissed you in the garden. You were angry at me, but your lips were welcoming."

I wanted you so desperately and couldn't have you. Instead of saying the words, she tugged her wrists free, placing her hands flat against his chest. Here was the warmth and life she'd not felt in the cold marble.

"Your diligence to your craft deserves a kiss," he said, his smile part rascal, part lover.

He matched the promise with the deed, and when the kiss ended, each leaned against the other.

"I could love you here," he whispered. "And caution the crew that I need time alone to reprimand you for your sins."

She pulled back and looked at him with mock indignation. "What sins would those be?"

"Too alluring," he said, kissing a path from one ear to the other, his lips dancing across her nose. "Too enticing," he said, moving one hand so that his fingers brushed against one clothed nipple. "Entirely too impudent," he added, kissing her once more, so deeply that she saw sprinkles of silver behind her closed lids.

Iseabal had thought him charming before, but she had not known that he might have a patch of wickedness in him. There was, evidently, still a mischievous boy trapped inside the man.

Once again he held her hands against the wall, but this time he shielded the backs of her wrists with his fingers so that they wouldn't become abraded by the planking.

They were unseen here, protected from curious onlookers, even had one of the crew been standing in the rigging.

Bracing one hand against the wall, he bent and lowered his head, kissing her gently. "I like kissing you," he said softly. Moving his other hand to her jaw, his fingers kept her prisoner there while he deepened the kiss, using his tongue to trace her lips before slipping it into her mouth.

His hands returned to her palms, although there was no need to restrain her. She was trapped by his kiss and by the feel of him pressing gently against her.

Her eyes fluttered shut again, and her breathing grew tight as her fingers curved toward her palms, trapping his fingertips. Below them, the ocean currents swirled, almost as if tenderly rocking the *Fortitude* as she sliced through the waves.

"The goddess of the sea," Iseabal whispered, feeling Alisdair's smile at the corner of her mouth.

Her smile answered his. Her eyes were still closed, and she could feel the heat of the sun's rays upon her face, and the warmth generated by Alisdair's touch. At this moment she felt like a creature of nature, all thought and reason vanishing beneath a greater need to be touched and loved. Not simply physically, but with her whole spirit.

Around her, the crew of the *Fortitude* worked. But leaning her forehead against Alisdair's chest, her hands flat against his waist, Iseabal realized that she truly didn't care if the whole world watched them.

Spreading her fingers wide against his jacket, Iseabal decided that she wanted to feel his skin instead. The fabric of his coat could not disguise the powerful curve of his shoulders, or his sleeves veil the strength of his arms. She wanted, almost desperately, to place her hands upon his stomach and lower, until his breath hitched in need. But more than that, she wanted him close to her, until one of them was part of the other, neither invaded nor commanding, but simply welcomed in the closest embrace of all.

"Love me," she whispered, the words awkwardly uttered, trapped as they were in the constriction of her throat.

He stepped back finally, as if knowing she needed room to breathe.

"Now, Iseabal?" he asked, his eyes sparkling.

She would have spoken her thoughts to him were she capable of having any. But her mind was oddly empty, even as her body warmed at the look in his eyes.

"Yes," she said tenderly, tipping her head back.

"Not here," he said, his face changing at the moment, his eyes narrowing slightly, and his smile disappearing. Without another word, he grabbed her hand, pulling her down the narrow corridor until they rounded the corner of the captain's cabin.

"Sir," Brian said, stepping into their path, "if I might have a word."

Brian had been promoted to fill Daniel's role while the first mate was in London. The young man had looked stunned, and since then slightly discomfited at his new role.

"Is the ship sinking, Brian?" Alisdair asked, frowning at the young man.

"No, sir," he replied, nearly jumping at Alisdair's tone.

"Are there pirates chasing us?"

The young man shook his head, his cheeks reddening.

"Sea monsters? Mermaids? Is the damn cat rubbing her tail on the mast?" Alisdair made no pretense at civility.

"No, sir."

"Then it can wait, Brian," he said abruptly, opening the cabin door and pulling Iseabal inside. The door snapped shut as he turned to her.

Her smile vanished as he stared at her, any thoughts of amusement melting away at his look. Her face felt flushed, her skin too warm, and her knees almost weak; her fingers trembled against the material of his coat. Her heart raced with a fluttering beat when she stood on tiptoe and extended her hands around his neck.

Slowly, gently, she drew his head down to hers, needing his kiss the way the world needed the sun. An elemental yearning.

She sighed against his lips, as if in relief. Her eyes drifted shut, but in her mind, she could see him. Tears dampened her eyes and nearly slipped from beneath her lids as she opened her mouth and welcomed him.

His blood was brandy, streaking through his body to rest in his fingertips and toes, making it impossible to walk steadily or to hold her without trembling.

Stepping back, he bent on one knee before her, and without glancing up, began to remove one shoe.

Wordlessly, Alisdair rolled down the first of her stockings, taking time with his task while he tried to regain his composure. For the first time in his life, Alisdair wished he had James's talent for words. He would tell her then how much he'd come to value her smile and their talks together. How her amusement charmed him, and her secret thoughts surprised him. Perhaps he would even confess how effortlessly she stripped him of his experience, rendering him as youthful and excited as a boy.

With one hand at the back of her knee for support, he lifted her foot and slipped the shoe and stocking free.

He had seen her naked before, had loved her both in the light of candles and in sunshine. Now Iseabal stood with only her legs bare, and he felt a surge of tenderness and desire that nearly staggered him.

Her toes were short and pudgy, and endearingly sweet. Placing one finger on each of the toes of one foot, he began tracing a path to her ankle, then upward to a knee.

Bending his head, Alisdair pressed his face against the fabric of her petticoat. His fingers trembled against her leg as his hand curved around her calf to steady himself.

A moment later he reached up and unfastened the bow securing her petticoat, sliding it from her gradually, almost reverently. She stepped free of it, her hands clasped at her waist. The look in her eyes was both vulnerable and trusting in a way that made his breath stutter.

I will protect you. I will keep you safe. I will place myself between danger and you, sweet Iseabal, he thought, the words the only poetry he'd ever composed.

Wordlessly, she watched while he tossed the stocking in the air to land where it would. Amusement vied with tenderness as she watched him finish with the other stocking and stand before her.

Alisdair tossed her jacket to the lid of her basket, her stays suddenly adorning the tansu against the wall.

What he did next, she would always remember. He reached out his hand, tracing the thin edge of lace on her shift. She felt his fingers tremble against her skin and closed her eyes, defeated by this sign of his vulnerability. At this moment, in this silent room, he was neither captain nor earl. Not the MacRae. He was simply a man, as mortal as she felt. Her husband, given to her not once but twice, that she might know the wonder of him.

She covered his hand with hers, stepping closer to unwind the stock at his neck. Once she had it unfastened, she allowed it to drift to the floor in a serpentine twist of fabric. His coat was next, and she pushed it off his shoulders, where it stubbornly resisted her efforts. He smiled finally, aiding her until it, too, fell to the floor, resting atop one of her stockings.

He removed his boots and stockings himself, but instead of stepping out of his breeches, Alisdair placed her hands on the button flap and held them there.

They exchanged another look, one of awareness and discovery. Breathing should not be so difficult, Iseabal thought. Nor should undoing one button, then another, her mind alight with anticipation. When he was freed from the restraining cloth, she held him cupped in her hands.

He had promised her pleasure and given it to her time and again, teaching lessons of love that had shocked and delighted her. She wanted to give him back the same joy.

Releasing him, she removed her shift, grateful that she no longer needed the wrapping. Her side was still discolored, but in this faint light the bruising would simply be one more shadow.

Her eyes were downcast now, a flush appearing on her cheeks. But Iseabal said nothing to halt him. She stood naked, making no move to cover herself. Her hands remained at her sides, the palms flat against her thighs. A statue of loveliness, he thought, but instead of stone, there were supple curves, and life in the pulse beat of her blood.

He wanted to flatten his palms against her, place his mouth on the inside of her elbow, gently suckle those impudent nipples, and stroke the back of her knee, the bulbs of her heels, behind her ears, the soles of her feet. All of it done with no sense of hurried haste. But that wish was impossible around Iseabal.

Reaching out a finger, Alisdair touched the tip of her breast, following it with a kiss. With the greatest of care, he trailed a path from her wrist to her armpit to her hip with one finger.

If he ever constructed a ship with Iseabal's grace and beauty, the vessel would sail across the water like the breath of life itself.

Bending his head, he kissed her. Sweetly, slowly, imbuing into the kiss all the unspoken words that cowered in his heart. Looping her arms around his neck, Iseabal moved even closer.

Nipples tight with arousal demanded the touch of a finger, the lave of a tongue. Lush, full lips coerced a kiss.

The ache that swept through him was one of incipient rebellion. His body longed for release even as his mind counseled restraint. Now, when the swell of her breasts beneath his hands encouraged his capitulation. His mouth encompassed a nipple, his body protesting the pace of this seduction.

Alisdair felt as if he would cease to be unless he touched her, would evaporate in the wind that sighed around them if he did not bury himself in her softness. Disappear, like a wraith, if he did not nourish himself in this one woman.

She stepped away from him, moving to the bunk. Glancing over her shoulder at him, she smiled in invitation.

Outside the cabin men were shouting to one another. Waves splashed against the *Fortitude*'s bow, and wind filled the sails. But in this shadowed room there was silence laced with a pandemonium of the senses.

Perhaps there were other men just as handsome, crafted of muscle and bone and beauty. But she had never seen one and would never look for his match. This man, erect and male, was all that she needed.

"You don't know how many times I've thought of you like that," he said, removing his breeches. "You were lit by candlelight," he murmured, coming to her side. "With your breasts just as they are now, tight and ready for my lips."

He trailed his fingers over one nipple, then the other.

Iseabal drew back slightly, lifting herself until she lay on the bunk, close to the wall. She held out her hand to him and he joined her. Here, in this comfortable nook built into the wall, they had loved before, and with each act she'd found a growing pleasure in his arms.

How would she articulate what she felt? She needed to feel him deep inside her, to hear his breath against her cheek, harsh and gasping.

Passion was as new to her as joy, both emotions swirling through her, along with an anticipation so powerful that it seemed almost wanton. She had expected to feel companionship and comfort from a husband, but Alisdair had given her so much more.

Something thrummed between them now, some mutual awareness that had not been there in those nights of loving.

Lying beside her, he turned onto his side. She wished, suddenly, that there was light, like on the morning after their wedding. He made her feel beautiful, as if her body were perfect and her flaws inconsequential. But more important, she wanted to see him. Glorious and male, strong and virile. He was hers, she thought in a surge of protectiveness.

She touched the edge of his jaw, drawing him to her with the smoothing of one fingertip against his lower lip.

His kiss was long and deep and eternal in its perfection. Pressing her face against his neck, she wound her arms around his back, pulling him close to her in a sudden, desperate wish to keep him safe. But he would always climb the rigging, or stand at the bow of the *Fortitude*, looking out into the world as if to welcome all its excitement and dangers.

Bending his head, he mouthed a nipple, scraping the edge of it with his teeth. He drew sharply on it, caressing her breasts with tender fingers, the contrast between the two sensations startling.

Running his palm over her stomach, he followed with a kiss, trailing a path from her throat to her navel. She shivered at the feeling, but he soothed her with a murmur.

He touched the tip of his tongue to her, the sensation so startling that her eyes flew open. His thumbs spread open intimate folds, before lingeringly tracing a path for his lips to follow.

"Alisdair," she said, but wasn't sure if she spoke in protest or entreaty.

A long, slow glide of his tongue silenced her.

Delight raced through her body, warming her. Her legs widened instinctively; her hips arched to meet his lips. He acceded to her unspoken demand, lengthening the strokes of his tongue, circling, then soothing.

Iseabal felt herself contract deep inside, a reaction to the soft puff of whisper as he spoke against her flesh. "Iseabal."

She wanted more, then less of the sensation, then more again. *Please.* Tiny arrows speared her, each one calmed, then incited again by the sensual motions of his tongue.

Gripping the sheets on both sides of her, she absorbed and accepted, adrift in pleasure so intense that her heart fell silent, her breath stilled. There was only Alisdair and need.

He drew slightly away and she murmured a protest, only to release her breath and her heart as he entered her a moment later. Her body bowed upward to meet him, her mind a midnight sky, deep and dark and empty. Her body held sway now, feelings dictating her movements, passion becoming both mind and heart.

Her hands gripped his arms, pulling him to her. She buried her face against his throat, opened her mouth against his heated flesh. Wrapping her legs around his, she held onto him as if he were both her captor and her savior.

Supporting himself on his forearms, Alisdair looked down at Iseabal as she blinked her eyes open. Did he wear the same dazed expression? He must, held as he was at the knife point of desire.

His fingers measured her shoulders, his hands trailing down to rest on either side of her breasts.

Iseabal widened her legs, lifting her knees slightly to rock gently beneath him. He felt a contraction around him, urging him toward completion.

"Don't do that," he said harshly.

"Did you feel that?" she asked, eyes closing. But a small, almost triumphant smile played on her lips.

"Yes," he said tightly, laying his cheek on hers. "For the love of God, Iseabal," he muttered, torn between mindless pleasure and capitulation.

"I didn't know I could do that," she said, and squeezed again, her internal muscles gripping him like a hot, damp fist.

An oath escaped him, a cry of surrender and mortality. He felt as if he were being split in two, and a second from now would need to gather parts of himself together with flailing hands.

Once more he pushed himself into her, reaching a place of darkness behind his lids.

Iseabal gripped him again, making him lose track of who was being seduced. He had wanted to grant her a moment of perfection, and was, instead, being led into an abyss of pleasure.

Please, his body urged. *Now.* He withdrew again, a second later surging into her in priapic demand. Her hips arched and he stifled his groan of pleasure against her breast, withdrew again. He had ceased being a thinking man, his body's urgings becoming a drumbeat he could not help but obey. *Now. Now.* The rhythm escalated as he gripped his hands on her shoulders and pulled himself deeper inside her.

His breath fanned against her temple as he closed his eyes and simply relished the unendurable feeling of need. Swirling through him like a hot tropical storm, it seemed replicated in the currents below the hull.

Alisdair felt trapped in a rhythm as old as the waves, as undulating and as fierce. He withdrew, then entered her again, the sound of her soft moan a counterpart to his own wordless wonder. He was rigid, painfully so, but it was a feeling he savored, like sailing before the wind. Dangerous, unpredictable, falling headlong into excitement and wonder.

The current beneath the hull, steady and relentless, followed his movements, the arching of his hips, the press of his swollen length inside her, his reluctant withdrawal. A tide of sensation, and she was his beach, a safe haven, a resting place.

The goddess of the ocean rocked them in long, sensual movements. He wanted to make this joining last, but Iseabal clutched his back suddenly, her nails gouging into his skin. Her eyes flickered open, wide and helpless in surrender. In that moment he was lost, his vision fading, his body and mind blinded in bliss.

Chapter 23

To Iseabal, the journey back to Gilmuir seemed to take only moments. Perhaps because she'd spent the voyage to London worrying about her uncertain future, while now she barely noted the passing of the days.

Alisdair stood beside her, but Iseabal didn't turn to look at him. His appearance was marked on her mind forever, just as his touch would always be imprinted upon her body. He stretched out his hand and instinctively her fingers threaded with his.

Over the past few days, the *Fortitude* had traveled without full sail, slowing her speed so that the *Molly Brown* could catch up with them. Now both ships were navigating Coneagh Firth. The wind welcomed them, batting playfully at the *Fortitude*'s sails, fluttering Iseabal's petticoat, and tossing her hair against her cheeks.

Silently they stood, hand in hand, watching as they neared Gilmuir.

From time to time they passed a village nestled close to the loch, as if the tiny hamlet sipped at the water like an animal slaking its thirst.

Alisdair's hand tightened on hers, and she knew he'd seen the castle. Standing like an impressive icon to heritage, Gilmuir glowed with the rays of a morning sun.

"Gilmuir seems to be welcoming us," he said, smiling.

She nodded, her attention drawn from the castle to Alisdair. Lately, he seemed even more handsome than he had at their first meeting, as if the character of the man had seeped outward from his soul and altered his features.

She wondered if their children would be graced with the MacRae eyes. Bringing their clasped hands up to his lips, Alisdair placed a tender kiss on her knuckles as if he'd heard her thought.

"The *Molly Brown* will dock here," he said, looking toward his left, where the land sloped gently to the loch. "In order to unload the horses and most of the provisions," he explained.

Understanding immediately, Iseabal smiled. "It would be difficult trying to lead the horses up the staircase," she said, amused by the mental picture.

Without warning, he bent to kiss her, in full view of his crew. A few men grinned at her when she glanced in their direction, but then turned tactfully away. Not one of the sailors had voiced an objection to her presence on this voyage, at least within her hearing. Perhaps, she thought, bending to pick up Henrietta, their approval was due in part to the cat's affection.

The *Molly Brown* eased behind them, the captain standing on the bow. A signal from the *Fortitude* was answered quickly with a similar flag.

"What are they looking for?" she asked, watching the men on the other ship peering over the side.

Glancing at her, Alisdair reached out and scratched Henrietta between her ears. The cat's purring grew louder and her body heavier, as if she'd relaxed every muscle in it.

"See the differences in shading?" he said, pointing to the shoreline. Iseabal lowered Henrietta to the deck and the cat wound herself around Alisdair's legs. Following his direction, Iseabal looked over the side, noting that, close to the shore, the loch was either a pale green or a deep emerald.

"The darker the water, the greater the depth. The *Molly Brown* is heavy and they don't want to chance going aground."

The spot where the captain chose to dock was within sight of the necklace of rocks. Easing the *Molly Brown* closer to shore, however, was not so easily accomplished. An hour later the merchant ship weighed anchor not ten feet from shore.

After the first plank was placed in position, one sailor nimbly walked across to the glen.

"What's he doing now?" she asked, fascinated by his actions. He seemed to be digging a hole.

"The landward side of the gangway must be rooted," Alisdair said, "so that it doesn't slip. He'll bury about an arm's length of each plank." The second and third boards followed, the area now wide enough to accommodate the horses and the numerous barrels.

As they began unloading, the *Fortitude* slid cautiously around the jagged rocks. The cove seemed particularly beautiful this morning with the sun sparkling off the surface of the cobalt-blue water and the cliffs towering protectively above them.

"Have a boat lowered," he said, turning to address Brian. "And ask the men returning to Nova Scotia to ready their gear."

"What about Daniel?" Iseabal asked.

"When he arrives, he'll take the *Fortitude* back to Nova Scotia. To send word to my family and gather what belongings I need."

"You would let him take your ship?" Her tone held amazement.

"There are others to build," he said, holding out his hand for her again. She placed hers in his, and he led the way to the rope ladder.

As Iseabal followed him down the rungs, she had the thought that this task was no more easily accomplished with practice. Gratefully, she lowered her feet into the flat-bottomed skiff, holding onto Alisdair for support.

She sat in the boat, watching him handle the oars. Her heart felt as if it were expanding to encompass not only Alisdair but Gilmuir itself.

If she were a fanciful woman, Iseabal would have believed that the old fortress gave a sigh of relief as they left the boat and entered the cave. The morning light, deflected by the water, illuminated the domed space.

Iseabal halted in surprise, noting the portraits. The first time she'd been here, a storm had shrouded her view, but now the portraits of a woman adorning the ceiling and wall were clearly visible.

"Ionis's lady," Alisdair said from beside her. His low voice seemed even more intimate in this quiet and shadowed place. "Do you know the story?"

Wordlessly, she shook her head.

"Saint Ionis was sent to live here hundreds of years ago, a penance given to him by God. It seems he strayed from his vows and loved a black-haired, green-eyed girl. From the looks of it, she haunted his dreams all the rest of his life."

Iseabal glanced at the woman who had been so well loved, only now noticing that there was a tinge of sadness to her eyes. Had she truly grieved, or had Ionis simply mirrored his own feelings in his paintings?

"Did God ever forgive him?"

"I don't know," he said, drawing her back against him. "Perhaps He did, simply because there is little left of the saint, but his lady remains."

For a moment they stood staring at the woman, Alisdair's hands gently moving up and down Iseabal's arms. Turning finally, they began to mount the steps in silence.

Once on the floor of the priory, Alisdair held out his hands for her, beginning to lift her free much as he had that first day, when she'd been trapped in the pit of the foundations. Only this time he held her close when she stood, his arms surrounding her, his hands flattening against the small of her back.

In this ruined priory once held sacred, Iseabal suddenly realized that she was more fortunate than a woman beloved by a saint.

Alisdair bent his head, resting his chin against the shimmering ebony of Iseabal's hair. Her hands wound around him, gripping the back of his coat. For a moment he was content to stand there, the wind gently whirling around them as if the priory itself approved of their return.

"Are you happy, Iseabal?" he asked, never having thought

to ask such a question before. The moments ticked by in an agony of seconds while he waited for her response.

"Yes," she said, the answer coming in a low, breathless voice. He moved his hands to her buttocks, pulling her even closer.

His new bride, once innocent and now an apt pupil, arched her hips against him as if welcoming his sudden uncontrollable reaction.

"If you continue, I might take you right here on the priory floor," he whispered.

"Not here," she said, teasing him with his own words spoken only days ago. She kissed his shirt, a sweet gesture in comparison to what her hands were doing. She was stroking her palms down his midriff, past his hips, her fingers trailing up and down his thigh in a maddening exploration.

When had he lost control over his sensual nature? When, for that matter, had he ceased to be a creature of intellect and one solely of bodily responses? When Iseabal spoke, he answered silently. When she moved close to him, the scent of her encouraged his erection. He could not, Alisdair thought in disgust, even embrace his wife without feeling a tinge of lust.

"Iseabal," he cautioned.

"Not here," she said again, then surprised him by drawing back. She held out her hand to him, a small, delicious smile playing on her lips and her green eyes sparkling with merriment.

When had she become a vixen?

He allowed her to take his hand and lead him unerringly through the ruins. Iseabal knew Gilmuir better than he, Alisdair decided as she wound through the fallen bricks and around deep holes caused by the missing floor. He was the ghost of Gilmuir; and she, the woman who fulfilled her promise of unearthly beauty within its shadows.

In that instant, his mind conjured up a figurehead for the first of the MacRae vessels constructed at Gilmuir. The form would bear Iseabal's face, her hair billowing out behind her. But he would not allow this ornament to be naked to the waist, breasts thrusting toward the waves. She would, instead, be gowned in silk, something green to match the beauty of her eyes. Some garment, perhaps, in the Chinese fashion, with a high collar and buttons down to her ankles, so concealing that only he knew what lay beneath the fabric.

"Here," she announced when they came to the mostly intact corridor. "I used to think that I'd heard lovers' whispers here, but now I think it was only a foretelling of what was to come." As she gazed at him, the smile vanished from her face.

She took a few steps toward him until her hands rested against his chest once more. "It's a place for lovers, Alisdair," she said. "For secret assignations."

"I would not have you shamed, Iseabal," he said gently. "And any of the crew might come to Gilmuir and see us. I've another locale in mind," he added.

She said nothing when he took her hand, walking from Gilmuir and across the land bridge to a place told to him in tales.

Crossing the glen, Alisdair was unsurprised to see evidence of recent sheep grazing. Drummond, evidently, was not a man of his word. Iseabal had warned him.

"I wonder what Drummond will say when he learns we've returned," he said.

Iseabal smiled. "He will take you to court," she said unhesitatingly.

He glanced over at Iseabal, wondering why he had never

seen signs of Drummond in her. She didn't have the nature to be devious, or contemptuous of others. In Iseabal there was a core of sweetness, as if she had learned the lesson of love well enough. From her mother? Or from another, one she might have loved before their marriage?

Alisdair halted in mid-step, the idea anathema to him.

"Was there anyone special for you?" he asked, more gruffly than he had intended. "A sweetheart you might have known before our marriage?"

"With my father guarding my virtue like a gorgon?" she replied, evidently amused.

He did not mean her body, but her heart.

Alisdair resorted to silence, leading her to the line of trees, wishing he had a more detailed map than his memory. His great-uncle Hamish had once told him of this place, bragging of standing atop the knoll and serenading the British with his pipes.

"Where are we going, Alisdair?" she asked.

"To the top of MacRae land," he said. "Where we might look out on Gilmuir and our new home."

Perhaps later he would lay her down on the ground and show her what he felt. Words could not express this feeling, but loving her might do well enough.

The strong scent of pine flavored the air as they entered the thick forest. Where perhaps there had once been a path, small saplings, decaying branches, and a thick cushion of fallen needles now layered the floor of the woods.

He was not a man, for all his thoughts of Gilmuir, given to whimsy. But it felt right, somehow, that he would be ascending this hill with Iseabal. As if this moment, perfumed and perfect, had been destined to occur from the moment of his birth and hers.

Glancing down at her once more, he marveled at her beauty. The dappled sunlight graced her with both shadow and sun, giving her a radiance he'd never before seen. Almost, he thought, as if she were a mythical creature, Iseabal of the forest.

Smiling at himself, Alisdair realized that if she were the queen of this place, then he was the fool.

Chapter 24

A t the top of the hill, Alisdair halted, his breath stripped
from him by the surrounding view. Brandidge Hall,
with all its magnificence, could not measure up to this scene.

Ahead was the glittering loch, and next to it, Gilmuir. To
his left were the rolling glens of MacRae land, the destruction caused by the foraging sheep softened by distance. To
his right was a thick line of trees, and beyond, a series of hills
stretching out like the humps of a dragon's back.

"Alisdair."

Turning, he smiled down at Iseabal. She imbued his name
with tenderness and passion, seduction and surrender.
Threading his hands through her hair, he pressed his palms
against her scalp.

His kiss was gentle but deep, promising both sweetness
and passion. "I want to love you here, Iseabal," he said,
pulling back. "Here," he said again as if enforcing the point.

The wind would caress their bodies; birds would sing in a joyous chorus as if to accompany their loving. Even the sun blazing brightly overhead seemed to approve of his plans.

His fingers stroked the corners of her lips, measured the beauty of her lovely smile. When had he become fascinated with the line of a woman's jaw, or with the sweep of curve from throat to shoulder? Touching his lips against her skin gave him two delights, one from Iseabal's sighing response, the other from his reaction.

He wanted to render her speechless with wonder, to see her eyes when she soared with him to a place beyond articulation or description.

Her heated breath against his throat required a calming kiss to her temple; her racing heartbeat, a soothing palm resting against one breast.

Slowly he unfastened the front of her jacket. Her only movement was to regard him with that solemn gaze of hers.

"May I love you here, Iseabal?" he asked gently.

She nodded, the color mounting in her cheeks. But with a deft movement she untied her petticoat, stepping out of it with easy grace. Her shift fell to the ground, until she stood only in stockings and garters. Slipping off her shoes, she moved her hands to the tops of her stockings and, in a gesture feminine and delectable, began to roll each one down.

As she undressed he matched her actions with his own. His coat joined her petticoat and skirt; his shirt, her shoes; and his pants, her stockings. *Hurry,* his mind counseled, and a far-off bell pealed, reminding him that he had never felt this way for any other woman. Only for Iseabal.

Raising herself on tiptoe, Iseabal stroked his skin with her palms, curving around him like a siren of legend and lore. A figurehead come to life, or a mermaid, stripped of her tail and given speech. Her hand flattened on his abdomen, her fingers splaying across his skin, the silken brush of her hair against his bare chest enticing.

Forcing his hands down to his sides, Alisdair stood in the position of supplicant. Or victim, he considered a moment later. She brushed her breasts against his chest in an evocative gesture, her eyes closed and the expression on her face one of rapt wonderment.

"Kiss me, Iseabal," he murmured. She opened her eyes, staring up at him, and for a brief moment Alisdair felt locked in her gaze. A thousand thoughts came to him, none of them coherent, each one enmeshed in a confusing puzzle.

He wanted to reward her for her acquiescence, praise her in some mindless way. Instead, he bestowed a fervent and heated kiss between her breasts.

The sun speared them, spilling over the forest and bathing the treetops. An enchanted land and place and time.

Slowly she sank to her knees before him, sliding her palms up the length of his thighs. He was so powerfully built, a warrior disguised by well-tailored clothing and the grace of his movements. Her thumbs brushed against his erection with a featherlike touch.

His hands fisted in her hair as his body arched forward. "Iseabal," he warned.

"Am I hurting you?" she asked.

He shook his head from side to side, moved his hands to her shoulders with a talonlike grip. "I'm too close," he said, his voice a pained whisper. Gently, he removed her hands from him before sinking to his knees.

Cradling her head between his hands, his thumbs brushing against the corners of her mouth, he whispered, "Shall I find my release with your touch, Iseabal? Or bring you pleasure?"

"Pleasure, please," she said, the words honeyed and languid.

She flattened her hands on his chest, pushing him back onto the ground. Harlot or wife, temptress or wallflower, it simply didn't matter. He was Alisdair and she was Iseabal, man and woman.

He was driving deep inside her, so fast and so full that she nearly screamed with the pleasure of it.

If her heart beat, it was incidental. If her blood ceased flowing, she would not have known, because every every sense was centered on him and this blessedly swift possession.

She rose slowly, then down again, savoring each pulsing beat of sensation. His hand bracketed her waist, his hips arched beneath her, but she refused to hurry, trapped in a feeling so perfect that it seemed as crystal as a raindrop, as fiercely bright as a rainbow.

Her head arched back, she crossed her hands over her naked breasts and clutched her shoulders, so intent was she in the pure selfishness of this moment, adrift in pleasure so acute that it skirted the edge of pain.

He stilled beneath her, the harshness of his breathing the only indication that he was as needy as she. No words passed between them, and the only place they touched was where he was buried inside her, intrusive and hard.

She rocked on her knees, the sudden spurt of delight almost too much to hold inside. Reaching down, she gripped his hands, placing them on her breasts. His fingers were cooler than her skin, and the feeling of his palms brushing back and forth against her nipples was a soothing relief.

Unexpectedly, he moved, toppling her in such a gracefully executed turn that she wondered if he was much practiced at it. One of his hands cradled the back of her head, the other her shoulder, so that she was protected from the ground.

She dug her fingers into the earth, pushing herself toward him. Gripping his back with nails grown sharp for the task, Iseabal suddenly felt that she was no longer simply a woman, but another type of beast, female and ferocious.

Her hips arched upward, her internal muscles clenching him tight. She had marked him as hers, and now she wanted everything. All of what he'd given her before, and more.

There were no shattering stars behind her lids, no rainbow hues on the ceiling of the cave. For a moment there was nothing at all, as if the entire world had collapsed around her. All she could feel were waves of pleasure so strong that she seemed to undulate with them.

Her body felt as if it did not belong to her in that instant, a strange metamorphosis accomplished as her hips arched and her shoulders drew back. Her lips fell open, preparing for a scream, but there was no sound of delight or satisfaction, only an openmouthed welcome to this new and different person she had become.

He lay stunned, his mind reeling from what had just happened. Loving Iseabal had not simply been an act of lust or seduction, but a passion so intense that Alisdair felt as if his body had been turned inside out.

Iseabal's head rested on his arm, her hand flattened against his chest beneath his shirt. He, in turn, held her tightly against him, closing his eyes with a sudden feeling of tenderness. If she moved, it would be with his permission, and if he wanted to rise, she would be the one to allow it.

Possession.

His eyes blinked open and he stared at the tips of the trees pointing the way to this bald patch of earth. That was what their loving had been, he realized. They'd each claimed the other. Not in gentleness or tenderness, but with a fevered passion that left his body thrumming.

Her fingers idly smoothed against his chest, making him suddenly wish that he had a half-dozen hands. One to guide her fingers to his erection, one to hold her face steady for his lips, another to feel the whole of her body. The core of her would require at least two hands to explore hidden hollows and welcoming secret places. But people waited, even as he wished they didn't, and duty summoned him, even though he would willingly relinquish it.

Alisdair helped her dress, each garment she donned rewarded with a kiss. Iseabal was breathless by the time her petticoat was tied at her waist, her blood heating once more as he helped her slowly fasten her jacket.

He had donned his clothes with greater speed than she, but then, he was able to do so without assistance.

"You dressed too quickly," she said absently, her fingers stroking the front of his coat. How strange that she should want to touch him all the time. A pat on his arm, a clasp of his hand, tiny gestures that reassured her in some odd way.

The faint light illuminated his eyes, sparkling like the water on the loch, and his smile, endearingly crooked. A lock of hair had fallen down over his brow and she pushed it back with tender fingers, thinking that he had never looked as handsome or as young as at this moment.

"Must we leave?"

"Shall we make our home here, Iseabal?" he asked. "Build a tiny cabin upon this knoll?"

"Yes, please," she said, smiling up at him. "We'll make a bower of this place, Alisdair. You'll hunt for our food and I'll cook it here."

His response was to grin at her.

One part of her, protected by caution all these years, watched with wariness, suspicious of this feeling. But the childish and impulsive and impossibly reckless Iseabal, gloried in loving Alisdair.

Happiness was enervating, making her feel as buoyant as a cloud, almost hollow inside, as if every despairing thought, any worry, any emotion less than delight, had no place there.

Laying her cheek against his chest, Iseabal knew that if memory should ever be stripped from her, she would forever be able to recall this day, and this particular moment, standing on a sunny hill with Alisdair.

"Iseabal," he said gently, and then seemed to falter for words much in the same way she did around him.

Instead of speaking further, he turned with her in his arms, surveying the vista in front of them. There was Gilmuir sparkling in the sunlight, and beyond, the glittering waters of Loch Euliss.

Feeling him stiffen, she glanced at his face. He was staring at the western horizon with a frown.

"What is it, Alisdair?" she asked.

He glanced down at her and then back to the rolling hills. "A fire," he said simply.

Iseabal studied the hills to the right. The sky above them was growing darker, thick black smoke curling into the air like a giant puff from a celestial pipe.

"Lightning often causes a fire," she said, feeling a curious sense of dread.

"There is no sign of recent rain," he replied, his hands sliding to her wrists. Iseabal stood so close that she could feel him breathe against her back.

"Someone might be a poor cook," she said faintly.

Alisdair squeezed her hands in wordless acknowledgment of her attempt at humor.

He came to stand in front of her, bending to kiss her lightly. "Will you wait for me here?" he asked.

"What are you going to do, Alisdair?" She held her palms against his chest, by will alone refraining from voicing her sudden worry.

Men do not like a complaining wife, a lesson she had learned well enough in her childhood. Men went off to defend their land, or to visit Inverness or Edinburgh, and, before her birth, to war itself. On such occasions as this, a wife knew well enough not to badger or cajole or even attempt to convince a man not to do his duty. Instead, a woman was supposed to stand, wait, and watch, just as Alisdair had asked of her.

"Must you go?" she asked, unable to forestall that one question.

"It's MacRae land," he said, folding his hand over hers. "Will you stay?" he asked again, and she nodded reluctantly, determined not to show her sudden and disconcerting fear.

Daniel was consulting his log when he was abruptly lifted off his feet from behind. In that instant of disorientation, a host of possibilities came to mind. Thieves or sailors impressing him into the British navy, or simply wharf rats about their mischief. He began to struggle, his legs flailing, when the sound of laughter halted him in mid-kick.

"If you're a MacRae," he said, his irritation swift and strong, "then you'd better put me down."

"You're an easy target for mischief, Daniel, when you're too intent on your lists," Hamish said, releasing him.

Daniel turned to face the four of them, every single one of the MacRae brothers smiling. He'd been the brunt of their jokes before, but he'd rarely been as annoyed as now. Because of the interruption, he would have to begin counting the barrels of rice flour again.

"Where's Alisdair?" Hamish asked.

"Where's the *Fortitude?*"

"What are you doing here on this floating jetsam?"

Question upon question was hurled at him and he refused to answer, choosing to frown at them instead. One by one, they seemed to notice his irritation, falling blessedly silent.

Before he answered their questions, he asked one of his own. "How did you find me?" The merchantman was one of several hundred vessels in London's port.

"We inquired of the harbormasters," James said. "Strangely enough, not one of them knew when the *Fortitude* departed for Nova Scotia, but the mention of the MacRae name brought about a very curious reaction."

"They all nearly spit when talking about you, Daniel," Douglas contributed, to the obvious annoyance of his older brothers.

"What have you done," James asked, "to merit such a reputation?"

"Refused to pay the prices some of these thieves fetch," Daniel said curtly.

All four of the brothers smiled.

"I'm wise with my money, not cheap."

"Parsimonious," James contributed, always the peace-maker.

"I think you made them mad with all your superstitions," Douglas said, his attention on kicking his shoe against the deck. "The harbor must not face in the proper direction."

"Not enough cats," Hamish said, without a hint of a smile on his face.

"Or too many," Brendan said. "All that meowing and such."

Daniel's eyes narrowed. "You'd be better off keeping such comments to yourselves if you'll be wanting answers to your questions."

Once again they fell silent, but not for long.

"Why would you be buying this stuff?" Hamish asked, kicking at one of the barrels. If he overturned it, Daniel vowed, he would make Hamish sweep every last particle from the deck. With his tongue.

"And where is Alisdair?" Brendan asked.

"You mean the Earl of Sherbourne?" Daniel said, giving in to an imp of mischief as wicked as any MacRae's.

For a moment Daniel simply savored the look of stunned surprise on the brothers' faces before adding to it. "He's married, you know."

A rare day, indeed, Daniel gloated, to best the MacRae brothers.

The ground rose gradually from Gilmuir's land bridge to a steep point far beyond the hill where Iseabal waited. To shorten the journey, Alisdair kept to the high ground, avoiding the forest. Even so, it took him nearly an hour to reach the place still marked by a plume of smoke.

Iseabal could be right, Alisdair thought. The fire could

have been started by a stroke of lightning, an accident, or any number of ways. Or it could have been caused by something less innocuous, a suspicion borne out by the sight before him.

Nestled against shale and rocks, on the opposite side of the hill from Gilmuir, was a clachan overlooking an inlet of Loch Euliss. The fields beyond looked to have once promised a plentiful harvest. A sturdy little village, with a series of small boats tied at the shoreline and nets draped among the square stone cottages.

Now, however, the homes were ablaze, the nets among them ladders of fire. The fields had been trampled, the animals slaughtered.

The air was foul with smoke and mixed with the stench of burning thatch and charred bricks. But none of the huddled villagers moved to extinguish the blaze.

Children stood beside their mothers, clutching the women's petticoats for support, while older people clenched their hands together and stared with repugnance at the five mounted men who'd fired their homes. The able-bodied men were rounded up and held at gunpoint when they would have moved to save their homes or offer comfort to their wives.

What cottages hadn't been put to the torch were being searched by two other men. Anything deemed worth saving was immediately pocketed or thrown over an invader's shoulder. The rest was set afire.

Alisdair strode forward, enraged that a Scot should do this to his countrymen. The identity of the attackers wasn't hard to ascertain, for each wore clothing he'd seen before at Fernleigh. Drummond's men.

An old man was suddenly being whipped, pushed closer to the fire by one of the riders as if his cruelty were a game.

He fell heavily to his knees in the dirt, his white beard trailing in the ground as he begged for his life. His tormentor simply continued to whip him.

Alisdair began to run, reaching the two of them. Jerking the whip from his grasp, he threw it to the ground before hooking his hand in the man's gun belt and pulling him from the horse. Drummond fell with a thud to the ground but immediately sprang to his hands and knees. Alisdair didn't wait, but kicked out with his boot, his heel connecting with a pointed chin.

"Strike someone who can fight back, not a man twice your age."

Unexpectedly, a woman emerged from the doorway of one small stone cottage, her apron aflame. He rushed to aid her, and with the help of the other villagers, pushed her down to the ground and rolled her in the dirt until the flames were extinguished.

"A good Samaritan," a voice said.

Alisdair turned, looking up slowly. Another Drummond attacker easily controlled the reins of his horse with one hand while he leveled a pistol at Alisdair with the other.

He'd seen the man before, on his first visit to Fernleigh. A thin face like a starving Scot's, narrowed eyes that seemed to mirror the flames behind him, and a grin that appeared almost evil in its incomparable glee. As if, he thought with a sudden premonition, the man anticipated the exact moment of Alisdair's death.

Only an instant had passed and already it seemed a lifetime. Speech was echoing, as if they were enclosed together in a Chinese jar. A specimen of nature. Killer and victim.

Abruptly, Alisdair heard a muffled sound, then witnessed the contained flash of spark and powder. Powerless to move quickly enough, he viewed his own death, felt the instant when the bullet struck his head. The second of consciousness left to him was filled only with regret.

Chapter 25

Iseabal remained seated atop the knoll, her arms wrapped around her knees. From time to time she would stand and look toward the place they'd seen the smoke, her sense of dread increasing with each passing hour. Telling herself that Alisdair MacRae was not a man easily bested did not seem to ease her mind.

The afternoon was advancing, the sun beginning its downward journey into night. But still there was no sign of Alisdair, only the fading tendrils of smoke curling into the air.

Perhaps the journey was farther than it had seemed. Or he was aiding in extinguishing the blaze. There was no reason, after all, to feel this fear, she told herself. She'd lived in caution so much of her life that it had become a habit.

Standing, Iseabal began to circle the knoll, her feet crushing the pine needles along the edge. The horizon was growing darker, not with smoke, but with night. The longer she stared, her eyes smarting, the more concerned she became.

Even the silence seemed ominous. The birds were quiet, and no sound came from the underbrush, as if nature itself stilled in anticipation.

There, at Gilmuir, was the only sign of activity, as the horses from the *Molly Brown* were being led across the land bridge and into the courtyard.

He might well be there, thinking, because of the lateness of the hour, that she would have returned to Gilmuir. Or he'd sent word to her in some way and the news waited for her below.

Doubting that either had truly occurred, Iseabal nevertheless clung to both thoughts as she began the descent to Gilmuir.

Gossamer rays of fading sunlight filtered through the trees, momentarily dancing upon the leaf-strewn ground as if to illuminate the way. But night was coming to the forest, draping the trees in swags of shadow. Saplings were no longer signs of new life, but taloned wooden fingers reaching out to snare her petticoat. Branches cracked beneath her feet with each step, the scent of decaying leaves sour and pungent.

Finally she was free of the forest, into the open air. Twilight misted the air as Iseabal followed a weed-strewn path, thinking it led to the land bridge.

Instead, she found herself in the deserted village of Gilmuir. At least ten cottages still stood, their thatched roofs damaged in the intervening years, but the stonework of the walls mostly intact. As a child, she'd come here, wondering what had happened to the MacRaes. Now she knew, and this lonely spot in the glen was a testament to the courage and tenacity of those people.

Here the ghostly whispers of voices lingered in the air just as they had at Gilmuir. But not sad ones. A sighing breeze seemed to echo the lilting laughter of long-ago friends. A leaf skittering on the ground mimicked a whisper of delight from one child to the next. If spirits lived here, they were happy ones.

Alisdair.

She could almost feel him standing beside her, smiling, his eyes wearing that look of pride when speaking of his ship or his family. He stretched out his hand to her and she wanted to take it, pull his image to her, rendering it from filmy and transparent to real.

Had something happened to Alisdair? Did his spirit bid her farewell? Gently and sweetly, with a smile that came from his soul? Pushing that thought violently away, Iseabal left the village.

The land bridge was illuminated by two blazing torches on either side. Lanterns had been set on poles around various spots in the courtyard. Scanning the area, Iseabal noted that the cook had already begun a meal. The men of the *Fortitude* were erecting a few small tents, and strangers, whom she took to be the crew of the *Molly Brown*, were stacking crates on the eastern side of the promontory. Farther away, closer to the land bridge, was a rope corral where the horses had been tethered.

But there was no sign of Alisdair.

The jarring clank of metal against metal made her realize how quiet it had become. One by one, the crewmen turned to stare as she walked to Brian's side.

"Have you seen Alisdair?" she asked, making no pretense of hiding her worry. "Is he here?" Holding her hands tightly together, she willed them not to shake.

"I haven't seen the captain, mistress," he said. His frown changed his face, made it oddly older. "Not since you and he left the *Fortitude*. Has something happened?"

She told him the story, willing her voice not to quaver. Brian listened without comment, then turned to study the horizon. If smoke still rose to the sky, darkness had masked all signs of it.

"We'll find him, mistress," he said grimly, signaling to another crewman.

Did he actually expect her to sit and wait? She left him, striding toward the horses.

"Let us go instead, mistress," Brian said, following her.

She didn't bother arguing with him, didn't attempt to defend her position or obtain his agreement; she simply ducked beneath the rope, selecting the nearest horse.

The glen would be treacherous at night, with uneven earth cropped clean by the sheep, and holes in the ground that a horse couldn't see. But Iseabal gave no thought to the animal that carried her, aware only that she must find Alisdair. Choosing a bridle and bit, she adjusted them, then led the horse out of the enclosure.

Using a fallen block of masonry as a stepping-stone, she mounted, feeling safer on the animal's back than in an unfamiliar saddle. Turning the horse, she retrieved a lantern from its pole.

"Follow me," she told Brian, holding the lantern at her side. That was the last thought she had for any of them. Her attention was focused ahead of her, to the place where she'd seen the smoke.

The unmistakable sound of hooves caused her to glance back. Three large and looming shadows followed her. Evidently, Brian and his companions had chosen to ride bareback also. What they lacked in experience, she thought, Alisdair's crew made up in determination.

Following the edge of the forest, the line of trees a guide, they turned southward, then west again. A longer journey than Alisdair might have made, since they couldn't cut through the thick trees. The earth began to rise beneath them as they rode, the terrain becoming more hilly. All of a sudden the stench of burning was in the air, and Iseabal knew they were close.

Her stomach tightened, one hand gripping the reins tensely, the other holding the lantern with such fierce possessiveness that the iron handle felt embedded in her palm. Fear was an icy feeling, leaving her cold and trembling.

She had never traveled this far before, Gilmuir marking the boundaries of her secret rebellions. Her skirts were bunched up in front of her as she rode astride, her ankles exposed, and her hair flowing behind her as if she were a maiden and not a married and chaste woman. Modesty, however, didn't concern her, the only thought in her mind to find Alisdair.

The horse's hooves on the rocky ground sounded like his name. *Alisdair. Alisdair. Alisdair.* An entreaty echoing through the empty glen until it was swallowed up by the forests.

There, on the slope of a hill, protected by an outcropping of stone, was a small clachan. Like lumps of still smoldering coal, the cottages glowed from within, their stone walls blackened. In the center of the village stood a clump of people, only dark shadows themselves, the only clue to their humanity an occasional faint sob.

Riding to the edge of the trees, Iseabal hung the lantern on a branch before dismounting. Her knees sagged beneath her, but she forced herself to pick up the lantern again and walk the distance to the crofters' huts.

Behind her, the three men from the *Fortitude* also dismounted, following her wordlessly, their silence a gesture of support.

"I'm looking for Alisdair MacRae," she said as the shadowy forms turned. She held up the lantern so that they could see her, and to better view them.

Soot marred their faces and hands, darkening the front of their clothing. They were all old, people for whom death waited with an outstretched hand. The elderly should be cherished for their wisdom, venerated for their age, not left without homes.

The question of what had happened here was second to her desperate need.

"Have you seen him?"

An old woman studied her for a moment. "There was a man here," she said faintly. "A stranger come to our aid, for all the good it did him."

"What became of him?" Iseabal asked, her palm flattening across her stomach. The lantern sputtered and popped as she waited. Instead of answering, however, the old woman looked confused.

"I don't know," she said uncertainly. "There were so many men around. I don't know what happened to him." Her eyes veered to one hut. Emerging from the doorway was a body, half consumed by the fire.

Slowly, each step measured by a ponderous beat of her heart, Iseabal neared the cottage, holding the lantern aloft. The only people she'd seen dead had been prepared for their lykewake, washed and readied for their burial in simple ritual.

The lantern jiggled in the wind until Iseabal realized it did so because she was shaking so badly. Forcing herself to look down, she studied the form. Long legs, half buried beneath rubble. But they weren't his boots, she noticed suddenly, feeling almost faint with relief. This poor man wore shoes so worn that the soles were nearly bare.

Turning away, she called out to the others. "Did anyone see what happened to the stranger?"

"They shot him," a quavery voice replied.

Her stomach calmed in the instant Iseabal stared at the old man. The breeze ceased to blow and the world might well have turned entirely dark. She could not look away from the sight of him slowly stroking his white beard, nor could she speak. Words had blackened in her throat until Iseabal tasted soot when she swallowed.

"They carried him off," another man said, stepping forward. "With the others. The able-bodied men and the women and children. They wouldn't have bothered if he were dead. Dead slaves don't fetch much coin."

"Slaves?" Iseabal asked faintly. She was beginning to tremble all over, as if the breeze were chilled instead of being as warm and as soft as a lover's breath. Inside, however, the cold mounted until Iseabal felt brittle with it.

"The glens have been emptying for months now," the first man said. "The Highlands are being stripped of its people. Whole villages disappear and in their place are sheep."

"We should be grateful to be old," the second man interjected. "We're supposed to die here."

"They carried him off," she repeated, the ringing sound in her ears making Iseabal feel if she were speaking beneath water. Perhaps she was drowning in grief. "Where would they take him?"

"We don't know," the old man said, shaking his head slowly. "There is no one left to tell the tale." He looked around him, then turned back to her. "Except for the aged, and half of them so confused they cannot be certain.

"He was shot, that's all I do know," he said, glancing at another man, who reluctantly nodded in agreement

"We should go back to Gilmuir, mistress," Brian was saying. "We'll send riders out to see where they might have taken the captain."

Iseabal said nothing, moving her horse to a fallen trunk and mounting. She left the lantern behind, feeling part of the darkness, a shadow as dim as the one now veiling the moon.

She turned her horse, wishing the mount were one familiar to her. But Iseabal could find the way well enough back to Gilmuir and on to Fernleigh.

"Where are you going, mistress?" Brian asked, calling up to her.

Staring down at him, Iseabal willed the words to come. "To find my husband," she said.

"We'll come with you." Raising his hand, he signaled the others.

"Go back to the ship," she said curtly. "See these people to Gilmuir," she ordered, glancing away from him and addressing the villagers. "We will see you fed and given shelter," she promised.

"And who, exactly, would you be?" the old man asked, his wrinkled face twisting into a suspicious scowl.

Instead of answering him, Iseabal positioned her mount toward Fernleigh and her father.

*   *   *

"Pick him up," Thomas Drummond said, pointing to two men with the barrel of his gun.

Glancing down at the fallen man between them, one of the prisoners spoke. "He's a heavy brute."

"Pick him up," Thomas said again. "You've carried him this far, you can finish the job."

The two men each hooked a hand beneath the MacRae's arms, pulling him along, his head lolling, his feet dragging in the dirt behind him. Either the journey to the ship would kill the MacRae, Thomas thought, or he would survive long enough so that Drummond was paid for his worth as an indentured servant. Either way, the MacRae would be gone from Gilmuir permanently.

Thomas had long ago surmised that his fortune lay not in what he could do, but for whom he could do it. Times were hard in the Highlands, and even more difficult for a man who wished to make a name for himself. There were no wars to fight, nothing to raid in this poor stretch of country. He owned no property, and no wealthy widow had yet agreed to wed him. Therefore, he had settled for aligning himself with his cousin Magnus. In serving him, Thomas reasoned, at least he was seen as an important person.

Any man who could kill without thought of punishment was powerful.

He rode ahead, following the line of villagers. By dawn they'd make the port of Cormech and would be loaded aboard ship.

As was his custom, he'd left the old behind, huddled near their burned-out huts. He wouldn't fetch a coin transporting them from Scotland. In fact, the ship's captain might well charge him for their fare.

The infirm would die, and the aged would age further still.

But that was the way of nature itself, and he only mimicked God in his actions. If the old ones learned to live in the open, like animals, they would soon become accustomed to it. Become stronger, Thomas reasoned, thinking that they might even be thankful for their trial.

Smiling, he rode to the head of the line.

Chapter 26

The stench of smoke was being carried with Iseabal in the breeze. To travel at night and alone was unthinkable, even if the destination was her childhood home. But there were considerations more vital than safety.

Where was Alisdair?

Fernleigh stood tall and ominous in the darkened countryside, not one glimmer of light penetrating its thick walls. No welcoming lantern was hung by the front door, and the moonlight, shining silver on its corners, made her childhood home appear like the chimney of Hell.

Iseabal dismounted, tying the horse's reins to the ironwork in front of one window. Rage and grief vied with each other, rising to fill her chest and swamping any other feelings. She pushed her way past the guard, determined that no one would stop her from finding Alisdair.

Inside the clan hall, a few tapers had been lit in a grudging concession to night. Her mother sat in her customary place beside the cold fireplace, her father drinking at his table. For once he was alone, his cadre of followers absent for the night.

Leah glanced up, her expression one of shock upon seeing Iseabal. She stood, dropping her needlework on the chair behind her. A second later Iseabal was enfolded in her mother's arms.

"I thought you gone, Iseabal," Leah said, patting her cheeks, examining her from toes to head in a sweeping glance.

The screech of wood against the stone floor made Iseabal turn. Her father sat back in his chair, surveying her.

"You're not welcome in this place, Iseabal MacRae. Go back to your husband and tell him that I'll not return his money for you."

"Where is he?" she said, standing in the middle of the clan hall. Her hands were clenched behind her, and her heart beat a pounding rhythm so strong she could hardly breathe. "Where is Alisdair?"

"Have you lost your husband, girl? Barely a month wed and he's already fled from you?" He glanced at his wife, and added dismissively, "I should have suspected as much, if that one taught you in the womanly arts."

As she took one more step toward him, Iseabal could feel the cold stone of the flooring through the leather of her shoes. Stone no more warm than this man's heart.

"Where have you taken him?" she asked, her voice level and harsh. Did he sense what she was feeling? Was that why he straightened in his chair, loosening his grip on the tankard? His eyes narrowed, his lips turned down, expressions of disfavor she'd seen every time they'd met.

"What has happened, Iseabal?" Leah asked.

Without taking her gaze from her father, Iseabal answered her.

"He burned a village, Mother. For the sake of his sheep. Alisdair tried to intervene. He's been missing ever since." She couldn't utter the other words, images that remained out of sight, just beyond thought. He had not been shot; he was not dead. She would know it, be feeling something other than this killing rage.

Drummond stood abruptly, striding to her side. He raised an arm to her and she smiled, the gesture halting him.

"Hit me," she dared him. "Silence me with your fists. I have thirty men at my command," she said in a low, threatening tone. "Thirty men who would willingly force you to reveal what you know. Or kill you. We'll see how brave you are when confronting someone other than my mother and me."

He struck her then, but Iseabal didn't flinch from the blow.

"Where did you take him?" she asked, wiping the blood from her lip. The pain inside was greater than anything her father could do to her.

"To Cormech," her mother whispered.

Iseabal spun around to find her mother staring at Drummond. Leah knew, Iseabal suddenly realized, wishing that the knowledge wasn't there in her mother's stricken look.

"He sells his clansmen at Cormech," Leah said, her voice trembling. "As bonded servants. Or as slaves."

"Shut up, woman," Drummond snapped. "You know nothing of my business."

"I know that you used to send them to the Carolinas, in the colonies," Leah said, "but with talk of the rebellion, you had to find another place." She pointed to her chair. "I sit there day after day at your command. Do you think that I don't hear you, don't know what you've done?"

She took Iseabal's arm, standing in mute defense of her daughter. Not the first time she'd done so, Iseabal thought, but the only occasion in which Iseabal had known the extent of her father's greed and crimes.

"I don't know where he sends them now," Leah said.

When her father raised his hand again, Iseabal grabbed his wrist. "Are you going to beat us both, Drummond?"

Releasing him, Iseabal stepped away. The anger she'd felt had deepened, altering her. She was no longer afraid of him. She felt nothing at all, neither fear nor conscience. In the depths of her heart there might have once been a wish for understanding, or a seed of compassion.

At one time she'd wanted to believe the best of him, had wanted him to be the kind of man who, instead of frightening her, would show some affection. Ever since she was a little girl, she'd thought that a piece was missing in the puzzle that was her father. All Iseabal had to do was find it and then she would understand why he was the way he was. Why he took so much pleasure in his power over others, why he treasured money over his family.

But there was, she abruptly realized, no missing piece of Magnus Drummond. He was always as he had been; the only difference now was that she was seeing him without hope clouding her vision.

Leah bowed her head, the arch of her neck rendering her vulnerable at that moment. She became, as Iseabal watched, a frail woman in a world that was not disposed to tolerate the weak. But there were other victims this night, people who might have been spared, had Leah spoken earlier.

"Why?" Iseabal asked, moving back from her mother. "Why did you never say anything? Or do anything?"

Leah raised her head, her eyes swimming with tears. "What do you expect me to have done, Iseabal? Do you think people would listen to me? There were enough to know what he was doing, and not one hand was ever lifted to stop it."

"Get out of my house, daughter," Magnus said, his voice slightly slurred.

Glancing over at him, Iseabal allowed her anger free reign. "Don't call me that again," she said sharply. "I wish to God I weren't of your blood. But rest assured, I'll spend my entire life making amends for it."

"You do that," he said, eyes narrowing. "I don't know where your husband is, but you can tell the MacRae that I'll be watching as he's driven from Gilmuir. I'll go to court and win that land back as rightly mine."

"I doubt you'll fare well against English magistrates," she said dismissively. "Alisdair MacRae is an English lord now. The Earl of Sherbourne."

"Is he, now?" he asked, striding back to the table. Sitting, he peered into the bottom of his tankard. "Or maybe he's just a ghost."

Iseabal knew, as she passed beneath the arch, that she would never come here again. The *Fortitude* had proved more a home. This had never been a welcoming place, and now it truly was an empty shell.

Looking back at the two of them, Iseabal wondered why she had never before seen her parents quite this way. She might as well have been a foundling, so removed did she feel from either of them.

She would go to Cormech with the crew of the *Fortitude* and search every ship in the harbor in order to find Alisdair. And if that did not prove successful, she would travel the world to rescue him.

Chapter 27

Moonlight illuminated the loch, granting a silvery hue to each undulating wave and touching Gilmuir with amplifying shadows. For centuries the fortress had stood, a welcoming haven to any MacRae and a warning to the invader. Tonight the lanterns glowed brightly, and when someone closed a shutter or moved the light across the courtyard, it appeared as if a dozen glowing eyes were blinking at her.

She crossed the land bridge slowly, noting the changes done in her absence. A triangular sail had been strung across a series of poles, providing an adequate shelter for the villagers, if not a luxurious one. A hot meal was being served, the cook waving a ladle at those not quick enough to come and eat. Blankets were being unrolled, old men and older women helped to what comfort Gilmuir now offered.

As she rode into the encampment, the noise seemed to fade until Iseabal realized that she was again the object of attention. Dismounting, she leaned against the horse, feeling a trembling need to surrender to the grayness for a while. Exhaustion drained her, made the journey from Fernleigh feel as long as that to London. Worry held her tight as if it were a rope wound around her chest. For an hour or two, however, she wanted to feel nothing, be numb, pretend that Alisdair was aboard the *Fortitude* and would soon join her. Or convince herself that she was in the midst of a dream and none of this was real.

But the fog of this grief was too thin and painful, allowing enough glimpses into the world to prove that all of it was actually happening.

She straightened, realizing that only after Alisdair was found would she be able to relax.

"You should come and rest," a voice said.

She glanced over her shoulder to find Brian there, a carefully bland expression on his face. Had she been rude to him? Had she offended him in some way? She couldn't remember, and if an apology were necessary, it seemed beyond her.

"Did you learn anything, mistress?"

"I believe he's been taken to Cormech." *If he's alive.*

"Cormech?"

"Where clansmen are sold as slaves," Iseabal said dully. If she could distance herself from her birth, she would have. What part of her was most like her father? She would find it and excise it, remove it—whatever it was.

"How soon can we leave?" she asked.

"It isn't safe in the darkness," Brian said, stepping away from her.

She would find Alisdair in a driving storm, at midnight, in the midst of a gale, she thought. Any time at all. But she understood the young man's fears well enough. "There's a road to Inverness," she said. "From there we should be able to find our way to Cormech. Even in the dark."

He nodded and walked away. Paying no heed to the stones littering the courtyard, Iseabal walked to the edge of the cliff. A barrier of rock, knee-high, either man-made or crafted by nature, warned the wary that beyond this point was a steep drop to the loch below.

Wrapping her arms around herself, Iseabal stood staring out over the water. Beyond her vision was Coneagh Firth, and still farther, the sea. Alisdair's ocean.

God would not give to her with one hand and take joy away with the other. Or perhaps that was how happiness came, in rare bursts that must be balanced with sorrow in order to appreciate them. Surely life was not set on such a delicate fulcrum of penance and pleasure. If so, she'd not valued those moments with Alisdair sufficiently, not nearly enough to offset the rest of her life without him.

Turning, Iseabal walked back to the other side of the courtyard, passing a group of men milling around Brian. Torchlight revealed their somber faces and the surface of the map the young man was unrolling.

Another group of men was placing lanterns around the perimeter of the ruins, working to the sound of their own thoughts. None of them, she noted, looked in her direction, and if they spoke among themselves, it was in such a hushed whisper she could not hear it.

Iseabal could have pointed out those treacherous spots, those places where the ground felt weak or a leaning column should be avoided. But such a warning needed voice, and at the moment, she was incapable of speech.

She kept walking, her feet smarting from the sharp

stones, her hands pressed together so tightly that her wrists ached.

At the cliffside once more, Iseabal stared out at the loch unthinkingly. The wind sighed low and mournfully around Gilmuir, as if fearing the depth of night. The stars seemed to blink as if the fast-moving clouds obscured their vision. Or perhaps they wept, each sparkle a droplet, each wisp of cloud a celestial finger brushing against a damp, starry eyelid.

For a moment, just a moment, she allowed herself to think the worst. How could she bear it if he were dead? Alisdair, of the teasing smiles and the glint of humor in his lovely eyes. The man who ruffled the hair of his cabin boy and laughed aloud at another of Daniel's superstitions. How easily it was to recall him bending over Patricia's hand, or gently kissing her faded cheek. How much more painful to remember him only hours before, standing on the knoll with her, his eyes filled with an expression that made her heart feel buoyant.

"If I might have a word with you, mistress?" Brian said from behind her. Iseabal turned, glancing over his shoulder at the small shelter the sailors had constructed.

"We've tried to make you as comfortable as we could," he said, leading the way.

A surprisingly cozy place, she thought, the oiled canvas offering protection against the night, the brazier giving off warmth with strangely little smoke. Someone had built a creative bench of rocks for her, and a sleeping pallet had been arranged. She might have been at ease here at another time, when her mind was not filled with thoughts of Alisdair and her heart was not a stone.

"Thank you," she said quietly.

Brian didn't seem to expect more. Unrolling a map, he tilted it to the light. "I've a suggestion, mistress." He curled the map back to show her. "We're here," he said, pointing to a spot. "And here's Cormech," he added, drawing his finger southwest. "On horseback, we'd have to circle Inverness and back up and around Moray Firth."

Iseabal remained silent, waiting for him to continue.

"It would be a faster journey by sea," he said, rolling up the map once again. "We can reach the port easier by taking the *Fortitude*."

"I gather it that the sail is from the *Molly Brown,* then?" she asked wryly, glancing over at the improvised shelter.

"The captain is an understanding man," Brian replied, a touch of wickedness to his grin. Iseabal couldn't help but wonder what kind of inducements had been offered for him to be so.

"Can we not leave now?" she asked quietly.

"We'd never navigate around the cove," he said, his eyes understanding. "But if we left at dawn, we'd still be there faster than if we traveled all night."

She nodded in reluctant agreement. "At dawn, then," she said, wishing that she had the power to command the sun.

He made a curious little bow before leaving her.

Sitting on the stone bench, her feet flat on the ground, her knees at a perfectly squared angle, her head bent forward so she could study her clasped hands, Iseabal wondered if anyone peering into the tent would realize how close she was to crying.

Alisdair blinked open his eyes, staring up at the sky above him. There should be stars, he thought, but in their place were gray clouds obscuring the moon like a gauzy veil.

His head ached abominably, as if it had cracked open and his senses were lying in a pool beneath him. He smiled at the errant thought, willing his headache away. But instead of vanishing as each moment passed, it seemed to escalate, the pulse beat of his heart replicated by the hammers slamming against his skull.

Along with the pain was another feeling, one rendering him even more uncomfortable. His thoughts were foggy, the very reason for his lying here unknown to him. He closed his eyes, focused on the last memory he had. Even that seemed elusive, as if the pain had taken over all of his mind.

Stretching out his hand, Alisdair touched a coat sleeve. Turning his head, he saw a man sprawled in exhausted slumber beside him, and beyond him yet another. Fighting back the pain, he raised his head. There were scores of people in the open field, not merely men, but women and quietly sobbing children.

Where was he? Who was he?

Alisdair MacRae.

He lay back down again, satisfied that his mind seemed to be working despite the pain. He captained a ship. More, he built them. His home? Cape Gilmuir, Nova Scotia.

Reciting a litany of knowledge about himself, Alisdair realized the words were not as reassuring as he wished. Something was missing, some great part of his life, like a black and shadowed void.

He lay flat, his legs straight, his toes pointed to the sky. A pose for his coffin, but even that thought was not as terrifying as the gaps in his knowledge.

"Get up!" a voice shouted, and people began to rouse around him.

A child cried and he winced at the sound, turning his head to see a woman raise herself up to shield her frightened child with her body. Above them stood the shrouded figure of a man. He drew back his boot and kicked again, but from here Alisdair couldn't see if the other man had struck the child or not.

"Didn't I tell you to get up?"

Alisdair felt his arms being jerked, and found himself being lifted by two men. He could stand, but the words to assure them of that fact wouldn't come. All at once he wasn't at all sure he could stand, let alone walk. But it didn't seem to matter, because he was being dragged like a dead weight between the two men.

He felt like a planed timber floating in the ocean. He was becoming waterlogged, sinking to the bottom of the sea, never to be found again.

Chapter 28

The journey to Cormech was swiftly done, the *Fortitude* speeding across Moray Firth to the port town in a matter of hours. The ship's sails were full and she seemed to skip over the water like a flattened stone.

Iseabal stood on the bow, in a position Alisdair had often taken, her arms folded behind her, feet apart to absorb the thrumming of the current below them. If the ocean was truly a goddess, then perhaps it was she who sped the *Fortitude* on, as desperate and as lonely for Alisdair as Iseabal.

Henrietta wound around her legs, and Iseabal bent to pick her up, feeling an odd comfort in rubbing her chin between the cat's ears.

The ruins of a castle greeted them from a nearby hill, not unlike the sight of Gilmuir itself. Only one tower remained of this place, a stark and lonely reminder of what had once been. There was so much destruction in this part of Scotland, ruins and deserted places that hinted at better times.

Unlike in London, they found easy docking. Iseabal was in a fever of impatience until the ropes were tied and the *Fortitude* berthed. She was the first off the ship, not waiting until the ramp was stabilized. Turning back impatiently, she saw Brian standing at the rail, speaking to another man. The sailor handed a pistol to Brian and he promptly tucked it beneath his vest.

She had the thought, as he joined her, that this past day had aged him. Perhaps she, also, had become older in appearance, bearing the signs of anger and grief on her face.

"Teams of four men will begin on each side of the harbor, mistress, while we visit the harbormaster."

Iseabal nodded, grateful that he had come up with some kind of plan. She'd not thought the harbor to be so large, but if necessary, they'd search all the ships here, and every port, every inlet, every dock in the entire world.

The visit to the harbormaster elicited the information that five ships were due to sail today, three had left yesterday, and a score more would sail tomorrow.

"It would help if we knew the destinations," Iseabal said.

"They may have already sailed, mistress," Brian cautioned, carefully averting his eyes.

Iseabal remained silent, unable to refute the young man's words since the thought had already occurred to her.

Brian walked beside her on the pier, two sailors whose names she had forgotten behind him. A woman and three men, not an untoward sight, except for her appearance, perhaps. Her eyes were gritty with unshed tears, and a night spent in prayers rather than sleep. Her feet felt leaden, and there was a fluttering in her stomach as if she trembled inside.

At the first vessel, Brian preceded her up the ramp. "Permission to come aboard," he called out. A weathered old man granted it with a nod.

Sailors milling about the deck stilled, watching them with interest. The ship was much older than the *Fortitude*, evident by her weathered rails and masts, but kept as neat as Alisdair's ship.

"I'm Iseabal MacRae," she said, stepping to Brian's side and addressing the man.

"And I'm Patrick Hanoran, the captain of the *Starling*," he countered, his brown eyes twinkling. He was not, she noted, as old as he had appeared at first sight. Although his beard was gray, his hair was only lightly touched with silver.

"Have you taken aboard any passengers since yesterday?" Brian asked.

"I've not," the captain said, his gaze trailing from the hem of Iseabal's petticoat to the collar of her jacket.

"I'm looking for my husband," she said frostily, irritated at his perusal.

"What makes you think I have him?" he asked, leaning nonchalantly against the rail.

"We think he's been sold into slavery," she said, the words so sharp they seemed to claw at her throat.

He straightened, folding his arms in front of his chest. "That's an insult you offer me, madam," he said stonily. "I'll carry powder for the English before I turn my ship into a slave trader."

"Do you know of one who might?" she asked, holding her breath at his answer. *The ship next to mine*, he might say. *Or the one down the pier.* Or he might even speak the words she feared, telling her that a ship had left this morning, carrying a cargo of human misery. Instead, he only shook his head.

"I've nothing to do with men like that," he said. "I trade tobacco and rum for wool," he added. "And that's all."

Moving away, he gave a series of orders to his men, effectively dismissing her.

Turning, she caught a glimpse of Brian's face, carefully expressionless. She had often looked the same in order to hide the truth of her feelings.

"He's here," she said, placing her hand on his arm. Perhaps the greatest act of courage might simply be voicing hope. "He's here," she said again, her voice strong and resolute.

Brian said nothing and she finally released his sleeve.

A bit of foolishness, perhaps, but she so wanted Alisdair to be within arm's reach that she could almost feel him nearby.

"You mustn't grieve for her, sir," the young chambermaid said. "She wouldn't want that at all."

James glanced over at her. For all her words, her eyes were bloodshot and her cheerfulness seemed forced. All of the servants at Brandidge Hall appeared similarly affected, as if the countess had not been simply an employer, but much beloved.

"She was an old lady, sir, and you and your brothers made these last days full of joy for her."

"Two days only," he said, wishing it had been more.

"An important two days," she said unexpectedly. "She died happy."

He waited until she left the library before directing his attention to his journal once again.

Patricia, Dowager Countess of Sherbourne, died in her sleep the night past. Surely Heaven will open its

gates to one such as she. She became a grandmother to
us all, gifting the MacRaes with a blessed sense of be-
longing in this strange land.

James laid down his quill, his attention directed to the
view. The desk he used sat before a large mullioned window,
and the vista revealed a misty dawn.

Brandidge Hall was a solemn place, as if peopled by
ghosts at this moment. Not a sound intruded, or a voice, and
if there were footsteps they were inaudible to his ears. He
might have been alone with only the fog for company.

Glancing down at the book in front of him, he began to
write again. The journal was the recipient of his most private
thoughts. In it he could distill to words the variety of his ex-
periences and thereby forever recall each minute. Sometimes, in rare moments like now, James wished that he might
be able to change the deed itself.

But as the chambermaid had said, Patricia was old, and
death comes more swiftly to the aged.

Their plans were to have left for London an hour ago, but
the news of Patricia's passing had altered their schedules.
They would attend the countess's funeral and only then return to their ship and to yet another distant destination, that
of Scotland and Gilmuir.

They had made their way to five ships, but on each one the
sailors had denied knowing of Alisdair's whereabouts.

"They won't tell us anything," Iseabal said as they walked
up the ramp to the next ship.

"Sailors are notoriously closemouthed," Brian replied.
"They won't tell tales, but they might slip a word or two at a
tavern."

She glanced at him. "Do you think it would be worth our while to seek out the nearest tavern?"

"Only if you remain aboard the *Fortitude*. Such a place is not for you, mistress."

She frowned at him, but decided that she would argue with him later. For now, Iseabal stood to the side as Brian addressed the sailor at the railing.

"I've no knowledge of the man you seek. The captain's ashore and you'll have to speak with him."

"Where?" Brian asked.

"I'll not be telling the captain's business," the man replied. "It's worth the skin on my back."

Iseabal and the three men turned to make their way back down the gangplank when she abruptly stopped, halted by a sound. The faint mewling of a kitten. Or an infant.

"Did you hear something, Brian?" she asked, glancing back at the ship.

"Yes," he said, nodding. "A child."

After making their way back on deck, Brian faced down the other man.

"How is it that there's a child aboard when you said you'd taken on no passengers?"

The sailor didn't answer, choosing instead to stare at them stonily.

"Give me your pistol, Brian," Iseabal said, holding out her hand.

When Brian only glanced at her, Iseabal snapped her fingers in a rude gesture, impatient for the gun. Grudgingly, he handed it to her, perhaps knowing that she had gone beyond morality and good judgment.

The pistol was heavier than she expected. Using two hands, she leveled the barrel at the stubborn sailor.

"Show me how to shoot it," she said. Brian whispered to her of powder pans and tinder. The barrel wavered, then steadied as she began to follow his instructions.

"It's just a group of Scots," the man said, backing away. "Wanting to make another start for themselves somewhere new."

Iseabal followed the sailor with the barrel.

"Did they come of their own accord?" she asked.

"I don't know," he said, evidently beginning to understand that she had no hesitation in using the weapon. Stepping back against the rail, he gestured with one hand toward the hold. "Look for yourself."

"We shall," Iseabal said, giving the pistol to one of the sailors from the *Fortitude*. "Shoot him if he moves," she ordered. Apparently, there was something of Magnus Drummond in her after all, enough cruelty to render her dangerous.

Brian climbed down the ladder first, Iseabal following. The hold of the ship was a dark and dank place, but it didn't take long for them to realize that it was also full. Not with barrels of provisions or crates of marketable goods, but with a living cargo, people huddling together against the curve of the hull.

"I'll go fetch a lantern," Brian said, the horror in his voice a mirror of her own thoughts.

"We mean you no harm," Iseabal said in his absence. Not one voice answered her, as if they knew she was the daughter of the man who'd ordered this done to them.

Brian returned, lifting a lantern. The faint light barely penetrated the shadows of the hold, but gave enough illumination to view the faces of the people staring back at her. A white-faced woman held her infant to her chest while her husband sat beside her, one arm around her shoulders, the other pulling an older child back as if to shield the boy.

Children sobbed, frightened, while the adults stared up at Iseabal with dispassionate eyes devoid of hope.

Brian walked ahead, making his way to the end of the hold, lantern held high.

"We're looking for a man," she said. "A man named Alisdair MacRae. He might have aided you yesterday. Have you seen him?"

Again only silence answered her.

"Here," Brian called out, raising his arm as he knelt beside a figure.

Iseabal felt as if her heart stopped, then started again. For a moment she couldn't move; then hope surged through her like Gilmuir's fierce winds.

Carefully avoiding outstretched arms and extended legs, Iseabal made her way to Brian's side. For a moment she didn't recognize Alisdair, he was so covered in blood. She knelt beside him, placing one hand against his shirt. Staring at his bloody face and matted hair, she would have thought him dead except for the rise and fall of his chest beneath her palm.

A child whimpered and she heard the sound from a distance. A man spoke and she noted his voice but not his words. The edges of her vision went gray as her eyes filmed with tears.

Something broke within her. The wall of her courage, quickly erected, was no defense against this abrupt, poignant joy. Tears slipped soundlessly down her cheeks, bathing her face in a baptism of gratitude.

"Alisdair," she whispered, his name sounding like a prayer in this dimly lit hell.

Brian handed her the lantern, moving to place his arms around Alisdair's shoulders.

"He's been in and out," a man lying at his side said. "We half dragged him here," he added, leaning back against the curved timbers.

"Who did this to him?" Brian asked, kneeling at Alisdair's side.

"My father," Iseabal said, feeling a strange sense of desolation as she spoke. The confession seemed to alter Brian. His shoulders stiffened and his wary gaze was fixed on her as if she were a stranger.

"Your father?" he asked tightly.

"Magnus Drummond," she admitted, fingering the placket of Alisdair's shirt.

"I'll go and fetch the other men," Brian said, lowering Alisdair carefully to the floor of the hold.

She watched him leave, heard the murmurs as people began looking in her direction. Her identity spread among those huddled in the hold, repeated until it was a dark whisper.

Iseabal had never felt so hated.

She wanted to explain to them, to offer excuses not for her father's behavior, but for her own. For not knowing the depth of his perfidy, for not suspecting that he would be capable of imprisoning children, of selling whole families into slavery.

A little girl smiled, unaware of the hatred directed Iseabal's way. The mother grabbed her daughter, cradling the child, a gesture of repudiation as telling as a slap.

Alisdair moaned, and Iseabal leaned forward, moving her hand from his face to gently touch his bloodied cheek.

He opened his eyes, wincing at the glare from the lantern.

"It's all right. We'll soon have you out of here."

After that? Iseabal realized she didn't know.

A litter, little more than a bit of canvas tied between two ropes, was devised to raise Alisdair from the hold. As the sailors from the *Fortitude* carefully lifted him, Iseabal looked down into the shadowed interior, gloomy even in the bright noon sun, and realized that she could not leave the others behind.

"How much did you pay Drummond for those people?" she asked the first mate.

"You'll have to talk to the captain about that," he said, surly now that she had no pistol aimed at him.

Nodding, she motioned for the others to follow. Once off the ship, Iseabal turned to Brian. "Find the captain and pay him whatever he wants for his cargo," she said. "We'll take those poor people back to Gilmuir with us."

He merely nodded in return, leaving her side as if he could not wait to be gone from her.

Fergus MacRae was determined that this would be the last of it. Smith or no, he'd find another way to make a living besides placing chains on his countrymen.

Reluctantly, he made his way to his ship and his new commission, passing a littered figure carried by two men. A woman walked at their side, her face wet with tears.

Turning, Fergus glanced after them, uncertain as to what he had truly seen. The recognition had been instant, but he had to be mistaken.

He began to follow them, coming abreast of the litter once again. Staring at the woman, Fergus felt as if he were in the midst of a dream. She bore the same features as the woman he loved, and the same shade of hair. This stranger might well have been his Leah at the time of their parting years ago.

A young man grabbed his arm, stopping him.

"Why are you following them?" he asked.

Fergus brushed him off easily, regarding the man with all the harshness of thirty years of unrequited dreams.

"Who is she?" he asked curtly. The woman had had the face of his beloved. Leah, of the subtle smiles and the gentle heart.

"Who would you be and why would you be wanting to know?"

"I know her," Fergus said, then realized how foolish that was. Of course he didn't know her. She was too young to be Leah. "Who is she?" he asked again, unwilling to give this man the secret of his heart.

"A Drummond," the younger man said curtly. "Married to a MacRae of Gilmuir."

"There are no MacRaes at Gilmuir."

"There are now, despite Magnus Drummond's efforts." The other man turned and strode away in the opposite direction, leaving Fergus staring after him.

Chapter 29

Alisdair was carried aboard the *Fortitude*, the crew left aboard ship moving to the rail to greet him. A flag was quickly raised to alert the crew members searching the other ships in the harbor. Men began racing back, the sound of their boots on the wooden pier like the far-off rumbling of thunder.

One by one, each man fell silent, noting the captain's condition. Iseabal walked beside Alisdair, her hand resting close enough that her fingers felt the warmth of his body. Proof that he still lived.

A funereal silence followed them as they moved across the deck. More than one man took off his cap, clutching it in his hands. Iseabal stopped, spoke to a man she recognized.

"Brian will be coming shortly," she said, willing her voice to remain even. "We're bringing the rest of villagers home with us." Speech had flown from her, those two clipped sentences the extent of her ability to communicate.

Her father had done this to Alisdair. She was ashamed of her birth, in a way she'd never before felt. Drummond's blood flowed in her veins. His capacity for cruelty lurked in her very nature, and because of her father's actions, she'd almost lost the man she loved.

"I'll tell the others," he said, his voice sounding too kind. She didn't think she could bear kindness at the moment.

Rory stood at the doorway to Alisdair's cabin, holding the door open wordlessly. The room was shrouded in silence and darkness, neither of which was comforting. Not once in all those times climbing the rigging had she seen the cabin boy afraid. But now he looked frightened and incredibly young.

"His wounds need to be treated," she said as the sailors brought Alisdair into the cabin. "Will you help me?"

Rory nodded, his gaze still fixed on his captain. As the sailors began to move him to the bunk, Alisdair groaned. Entering the cabin, Iseabal stood behind the men, wishing that she could ease any pain he might be feeling.

Finally, he was placed on the bed, the white sheets a stark contrast to his bloodied face.

She nodded her thanks to the sailors, knelt beside Alisdair, and impatiently brushed her tears away. Her weeping would do Alisdair no good and could not ease the situation.

Glancing behind her, Iseabal realized that Rory had left. Just beyond the open door, however, the crewmen were gathering in silence.

Iseabal went to Alisdair's chest, removing the Chinese jars. From the third door she retrieved the poppy juice and put all three containers on the floor in front of the bunk. Another drawer yielded a stack of toweling, that she began to tear into squares.

Rory entered the room a few moments later bearing a ewer filled with warm water, carefully placing it on the floor next to the jars. Standing, he manfully waited for his next order.

What needed to be done? Each man's gaze was directed either to Alisdair or to her. And she, the one they looked to with such hope in their eyes, was filled with mind-numbing fear. If she were capable of giving them a miracle, she'd say another prayer and Alisdair would sit up, rub his palms over his face, and smile with his usual morning greeting. But he remained motionless on the bunk, so still and quiet that his pose mimicked death.

"He needs to be undressed," she said, considering her words. "So that we can check for other injuries. If you will remove his clothing, then I shall see to the wound on his head."

A plan, then. Something to keep her mind and hands occupied.

"Daniel says a sick man never dies at sea, mistress," Rory said, his voice too young for this place and these circumstances. "Only when he reaches port."

"I'll have no more of Daniel's idiocies repeated in this room." Iseabal said curtly, pushing up her sleeves. "He's Alisdair MacRae and he isn't going to die."

Kneeling at his side, Iseabal began to bathe his face carefully, cleaning it of blood. Only then did she begin on his wound. The depth of it would reveal whether or not Alisdair would gain his senses or would fall into a deep sleep, never to awake again.

Once his hair was clean, her fingers trailed gently over the edges of the wound. Although the gash was long, it did not appear deep, as if something had grazed his scalp. Perhaps he had truly been shot.

"Will he be all right?" Rory asked.

She glanced over at him, only now realizing that Alisdair's boots and breeches had been removed.

"The sooner he wakes completely, the better a sign it will be." And when he awoke, hopefully, he would recognize her and his circumstances, but that was a thought she kept to herself.

Rory nodded, satisfied for the moment.

Removing the stopper from the tallest of the vials, Iseabal poured a little of the yellow liquid onto her fingers. Gently she applied it to Alisdair's wound, hoping that the Chinese medicine had the same healing effect on him as it had had on her.

Her eyes watered from the contents of the next vial, but she coated the wound without hesitation. She worried about the poppy juice, deciding to give it to him only if he awoke in pain.

Rory came beside her, beginning to remove Alisdair's shirt. Setting the container of poppy juice down, she began to help him.

"I'm thinking I'd be better off burning that instead of trying to clean it," Rory said, staring down at the bloodstained shirt.

A profligate gesture, but one of which she approved.

"He's not been stabbed, mistress," the boy said, a conclusion she'd reached as well. "And other than this bruising about his arms, there's not a mark on him."

Then there was only the head wound to concern her.

She couldn't leave him naked, Iseabal decided, standing and retrieving the nightshirt from the tansu. Her hands wrapped around the soft fabric, warming it. There were so many memories associated with this garment. The first time he'd treated her and every night thereafter, the morning after their wedding.

As they dressed Alisdair, Iseabal's thoughts were errant and half formed. Was there anything she'd neglected to do? What should she do now? Nothing further came to her mind. Time itself would have to do the healing. Tenderly she touched his cheek, felt the stubbly growth of beard. Her palm cradled his face, her thumb lightly stroking his bottom lip.

"All we can do now, Rory, is wait."

Rory nodded, picked up the pitcher, and left the cabin.

She turned, glancing at the doorway, where the sailors still crowded, watching their captain. Each face was somber, eyes filled with worry. Alisdair was not only respected, he was well loved.

"How is he?" Brian asked, gripping Rory's arm after he left the cabin.

"He has a wound to his head, but that seems to be all," Rory said.

A smile began to dawn on Brian's face, the expression sent as fast as a thought across the ship. Iseabal wanted to reach out one hand and capture it, to caution him that such optimism might be unwarranted. But his quick glance toward her left Iseabal no doubt that he would refute any of her words. An hour ago he had been her companion. Now he watched her almost suspiciously.

"He is still very weak," Rory admitted.

"But you think he will survive," Brian said, less a question than a request for reassurance.

"Yes, I think he will," Rory said, glancing back at Iseabal. Brian nodded in her direction, a wordless acknowledgment of her presence. He said something she couldn't hear to Rory, and the boy swiftly turned to look at her, anger in his gaze. Another link in a chain her father had forged.

Iseabal stood, walked to the door, and slowly closed it, blocking out derisive looks and whispered disdain.

She watched Alisdair sleep, imprinting his face in her memory. His jaw was stubborn, his lashes long and black, his cheekbones seeming to point the way to a mouth made for a thousand expressions and a hundred types of kisses. A man of great attractiveness, made even more so by his character.

Iseabal trailed a finger around the rim of the basin, chasing a water droplet, immersed in thoughts of what might have been. If their lives had been different, he would have been her companion in youth. They might have raced together through the glens or explored the forests. She would have shown him her necklace of blue rocks, the treasure she'd found at Gilmuir. And he, as youthful laird, would have granted her the jewelry as a gift for loving the fortress as he did.

Perhaps one day their affection might have changed, become something greater, deeper.

Now, however, anything they might have begun to feel for each other was submerged beneath the truth of their lives. Alisdair was a man of principle and she was Drummond's daughter.

Laying her head against her arm, she closed her eyes, listening to the soft sound of Alisdair's breathing. The afternoon waned into evening, the lap of the sea as it cradled the *Fortitude* on her voyage almost lulling. But Iseabal remained awake, her fingers resting on Alisdair's wrist, warming him with her touch and guarding him with her presence.

Loving Alisdair had made her feel invincible. Losing him would be like death.

*   *   *

"I don't see why I have to stay behind," Douglas complained, watching the MacRae ship sail away from London.

"It's because you're the youngest," Daniel said matter-of-
factly. "The youngest always gets the short shrift. Or," he
added, eyeing the boy, "they're spoiled. Given too much."

Douglas clasped both fists on his hips and stared at
Daniel. "You'll not be calling me spoiled, Daniel," he said.
"I'm a MacRae, whatever my age."

The boy had a way to go before knowing as much as he
bragged he did, Daniel thought. As to why his brothers had
left him behind in his care, the older man had only an inkling.
Perhaps they had wanted their youngest brother to obtain
some additional experience in seafaring. Or it could be that
Douglas was growing tiresome and it was either leave him
with Daniel or throw him overboard in disgust.

Daniel stifled his smile, thinking that it wouldn't be wise
to let the young man know how amused he was. Douglas was
just like a MacRae, part and parcel of the entire clan. Stubborn, and more than a little proud, despite his years and his
lack of knowledge.

But he would learn, Daniel thought, as long as he wasn't
allowed to get the upper hand.

"It will be weeks before I see Scotland," Douglas said in
disgust.

"Not that long," Daniel said, checking his manifest. "And
you can make the journey speedier still," he added, glancing
at Douglas.

"How?"

"By being my clerk," Daniel said, ruffling the boy's hair.
Douglas pulled away, his chest puffing up like a banty

rooster. "I'm going to be the captain of my own ship," he boasted. "Not a clerk."

"They're sometimes one and the same." Daniel made no effort now to mask his smile. "Who do you think guarantees the contents of a ship's hold? And whose word is taken when a cargo is given to a ship? And who is to blame for as much as a handful of tea missing?"

When Douglas didn't answer, Daniel handed him a sheet of the manifest. "The captain, that's who. On this voyage I'm acting in your brother's stead, and I'll not have any mutiny from you, Douglas."

Douglas looked rebellious, but he took the sheet nonetheless.

"It's better than being a cabin boy," he muttered.

"You might not think that at the end of the day," Daniel said, nodding in the direction of the adjacent pier. "There are over a hundred barrels to check, and that's before the wagons arrive tomorrow.

"Harness your irritation, Douglas," he said, hoping that the young man had the sense to take his advice. "Use your energy to begin to count the crates and casks before they're loaded aboard ship. It's a chore better done here than in the hold."

Daniel watched as the youngest of the MacRae brothers stomped across the deck and down the gangplank in a display of temper.

Exactly, Daniel thought, like one of the MacRaes.

He was, perhaps, a fool, Fergus MacRae told himself. This journey to Gilmuir would, no doubt, result in a blistered stump and aching arms. Because of the distance, he had tucked his cane into the pack slung over his shoulder and used a crutch he'd made himself of three pieces of wood bound together. He'd welded the middle of it with an iron bar, and padded the top with a bit of worn cloth. He'd not made the cushioning thick enough, he realized as the top of the crutch began gouging into his armpit.

Who was the woman he'd seen in Cormech? Was it possible that there were, after all these years, MacRaes at Gilmuir?

Best leave the wishes to others, Fergus, he counseled himself. Life was hard enough dealing with the why of it without asking for more grief.

But wouldn't it be a grand thing to walk back to his home and see, not the English squatting there, but the sight of his kinsmen? The loneliness had not been easy to bear, ladled on top of the loss of Leah. He'd like to find just one person still alive who had known him as a boy. Who might even say to him with a teasing wink, *What a clumsy oaf you were, Fergus.*

Memories flooded his mind, of times racing in the sun with his brother or trying to rid himself of his bedeviling younger sister, of picking harebells for Leah and sliding them beneath her chin to tickle her throat. Now these recollections seemed doubly precious, since all the people he had loved the best had been lost to him. Leah, because of his pride. His brother, James, at his side at Culloden, and Leitis, vanishing as she had all those many years ago.

Resolutely, he picked up his pace, forcing himself to cover the distance he'd allotted for each day. Such was the way he'd lived his life in these past years, by choosing one goal and achieving it, ignoring all the setbacks and the naysayers. Fixing his gaze on a spot on the horizon, he vowed to reach it before nightfall.

One thought pushed him forward. He was going home to Gilmuir.

Chapter 30

Alisdair awoke gradually, sleep falling away like layers of wispy clouds. For a few moments he lay in his bunk, staring up at the wood-grain pattern above him, taking a careful bodily inventory.

He moved his head from side to side, relieved to find there was only a dull ache where before a thousand anvils had rung against his skull. Carefully, he sat up, dangling his feet over the side of the bunk, surprised, then amused, to find himself attired in the voluminous red nightshirt.

"You'll wear it, Alisdair. Nights are cold aboard ship."

"Thank you, Mother," he'd said politely, taking the wrapped garment from her. He'd store it in his chest, as he did all the others.

"He'd be better off finding a mermaid to companion him," one of his brothers said.

Leitis MacRae had arched one eyebrow and the room had

fallen silent. Grown men all, they were easily chastised by their mother.

All thoughts of his family vanished when he saw Iseabal huddled on a pallet in the corner of the cabin. He'd slept in a similar position many nights at the beginning of their marriage and could attest to the discomfort.

Why, then, had she chosen not to sleep beside him?

"Iseabal," he said softly. She woke easily, her eyes blinking open to meet his gaze.

He raised his hand, surprised to find that it trembled in the air. Two short steps and she'd captured it between her own, placing her cheek gently against his palm.

"What happened?" he asked gruffly. Why did his throat taste of fire and his arms and sides hurt? As if he'd been kicked by a horse, he thought, or dragged across Scotland.

Once, he'd seen a French privateer attack an English merchant ship, her cannons firing from bow to stern in a regulated barrage. That was how his memories came to him, each giving Alisdair back a piece of himself.

The stench of fire, the caustic smell of thatch burning, the whimpers of children, were only a backdrop for the image of a face, disdainful and mocking.

"We're at Gilmuir," Iseabal said. "Aboard the *Fortitude*."

Bending down, she brushed a kiss to the back of his hand, a warm tear anointing his skin.

"I'm fine," he said in an attempt to reassure her. She merely smiled again, placing her cheek against his cradled hand as if she recognized the shallowness of his bravado. He felt incredibly weak, as if he were a newborn babe and innocent to the world.

"How long have I been asleep?"

"A few days," she said, reaching up to cup his bearded cheek.

He stared at her. "A few days?" he echoed.

"You needed the time to heal," she explained. "Your eyes are clearer," she added, "and you don't look so pale." Reaching up, she brushed her hand over his brow, sweeping his hair away from his face. Her skin smelled of herbs and sandalwood.

"You used the Chinese medicines."

"Yes," she softly said. "Do you feel any better?"

"I feel as if I've been kicked by ten horses," he answered. Looking down at the nightshirt he wore, Alisdair began to smile. "Do I also have you to thank for this?"

Her cheeks deepened in color, as if she were sharing his thoughts and his pleasant memories of this particular garment. Iseabal, in the morning after their wedding night, bathed by sunlight as she sat there smiling at him and nibbling on her toast. Iseabal, defiant and attempting to hide it while he treated her ribs and then covered her body before temptation loosed him from simple lust to unacceptable behavior.

"Brian's left word that he would like to see you as soon as you are awake. Do you feel strong enough?" she asked, her voice low and oddly seductive. A siren's voice, he thought, raising his eyes to meet her gaze.

Alisdair nodded to cover his sudden wish to touch her with hands that retained memory of her curves and lips that knew the flavor of her kisses. Perhaps he felt like this because death had come so close to him, and this was a way to celebrate his life. Or perhaps it was simply Iseabal.

Amused at himself, he crossed his legs and placed his hands on his lap in a nonchalant attempt to hide her effect on him.

"Not before I wash and dress," he said, determined that none of his men would see him in his nightshirt.

"I'll send Rory to you," she said, standing and slipping from the room before he could stop her.

A few minutes later Rory appeared in the doorway. The boy halted there, a tray balanced on one hand, his attention fixed on Alisdair.

"I knew you would come to yourself, sir," Rory said, entering the cabin. "I've fetched your breakfast," the boy added with a grin. "Are you up to eating?"

Surprisingly, he was hungry. No, Alisdair thought as he sat at the table, he was famished and could cheerfully eat the tray Rory was unloading.

Once the dishes were arranged, Rory set the pitcher aside as he opened a door in the tansu. Retrieving a turtle-shaped jar that held Alisdair's sandalwood soap, he placed it beside the pitcher, basin, and toweling.

"Can I do anything else for you, sir?"

"Send word to Brian that I'll meet with him in an hour."

Rory nodded and began to leave, turning at the last moment to smile at Alisdair. The expression was so engaging that he had no choice but to smile back at his cabin boy.

"Get dressed, you drunken fool!"

Thomas's first reaction to being shaken awake was to pummel the man whose hand was on his shoulder. His second, more cautious approach was to slit open one eye and then quickly sit up, facing Magnus Drummond.

"You stink of ale, Thomas. Proud of your night's work, are you?"

He nodded, peering through the fog of sleep. Drummond's bloodshot eyes narrowed at him as he yawned.

Drummond looked as if he'd not slept the night, either, Thomas thought, but he doubted his cousin had been engaged in such enjoyable pursuits. The older man's clothes were wrinkled and dusty, his face shadowed by a stubble of beard. Even his hair was askew, and Magnus liked a neat and tidy appearance.

"Where is he?" the older man asked, his face florid. "Where is MacRae?"

Thomas narrowed his eyes. "How did you know I had him?"

"Never mind that," Drummond said. "Where is he?"

"With the other villagers," Thomas said, standing and stretching. The night before had been one of revelry, such as Cormech offered. He'd been treated to more than one glass of ale by the captain of the *Harriet*, and had celebrated in another way with one of the barmaids.

"I want him killed," Drummond said. "And his body taken to Fernleigh for proof."

"Do you want to discuss this here?" Thomas asked cautiously, glancing around the attic space. The inn was full, and this chamber currently shared with five other sleeping men.

"Where is he?" Drummond demanded, obviously uncaring that his orders were overheard.

Thomas began to fasten his breeches, thinking that he'd never seen the other man so worked up about anything, unless it was the loss of a coin or two. "Aboard the *Harriet*," he said, pulling on his boots. "And it's a lucky thing you've come now," he added. "She's due to sail today."

"Nothing's been lucky in my life since the MacRae arrived in Scotland," Drummond said with a scowl.

Thomas walked with his cousin to the ship, explaining how MacRae had come to be in his possession.

"You should have killed him," Drummond said angrily.

"Why should I, Magnus?" he asked, facing him squarely. Behind him, the dawn sun glinted off the waters of Cormech, illuminating the ships lined up at the pier like greedy nurslings. "I sold him instead and made you richer. He'll never return to Scotland. Instead, he'll be working at hard labor for the rest of his life. If he survives the voyage."

Drummond nodded grudgingly. "I suppose I'd have done the same."

Thomas led him aboard the *Harriet*, introducing him to the captain.

"Drummond wants one of your passengers," Thomas said, exchanging smiles of greeting. "One you took aboard yesterday."

"Feel free to search the hold," the captain said, "but you won't find him there. You won't find anyone there."

"Where are they?" Thomas said, suddenly aware that Drummond had taken a step away from him. At no time was it wise to be on the man's long list of enemies. In Magnus's current mood, it was dangerous. "We delivered and you paid," he said. "Seventeen men, women, and children."

"Gone," the captain said. "And me compensated prettily for them, too."

"Where?" Drummond asked, looking as if he'd eaten a breakfast of nails.

"I don't know," the captain said, "and I don't care, unless you want to sell them back to me. I'm looking for another cargo." He smiled, the expression seeming to annoy Drummond further.

"I heard them talk," the first mate interjected. "They're going to a place called Gilmuir."

Drummond nodded, as if the news had been what he'd expected.

"A woman freed him," he said, the statement verified when the first mate nodded.

"A nasty piece of work," the sailor added, scowling. "Someone should take her by the hand and teach her how to behave."

"Someone will," Drummond said, his mouth thinning. He turned and walked off the ship, leaving Thomas to follow him.

"Once the Drummonds fought the MacRaes," he said. "But there's not been discord between us for decades. It's time that changed. The MacRaes have their footprints all over my life and I'm done with it."

"What are you going to do?" Thomas asked, grateful that Drummond's anger was directed at someone else.

"Lay siege to Gilmuir," Drummond said, smiling.

Thomas halted, staring at his cousin. Had the man lost his mind? From the gleam in his reddened eyes, it was almost possible to believe it.

"We've not enough men to lay siege to Gilmuir," Thomas said, wondering if he took his life in his hands telling Drummond the truth. "Especially if he has the villagers on his side."

"Then hire them for me," Drummond replied, surprising Thomas. "I'll see MacRae die on his precious land." He stared out to sea in the direction of Gilmuir. "My daughter will be made a widow, Thomas, and ripe for marriage once again. I'll give her to you as a reward for your loyalty."

"You would marry Iseabal to me?" he asked, startled.

"What better man?" Drummond said, turning to grin at him, his expression oddly malevolent.

* * *

Dressing was not done as quickly as Alisdair wished. From time to time dizziness threatened to topple him, forcing him to flatten his hands against the bulkhead in order to maintain his stability. He sincerely hoped that the headaches and this unwelcome disorientation were not permanent reminders of how close he had come to death.

He dismissed that thought before it could take root, fastened his shirt, and slipped into his boots.

Annoyed at his own weakness, he called out a gruff greeting when someone knocked on the door.

Brian stood on the threshold, his smile stretching from ear to ear and his hazel eyes alight with happiness.

"It's good to see you up and about, sir," he said, looking more like an enthusiastic boy than a young man promoted to a position of authority.

Alisdair was doubly grateful that Brian had not been present fifteen minutes earlier, when he'd struggled to maintain his equilibrium while donning his shirt. Buttons were a chore, and pulling his boots on had been likewise as difficult.

"I'm grateful to be up," he said, voicing the truth. If the bullet had been an inch deeper, he'd be buried by now.

"We've moved to Gilmuir, sir," Brian said, "and are in the process of building temporary shelter."

Iseabal entered through the opened door quietly, but Brian turned at her entrance. In a second his face changed, becoming more severe, almost taut. As if, Alisdair thought, he'd suddenly become a statue.

"For the people of Lonvight," Iseabal explained, moving to Alisdair's side. "Where you were hurt."

"Is the village intact?"

"Lonvight?" Brian asked. "Burned to the ground, sir." He

did not, Alisdair noted, look in Iseabal's direction. Nor did she look at him.

"Not Lonvight," Alisdair said impatiently. "The old village of Gilmuir."

"Yes," she said softly. "The village still stands. And large enough to accommodate all the people of Lonvight," she added, glancing toward the door.

"Why will neither of you look at the other?" Alisdair asked, annoyed at their behavior.

Brian stood rigid, looking at the bulkhead in front of him, while Iseabal said nothing, only smiled gently as if to dissuade Alisdair from further questioning.

"At the end of the land bridge there's a path to the left. It's overgrown, but you can find it if you're looking. Follow it and you'll come to the village," Iseabal said, concentrating on the view of the cliffs beyond the rail.

"I'll see to the state of the old village," Brian said, bowing slightly. "Unless you wish me to perform some other duty, sir."

Alisdair stared at the young man, seeing in his eyes a flat, obsidian look that warned he'd get no response to his original question.

"No," he said, waving him away. "Do what you will."

The door closed softly behind Brian, leaving the two of them alone.

"Well?" Alisdair asked. "Are you going to remain mute also?"

"There isn't anything to say," Iseabal replied easily, beginning to tidy up after his bathing and dressing. She smiled at him, a closed and bland expression no doubt meant to be amiable.

Alisdair realized that he'd seen that expression on her face before, when she'd greeted her father.

*   *   *

He was looking at her as if he'd never truly seen her. That studied glance seemed all the more intent for his stillness.

What could she say to him? The truth? Stark and un-adorned, it would strip her of all defenses, just when she needed them the most.

My father did this to you. There, the crux of the matter. And she, as a Drummond, was anathema to his crew. The past days had proved that well enough. When she ventured outside the cabin, she was greeted by silence and distrustful looks. Rory acted as grudging intermediary, passing along news of Alis-dair's condition to Brian and relaying word of the plans to leave the *Fortitude* and begin building the settlement at Gilmuir to Iseabal. Only Rory had remained aboard the *Fortitude* now and she'd managed, until this moment, to ignore Brian's antipathy.

She bent, picking up the empty pitcher in the awkward si-lence. They might never have been intimate or loving; the nights in this cabin could have been no more than a wistful dream.

"Iseabal," he said, holding out his hand. A small smile played around his lips as if he coaxed her to confidence.

Speaking would only lead to unfriendly truths.

Moving toward the door, she stared at the pattern of wood rather than look back at him.

"You should rest," she said. "You mustn't tax yourself too soon."

"I've rested enough."

As she opened the cabin door, she heard him get up from the bunk.

"Iseabal." His hands were suddenly on her shoulders, his cheek placed against the braid of her hair. A warrior's body pressed against her, warming and promising.

Iseabal opened the door before he could turn her, before they kissed, before a dozen cautions went flying from her mind.

"Rest," she said, slipping from his grip and escaping.

Chapter 31

"You cannot expect me to keep feeding all of them," the cook said, waving his wooden spoon in the air. His voice was raised, his cheeks pink with emotion, but Alisdair noted that his eyes were sparkling with excitement.

"Only you could accomplish such a feat, William," he said tactfully. "And not for just now," he added, certain that the cook understood the demands on his time. "We'll need your services until the village can be repaired."

"I'll be feeding hundreds!"

Not quite hundreds, he thought. Merely forty-two, in addition to the twenty crewmen of the *Fortitude* who had chosen to live at Gilmuir. But he wisely remained silent, allowing William to express his displeasure along with his secret delight.

The cook was French and took great pleasure in his tantrums. William had been angry all day, throwing implements down on the ground and then, when no one would continue to pick them up, resorting to rocks. The best way to calm him was to simply listen, and agree with William that he was the most maligned and underappreciated member of the crew.

"I should go back to Nova Scotia," William said, but his voice was not quite so loud now, and his sideways glance was more testing than threatening.

"I, for one, am grateful that you're not leaving," Alisdair said. "Who else could handle such a monumental task?"

"No one here," William said, looking around him. Three of the crewmen had been pressed into service to assist him, and although their intentions were good, they had as much expertise in the kitchen as Alisdair had with needlework.

"I guess I must stay," William conceded grudgingly. The wooden spoon tapping against the palm of his hand seemed to measure the beat of his words. "If I don't, you'll all starve."

Alisdair smiled, reaching out to grasp the other man's shoulder. "I appreciate your loyalty, William."

The cook nodded, beginning to shout orders to his helpers for the noon meal.

Turning, Alisdair discovered Brian standing beside him. Nodding to the young man, he walked briskly away in case William should change his mind and voice yet another complaint.

The two men halted in the courtyard as Alisdair glanced around, surveying the activity.

The land bridge was a thoroughfare of constant motion, the villagers of Lonvight crossing back and forth from Gilmuir to their new homes. Building materials were being shared, and the old village was being refurbished by shoring up sagging roofs or repairing holes in the mortar.

The crew of the *Fortitude* was occupied in building a structure on the site of the old fort to house those men remaining at Gilmuir. A more private, and smaller, cottage would be his and Iseabal's home until Gilmuir was rebuilt.

If she ever consented to leave the *Fortitude*.

"Are there any more problems that need to be addressed?" he asked.

"Only that a certain wife in the village is positive her husband is lusting after another woman, but I expect that's a conundrum they will have to figure out themselves."

Alisdair raised an eyebrow, effectively smothering Brian's smile. He had his own marital discord to deal with, and it was not a humorous subject.

He left Brian then, taking the staircase to the cove. He was forced to wait for several minutes as the crew from the *Molly Brown* lifted another enormous barrel up the staircase. The task, cumbersome and time-consuming, was nevertheless faster than dragging the heavy casks overland behind two horses.

The cove was peaceful today, aglow in sunlight and with few currents. Alisdair tied the skiff to the side of the *Fortitude*, climbed aboard easily. Except for his healing wound, he might not have suffered any effects of nearly being killed. In his memories, however, he could not quite forget the moment or the man.

Standing on deck, he felt caught up by another type of recollection. He'd manned this ship on voyages across oceans, to countries both alien and enthralling. He'd stood at the bow railing wondering what tomorrow might bring. In that very same place, he'd prayed at times, to be delivered from a merciless gale, or for the wisdom to steer them around typhoons.

Could he give it up so easily? Change his home from the sloping deck of his ship to the solid grandeur of Gilmuir? Surprisingly, yes. His travels had been right for a young man eager to explore and make his way in the world. Now, however, he was prepared to build. Not only Gilmuir, but the foundations of what would be the rest of his life.

The faint sound of stone hitting the bulkhead alerted Alisdair. The noise came again and he followed it, circling the cabin and heading toward the stern. Iseabal sat on a chair, her attention directed at the block of marble in front of her.

Tapping on the mallet, Iseabal sliced through the marble as if it were a loaf of newly baked bread, the ringing sound of the chisel against stone ricocheting against the cliff walls. A shard flew against the bulkhead, falling unheeded to the deck.

A face was emerging from the ebony stone, a chin only partly chiseled, a nose jutting out imperiously. Recognizing himself in the brow not yet fully formed, and in the shape of the head, Alisdair felt a surge of embarrassment.

"Do you not need to measure me in some way?" he asked a moment later. "The length of my nose, perhaps? My chin?"

She turned, dropping the mallet, and stared at him.

"I know your face well." A simple statement, made as one would speak of the day, the moment, the climate. A wary response, carrying no emotion at all.

He studied her, wondering what she would say if he spoke his thoughts. He, too, knew her face well. She was a woman possessed of average features. Her nose was unremarkable, her cheekbones slightly higher than normal. Her mouth was not distinctive in any way, save that the lower lip was slightly fuller than the upper. There was nothing of her face that people might remark upon or marvel at. Her eyes were green, but not so vibrant that they caused comment. Yet, average in each of her parts, she was nevertheless exquisitely beautiful assembled.

Leaning against the corner, his hands tucked behind him, Alisdair watched her. The afternoon sun brought color to her face, tinting her cheeks a delicate rose. She'd tied back her hair with a ribbon to match her pale blue jacket.

The longer he was married to her, Alisdair thought wryly, the more beautiful she became, as if her character altered her appearance somehow. Or perhaps it was simply that he could see her more clearly the better he knew her.

"You should have come to Gilmuir," he softly said.

She said nothing, no demurral or teasing response. Simply nothing, like the Iseabal she'd once been, silent, watchful, and eternally cautious.

For days she'd been oddly distant, treating him in the same blandly compassionate way she would a stranger. Gone was the easy camaraderie they were beginning to build together, and in its place was an awkwardness he'd not felt since the beginning of their marriage. She guarded her thoughts well, holding them inside so tightly that he'd no inkling of them.

"I wished to work," she said, addressing her tools. Slowly and carefully, she arranged her chisels in a neat pattern of militaristic rows.

"It takes a great deal of your time lately, Iseabal."

She glanced at him then, the worry in her eyes disturbing him. He knew there were words she did not speak and emotions she chose to conceal. Her reticence was grating, but not as much as her lack of trust in him.

"Do you object, Alisdair?" She stood, covering the bust with a square of hide. He moved to her side, slid the leather from the stone.

"I have no objection to your carving, Iseabal," he said. "I only wish to know the reason for your sudden aversion to my presence and to Gilmuir."

"Why would you think that I'm averse to either?" she asked carefully, once again shielding her work. He smiled grimly at this evidence of her gentle obstinacy. When she wished, she could be as opaque as marble and as stubborn as stone.

"Because you've avoided me as aptly as you have going ashore," he said, clenching his hands together at his sides.

"I wished to work on my carving," she murmured, looking away again. Standing, she moved to the rail, studying the pockmarked cliff face as intently as she had her statue.

After their marriage, she'd ceased being tentative with him. Instead, they'd shared laughter and conversation, delighting in the other's nature as well as in moments of loving. He wanted that other Iseabal back, not the quiet woman with hints of anger in her gaze, and not this one whose defiance had been replaced by a solemn sort of misery.

"Why do I think that's not the full answer, Iseabal?"

How could he solve a problem that was never mentioned? Or respond to a question never voiced? Her silence irritated him, so too her meek acceptance of his burgeoning anger.

She'd acted the same with Magnus Drummond.

He turned on his heel and left her, striding to the cabin. An act of restraint had him closing the door softly behind him when he wanted to slam it. He didn't have Iseabal's nature. What she achieved by endurance, he gained with more forthright tactics.

He should go to her, convince her to speak to him, utter words that would reassure her. Except, of course, there were none. He suspected the reason for her reticence well enough.

Despite her fear of Drummond, the man was still her father and parental bonds were difficult to sever. She was torn in her loyalties while his had never been clearer.

If she wanted to extract a promise from him that he would do nothing to Drummond, he could not give it to her. Any more than he could agree to refrain from protecting his home or the people who depended on him. He couldn't ignore her father's actions.

Drummond had effectively declared war on Gilmuir.

James MacRae stood at the bow of his ship, the *Cuideal*, two of his four brothers beside him. They were as silent as he, awed by the sight of Gilmuir, the place they'd heard about all their lives.

Golden light poured over the ship, as if welcoming them home. A riotous morning sky, replete with pink-and-orange streaks, announced their silent arrival.

Noting the merchant ship anchored at the side of Loch Euliss, James wondered if the *Fortitude* was moored in the cove. If so, attempting to navigate the narrowing waterway would be foolish, if not dangerous. His ship drew more than either vessel, being designed to carry cargo across the oceans.

Turning to his brothers, he made his decision. "We'll anchor here," he said.

"You'll be rowing us to the cove, then?" Hamish asked sardonically.

"You should be the one doing the rowing," Brendan answered. "You've taken it easy on this voyage."

"I'm all for walking to Gilmuir," James said, "if only to escape the two of you." With that, he left to relay the orders.

* * *

Iseabal stood at the door of the cabin, fist raised to knock. How fleeting courage was. A week ago she'd faced down her father and was willing to shoot a man to find Alisdair. Now, however, she felt as frail as a new lamb and about as brave.

She rapped on the door with her knuckles, but there was no answer.

"You do not have to knock," he said irritably when she hesitantly opened the door. "This is your cabin as well as mine."

"Your wound needs to be treated," she said, coming into the room. "Unless you would rather do it yourself."

"Why should I object to my wife's ministering care?" he asked tightly. "It is better than her fleeing from me."

"I haven't left the ship," she said quietly, moving to the tansu and retrieving the articles she needed.

"No, but you've been as distant as if you had."

Some words cannot be voiced; some fears are too terrible to speak. She'd found it easy to be brave on his behalf, but facing him now was more difficult than holding a pistol on a sailor. She didn't want to see the same look on his face as she had seen on Brian's or the other crewmen's. She didn't want to watch while he slowly withdrew from her, as if her touch were plague-filled.

She'd lose too much for her courage now; it was easier to remain silent.

Placing the jars and vials on the table in front of him, she began to examine his wound. A nasty blow, one designed to kill, yet he had escaped death to sit in front of her now.

Their life had been a circle, Iseabal suddenly thought. Once, she'd sat where he did now, trapped in fear and reticence as surely as she was at this moment. He had been the caregiver and she the reluctant patient. But where their circumstances might have differed, their natures had not.

He was still brave; she was yet a coward. Alisdair demanded of life; she accepted. He saw possibilities, while she felt boxed in by her own limitations.

She glanced down at him. His eyes sparkled at her like a sunlit morning sky, but his mouth was unsmiling. At this moment he was simply Alisdair MacRae, stripped of all his honors and titles. Impatient, stubborn, insistent, occasionally demanding. A mortal man, after all.

How odd that she should find him even more fascinating for all his faults.

Her hands came into his field of vision, her fingers long and tapered, callused fingertips sliding delicately through his hair. She was careful but relentless in the exploration of his wound.

"We have not loved enough, Iseabal," he said, his gaze lifting to hers.

Her fingers halted against his scalp. Her breath seemed trapped on a sigh; her full breasts, sedately covered, were suddenly too close. His inclination was to bend forward, brush his lips against the swell of fabric.

"We've not been married long," she said finally, her gaze on his hair.

"Do I please you?"

Now there was a longer pause, as if she were framing the words. Surely he was not that bad a lover. Inconsiderate? He could imagine that, he thought wryly, with his body's intractable reaction to her even now. Alisdair the quick.

"Yes," she said shortly.

As she applied the medicines, he traced a path from her wrist to her elbow, gliding over the sleeve of her garment with a remembering finger. Her arms were straight and muscled from her sculpting, her wrists supple yet delicate.

She pulled back, capping the jars and placing the stoppers on the two vials.

Leisurely, he reached up and began to unfasten her jacket, saying nothing as he did so. But his gaze never veered from her face when he opened the buttons.

"I want more, Iseabal," he said, pressing his face between her breasts. His breath felt heated against the delicate lace shift. "I want the woman I was beginning to know. Where has she gone, Iseabal? Where have you sent her?"

Her eyes widened, but still she didn't speak.

At her silence, he reached around her legs with both arms, leaning his head against her hip. She placed her palms against his temples, her fingers speared into his hair.

"I am here," she whispered.

"Are you, Iseabal? Then why do you fear me?"

"I do not," she said, her voice sounding as if she trembled. He pressed a finger against her inner wrist, felt the fluttering beat of her blood.

"I promised to kiss you the next time you treated me to silence," he said, standing. He leaned down, holding her head still with his hands.

There was something magical in the way his mouth fit against hers, he thought. He saw sparks behind his eyelids, but reveled in the sensation of losing himself in passion. His breath was constricted, his heart matching hers beat by beat, his senses focused only on Iseabal.

If they could not have trust between them, at least they had this.

"Damnation, Alisdair, what's all this about you getting married? And to a Scot?"

Alisdair stiffened, pushing Iseabal behind him. Her jacket

was unfastened, and her shift and what was beneath it were not for public viewing.

"It wouldn't hurt for you to knock, James," he said curtly, glancing at them. Three of his brothers stood there, various degrees of surprise flickering over their faces. Only James, he noted, had the sense to look chagrined. Brendan and Hamish were as slack-jawed as envious hounds. He should have been surprised at their appearance, but all he could feel at the moment was rage.

"Shut the door, damn it!" he roared, and they finally had the grace to step outside, closing the door behind them.

"Forgive me," he said, glancing down at his wife. "My brothers are oafs."

She only nodded and, as he watched, retreated into herself once again.

Alisdair sat before her on the floor, his back against the bunk where she perched. His wrist rested nonchalantly on his drawn-up knee. A casual pose, Iseabal thought, wishing that she could appear as nonchalant.

The three MacRae men—James, Hamish, and Brendan— sat on the floor opposite them. There was something about the brothers that linked them—a curve of chin, a proud nose. Yet they were each so dissimilar in appearance they could easily have been cousins instead of brothers. James was tall and slender. Hamish was gifted with broad shoulders and an oddly squared physique. Brendan was simply average, but possessed of a more ready smile than his brothers.

Beneath their surface amiability, however, lurked an almost palpable anger, as if listening to Alisdair's tale had further united them.

"The bastard tried to take the land again?" Hamish asked

gruffly. "I think this Magnus Drummond needs to be taught his own boundaries."

"And soon," James added.

"I'll volunteer to help." Brendan grinned, as if in anticipation of the encounter.

A formidable group, the MacRae men. Iseabal couldn't help but wonder if her father suspected the degree of his own danger. And her own? Alisdair's tale had been filled with omissions, especially concerning their marriage.

Giving in to an impulse, she placed her hand on Alisdair's shoulder. Absently, he reached up and covered her hand with his, a wordless gesture of support. His other hand began idly stroking her knee as if he sensed her feelings of dread.

"How did you learn I'd come to Gilmuir?" Alisdair was asking.

"The countess," Brendan said. "She liked you very much, Alisdair. I think you made a conquest there."

"Liked?" Alisdair asked.

"We've come with bad news," James interrupted before Brendan could answer. "The countess died two days after we arrived at Brandidge Hall."

Iseabal bent her head, overwhelmed by a quick, spearing sadness. The news was not unexpected, but all the same, Iseabal wished that she'd never heard it. Ignorance would have given her the ability to place Patricia in the wondrous setting of Brandidge Hall in her imagination, living endlessly.

Closing her eyes kept her tears at bay, but nothing could ease the ache inside her. She felt overflowing to the brim with emotions, all of them raw.

Alisdair was rubbing her fingers beneath his, a deliberate exploration from nail to knuckle. Iseabal traced an answering pattern against his fingertips. Memory joined them, a curious bridge that transported them from here to Brandidge Hall.

"We'll send the *Molly Brown* back to London, then," James was saying. "There's no point in her making the voyage to Nova Scotia when we're here, after all."

Alisdair nodded.

"How is it that you came to be wed?" James asked. Glancing up at Iseabal, he smiled, and she had the oddest thought that he, of all the MacRae men, might be the most perfectly handsome. He was the only one besides Alisdair who had the MacRae eyes. Set into his narrow face, they were dramatic and intense.

"How did we come to be married?" Iseabal repeated, feeling oddly trapped by his friendly gaze.

"Iseabal is Drummond's daughter," Alisdair said. A statement that had the effect of turning the brothers' attention directly to her. Iseabal felt as if she'd been stripped naked and made to walk a crowded thoroughfare in Edinburgh.

Slowly she withdrew her hand, clasping both together on her lap. Her demeanor was proper, knees at a perfect angle, feet together. The heavy silence lingered as if filled with unspoken words.

She met each gaze separately, looking from one face to another. Even though nothing was said, their narrowed eyes and thinned lips betrayed what they thought well enough.

Iseabal stood, knowing that if she didn't leave this place, she would shame herself. All of the worry and fear she'd felt during the past week would come spewing out in a torrent of words and tears. Alisdair held out one hand as if to stay her, but she brushed past him and through the open cabin door.

Walking to the stern, Iseabal cast off the rope that held the skiff. Henrietta came to stand at the rail, licking her paws and generally appearing satisfied with herself.

"How do you do it, Henrietta?" Iseabal asked, glancing down at the cat. "Do you never wish for more of life than you have?"

Henrietta paused in her grooming to look up, disdain in her eyes. As if to say, Iseabal thought, that a bit of fish was all she needed to be content.

"My wife is a MacRae," Alisdair said tightly, standing and staring at each of his brothers. "She's been a MacRae from the day I married her and you'll treat her that way."

"How can you trust her, Alisdair?" Hamish asked.

The question jarred him, and for a moment Alisdair was stripped of words. *I just do.* But he doubted that was enough of an explanation for Hamish.

"She saved my life," he said finally, knowing that the answer was deeper than that. But surely love didn't come that suddenly; it was nourished in decades, made solid by years of friendship, bonds of family and friends, a commonality of the past and plans for the future.

A past? One of heritage, perhaps. Friendship had already come to their marriage. The future stretched out before them, filled with companionship. And love, he abruptly realized.

He turned at the doorway, glancing back at his brothers. "She's a MacRae," he repeated. "And my wife. If you cannot accept that, then you're not welcome at Gilmuir."

Leaving them, Alisdair went in search of his wife.

"He's got near to a hundred men with him," the stableboy said, clutching his cap between his hands.

Loyal to Iseabal, and complicit in her acts of freedom, Robbie had proved invaluable to Leah over the past few days. He was the one who had warned her of Drummond's approach, and now delivered this startling news.

Each delicate stitch seemed crimson, Leah thought, instead of the pale saffron it was. The flower petal appeared before her eyes magically, as if her hands continued to work while her mind seemed frozen.

"He's not stopping at Fernleigh," the boy said.

"He's going to Gilmuir," she finished for him, knowing her husband's plans all too well. He'd sent Thomas back to Fernleigh for his money box, and at her questions, the other man had bragged to her of Drummond's intentions.

"MacRae's alive now," Thomas had said, grinning. "But he'll not be for long."

"And Iseabal?" she had asked. Casually, so that Thomas would not know how much she waited upon his answer.

"Well enough," he said. "She's taken him back to Gilmuir, but she'll be freed of that place soon enough."

He'd grinned again, turning away.

More than a week had passed since Iseabal had come back to Fernleigh and stood looking at her with contempt in her eyes. More than a week since Magnus had left, leaving Leah safe from his rages.

He'd not taken the time to punish her for her words, but Leah had no doubt that Magnus would remedy that oversight upon his return.

He'd taken his pistol. An alarming weapon, one too large to be tucked inside his vest. A curiously beautiful piece of wood and metal, made to his specifications in Edinburgh by a gunsmith of repute. How like her husband to spend his hoarded money on an instrument of death. Or on hired assassins.

She smiled her dismissal, and the stableboy left her. Standing, Leah walked to the front door of Fernleigh. The ever-present guards were gone, summoned by Drummond to Cormech.

Gilmuir was a place she'd never wanted to see again, the ruin of Fergus's home reminding her too much of him.

They'd met accidentally, at a fair near Inverness, their love a secret, not for lack of propriety or due to shame, but because his family had argued for the rebellion and hers had not. How strange that an event of such importance should have no value now.

Why did you never say anything? Or do anything? Iseabal's words, truthful and hurting.

She'd not once sought to change her life until her sadness had become a habit more than a choice. Over the years, she'd been comfortable within the dungeon she'd created of Fernleigh and quietly and stoically accepting of Magnus's abuse.

Her life had stopped all those years ago when she'd preferred to live an existence in which Fergus was a dream, a giant angel with blazing red hair and a grin like Satan's.

"I did something, Iseabal," Leah said to the air. "I prayed a path to Heaven itself."

But prayers alone would not solve this situation. She needed to warn Iseabal, and prevent the death of another MacRae.

Chapter 32

In the few minutes elapsed since Iseabal had left the cabin, she'd entered the skiff and was halfway across the cove. What she lacked in skill in rowing the small boat was more than made up in determination, Alisdair realized. Irritated, he commandeered his brothers' boat and followed her.

"Iseabal!"

She looked back once, frowned at him but didn't answer.

When he called out again she didn't bother to turn, simply beached the skiff, and disappeared into the cave. With any luck, the men would be hauling another cask up the steps and she'd be forced to wait. But she'd accidentally timed her ascent well, he discovered upon reaching the cave. One barrel had just been lifted and another was being tied to the winch ropes.

She had escaped while he was being forced to wait.

* * *

Leaving the priory, Iseabal halted, startled at the transformation that had occurred at Gilmuir in the past ten days. Barracks were being erected where the English fort had once stood. The cook was commanding his encampment while Brian and the other crewmen of the *Fortitude* were finishing up four stone walls of a cottage built away from the other structures. Dozens of barrels were aligned along the old castle's roofed corridor, along with extra tools. Wood was being culled from the forest and used for supports for yet another large structure, designed, she thought, to act as a community place during the time it would take to rebuild Gilmuir.

Sound gradually eased as saws and hammers, shovels and mortaring tools, were lowered. Even the flap of laundry along a line strung from two supports grew mute, as if the wind had suddenly ceased to blow.

Pockets of silence met her as she stood there, arms folded around her waist. The training of her childhood came to her aid as she slowly made her way past the villagers and the crew. Studiously ignoring them, Iseabal walked toward the land bridge, each step marred by the glares of men she'd thought she had come to know and strangers who hated her simply because of her birth.

If she were truly brave, as she'd once thought, she'd turn and address them all, tell them that they were wrong to judge her by kin alone. But her courage was not renewable, Iseabal discovered. Once spent, it was simply gone.

Her isolation would stretch out for a lifetime, a mirror of her childhood. Suddenly she couldn't bear it. Running across the land bridge, Iseabal headed for the forest.

Finally able to ascend the steps, Alisdair began looking for Iseabal. The crew and the villagers were looking toward the land bridge, expressions of anger on each face. As if, he thought, Magnus Drummond had strode onto MacRae land.

Not the father, Alisdair realized, following their gaze. But the daughter. The revelation was not a pleasant one. He'd been too selfish in his thinking, believing that Iseabal's restraint was directed toward him. What an idiot he'd been.

Alisdair found himself suffused by two emotions—regret and irritation. Brushing aside questions and ignoring the looks of his crew, he began to run, intent on reaching Iseabal.

Glancing over her shoulder at the sound of footsteps, Iseabal began running faster on seeing Alisdair. While she didn't fear her husband, neither did she wish for a confrontation at this particular moment. She felt on the verge of tears and too vulnerable for detachment.

Finding the overgrown path easily, Iseabal began following its winding course upward.

"Iseabal!"

She jerked, startled by the proximity of his voice.

Desperately, she glanced from right to left, looking for a thicket or some large boulder where she might find cover. Nearly obscured by thick branches and overgrowth was an entrance to a cave, a yawning shadow and a possible refuge.

Racing up the bank, Iseabal slipped inside. The cave was curiously intimate, graced by both darkness and filtered sunlight. The wind soughing through the trees whispered nature's poetry, the scent of pine and earth almost welcoming.

She peered out to find Alisdair closer than she'd thought. He stood, feet planted apart, both hands on his hips as if he commanded the forest itself.

A moment more and he would have seen her.

*   *   *

"Are you a ghost?" Alisdair called out, deliberately recalling their first meeting. In the sun-dappled shadows the pale blue of her skirt acted as a beacon against the slate walls of the cave.

"I remember the last time we were in this forest together," he said, taking one step closer to the incline. "We were laughing."

Iseabal didn't answer him, but then, he'd not expected a response. After all, she'd taken great pains to avoid him.

"I can understand why you might want to avoid people who are rude to you, Iseabal, but what have I done to hurt you?"

Slowly, he mounted the sloping ground in front of the cave.

"Perhaps I insulted you when I was senseless? Said something that you took amiss. Did I do that, Iseabal?"

No answer.

"Then perhaps it was a gesture. A look, a movement, some wave of hand that made you angry?"

Another step and he was on the shelf of stone leading to the cave. The place seemed oddly familiar to him. Words from a dozen years ago slipped into his mind. "It's a secluded place," his father had said. "One with many memories," he'd added, winking at Leitis.

"I'd not pursue that, Ian," she'd teased him back. "Not with all your sons listening."

"It's where we kept the MacRae treasure," his father explained.

"The MacRae treasure?" Hamish had asked eagerly.

"Not what you might think, Hamish," his mother had corrected, brushing a hand over his curls. "Not jewels, gold, and silver, but the possessions of simple people. Those things that made life worth living."

"A plate with a blue-and-white pattern," Ian had said, bringing his wife's fingers to his lips.

"Or a set of pipes once played by a gruff old man," she'd added, smiling at him as her cheeks bloomed with color.

Alisdair surveyed the entrance, turning to see what stretched in front of the cave. The pine forest had grown up around the cave opening, obscuring any view that might have once been possible of Gilmuir and the loch.

"Now," he said, anxious to solve a more pressing riddle than the MacRae treasure, "if I have done nothing, why are you running from me?"

"Perhaps I don't wish to speak to you," she said as he stepped into the cave.

"When is going to be a propitious time, Iseabal?" he asked dryly. "These last few days you've done nothing but ignore me."

Placing her palms against his chest, she suddenly pushed him with all her strength. He only rocked back on his heels, an action that seemed to further anger her.

"Don't you understand?" she shouted. "You've married a Drummond, and however much I might want to change that, MacRae, I can't!"

He shouldn't be so surprised. Her temper had been hinted at often enough, the flash of fire in her eyes demonstrated on numerous occasions before now. But the faint light sought out the sheen on her cheeks and it was only then that he realized she was crying.

"You're a MacRae, Iseabal," he said, reaching out to trap her wrists. She pulled away from him easily, took a few steps back until she was in the shadows once more.

"Tell that to your men," she said, wiping at her cheeks. "Or the villagers. Or your brothers. I notice you had no words to correct them."

"I don't comment every time an ass brays, Iseabal," he said, conscious that she was right; he'd not defended her as quickly as he should have.

"Every time I see one of your men, MacRae, they stare through me as if I'm not there."

"I am sorry for that, and for the hurt it caused you," he said, moving toward her. "But perhaps it isn't solely your birth they distrust, Iseabal, but your actions."

"So this is my fault, MacRae? My behavior that is wrong?" she asked, folding her arms in front of her and gripping each of her elbows. The tap of her foot against the slate floor warned him that his next words should be wisely chosen.

"It is not, Iseabal," he said, hearing the echoes of her childhood in her question. "If my men had not trusted you, they wouldn't have left you alone with me."

Threading his fingers through his hair, Alisdair wondered how to explain. "I've been with my crew through countless battles, Iseabal," he said. "Men form bonds when they're trying to survive. Bonds sometimes even stronger than family. I don't know if I can explain it." Placing both his hands on her shoulders, he drew her closer. She stiffened, but allowed him to put his arms around her.

Leaning forward, Alisdair pressed a kiss to her forehead, an absently fond gesture that amused him. The last emotion he felt at this moment was detachment. Instead, he was irritated, even angry, both at his own actions as well as Iseabal's.

"Nothing matters when you're trying to survive but the fact that a man is willing to support you, fight beside you. You don't see his nationality or his race, don't care about his language or his character. His appearance, his habits, his ancestry, none of these are important. Iseabal, you were in battle with my men. Rory told me what you did. You became one of them."

"Is that why they look at me as they do, Alisdair?" she asked, pulling away once more. "Or why they treat me with such disdain?" She began to walk away, as if wishing to keep the maximum amount of distance between them.

"But instead of protesting, Iseabal, you chose to allow your distance to speak for you." He turned toward her, impatient with his own inability to explain. But he was not prepared to live the rest of his life this way, with Iseabal remaining silent and cloistered in her thoughts. "What else are they supposed to think, but that you were repudiating them? I felt the same," he added. "I can't understand your silences or know your hidden thoughts. Am I to divine them, Iseabal? I am only a mortal man without the gift of hearing what you don't say."

"Where do you get your courage, Alisdair?" she asked quietly.

The change of topic annoyed him, but he answered nonetheless. "What makes you think I have an unending supply of it?"

"Because I've never seen you afraid."

"There are numerous occasions in which I've been afraid, Iseabal. More than I wish to recall."

"Yet I've never seen you doubt yourself, Alisdair, or seem unsure."

"Do you wish to see me weakened, Iseabal?" Her tears could accomplish that, he thought.

"You want my thoughts, Alisdair? They are terrible things sometimes, requiring a courage I don't know that I have."

"You are as brave as any of the men of the *Fortitude*, Isea-bal," he assured her gently. "But instead of knowing that, you are acting like a freed bird who still sees the bars of her cage."

"Then here is the truth, Alisdair. I hate Magnus Drummond. I hate him for making me feel afraid, and I hate myself for being a coward. But I hate him even more for trying to kill you."

He said nothing as he followed the sound of her voice.

"I can bear the disdain of others, Alisdair; but I don't want to see you look at me as if you hate me."

"I wish that I could say I've always treated you well, Isea-bal," he said, uncomfortable with that particular truth. "But my anger was never because of your birth."

"Why did you wish to stay married to me?" she asked, voicing a question he wished she had not posed.

"I could tell you it was your beauty," he said slowly. "Or," he continued, laying his palm against the warmth of her cheek, "I could say it was because this marriage was no fault of yours, and I could not punish you for it." He moved his hand to the back of her neck, fingers burying themselves in the hair at her nape. "Or even that it was the proper thing to do."

"Was it that?" she asked dispassionately.

"All of that, Iseabal," he said, suddenly wondering at the true meaning of courage. The words he wished to say were trapped behind a restraint as formidable as Iseabal's.

Her hands gripped his sleeves as she rested her cheek against his chest. Raising her arms, she linked her hands around his neck, held onto him in a way she'd never done before.

"We are man and wife, Iseabal," he said. "Partners in life.

We must trust one another with our fears and our hopes and our wishes."

"Do you trust me?" she asked a moment later.

"With my life," he said easily. "But I want all of you, Iseabal. Your fears, your hurts, your uncertainties. I want your opinions, even your anger. Not coldness."

Standing on tiptoe, she gave him a quick, lighthearted kiss. But he caught her and held her close, deepening the kiss.

Steadying her chin, he widened his mouth, encompassing hers, touching the edge of her lip with his fingertip.

Her fingers felt for the opening of his shirt, but his hand halted them, raising each one to his mouth to stroke his lips across each knuckle.

Hands smoothed over her back, pressed against her waist, measured the curve of her breasts, as if he'd never before touched her body. The hunger he'd felt for her earlier had been interrupted by his brothers' arrival. Now it roared to life again in the darkness and privacy of this cave.

He kissed her once more, capturing her breath on a sigh and transmuting it to another sound, one of almost pained need. He wanted this, as his body craved air and food and water. He felt as if he were too slow in his ministrations, too delicate in his touch.

He gripped her suddenly, pulling her up until she could wind her legs around his waist. Slowly, he pressed her to the wall, reaching out with one hand to raise her skirts while bracing the other on the wall beside her.

An object fell to the floor with a heavy metal clang. Another sound immediately followed the first, this a soft, muffled groan of air so plaintive that it seemed like a woman's wail.

"What was that?" she asked as Alisdair gently lowered her to the floor. Iseabal fluffed her skirts before touching Alisdair's sleeve.

"I don't know," he said, moving to the side. He stretched his arms outward, then down, feeling the way in the blackness of the cave.

His earlier thoughts came to mind as he bent and fumbled on the floor for the object. His fingers traced the filigree design while he smelled the sour odor of pitted silver.

"It's the MacRae treasure," he said as his hands felt the lip of a stone shelf. In the Stygian darkness he encountered a variety of objects, their purpose and their design easily determined.

"A treasure?" she asked, her voice sounding amazed.

"A silver tray," he said, handing the fallen object to her. "Bagpipes," he added, his fingers moving across the sticky bag of a long-unused set of pipes. "A metal cup with an elaborately carved handle and an initial etched in the pewter."

Carrying the tankard to the cave's entrance, he held it out in the faint light.

"R?" Iseabal asked, coming to his side.

"I think it belonged to my great-grandfather," he said. "Ranulf MacRae."

"I found a necklace of blue rocks in the ruins one day, but I thought it was the only thing left of Gilmuir."

He linked his hand with hers and walked back to the shelf. The slate floor beneath his feet was pocked and worn, leaving Alisdair to wonder how many centuries his clan had hidden their wealth here.

What he had originally thought to be dozens of items turned out to be hundreds. Goblets and bowls, dusty fabric, the tight woolen weave beneath his fingers hinting at a tartan pattern. A wooden platter, bowls carved from MacRae trees. All items salvaged from a life lived at Gilmuir.

"Why did they leave all these things behind?" Iseabal asked.

"When they left Scotland with the Raven, they could only take one pack," he explained.

"So they left the rest here for safekeeping?" she asked wonderingly.

"Yes," he said, "and here they've stayed all this time."

The day, bright with sun and summer, lured him forward. Gritting his teeth, Fergus obeyed the summons.

His stump was inflamed, the pain constant and irritating. With small steps he'd made the journey, telling himself that Gilmuir was just over the next rise. In such a way he'd come this far, and he wasn't about to stop now.

He was a MacRae and not a man easily vanquished.

Only a little hill, Fergus. Don't look at the top, but at your foot and the crutch. Better yet, count the damn sheep. Where once the glens had been green and thick, now there was only a continuous flock of dingy sheep, moving from one hill to another like a great glutted worm.

Counting a beat in his mind, like the swing of his hammer against an anvil, Fergus measured his steps. A hundred and he was nearly halfway to the top. Another hundred or so more and he was there.

The sunlight glittering on the waters of Loch Euliss was a magical sight. So, too, the moment he turned to his right, shielding his eyes.

Gilmuir. He blinked several times, realizing that he was acting the fool. But, idiot or not, he felt his eyes mist over and a yearning fill him.

Where was the English fort? The last time he'd seen his home, the structure had sat so close to the old fortress that it looked to be nudging it over the cliffs. This wasn't the place of his dreams, Fergus realized. Still a ruin, but teeming with people and activity.

A movement to his left caused him to turn his head. Streaking across the glen was a mirage, a vision given to his willing mind in payment for his efforts. Leah, as she had been so long ago, racing to meet him in their secret spot. Her hair flew out behind her, her body bent over her horse as if she and the animal were one at this moment, flying over the ground with more joy than sense.

Watching her, he was taken back to another time, when he'd waited anxiously for her to join him. Secret lovers and public friends. He'd felt the same back then as he did at this moment, captivated and eager, love lodged so deep in his heart that it would never shake free.

Not a mirage, his mind told him, even as his heart warily acknowledged the truth. Not a vision from his past, but a woman, after all, her destination obviously Gilmuir.

Behind her, just emerging from the curve of land, was a troop of mounted men. But the twenty or so riders didn't concern him as much as those who followed on foot, their ranks uneven but their numbers impressive. They, too, were headed for the promontory.

Several questions needed to be answered, Fergus thought, beginning his descent to the glen. The first of them was why Gilmuir was being besieged. The second was the identity of the woman.

Measuring the distance, Fergus ignored his throbbing leg. Instead, he began planning a shorter route, if a more difficult one. As a boy, he'd been familiar with the forests surrounding his home. Now he'd discover how much he remembered.

"The least he could have done was leave our boat," Brendan complained, sluicing the water from his face. "It was a damn cold swim."

"I doubt he was thinking of us," James replied, his attention fixed on the cave paintings around him.

"Ionis's lady?" Hamish asked, moving to his side. James nodded. "The image of Iseabal."A tie to Gilmuir more fixed and real than their presence.

"Are you going up, then?" a man asked, threading three strands of rope through his hands. Behind him, a barrel was being fitted with two thick lengths of rope.

"We are," James said, leading the way up the staircase. The journey was made in silence as they navigated the ropes, pulling themselves up into the priory.

"I'd envisioned it differently," Brendan remarked, walking across the slate floor and peering through one of the fallen arches into the water below. "Less ruin and more building."

"I'd be careful if I were you, Brendan," Hamish cautioned. "You're standing where the major fell."

Brendan's face blanched and he stepped back carefully.

"She'll be sad to hear of its destruction," James said, his two brothers turning to look at him as if they'd shared that common thought.

"It's true," Hamish agreed. "Our mother does have a fondness for Gilmuir."

"I'll not tell her," Brendan said.

"And I'll not lie to her, Brendan," James countered. "Especially since Alisdair has plans to rebuild the old place."

"Do you think he can?" Hamish asked, looking around him at the ruins of the once great castle.

James began to smile, knowing his brother's obstinacy. "I do," he said, striding through the priory and out onto the rocky ground.

There, ahead of her, was the fortress of the MacRaes.

At first Leah thought that her eyes were playing tricks, but then she realized that it was no illusion after all. There weren't ghosts milling about in Gilmuir's courtyard, but people. A white canvas shelter stood just beyond the bridge of land linking the promontory to the glen, and still farther, it appeared as if some men were in the process of putting a thatch roof on a long, rectangular building. This was not a scene of despair or mourning, a fact which gave her some measure of hope.

At the land bridge, she slowed and dismounted, walking her horse across to the courtyard.

"Can I be of some assistance, mistress?"

Turning her head, Leah saw a young man with earnest hazel eyes standing in front of her. "The afternoon meal is being served now," he said, his arm sweeping out to indicate an encampment obviously dedicated to feeding all these people.

"I've not come for your food," she said brusquely, "but to find my daughter."

"Who might she be?" he asked kindly.

"Iseabal MacRae."

His face changed in that instant, becoming fixed, his lips narrow and straight. Even his eyes seemed to ice over.

"Drummond's daughter. And you're Drummond's wife?" he asked curtly.

She nodded, familiar enough with expressions of contempt. Drummond's power came with an unsavory reputation.

"I'm here to deliver a warning," she said. "My husband is on his way to Gilmuir with a force of men."

Turning, he signaled to a group and in moments, it seemed, she was being surrounded.

"Why would Drummond be coming here?" a tall young man said, stepping forward. His eyes were the same shade as Alisdair's, a feature that she hoped marked him as a relative.

"You're a MacRae?" Leah asked, feeling the tightness in her chest ease when he nodded.

"One reason only," she said bluntly. "To kill Alisdair."

"Why should we believe you?" another, shorter man demanded.

"Because of that," Leah said, half turning in her saddle. Slowly she raised her arm, pointing toward Fernleigh. One by one, they all followed her gaze, contempt and doubt vanishing as they stared.

There, on the horizon, was Drummond, his troop of mounted men and hired soldiers behind him.

Chapter 33

❧

The inventory of the cave yielded several surprising finds, among them a store of silver objects and a set of porcelain delicately etched with celtic symbols.

"What will you do with all this?" Iseabal asked. She sat beside Alisdair, handing him object after object. Their inspection would have been much better performed in the light of a lantern, but this solemn darkness felt oddly right for this moment. Alisdair could almost feel the members of the MacRae clan march into the opening one by one, as if their shades appeared to claim ownership of their once beloved treasures.

"Send everything back to Nova Scotia with James," he said. "These items belong to the people who settled there."

"I wonder what they'll think, to get their treasures back."

"I don't know," he said, imagining the response. "It will

probably make some sad, perhaps bring back memories they don't want."

"Or give them happiness," she suggested, leaning her head against his shoulder.

"Yes," he agreed, "or give them happiness."

Iseabal seemed to know how he felt, because she gripped his hand tightly in a silent gesture of comfort. She did that often, speaking words that could not be spoken, transforming them into gestures instead. But this time she spoke, mirroring his thoughts so exactly that he was startled by her prescience.

"I wonder if they will think it a discovery or a burden," she mused quietly. "Will these treasures bring good memories or sad ones?"

"I cannot choose for them," he said, entwining his fingers with hers. "All I can do is ensure that all these items return to their owners."

"I would make the choice to be happy," she said. "This would be a link to the past," she continued, releasing her grip to place the tankard in his hand. "It's how I feel about the window at Fernleigh."

"The one with the knight," he said, remembering the one item of beauty in the great hall.

"Yes," she replied softly. "I could choose to bemoan the fact that our family is not what our ancestor might have wished it to be. Or I can simply take pleasure in the notion that, at one time, the Drummonds were loyal and brave men."

"Do not judge yourself by your father, Iseabal," he chided gently. "A man or a woman has no power over his heritage."

Pressing her hand on his arm, she leaned forward, brushed his cheek with a soft kiss. "Spoken by a man who has nothing but greatness as his legacy," she teased.

"If I did not?" he asked, suddenly and unwisely curious. "If I had no ties to Gilmuir, or was not a MacRae?"

Instead of answering him, she spoke, her words startling him. "Do you know why I want to carve your face? I want the image of you to always be seen, like Moira's portrait and Gerald's miniature. People may not know your name, but they will wonder at your nature, and know somehow that you were a great man, a man of purpose and dreams."

"You embarrass me with your praise, Iseabal. No man could live up to your expectations."

"You already have."

"It's a tender scene, I'm thinking, but I cannot understand why you choose the darkness for your courting."

Alisdair turned his head to find a giant in the cave's entrance, his height and breadth nearly obscuring the faint, greenish light. One leg of his breeches was pinned back to the thigh, his leg missing from the knee down. Although he stood balancing on a crutch, there was no doubt of his strength, or his potential danger to both of them. Getting to his feet, Alisdair extended his hand down to Iseabal, helping her to rise.

"Who are you?" he asked, discomfited by being caught off guard.

"It's a hidden place you've found, it's true, but even a whisper would sound loud to a passerby," the man said.

As Alisdair reached the opening, the other man flinched, drawing back quickly.

"Who is your mother?" the giant asked unexpectedly.

"Why would you be asking that?" Alisdair replied impatiently.

"Because I've a notion we're no strangers. Would she be Leitis MacRae?"

Alisdair said nothing, only stared at other man.

Iseabal came to his side, placing her hand on his sleeve as she studied the giant in the faint light.

"Very well," he said, when neither spoke, "I'll be the first to introduce myself. I'm Fergus MacRae and I'm thinking you're my nephew."

"You're dead," Iseabal blurted, her words the same Alisdair had been about to use.

"As you can see, I'm not," Fergus said. "But there was a time when I wished it to be true enough."

"What color are my mother's eyes?" Alisdair asked.

"The same blue of your own," Fergus answered, his smile broadening.

"And her talent?" he asked, wondering if the man was indeed his uncle.

If so, he was as his mother had described him, tall, broad-shouldered, and sporting a head of hair as red as the setting sun. His beard was of the same color, although liberally spiced with gray hairs.

The other man's smile faded. "I can see why you'd be wanting to know for sure who I am," he said. "The years have not been trusting ones. Your mother loved her loom. And spent all her time upon it when she could."

Alisdair nodded.

"And your father? Who might he be?"

"Ian MacRae."

"They always did have a fondness for each other, although I'd like to hear that story well enough," Fergus said. "I'll give you another memory to make you certain. Leitis gave your father a brooch to wear on the day of your grandmother's death."

I was a young boy and badly hurting. His father's voice

spoke in Alisdair's memory. *But such is not the excuse for wounding another. I crushed it with my boot, and made Leitis cry.*

"She speaks of you fondly," Alisdair said, reaching out his hand. "I am Alisdair MacRae, her oldest son."

The other man blinked a few times, looked away and then back again. "She's alive, then?"

"They both are," Iseabal added.

"And you've four other nephews," Alisdair contributed.

For a moment Fergus said nothing, but his eyes glinted as if they welled with tears.

Suddenly, Alisdair was being enfolded in a one-armed hug, the older man beaming at him through the forest of his beard. Alisdair was a tall man, but Fergus was his equal in height and strength.

Releasing him, Fergus glanced at Iseabal. "And who might you be?" Turning to Alisdair, he fixed a stern look on him. "You've not ruined the girl, Alisdair?"

"Iseabal is my wife," Alisdair said tersely.

Fergus smiled in approval, stepping aside for the two of them to leave the cave.

The descent to Gilmuir was made at a leisurely pace, the moments filled with explanation and shared memory. At one point Fergus turned to Iseabal, his smile fading the longer he stared.

"You remind me of a girl I knew," he said somberly. "Leah was her name. Do you know of her?"

For a moment Iseabal wished he had not asked, or put her in the position of telling him that the woman he loved was married to another. A lie, however, would not serve this man with hope so fervent in his eyes.

"She's my mother," Iseabal said quietly.

He said nothing, directing his attention to the ground as if the hollows and swells of the forest floor were of more importance than his memories. Because she knew how it felt to love so fiercely, she spoke again. "She has not forgotten you."

"She has not?" he asked, carefully not raising his eyes. "What does she say?"

Her words were halted by Alisdair's oath. He had stopped at the perimeter of the forest, his attention fixed on the glen to their left. Marching across the glen were what looked to be hundreds of men, led by her father and his troop of men.

"I'm thinking your visitors have not assembled to welcome me home," Fergus said, frowning at the group.

"Nor me," Alisdair said. "If it's a battle he wants, it's one he'll get."

Iseabal frowned at their shared grins, but before she could say a word, Alisdair bent to kiss her lightly.

"We'd best get home, Iseabal," he said. "It seems your father has come to call."

"Father?" Fergus echoed.

"A long story, and one best told at another time," Alisdair said.

"I've only got one leg, but I've two arms, and I'll fight beside you," Fergus said.

Once across the land bridge, Alisdair nodded to his brothers, leaving Fergus to introduce himself.

"How many men do we have?" he asked.

"Seventy-three, not counting my crew, but they're still aboard ship," James said.

"How many pistols?" Alisdair glanced at Drummond's men. They might be outnumbered, he thought, but he

doubted they were out-armed. The army following Drummond carried sharpened sticks and iron staffs.

"Sixteen," James answered.

"Are there any people in the village?" Alisdair asked
Brian.

"They're all here, Captain," Brian said. "It's the noon
meal and they come here to eat."

"We've put the women and children in the priory, Alisdair," James said.

Alisdair nodded, and a few moments later Iseabal found
herself being walked across the courtyard.

"I want you to stay here, Iseabal," Alisdair said at the entrance to the priory.

"Where are you going?" When he didn't answer, she
took one step back. "No," she said resolutely, her hands
clenched into fists as if she would go to war with him. "The
last time you left to be a hero, I nearly lost you. I'll not do it
again."

"I want you safe, Iseabal," he said, his mouth thinned.
"Now is not the time to argue about it. You must trust me."

"I trust you, Alisdair, but not my father. Or what he might
do."

He smiled then, as if amused by her caution. "I have no intention of letting Drummond win," he said, bending down to
place a light kiss on her lips.

Without another word, he walked away.

Your actions count more than your birth. The words
seemed to linger between them as Alisdair glanced back at
her. He'd asked her to see herself as others saw her. An odd
time to realize she'd given the crew and the villagers nothing

by which to know or judge her except silence, endurance, perhaps even acquiescence.

But that wasn't who she was.

Unlike her father, she wanted to squander her emotions, feel wild joy and deep passion. She wanted to hold nothing back, not happiness or sorrow, not even money. Each day of her life would be as a spendthrift.

Nor did she wish to be like her mother, greeting any disaster with silent acceptance. Iseabal wanted to rail against misfortune and fight oppression as well as sadness.

She began to smile, lightly at first as the realization came to her, then more brightly when she decided what she must do.

Stony faces greeted her as she turned, taking a few steps into the priory. The women of Lonvight were not a forgiving lot.

Bending, Iseabal gathered up the material of her petticoat with one hand, creating an improvised sling. "If you'll not join me," she said, "I'll fight alone."

Silence was the only response to her words. Children stood beside their mothers, hands clamped to skirts. A little boy peeped shyly around his mother's legs, then ducked behind her again.

"Set aside a few of you to care for the children," she suggested. "And join me."

Not one of them spoke.

"Then do as you wish," she said in a voice as rough as the faceted rocks she placed in her skirt. "But I will not have my husband harmed and my home destroyed."

Courage, Iseabal suddenly discovered, was not simply accepting in stoic silence what came to you. Nor was it the absence of fear. At this moment, standing here in front of these women while the sounds of battle escalated, Iseabal was as afraid as she'd ever been. But the choice was stark and clear; she could remain here or be at Alisdair's side.

"I'll come," a woman said, pushing her way out of the crowd.

Iseabal stared at her mother in disbelief. "What are you doing here?"

"Listening to you, Iseabal," Leah said gently. "You were right. I had accepted too much for too long."

They exchanged looks, Iseabal seeing in her mother's face all that she had experienced in these past days. The grief, the anger, the resignation each felt were the same, but her mother's anguish had been lengthened by years.

"Forgive me," Iseabal said. "I was wrong. I should never have said such a thing to you."

Leah smiled. "The truth can be vicious thing, Iseabal, but that doesn't mean it shouldn't be said." She bent, duplicating Iseabal's actions in gathering up the rocks.

Iseabal had no chance to mention Fergus's resurrection, because another woman moved beside them, picking up a few bricks that had fallen from the archway. Then another of the Lonvight villagers walked to Iseabal's side, arming herself as well.

"We'll not let Drummond take our home again," one woman said angrily, her hostile gaze fixed on Iseabal. "Any Drummond." Others behind her nodded.

"My name is Iseabal MacRae," Iseabal said, raising her voice so that the women in the back could hear her.

An eternity seemed to pass before one of them moved, pushing forward to stand with the other women. Silently, she bent, tucking a few stones into the fabric bowl of her apron. One by one, each woman stepped forward, nodding at Iseabal.

Alisdair was right; these people were judging her by her actions, not by her birth.

They might have been outnumbered, Iseabal thought as she turned and walked toward the courtyard, but the women behind her were a determined group, armed with their rocks and their rage.

Setting the men in a half-circle formation facing the land bridge, Alisdair began passing out the guns Hamish had acquired. Moments later, the first of the riders began thundering over the land bridge.

"Is that him?" James asked, staring at their leader. Most men looked well suited for horseback. Drummond appeared oddly misshapen, his broad shoulders and barrel chest contrasting oddly with his short legs sticking out at an angle.

"It is," Alisdair replied tightly.

"Someone should shorten his stirrups," James said with a smile.

Men were fighting hand to hand, some with clubs, others with nothing more than rocks. A few pistols had been fired, but they took long to reload, and a man was not about to wait patiently while his opponent readied his gun.

The chaos was overwhelming. The shouts of men, the clash of pikes, the occasional sound of a pistol being fired, rang in Iseabal's ears.

How a man could tell a friend from foe, she didn't know. But it seemed that killing was not the aim as much as was survival. A man fought back when he was struck, and fought again to prevent yet another blow. From the look of the combatants in the courtyard, she was as well armed as the others.

Searching the crowd, she couldn't see Alisdair, but she spotted Fergus easily enough. He was plowing through the men, brandishing a cane as a weapon and using it expertly from the bodies in his path.

Suddenly she saw him. Alisdair was encircled by men, each of them intent upon striking him. She watched, panicked, as he turned, his reaction slowed by surprise when he saw her.

Someone struck him on the shoulder and he went down to his knees, one hand flailing against his attacker. She saw his mouth open, knew he called her name. Too many men moved between them, separating him from her sight.

She wanted to rail and fight and weep and scream, scratch each face with her fingernails and dig in the ground with her hands in order to reach him. Dropping her store of rocks, she jerked a staff from a man lying still on the ground, and began to make her way to her husband's side.

Swinging blindly, she made a path through the men. At one point, a man stepped in front of her, determined to stop her. He gripped her pike and wrenched it from her grasp, only to fall to his knees a second later. She and Brian stared at each other over the other man's body. He'd struck the man over the head with the butt of his pistol and now stood watching her as if she were a ghost.

Retrieving her weapon, Iseabal stood facing the young man who'd once been her friend.

She would have spoken had the noise not been so great. Her lips tightened as she widened her stance, gripping the pike in front of her at an angle. Whether the obstacle was Brian or an enemy, it didn't matter; she was going to be at Alisdair's side.

For a moment she thought he was going to block her way, but he only stood aside. The moment, slowed and silent, lasted just that, until Brian was caught up in the melee and she was free to reach Alisdair.

Whatever happened today, she was not going to lose him again.

He should have known she wouldn't stay safe, Alisdair thought, standing. She'd never done anything he'd expected. Another blow struck him, and he fought back, using his dirk, his feet, his balled-up fist.

The fight reminded Alisdair of another war, one his father had described out of hearing of his mother. Culloden had been fought by Scots armed the same, with clubs and hoes, and with pikes created from the upper branches of saplings.

They had cried aloud in the same rage, yet their enemy this time was not the English, but a man so greedy that he saw the cost of a single sheep, and not the damage done to innocent people.

Drummond's men didn't seem as enraged as the villagers of Lonvight and the crewmen surrounding him. Although they fought well, they did so more defensively than aggressively.

Alisdair spun around, fighting off another attack, a wound on his cheek bleeding, his arm aching from where he'd been struck by a pike. Out of the corner of his eye he saw Iseabal now armed with a wooden spar. But before he could consider her inopportune bouts of courage, a shadow fell over him, and he heard Iseabal's shouts of warning.

Looking up, Alisdair realized that one of Drummond's mounted men was nearly on top of him. He saw the man's face, thinking instantly that he had been here before, had viewed that sharp-toothed, feral grin. The day had been the same, with a warm breeze in the air and the sun in the exact position in the sky.

But here there was no smoke.

Yet the pistol in the other man's hand was steady, just as before, and the look in his eyes was the same, as if the granting of death were a pleasure.

Alisdair rushed his horse, surprising him. Drummond's man held onto his pistol with a tenacious grip as Alisdair pulled him from the saddle, but he lost his hold on it when Alisdair smashed a fist into his face.

"That's for the villagers," he spat out, feeling the man's nose soften beneath his fists. "And that's for me," he added, hearing the crack of a jaw.

"Give *us* a chance," someone called out. Alisdair turned, recognizing him as one of the men he'd seen in the village. Now he was holding a club the size of a small tree trunk and grinning at him.

Alisdair tossed Drummond's flunky in his direction, thinking that when the villagers were finished, he'd send the man off with the *Molly Brown*. The British navy could use a person of his dubious worth.

"Fergus."

He turned at the sound of his name, as if able to hear her voice over the cacophony of battle. In the midst of the fighting, the two them stared at each other, the seconds lengthening until it seemed an eternity.

Her mother would have stood there forever, Iseabal thought, had not Fergus moved, limping through the fighting

WHEN THE LAIRD RETURNS

men, easily pushing those aside who would have separated him from Leah.

Iseabal felt like an interloper in this poignant scene, but she was not alone, she abruptly realized. Her father sat so still on his horse that he might have been carved from stone. His eyes were slits, his face twisted by rage. With a roar, he suddenly spurred his horse on, lifting his pistol and aiming not at Fergus, Iseabal realized with horror, but at her mother.

All of it happened so swiftly that Iseabal was hard pressed to recite the details later.

Fergus moved quickly, pushing Leah behind him, squaring his shoulders, and bracing his legs. Before her father could shoot, Fergus, brandishing his crutch like a weapon, knocked the gun from Drummond's hand, sending him flying from the saddle.

"What kind of man tries to kill a woman?" Fergus shouted, standing over him. "Are you that much of a coward?"

Drummond kicked at Fergus's good leg, the larger man toppling to the ground like a felled oak. Scrambling on his hands and knees for his pistol, Magnus reached it, turning and once again aiming for Leah.

A shot rang out, as loud as a clap of thunder. Her father arched back, a blossom of red appearing on the front of his shirt. His face seemed to change, to relax in the instant before he crumpled to the ground.

Her mother collapsed as well, falling to her knees beside Fergus.

Iseabal glanced toward Alisdair. He stood there, his pistol leveled in her father's direction. On his face was a look of steely determination, his eyes fixed and wintry. But James stood beside him, holding a similar weapon, smoke still wafting from the barrel.

"He didn't pay me enough to die with him," a man unexpectedly said, throwing his pike to the ground.

"We'll never see the rest of our money," another man said, doing the same. He began walking toward the land bridge. A mumbling assent followed him as one man after another dropped his weapon and began to leave Gilmuir.

James walked to where Iseabal's father lay, kneeling at his side. Stretching out a hand, he held it against Drummond's throat as if hoping the other man still lived.

"Merciful God," James said dully. "I meant to strike his shoulder, not kill him." He bent his head and closed his eyes, visibly shaken.

"We'll work on the God part, but I, for one, thank you," Fergus said, rising to one knee with the aid of his crutch and Leah. "He would have killed Leah if not for you."

Alisdair strode to Iseabal's side. She stood motionless, her gaze blank and fixed on the body of her father. For an instant she'd felt a killing rage, the same emotion mirrored on his face an instant before he died.

"God forgive me," she whispered.

Alisdair enfolded her in his arms, and when she remained straight and unbendable, he remedied that by picking her up and carrying her some distance away. "What sin have you committed, Iseabal?" he asked tenderly, rubbing her arms.

"Too many," she confessed. "I wanted to hate him with all my heart, but instead, I find myself too much like him."

He said nothing, simply wrapped his arms around her again. "How are you like him?"

She leaned into his chest, pressing against him to feel his warmth. "I would have killed to protect you."

"And I you," he said, holding her close. "Are we both to be condemned, then?"

She didn't know. The question was beyond her at this moment.

"I'm sorry," he said gently. "For his death."

Iseabal nodded.

He was her father, and for that alone, he would be mourned. Not for who he was, perhaps, but who he might have been. And when she buried him, Iseabal thought, she also would put to rest any hope. Only the living can change.

Together they stood, man and wife, in a joint embrace. One not simply of lovers, she realized, nor only of friends. Companions, perhaps, but that word did not quite suit, either. They were partners, and thinking that, she smiled and closed her eyes, feeling him place a kiss on the crown of her windblown hair.

"Is that why you never came home to me, you daft idiot?" Leah shouted, pointing to his missing limb.

Fergus frowned at her. "I never came home to you, Leah, so that you might have a whole life with a whole man."

"With him?" she asked in disgust, glancing at the corpse of her husband. "He beat me, Fergus."

"I'd no way of knowing that, Leah, and sorry I am for it. By the time I realized how bullish I'd been," Fergus said, cautiously walking toward her, "it was too late. You had already married. It would've been worse to see you and know that you loved another."

"It would have made me miserable," she conceded, "to be married to one man and love another."

Despite her words, however, she took one step away from him, her hands clenched into fists and resting on her hips.

"And now, Fergus? What will you do now?"

"I've nothing to offer you, Leah," he said gently. "Unless"—
he glanced behind him at Gilmuir—"you count one ancient
fortress and a man as badly beaten."

"Leave Gilmuir to Alisdair," she said firmly. "I've Fernleigh as my dowry. And you shall be lord there."

She began to smile, stretching out her hand to him. Since
he had no wish to tumble to the ground again, Fergus kept
one hand wrapped around his crutch, the other gripping hers.

"I'll be a rich widow, Fergus MacRae, and I intend to
spend every coin Drummond ever hoarded."

"You're testing my pride, Leah," he told her softly. "I'm to
let you support me?"

Once more she glanced at Drummond. "I'll take him
home, Fergus, and give him a proper mourning. Not because
he deserves it, but because I'm a good wife. I'll be expecting
you after that time."

They stared at each other, Fergus thinking that it wouldn't
be such a bad thing to have a wealthy wife. Besides, he'd already discovered that pride was a foolish thing when compared to love.

"I'll be there, Leah, money or no."

"Good," she said, standing on tiptoe to kiss him. He bent
his head, and this moment, yearned for all these decades
long, seemed perfect and just right.

Epilogue

She and Alisdair walked slowly up the hill to the cairn stones, a place Iseabal had come to only once in all her visits to Gilmuir.

The battle at Gilmuir had ended as quickly as it had begun, the sailors from James's ship coming to the brothers' aid. But there had been little need for them by that time. Most of the men her father had hired had left, only those loyal to Drummond fighting on.

Her mother had surprised them all by standing in the middle of the courtyard and shouting, "I'll not have any more fighting while Drummond lies cooling on the ground." Shamefaced, his men had draped his body over his saddle and followed her mother back to Fernleigh.

There were duties to perform, and buildings to build. Bridges to be mended, Iseabal thought, recalling Brian and the other crewmen. But for now, everything else could wait.

KAREN RANNEY

Both of them needed this stolen moment, not for passion, but for peace.

Placing one hand on Alisdair's arm, she felt the heat from his body, a warmth that seemed to reach out and envelop her as well. Although bloodied, he was safe. Bruised, but not broken. Only one other emotion besides gratitude could find its way into her heart. Love.

She would protect him with her life, shield his body with her own, defend him and support him. The essence of love in all its guises—wanton, maternal, supportive, passionate, and courageous.

"I need to find myself a wife," Brendan said, staring at Alisdair and Iseabal as they crossed the glen and walked up the hill hand in hand. "Do you see how he keeps touching her?"

"And she him," Hamish added, his attention also directed at the couple.

"They need an hour alone," Brendan said with a grin.

"Not an hour," Hamish corrected. "A day, maybe a week."

James silently watched Alisdair and his wife. Never before had he been jealous of any of his brothers, accepting and understanding that each had his strengths and weaknesses.

"No," he said, certain of his words yet feeling a disquieting pang of envy. "They need a lifetime."

He'd never come here before, but it seemed fitting to Alisdair that he did so now, paying homage to his Scots ancestors. His grandmother's grave appeared especially honored, a wooden cross inscribed in childish lettering marking her resting place and protected by a stone shield erected on three sides.

He knelt and, to his surprise, Iseabal moved into place beside him. He glanced at her profile, backlit by a fading sun. She was more than his wife, Alisdair suddenly realized. She was the woman he had never sought and yet always expected in his life.

He'd grown up witnessing the looks between his parents and sharing in their love. Instead of falling in love as a child as his father had, he'd felt the emotion creep up on him, coming to him in the form of a black-haired Scots lass, Iseabal of the shy smiles and hidden thoughts. Iseabal of the stubborn nature, he amended, and surprising passion.

Their marriage, instead of linking them, had created a rift. Yet their courtship had begun even so, occurring beneath the surface like an ocean current—beginning with curiosity, emboldened by interest, and finally resulting in a growing respect and admiration.

Alisdair felt as if the two of them had merged to become one person and then had split apart again, each carrying pieces of the other. She had the courage he had always possessed, and in his heart was the vulnerability that had once belonged to her.

Bowing his head, he said a prayer for Moira MacRae, the grandmother who would remain forever young in his mind. And for Patricia Landers, the woman who'd taken her place and loved a family so well. A fitting moment, he thought, to realize that there were other words he needed to say.

Reaching out, he placed his fingers over Iseabal's hand, tracing a path across her knuckles. Her hands were dirtied, her knuckles bruised. If he examined each palm, Alisdair was certain he would find splinters embedded in her skin. Marks of courage, determination, and perhaps stubbornness, too. This woman, with her somber looks and secret thoughts, was the only one he wanted in his life, for this day and forever.

Her gaze was on him as he stood, stretching his hand down to her. The moment reminded him of the first time he'd seen her, so solemn and wide-eyed, staring up at him as if he were the ghost of Gilmuir.

Slowly she stood until they faced each other. Iseabal stretched out her fingers to touch the edge of his jaw. Her gaze was steady, relentless in its offering of her deepest emotions. Something he should have seen long before now.

What did a man say when a woman had reduced him to wonder? Did he thank her or bless Fate itself for giving her to him?

The words were held there on his tongue, trapped by a sense of restraint. Alisdair felt as callow as a young boy, suffused with feelings aching to be said and at the same time terrified to speak.

At that instant he understood what Iseabal had felt, why she'd surrounded herself with a cocoon of silence and withdrawal. Standing before her, he felt nearly naked, baring his mind and soul wordlessly to her.

Her eyes had never looked so green, the color of the forest that enveloped them, or perhaps the shine of newly mined emeralds. Where her cheeks had been subtly colored before, now they were a fiery red, her lips the same shade and swollen, as if he'd kissed her a thousand times.

How could he tell her what he felt? Which words would be suitable? He didn't know, the blankness of his mind almost frightening.

Gripping her shoulders, Alisdair pulled her forward until, her cheek was pressed against his shirted chest. Her shoes were aligned next his much in the way their fingers had often entwined, and for a moment tenderness spiked through him.

"I wasn't entirely honest, Iseabal," he said, his words strung together with the delicacy of a spider's web. "It wasn't because of honor or responsibility that I wished to marry you again."

Reaching down, he brushed the hair from her cheek, tucking it behind her ear as his thumb gently removed a smear of dirt from her chin.

"I fell in love with you," he said softly, his voice little more than a whisper.

He drew back and looked into her eyes, thinking that he'd been more blessed than a saint. Ionis had lost the love of his life, while he had been granted Iseabal.

"Alisdair." She made his name an endearment, but then, she had a way of invoking so many emotions with only a few words—tenderness and passion, wonder and gratitude.

Her smile was luminous as her hands reached up and framed his face. Words were unnecessary; all he needed to know was shining through her eyes.

Turning, they looked out at MacRae land rich with color and history. The day was ending, the last rays of sunlight lending a golden color to Loch Euliss and illuminating Gilmuir. They'd have months, if not years, of hard work ahead of them, but the result would be glens as fertile as they had once been, and inhabitants who need not worry about survival.

Alisdair had a revelation at that moment, one not of sight but of heart. His home was not Nova Scotia, or the ship he loved to sail, or even Gilmuir.

Iseabal was his home, his haven, and his harbor.

Afterword

Nat Palmer, a ship's captain from Stonington, Connecticut, was credited with having the keenest eyesight of any sailor of his time. During a blinding snowstorm off South America, he took refuge at Deception Island. From there he saw a small smudge on the southern horizon. Sailing toward it, he became the first person since Columbus to discover a new continent. This portion of Antarctica was subsequently named Palmer Peninsula.

The true clipper ship did not make its emergence until the mid-nineteenth century, and Scottish shipyards, such as Robert Steele & Co. of Greenock, built some of the most famous vessels of their day.

Prior to that time, however, many shipbuilders experimented with various designs, including one similar to that of the *Fortitude*.

In addition to Daniel's superstitions, there were some other beliefs that fascinated me, such as the fact that it was unlucky to use the word "church" while at sea or to mention rabbits, hares, or other wild animals.

The Highland Clearances, the acts of stripping the land of its people in favor of sheep, took place in two main time frames—the late-eighteenth century and the mid-nineteenth century. People were burned out of their homes, and sometimes within them if not quick enough to leave. What then remained was leveled, leaving foraging area for the Cheviot sheep. An irony of history is that during this same time, the Highland Regiments were serving with distinction in foreign wars.

Some Scots were indeed sold by their lairds as indentured servants in the Carolinas. Both MacDonald of Sleat and MacLeod of Dunvegan are reputed to have been guilty of this act.